ARE YOU STILL MY GIRL?

A POST-APOCALYPTIC LOVE STORY

J. R. TOOTILL

Write Camp llc

 Formatted with Vellum

CONTENTS

Love you, Schmoopy...

I'll Always Be Your Girl

PROLOGUE

After the third civil war, the fracturing began when the regions physically broke off and were dismantled. The president's power was reduced to a last-ditch escape to the Pentagon building in the company of one badly injured Secret Service Agent, an elderly maid, and a terrified groundskeeper. They huddled in the ill-named safe room but were overrun after four days. They were half-starved, dehydrated, and exhausted from waiting for the president to pull the trigger on the handgun he held at his temple with trembling hands. And if he had been the kind of man to rise and run the country, he would have found the courage to blow his brains out. But he was a weak and scared little man without the generals that usually surrounded him. He didn't use the gun in his hand when the Eastern sector raiders rammed in the door or when they killed everyone else in the room and dragged him out and onto the grounds of the burning White House. The makeshift gibbet was hammered together in less than an hour while he merely sat in a whimpering puddle on the grass. They placed the rope loosely around his neck so that he hung, suffocating for hours, watching the white house burn to the ground. Most of the President's cabinet had fled days before, leaving him stranded and unprotected. A few supporters, lost in the scuffle and unable to go when it was safe, were found huddled in a storage room in the basement of the Pentagon. They were led out and executed before the now-dead president's swinging body as the White House roof collapsed into ash.

Then everything became chaos. With all authority gone, food and water reserves scarce, and no one in control, there was little hope. The self-appointed leaders of the Northeast, Southwest, West, and Midwest states failed to reach any accord. They returned to their territories without anything to offer the starving people in their cities. They intended to regroup as independent separatists, but, lacking resources, had little chance of accomplishing anything. That was when the sector perimeters were defined. With no one left to transfer military power, the fiasco in DC was seen as a costly blunder, and they could only operate as independent entities. They expected all reserves to be equally distributed, but with no one in charge, the military supply stations were looted and left empty. Minor skirmishes turned into more significant, detailed battles until all four regions invaded one another daily to siphon off any supplies they could. When this did nothing, and people became desperate for food and medical supplies, the idea of taking over the other sectors escalated into The Chemical Wars. But this accomplished little more than weakening an already depleted population whose immune systems were devastated by the chemicals seeping into the soil and the air.

The outlining areas around the cities, where most battles occurred, were reduced to little more than rolling dust clouds. After the chemical wars, only a few towns remained somewhat intact: New York, Chicago, Seattle, Los Angeles, Atlanta, and Philadelphia. They were quickly overrun by survivors who flocked to the cities for food and shelter. But there was no way to accommodate everyone, especially the sick and elderly. The city populations were divided into those who could work and those who were ill. This was the next internal sectioning: sealing off the diseased into chained communities outside the cities, where they were left to die without food or medical treatment.

Shortly after the sectoring, The Virus swept through and killed millions. The sick were transported to makeshift camps of less-than-suitable barracks-style houses miles away from the cities and crammed far beyond capacity. Everyone not showing symptoms was quarantined, but it was too late. The Virus spread, and the reek of infection soon permeated the city. Without the workforce or the time to bury the victims, steel wagons roamed the streets, ceaselessly collecting bodies. The wagons served as mobile crematoriums, burning hot enough to char the bodies to ash, gushing out a cloud of carbonized human ash from the scorch bins that clung to everything. The squatters fled into the upper floors of whatever high-rises were still standing. The military in each sector shut down all borders. No one was allowed into any city unless they had a medical certificate. Anyone who had traveled through the unprotected sectors was turned away unless being transported by a military escort.

The barren land areas between the sectors were damaged in the chemical wars and were thought to be highly contaminated, unprotected zones. Few traveled them anymore. The rumors of lingering chemical contamination and closed cities made travel useless. A hypothetical cure had been administered, but no one knew whether The Virus had finally been eradicated. The military in each sector sealed the people into the cities. They said they did it to keep everyone safe. But many believed it was an excuse for a complete military takeover. The populations in each city were segregated by job description and used as forced labor to rebuild. But they were sick and weakened by the years of war and chemicals, so progress was slow. Then SyntH, a synthetic form of street heroin, hit the street. Violent crime and addiction soared, forcing the creation of The Committee's Violent Criminal Division, whose sole and immediate purpose was to get the SyntH off the street. Then they were tasked with clearing out the overcrowded prisons. But the constant flow of released prisoners only began another cycle of violence, and it became apparent that what was needed was some form of aggression control and rehabilitation.

Saige and Thad Bodaway were the physicians assigned to develop the original aggression control medications. Saige was on the mandatory participation list for The Committee. It satisfied the terms of her licensing contract and assured her of a continued research grant to develop new medications, which was her real work, the research. Any failure on their part to participate in the program or any criticism of the rulings of The Committee resulted in forfeiture of her license and research funding. They had gone along on their collections, administered the prep drugs, and rode with the transports.

Their job was research, sedation and administration of the prep drugs, ensuring a successful Memory Shift, the new preferred method of realigning the guilty without their consent. The Committee's power became the rule when the looting and riots in the streets were out of control. But pulling criminals off the street only meant overcrowding of the prison populations. They had no choice but to release prisoners, which began an unproductive revolving door effect. The violent repeat offenders were constantly being cycled in and out of the system, which did nothing to decrease street violence. The Memory Shifts were initiated to control them so they could release the most violent offenders. Only the drug-resistant or extremely violent multiple offenders remained incarcerated.

The Committee's initial purpose was to weed out potentially dangerous offenders and rehabilitate them into more productive members of society. There were no accusations. No trials. No confronting a jury of their peers. That costly and unpredictable practice had been nullified years ago. There was a simple hearing before a committee consisting of one man, one woman, and one TALUS, an Artificial Intelligence moderator specifically programmed to intervene in the event of a deadlock. The TALUS provided services as an impartial observer and an advocate for the accused. Each TALUS served in their capacity for six months and was then replaced. It was believed that the TALUS began to internalize empathy and sympathy for the accused after six months and was no longer a reliable source. Although the hearings seemed impartial, the verdict had already been reached when orders were issued for the person to be collected.

Memory Shifting was the device of control.

But no one was there to control The Committee.

1

hase slid his hand up the side of the pipe, hoping his glove wouldn't slip as he wedged the toe of his sneaker in between the loose mortar of two bricks. He had knocked all the lights out along this side of the high-rise. Without any light to reflect, he would blend in with the brick wall as he scaled the side of the building. He reached the top ledge and inched his arm along the roof cap until he could get enough of a grip to pull himself up and over. And for a split second, he was an obscure silhouette held in suspended animation against an even darker night sky. The specks of reflected light glinting off the zippers of the black, well-worn leather jacket fragmented him. It was the only thing he had brought with him when he left; it was a not-so-subtle reminder of how easily things got lost in his world. He arched his back as his legs followed through. His feet landed lightly on the roof. A mesh of deep, black curls fell onto his forehead, obscuring the dark blue of his eyes, already dimmed to black in this shadowed light. He stood, took in the entire roof with one sweeping glance, and let out a slow exhale, and with it, all of the tension in his lungs from the energy surge that always shot through him as he climbed the last two levels of this building. He shifted his shoulders back to stretch them and took a deep, cleansing breath. He didn't know why, but it always stopped his breath when he pulled up and over the crest of this roof cap as if something was waiting for him on the other side. He didn't know if it was relief or disappointment every time he found the roof empty.

A pink polka-dotted glove came up over the side of the roof and felt along the edge for a place to catch. He reached down, locked fore-arms with Jo-Jo, and pulled her onto the roof. She slipped as she planted her tightly laced, high-topped foot, sending tiny pieces of gravel cascading over the side of the building.

"Shhhh, careful." Chase looked over the side of the building to be sure no one in the alley had heard the falling stones.

Jo-Jo was new to these excursions, but she was getting stronger. She was tiny but quick on her feet and could think in a crisis; he was happy to have her along tonight. Wisps of pink hair, matching the pink in her gloves, poked out of the dark hoodie, framing a cute face. She pushed back her hood, scratched her scalp, and shook her head back and forth as a giant shock of curly pink hair sprang out and fell to her shoulders like a shaggy, unclipped poodle. She pulled off her hoodie and tied the sleeves around her waist.

"Ah, that's better. Much cooler up here."

The dark was good for cover, but they could only see the subtle ridges along the brick and had to do everything by touch and instinct until they reached the top. Then they could see the roof edge and the street below, illuminated by reflected light from the building across the street. He had taught them how to feel along the ridges of the drainpipe and hook into the brackets that held the pipe against the wall, how to scrape their feet along the brick and burrow into the smallest crevices for balance.

Chase had learned to climb when he was fourteen. Five years later, he had a powerful center core from all those years of scaling buildings. He liked the control these lean, long muscles gave him, defining his frame. They gave him the speed and the strength he needed to scale just about anything. He was so much stronger now. Not like five years ago when he was a weak, skinny kid. Now, he was strong enough to do whatever was necessary. And that was exactly what he did: whatever was necessary.

Chase moved to reach down to grab Kalare's arm, but she had already hooked onto the roof ledge cap with a military-issue ballistic glove, and he watched her pull herself up and over. She dropped into a crouch in one swift motion. Her dark hair fell around her face as she grinned at him. She wore dark brown leather riding boots that snugly fit her calves. The straps were pulled tight so the boots would support her ankle and leg muscles like an extra layer of skin. She was a sultry blend of feminine and military layers of clothing that hugged a sturdy body. A frilly, layered, flowered skirt was topped with an olive military-issue jacket with the sleeves hacked off. It held a collage of compartments where she stashed supplies and ammunition. She was as much of a contradiction as her clothing: as strong and precise in her movements as she was soft and understanding with Chase. She changed everything. He was lost when they met, and she helped put him back together. But, even now, there were things he couldn't share. He felt guilty about that. He always felt guilty about something, although he vowed to tell her everything one day, but he couldn't face that yet. Not yet.

But how he loved to watch her move. The world slowed when he took her in. Her dark eyes were feathered with long bangs, which blended into long, deep brown hair that framed her rounded face. All the browns were variations of the same shades, like a cat whose fur and eyes camouflaged it from its predators. She moved in a sinewy motion that hypnotized him. He wished he could fall into her, block out the rest of the world, and never want or need anything else.

He slid the gun strap off his shoulder, unzipped his jacket, and retightened the gloves around his wrist. He loved the feeling he got from this vantage point, standing on this roof, above all the movement and noise on the street. He could see almost to the river from this side of Liberty Place One. The Committee had confiscated the buildings along Liberty Place and renovated most of them for their employees. The few buildings with lights cast an eerie shimmer onto the demolished buildings alongside them. It gave the city a kind of schizophrenic feel, as if they were living two lifetimes at once: one of destruction and one of rejuvenation.

He stared down Broad Street to the remnants of the old City Hall, now completely dark with just two feet and one thigh left of the statue that once stood high on a center column. The left side of the building had been demolished in one of the raids from the Southwest sector. He liked the idea of the statue's feet remaining there; it reminded him of the stories his father told him about when the city was not a war zone. It was one of his favorite places; he would climb up and sit for hours next to those feet, wishing he understood who this had been and why this statue once stood so tall in this city. He pulled his eyes from the dim lights to join the rest of them on the other side of the roof. This was the third and last building they would hit tonight. The take hadn't been very good so far.

"All good?" Sam, the last to pull up onto the roof, gave an affirmative nod to Chase. Sam was like a brick wall. He seemed to tower over Chase as he stretched to his full height, but it was an illusion of body mass, not height, as they stood eye to eye. Sam was a muscled mountain man with weathered features, hidden behind a reddish beard and a slicked-back mane of reddish-blonde hair that fell slightly below his shoulders. He usually wore sunglasses to hide the quietness of his grey eyes. They gave away a softness he tried to keep hidden from the world that others would misjudge as weakness. He wore a frayed and patched denim jacket. Strips of Velcro lined the inside flaps of the jacket and the bottom hem so he could tack down guns, knives, or anything else he needed. He was always prepared with a weapon or necessary tool and found a way to slip compartments into everything he wore. He slit the seams of his leather boots and slid various lengths of blades in between the padding along the top of the boot. He formed a wider compartment inside the ankle that concealed a Chinese throwing star he had stolen from a dead Collector a few months ago.

Chase and Sam had been hanging out along the docks for about two years. The first time Chase realized he could count on Sam was a few months after they met. Chase was rummaging through a building one night when he rounded a corner in a dark hallway and bumped into a collector so hard that it knocked him to the ground. The Collector pulled up on his weapon, but Sam, who had been following Chase, stepped out of the shadows, leveled his gun, and without taking a breath, shot the Collector in the head and simply said: "I have you, Brother." As he reached down, clasped Chase's forearm and pulled him to his feet. When everyone else ran from The Collectors, Sam stood his ground and happily ran toward them. It scared Chase, on the one hand, Sam's defiant stare in the face of death, but he was glad to have someone on his side with so little fear. Chase instinctively knew that Sam had his back. They moved together as if they could read each other's minds. When Chase moved in any direction, Sam moved with him seamlessly. Their friendship was forged in their inherent trust, which they shared with no one else.

They stood still on the roof for a few minutes, listening for movement. This building was so familiar to Chase. It was as if he could hear its heartbeat in the grumbling, outdated heating system that sputtered and rumbled through the loose pipes climbing within the walls and up to the colossal exhaust fans humming incessantly on the roof. The scent of the hot air pushed out with the exhaust was as familiar to him as the movement of Sam behind him. But this familiarity was always two-sided for him. On the one hand, it gave him a sense of security; on the other, it was always a fight not to sink into the sentimental attachment to his past life here. He knew that life was gone, but this place had prepared him for what he had to do now. He tried to see it as that and nothing more. He tried every time he came back. Some nights, the past was quiet, but on nights like this, ghosts seemed to rise with the steam pushing out of the vents, and when he breathed in, they encompassed him.

Everything changed after the Shifting began. He had escaped before they Shifted him, but his family hadn't been so lucky. And even though he remembered them and the life they once had, some days, it was like a dream that had never happened. He left everything behind the night he left, even his name. He only took his father's jacket. The first time anyone asked his name after he left, he absentmindedly blurted out *Chase* and winced to hear it out loud again. It was the Shift of his childhood friend who had given him the nickname that opened his eyes. But it was the attack on his parents that forced him out of this building and into a different life.

Anyone who had known him by that name was gone now. He had lost them all. But he didn't lose the speed and strength he developed during those little kid dares of building-jumping and pipe scaling. And when he first left, when he was alone, it was the only thing he had that he could depend on to outrun The Collectors and the Shiftings. Now he had these friends; he would trust them with his life if needed. But he missed the things and the people he had left behind. And at times like now, he missed them more desperately than he could ever admit out loud. He shook his head. *Focus,* he thought, *Focus on this. Focus on now.*

His eyes scanned the roof and stopped at the large metal door. He motioned for the others to follow and crossed the roof, crunching through the concrete gravel covering the older tarred roof. He crouched down at the metal door, pressed his ear to the doorjamb, and reached up to turn the doorknob, and it opened with a soft click followed by a high-pitched scrape of metal on metal. Chase slid a thin piece of wood under the corner with his foot, pressed his back against the doorframe, pulled in a deep breath, waited for his eyes to adjust, and headed into the hallway.

They had already made their way through the apartments on the top two floors when Chase heard the commotion as one of the apartment doors opened about ten feet in front of him. He stopped, pressed against the wall, and threw his arm up for the others to stop. A man with a medical bag walked to the elevator, followed by two armed men. *Collectors.* One was dragging an obviously sedated man; the other was pushing someone by the back of his collar. *Ziph.* Chase clenched his jaw and narrowed his eyes. Ziph, in striped pajamas that barely covered his lanky arms and legs, his pale ankles and wrists poking out like those stick-figure manikins piled in the trash by the old department stores that now housed squatters along Market Street.

Usually, seeing the Collectors at work would upset him, but not this time. Watching Ziph being pulled along by a Collector made his night. He couldn't see the man's face, but Chase felt the familiar twinge of sadness come over him. *Shake it off,* he thought, *you don't have time for this sentimental crap tonight.*

Chase motioned back with his thumb three times, slung the break-action single-barreled shotgun to his back by the strap, and then pulled the Sig Sauer 9MM from his waistband. He needed short-range accuracy for this one; its smooth pull would be good in this small hallway. He brought his left arm across his chest and steadied the Sig on it for stability. After pushing a slow breath out to steady his nerves, he slid his left foot back and slowly moved backward down the hall so he wouldn't bump into everyone behind him. He continued down the hallway until he reached the next angle, slid around the corner, and pressed into the wall as he heard the elevator door close. The door to the stairs was propped open, and he slipped into the stairwell where the others were waiting.

"Collectors. That was too close. Ready to get out of here?"

"Your call." Running into Collectors in the middle of the night was nothing new for Sam. The first time he saw a Collector was when they took his father. Never a person to hold his liquor, his father started a heated political discussion with friends in a bar one night, and someone turned him into The Committee. Sam had climbed out onto the ledge outside his bedroom window to smoke. When he heard the Collectors, he wedged into an abutment between his bedroom window and his parents' bedroom. He learned a lot about how they worked that night. The injections, the rummaging, and the removal of so-called subversive material. But what they did in his room was just cruel. Within ten minutes, his room, everything in it, his entire existence, was wiped from his home. His room became a storage space, and he no longer existed. He fell asleep wedged in the abutment, and when he woke up, his parents were just having breakfast, chatting away like any other day. They didn't remember him, and he had nowhere to go.

Sam started hanging out at the docks, where he could steal food from the trucks or grab half-decent stuff from the trash while it was still fresh enough not to poison him. He had gotten sick a few times from spoiled food, and it was something he didn't want to revisit. Luckily, no one bothered a guy who looked like Sam. He was willing and able to beat you down for food, weapons, or just for the hell of it. He was a formidable thing no one wanted to run into in a dark alley. Over time, groups of runaways, or more precisely, throwaways, squatted in the abandoned houses. They pooled each other's talents to survive. Kids who were good at stealing went into the stores during the day; those who knew how to pick locks did late-night break-ins wherever they thought they could get in and out without getting caught. They found that squatting together gave them an advantage, even if just in numbers. The abandoned houses and factories kept them slightly more isolated, with the river bringing up the entire back end. It wasn't always pretty or clean, but at least they were indoors and could stay away from the creeps trying to hurt kids or try to sell them out on the street.

The first time Sam met Chase, he was scoping out a new building on Front Street when he heard screams coming from the back of an alley. Three guys were getting rough with a girl, and Chase pushed into them like a maniac to get her out. He was outnumbered, and he didn't care. That's when Sam stepped in. Sam and Chase didn't take much effort to overpower the three guys and send them running out of the alley. They relied on each other after that. Chase was speed and brains; Sam was brawn and defense. Chase was on point; Sam brought up the rear. It was a good pairing for both of them. They switched from dumpster diving and shoplifting to raiding newly renovated apartment buildings. This seemed safer because they could get out of the building by ducking into the stairs and moving up to the roof before anyone caught them. But then they risked running into Collectors. Sam wanted blood, but Chase wanted to avoid The Collectors at all costs. Neither Sam nor Chase had been Shifted, and they wanted to keep it that way.

Whether looting the high-rises or hiding in abandoned buildings, The Collectors were a constant threat. One thing they did have going for them was that the Collectors hated dealing with the screaming kids. They usually just pushed them out into the street to fend for themselves as they loaded their parents into the trucks on their way to Shifting. Sam and Chase tried to get as many kids as possible to stay in the houses where they'd be safe. But getting them to trust that they wouldn't hurt them was harder. They would lose more kids whenever The Collectors wandered in and forced them to move. Most days, there just wasn't enough to go around for everyone, and as the city became more deserted near the docks, there was less food to find. Raiding the high-rises was getting more dangerous every day. When the Collector raids became a daily threat, staying along the river was even too dangerous. They decided to take their chances, packed everyone up, and moved out into the unprotected sector near the ocean. They found a secure place near the beach that was relatively safe because The Collectors rarely left the city limits. The hardest part of being out along the ocean was coming back into the city several times a week for supplies. But without electricity or running water, they had no other choice. Chase had made a few connections with people who could get medicines and first-aid supplies, but they were always running low on something, and someone was always sick.

Sam never really got the whole story about how Chase ended up on the streets. It always seemed odd; he wasn't a typical street kid. He was smart and knew how to do things most of the other kids didn't, so after a while, everyone naturally looked to him as the leader. But even with everything he had done, Chase kept to himself; he wasn't big on sharing. And there was always something boiling under the surface. It wasn't so much that Chase was angry; it was more like he had lost something that still owned a piece of him. He wandered the streets alone or sat on the roof for hours, staring into the night sky. It would have been easy to see him as a loner, but he wasn't that either. He was searching for something, and Sam had the feeling that even Chase didn't know what he was looking for while wandering alone out into the city's darkness.

A lot of that changed after Chase met Kalare. He wasn't off by himself so much, and she brought something calmer out in him. She was strong. He trusted her. It balanced him.

"Let's head out." Chase nodded his head upward toward the next landing, but Jo-Jo was heading in the opposite direction toward the hallway. "We still need some meds. Isn't it safer to go back in now that they left?"

"No, just the opposite. It means they are working in this city sector, and we should get out." Chase was taking the stairs two at a time. "So, JoJo, how do you feel about building jumping?" Chase called over his shoulder as he went through the door and onto the roof.

"Say what now? You mean like from here to there?"

"Exactly. Get a running start; push your momentum into your legs and just jump. Easy, right?" Chase said, grinning.

"You first." Jo-Jo thought they were joking. Sam laughed. This was Chase's home turf; he had been jumping these buildings forever. This was not the challenge Jo-Jo thought it was.

"Okay." Chase backed up about twenty feet, took off running, hit the air, and landed solidly on the other roof. "Piece of cake." He shrugged.

"Come on."

Jo-Jo looked at Sam and then at Kalare. "Oh, you guys are serious?"

"Serious as a plunge to our death. Do you want to go next?"

"Kalare? A little help here?"

"Sorry. This is pretty typical around here. What is this? Your third run now? I'm surprised this is the first time. He usually likes to show off." Kalare was laughing, holding her gun across her chest like it was the most logical accessory she could have. "Okay, I'll go next. Jo-Jo, it's really not that hard. Just get a good running start and commit to it. It's a rush." Kalare glided effortlessly across the space between the buildings.

"Oh great, another rush." Jo-Jo backed a little further than Chase and Kalare had and broke into a run. She cleared the ledge and was in the air between the two buildings when she squealed, looked down, and dropped her left leg. Her shoe caught on the lip of the other building, which pulled her face down, and she skidded across the other roof flat on her stomach. Chase ran over, half laughing, half concerned.

"See, I told you it was a rush." Chase let out a laugh that rumbled deep in his chest. It felt good to be light. Tonight, had brought back too many ghosts.

"Yeah, except for that last part where I hurtle to my death." But JoJo had loved it. Loved every minute of being with these guys. She didn't have any Shifting horror stories of parents being carried away in the night.

She was just an old-school runaway. Hated her parents and ran away with her boyfriend, who said he had a job lined up in the city. He dumped her for the first pretty girl who offered him free SyntH that cut through his veins like rat poison. It made him mean when he took it, and she knew she should leave, but had nowhere to go. She woke up one morning, and he had stolen all her money and anything else he thought was worth selling and left her alone in an abandoned building. She was kind of relieved that he was gone. She wandered around the city alone for a few weeks. She thought she was safe sleeping behind dumpsters at night until those three goons found her on Front Street and jumped her in the alley. Chase and Sam showed up like two superheroes from a comic book and fought the guys off. She was bruised and cut, but it would have been a lot worse if they hadn't shown up.

She wanted to pay them back for saving her and taking her in, so she helped with the supply runs. Kalare taught her how to handle the small cache of guns they had managed to gather. She took over the care and cleaning of the weapons, refilled ammunition, and locked everything up so the kids couldn't get to them. She pushed herself every day to be stronger, faster, and better. She had found a family in this group and would defend them to her death if necessary. So, when Chase said, *jump a building*, she jumped a building.

2

The Collectors always came in the dark, long after the world powered down. Faces obscured by an opaque sheath that blended into a black, tightly fitted hood. Dark gloved hands with shortened laser rifles that were strapped down to interchange as a natural extension of the arm. They were silent and nondescript except for a slight rustling of cloth against cloth until they stepped from the shadows to pull someone from their home for Shifting.

Saige heard them in the bedroom. Felt the change in density as Thad was hauled from his side of the bed. She opened her eyes slightly and saw his head slumped onto his shoulder and thought she saw the flash of iridescent blue through uncombed black hair that had fallen over the side of his face as he passed through the doorway. Or was that just her imagination? She watched his bare feet disappear as they dragged him into the hall. Ziph was stumbling, half-asleep, and rubbed his eye with the heel of his right hand as he scratched short-cropped blonde hair with his left. Had she heard him say *Mom?* as the gloved hand propelled him past her doorway? Or was her mind filling in the things that could not possibly be there again? Was this her world now? A world where Collectors crept into her home in the middle of the night to pull her family from her? *This is not how it was supposed to be, she* thought as she listened to the muted sounds of moving furniture and the rustle of things being gathered in Ziph's room. So, this was why they were here: Ziph. She held her breath as they passed her bedroom door, grunting with the heft of the things they carried off. Then, the apartment settled into an unnerving calm after the click of the door. The rooms felt empty and surreal without Thad and Ziph.

She rubbed in her arm where the hypodermic had slid in; she remembered the temple throb and electric flash across her forehead, the hand at her throat checking her pulse, and the Collector bent so close she could still taste his breath when he began the whispered reprograming, telling her she never had a son named Ziph.

I know, you bastard, she thought, *you already took him.*

Three years ago, she started dosing herself with the combination of drugs she hoped would prevent a Memory Shift. She woke up one morning with a feeling that something wasn't right. That something was missing. But she couldn't quite remember what it was. She began dosing Thad six months ago but resisted the urge to dose her son Ziph, fearing this would result in a slip. Ziph was different lately: surly and angry. He had become argumentative and often resorted to violent outbursts when he felt he was not being taken seriously, which was pretty much all the time. He asked too many deliberate questions about her opinions, and Saige knew this was more than curiosity. She had the distinct feeling he was looking for something. She feared he would turn her or Thad into The Committee if he thought there was a less-than-loyal response to any of his questions. There had always been a disconnect with Ziph, an uncomfortable uneasiness of unfamiliarity between them that she could never explain.

She wasn't sure where Thad's loyalties stood; she never expressed discontent with The Committee's direction. On the surface, Thad was a model citizen, father, and husband. Her need to share her disillusionment about this system with him could jeopardize everything if he disagreed. He would have to report her, and if he were loyal to The Committee, he *would*. She had seen it time and time again. Husband turning against wife. Wife turning against her children. So, for now, even though she felt guilty about hiding her feelings and, worse, dosing him without his consent, she was alone with her fear.

Would Thad even remember her tomorrow?

And if he did remember her, would he still be her Thad?

Or would he be lost to her forever?

T *had* came awake as his head thudded on the floorboards when the transport door slammed. Strangely, it was not Saige's eyes filled with fear that he remembered as he came out of the fog from the injection. No. It was her dark, fixed, intense eyes staring at him through the rear-view mirror the first time they met. Those unrelenting eyes gave him the strength to focus, and he would focus only on tomorrow. *One way or another, Saige, I will see you tomorrow.*

He knew they had tested him the night he was called to assist the Collectors who stopped in front of his brother's complex. Everything he had eaten for dinner had soured and started to rise up his esophagus before he even got out of the transport. The ride up the elevator was an exercise in claustrophobia as he tried to figure a way out. He tried to swallow back the rising gorge, but the elevator's heat was stifling, making him dizzy. He hadn't felt this kind of anxiety since... since... *when?* That had been happening to him a lot lately; little glimpses of memory flashed at him and then were gone. It gave him a hot shooting pain at the base of his skull. Thad hung back until the Collectors had gone a few feet down the hall before he leaned into the trash can by the elevator and threw up. *Maybe,* he hoped as he swabbed a handkerchief across his forehead; maybe, *it was for someone else.*

But he knew the minute Thomas had referred to medication overuse in violent patients as a form of population control. The Committee would assume it was a less-than-veiled message of discontent. And more, that it was an overt effort to rally supporters to oppose the new protocols. There were quiet grumblings in the medical community, but Thomas had been the first doctor who had dared to take on the trials in a public forum. Thad hoped this would be a partial Shift to ensure Thomas' continued research on biological regeneration, which showed incredible promise. Thomas may have some advantage since everyone assumed it was years away from being even slightly effective. The Committee was willing to take some leeway; they had invested a great deal of time and money into Thomas' research. It was always about money invested and the need for future results. Thomas was still valuable, and Thad hoped they would allow him to keep his life with only a slight adjustment. *God, he was even beginning to think like them.*

Thad leaned over the fountain and swallowed gulps of water, trying to thin out the slime of bile coating the back of his tongue. He lifted his medical case and followed the Collectors, who had already made it halfway through Thomas' apartment. Even though the room was pitch dark, the familiar aroma rose from the richness of the furnishings with a faint scent of leather and fine woolen tweed. Thomas liked natural fabrics and colors that had comforted him as a child: various muted green and gold hand-woven fabrics with the occasional pop of crimson covered the heavily layered chairs and sofas in his study. He spared no expense in decorating the house to his comfort. The contrast of Thad's dread was coupled with his desire to sit in the overstuffed brown leather easy chair while his brother contemplated the end of a well-chewed pipe as smoke from a tartly scented cherry tobacco haloed his head. Thomas inhabited the tradition of the old in everything he did; he was out of place in this new configuration of government control and disintegration.

Thad dropped his case onto the chair next to the bed and

searched his pockets for anything to get the taste of bile out of his mouth. He was surprised to see Thomas' eyes open and watching him. He unlocked the case, withdrew the hypodermic, and let his hand stop over the vials in the top level. He shifted the hinged shelf, pulled out two vials, withdrew a small amount from a blue vial, and filled the rest of the chamber from a clear vial. Thad shook the hypodermic until the liquid turned a soft amber.

"Thaddeus, I think you've made a mistake."

Thad met the dark eyes of his brother as he withdrew the syringe from his arm and wiped away the tiny pearl of blood at the tip. He rolled the drop of blood between the thumb and forefinger of his gloved left hand, stalling, but he knew he was caught. Instead of the usual pre-shift cocktail, he only added a small amount of barbiturate to the saline solution. It was enough to fool the untrained eye of The Collectors or someone who had never been Shifted but wouldn't get past anyone who knew the potency of the prep drugs. What else could he do? This was his brother about to be Memory Shifted. Thad was motionless as he stared down at his brother's tranquil eyes. He looked for some familiar flick of an eyebrow or twitch of the mouth, anything to tell him he was not about to be betrayed. But Thomas simply stared indifferently past him, an eerie shine bouncing off the glistening white of his eye with a refraction of the only light cutting through a slit in the curtain of the otherwise dark room. Thad's chest tightened, and he fought against the heat rising at his collar and swallowed hard. He stared helplessly at Thomas but saw nothing to tell him what to do next. He had to keep going now; he had no other choice but to administer the correct pre-shift drugs.

And why the Thaddeus? Thomas hadn't called him that since he was sixteen, when, after a nasty remark about a girl he was utterly infatuated with, Thad had landed a fist halfway up the bridge of Thomas' nose, breaking it and tinting his face into a deep purple and green bruised butterfly for two weeks. *That's the last time you will ever get the best of me,* was what Thad meant to say, but, as dazed as his brother was that he had taken the swing, he just stood there staring down at his hands. Thomas, on the floor, stared up at him with round, swelling eyes, cupping his hands under a gushing nose. He knew he should feel bad or apologize, but Thad had liked that surge of adrenaline pumping through his heart. He flexed his hands, staring at them as if they belonged to someone else, and watched the muscles pop out in reflex along his forearms. Pushing his hands to his sides, he shifted his eyes down as he stood over Thomas with his fists still clenched and his fingers pulsing against the urge to hit his brother again. Even at sixteen, Thad knew he would never reach the intellectual heights and respect that Thomas would. But this pristine sense of physical power was something new. And it was Thad's moment to cherish. He liked the feel of it. He liked it very much. They both knew that this moment had changed everything between them.

"A mistake?" The Collector closest to him was now hovering over the medical kit as if he knew what should be there. "What do you mean by mistake?"

"No. No mistake." Thad picked up a second needle and filled it from the correct vial. "I sometimes use a mild sedative before giving the cocktail."

"That's not protocol. This has to be reported." Thomas spoke over Thad's mop of dark hair and into the black-masked helmet of the Collector. "This has to be reported," Thomas repeated as Thad slid the needle into his brother's vein and pushed in the plunger, keeping his eyes down so he wouldn't meet his brother's gaze. What if he saw some sign of remorse before the drug took Thomas away? Then it would be too late.

Thad had been doing collections for The Committee for only a few months when he realized most of the victims of the new protocols were people who simply voiced an opinion, not the dangerously violent prisoners the Shifting was intended for. The new director was going off in a new direction, which no one questioned. To question was to be reprogrammed. Silence was preferable if you wanted to keep your present life, which Thad, above all else, wanted to keep his life just the way it was. So, he went along with the forced collections. Even the prominent were not immune. They were simply readjusted and returned to their pegs on the smooth-gliding wheel. The Committee insisted it merely oiled.

He was convinced he had been called to assist in his brother's collection to prove his commitment. He thought Thomas' stance on the protocols was a back-door nod against the rampant usage of Memory Shifts and, as a result, loaded the syringe from an alternately labeled barbiturate. The Collectors would never know the difference. He assumed his brother, faced with reprogramming, would simply go along with it, and The Committee would be content with his responses. Instead, he now knew that he had misjudged.

Thad flinched as the Velcro tore apart behind him. The Collector pulled off his glove and reached over in front of Thad, pushing against him as he pressed the slowing pulse thump in Thomas' neck. Satisfied that the correct medications were administered, he regloved, tightened the Velcro at the wrist, and backed up with a small, satisfied grunt so Thad could finish. "You do understand that this will have to be reported?" The Collector cleared his throat. "Any breach of protocol must be reported."

"I wouldn't exactly call it a breach. Do you want to inspect my kit?" Thad matter-of-factly opened his hands and waved them over his medical bag. "I'm sure you will find everything in order. There is a reason they have doctors administer these medications. We do know how to sedate and prepare for Memory Shift. He's a big guy, and I thought the sedative would have helped in the collection."

"Look, Doc, we've worked together for a long time, and I've never seen anything to question you, but I have to report this. I know you're not supposed to know who you are assisting to collect, but this is an accusation from your brother. Understand? There are implications here. I have no other choice but to report it."

"I know, I understand." Thad's voice was casual, but his heart was pumping hard, and the blood sped up and crashed into a headache in his temples. He hoped it was dark enough they didn't see the resultant flush.

The Collector motioned to the others to pick up Thomas. Thad continued to move vials and needles around in his kit, trying to act as naturally as possible. But this wasn't good. This was really bad. His hands began to shake, and he slammed the lid down harder than he wanted to, but they were already moving toward the door and didn't seem to notice. "I'll place this incident and your response in my report." The Collector had stopped at the doorway and motioned forward with his weapon. "We're through here."

Thad looked on helplessly as Thomas was placed into the truck. It was always surprising to him how loyal so many were to The Committee, even when faced with their own Shift. Thad had tried to save Thomas out of brotherly loyalty, and now he was in danger of losing everything and would probably be the next one to be collected. He climbed into the car and sat for a long time, letting it idle. His first instinct was to drive home, make Saige pack a bag, and just leave it all behind. But he had no idea where to go. And there was the work. There was always the work. And Saige would never leave it. They had been through all of this before. He had tried to get her to quit so many times, but she would never budge, even when it almost killed her. No. That wasn't the answer. He had to find another way. He knew this time he would be brought before the Committee; he only hoped they would give him time to explain. He thought of Saige, and fear formed that familiar jagged knot in his chest. He would never forgive himself if he lost her in trying to save his brother.

Thad waited three days for the call from The Committee. He had almost convinced himself he had escaped their repercussions when he had heard the familiar soft scuffle of movement in the shadows of their bedroom. He knew they were here for him. Before he could reach out to hold Saige one last time, he felt the pinch of the tip of the needle slide into the vein in his hand. The heat of the liquid moved up his wrist and into his upper arm. The coppery, salted taste landed on the back of his tongue, making his mouth water as the fuzzy, medicated hiss hit his head. He stole one last glimpse of Saige as they pulled him from the room. He thought their eyes had met for a second: his in panic, hers in fear. He hoped this wasn't the last time he would remember her as she was now, as they were to each other. His body went limp even though he fought the effects of the meds.

But they were seeping through him fully now, and he couldn't keep his eyes open or his mind clear any longer. He hoped that double-dosing Saige with the new anti-shift concoction he was using would keep her from the Memory Shift. He guessed this was as good a time as any to test it.

He hadn't told her he had been slipping his mixture of anti-shift meds into her drinking water for months, just *her* water, not the boy's water. Their boy, Ziph, would know. He would report. He would have them Shifted and reassigned, and he would enjoy it. He was loyal to the detriment of his own parents because that was the simplest route to the top; he wanted to head The Committee. It was like he wasn't even theirs. He probably wasn't. It was hard to keep track of all the Shifts. Either way, the boy would be Shifted tonight and might or might not be placed back with them. But Thad hoped that he and Saige would wake up in their bed tomorrow, still together. And, as much as he regretted admitting it, he hoped they woke to each other alone. The boy asked too many questions, which could only mean danger to him and Saige.

The first time he saw Saige standing on that demolished train station platform in Washington, DC, he had no idea that everything would change for him in an instant. At first, she seemed almost nondescript: brown hair tightly pulled back, brown eyes lowered behind thick-framed glasses, hiding in the folds of her upturned trench coat collar. She had pulled her arms into the jacket, tucking her head down like a turtle afraid to leave its shell. Her back was hunched over to brace her against the wind, pitching the pouring rain at her. She seemed frail enough to be hurled up and tossed into the wind, so tiny, lost, and alone. At least, that was how she had seemed standing alone on that platform, soaked through to the bone. He would learn she was much stronger than she appeared. And she used that easily misunderstood meekness in her demeanor to her advantage. They always underestimated her; it was always a fatal mistake.

He had hurried around the vehicle and opened the door for her, taking her hand and elbow to help her over the puddle and up and into the car. Her hand felt so small in his big, knuckled hands. He felt clumsy and awkward as she slipped by, leaving him in the wake of a subtle aroma of lightly flowered incense, which caught him off guard. She was like a room full of scented candles that blended to leave a trace of something he could not describe. It filled his lungs, invigorating him. He was loading her bags into the back compartment when she turned, thanked him, and smiled; it broke his heart into a thousand pieces. He didn't even remember what she said after that smile: *awful weather, terrible weather,* or something else that was so casual but seemed to be the most important thing he had ever heard.

The sound of her voice and the intensity of her essence were the only things that existed in the world. It took all his strength to break eye contact, shut the door, walk around the car, and open the driver's side door. It was as if he had forgotten everything. He had to think about how to walk, how to place one foot in front of the other, and how to move. His hands fumbled with the keys and missed the door lock, gashing the plastic plate around the keyhole. He finally got into the car but forgot what he was doing. Then he tried to start the already running car and ground down on the starter. If she noticed, she didn't say. Her wet coat soaked into the seat's leather, which only intensified every fragrance already swimming around in his head. The car was filled with her scent: flowers, incense, rain, and a million candles, all shimmering at once. He avoided the rear-view mirror and willed his eyes to stare out into the pouring rain, up the street, into oncoming traffic. He knew that once he locked eyes with her again, he wouldn't be able to tear himself from her dark, bold, unblinking stare. When he finally looked into the mirror, her eyes were already there, searing off his outer layers and plunging straight into his soul. His hands were like jelly as he pushed the vehicle into gear; his leg pressing the clutch began to shake. It wasn't so much that he didn't want to move; he couldn't move. He was afraid he would break the spell, and the thought of losing her, falling out of those eyes, and not having her in his arms suddenly became the most desperate thing in his life.

Thad Bodaway had been eager to fight in what everyone thought would be the final massive strike of the Chemical Wars. He was a junior officer and had risen quickly through the ranks by proving he could get specific jobs done with a handful of specifically trained troops. He was commissioned to head up a division deploying to the southwest to take over and dismantle the last known chemical plant. The night before the deployment, Dr. Regent, the acting head of The Committee, offered him a particular detail in Military Protective Services. Offered was a slight exaggeration. It wasn't as if he'd had a choice. He resented having to leave his men, and, worse, he was angry that he had been reduced to a military escort after finally being given the commission he had worked so hard to prove himself capable of commanding. But he was a soldier. Soldiers took orders. His duty was to be willing to give his all, no matter the assignment. To do any less was considered cowardice. And he was many things, but a coward was not one of them.

So, he took the assignment. And then Saige changed his life forever. Saige was everything. Or, more accurately, she was the key to everything. And although he at first resisted the assignment, he knew, even if Saige didn't, that he was protecting the future. She had been the only light in this whole mess. She was their only hope. Thad could never forget that he was a soldier first, and that sometimes following orders meant hurting those he loved the most. He could always walk the thin line where duty and life collided, and duty always won out. That was, duty always won out until Saige. That mission had saved them both from the chemical wars and the harsh aftermath of a world that had changed into something that no longer touched them because of who she was and the protective sources that kept her safe.

But now, that world that had enclosed them so securely was falling apart. He wasn't so sure his deceptions were essential to keeping her safe. They had kept her secure. Then. But Thad quickly realized that the very thing that brought them to this moment was the thing that would also drive them apart. And what would Saige do with all that now if she remembered it all?

4

Even though Saige disagreed with The Committee's politics, she provided the services as required under her contract. She tried not to think about what happened to the people who were Shifted once she left them with the Collectors. This was her only option if she were to keep her research and her family together. Saige was determined never to put herself in a position where she would be reassigned without Thad. She would do whatever was necessary to keep her and Thad together.

The first time she saw Thad standing in the new lab in Philadelphia, filled with boxes of unpacked medical equipment, he looked awkward and uncomfortable in the white lab coat. His curly black hair caught in a button-down collar pulled too tightly across his chest and shoulders. The lab coat sleeves were about four inches too short for his arms, and she giggled at him and said, "Take *that thing off; you look ridiculous.* He turned and smiled at her, and, as always, his eyes in that devastating blue that shifted into shades of green and smoky grey, depending on his mood, made her catch her breath. From the first time she had locked eyes with him, she knew there would never be anyone else for her. Even though he towered over her, she felt instantly safe with him, as if she had known him for much longer. She had spent most of her life either in school or a research lab and never thought there was room for anything else. But something happened when she met Thad. He made her feel protected in a way that didn't control her. She loved how he held himself in that self-assured, casual way of being comfortable in his own skin. But it was more than that; that serene aura of gentleness she sensed within his eyes had won her over. She was so sick of these military men who surrounded her with a pushy need to control; with Thad, it was different. He let her breathe.

She had been relocated to Philadelphia to research and develop medications for violent multiple-offense prisoners. The aggression protocols were doing well in early trials, and there was a massive reduction in repeat offenders as they were released from the prison population. When they realized their job was coming to an end, the flaw in the system became apparent. Without monitoring, the released prisoners would stop taking their medication, and the number of repeat offenders rose in ever-increasing numbers.

Then, The Committee proposed the idea of Memory Shifting for those about to be released. It seemed like a good proposal. This cost-effective, permanent solution eliminated the need for further medication and reduced government costs. It also gave prisoners, who would never have a life outside the system, hope for a normal life. As the new measures rolled out, success followed upward trends. The program was seen as a new hope for a violent society. Discharged prisoners were Memory Shifted and released into job programs to become productive citizens. But new leadership changes expanded the Shifts beyond the violent offenders. Then they rolled out the Shifts on a massive scale.

Saige never agreed with the new rollout protocols. But it was hard to disagree with the numbers. Crime was down. The immense cost of incarceration and continued medications had been eradicated. The Shifted were returned to their homes and placed in productive jobs. But as mass population Shifting became the norm, more severe adverse reactions occurred, especially among those who were repeatedly Shifted. The searing pain caused by bleed-backs and nasty

hemorrhages resulting from electrical impulses in the brain recon-
necting caused damage to both memory function and motor skills.
Even if the victims of the bleed-backs survived, there was no choice
but to reassign them to low-level jobs with simple repetitive tasks that
varied little from day to day. And yet, argued The Committee, even in
extreme cases like these, the results, in general, were still the most
beneficial for all in this new system of layered classes without specific
distinction.

Saige knew the reasoning, but she also saw the increased
randomness of the decisions, the silent night raids on the unknow-
ing, the resulting Shift of the so-called guilty, and the possible reloca-
tion of family members. It all seemed harsh to her, especially when
The Committee acted on all tips, with at least a memory reorganiza-
tion or full Memory Shift and reassignment. By the time they were in
front of The Committee, they had already been administered the
drugs and were halfway through the process.

But Saige knew that any out-of-place word or action, especially
while in the presence of The Collectors, could mean her own night-
time extraction from her home and loss of her family. Saige tried not
to give in to the always-present pressure of guilt in her chest: if they
had never developed the meds, the Shifting would have never
happened. But if the drugs had never been devised, the city would
still be overrun with violence and crime. It was an endless circle of
doubt that was rooted deep within her. But one thing she could never
get around: she knew she and Thad were responsible for it all. They
had been accountable since administering the first test drug to the
first patient in their original drug trial. The culpability of it all was
slowly eating away at her. But if guilt were the price she paid for
having Thad, she would gladly suffer it because everything always
came back to Thad.

5

T had was pulled from the transport by the back of his shirt and jostled onto the elevator floor. The fog from the injection was lifting. He didn't know if the anti-shift drugs were working or if he had been merely sedated. He didn't know if he would give anything away if he tried to stand, but his legs and arms were still rubbery, useless accessories. He may as well still be unconscious for all the good they would do him. All he wanted right now was to lie beside Saige, warm and safe in their bed. He tried to conjure up the smell of her hair, the line of her back, the feel of her lips. The elevator stopped, and the doors opened into The Committee hallway. This wasn't right. He was not brought into the Shifting holding area. The Collectors pulled him down the left hallway, through another set of double doors, and finally into a dimly lit room with one chair in the center and a large six-foot high alter-like monstrosity filling the entire front end of the room. He could see how it would be intimidating to have The Committee staring down at you on a solitary chair in the center of the room. If he was honest, it was working his nerves pretty good right about now.

Then the light switched on and blew everything out to a hazy white. His eyes immediately began to tear, and he resisted the urge to cover his face with his hands to push out the light. He felt as if he had been stabbed in both eyes and finally gave up trying to stop them from tearing. He could barely make out the heads of The Committee seated at the table, which he assumed was the intent. Then, the metallic whir of the TALUS circled through the room.

"No need to restrain him. Leave." A woman's voice dismissively commanded. The Collectors dropped him unceremoniously onto the floor and left the room.

"Dr. Bodaway, are you clear-headed enough to speak?" Her voice seemed familiar, but he couldn't quite place it yet.

"Yes," he coughed out. He blinked furiously, trying to push back the fog and ease the burning in his eyes from the caustic light.

"Dr. Bodaway, do you know where you are?"

"Yes, Ma'am, I think so."

"And Dr. Bodaway, do you know why you are here?" She said this with a slight sigh afterward, as if it were so much tedious nonsense.

"I think so. I think there was a misunderstanding in my last Shifting prep." *No sense in playing coy; let's just get to it.* He was too disoriented for this and hoped the pressure from jamming his palms' heels above his eye sockets would clear his head so he could think clearly.

"Well, Dr. Bodaway, we are very pleased you are being so forth-right. And by now, you realize you were just given a sedative, not the prep for Shifting. We have always seen you and your family as loyal and faithful to The Committee, so getting this report about your brother, Thomas, was rather disturbing."

"Yes, Ma'am." Thad was trying not to give anything away, but the lights, his stinging eyes, and his pounding head interfered with everything.

He couldn't think.

"So, Dr. Bodaway, we would like to hear from you exactly what happened. We have already spoken with Thomas and the Collectors who were present. But anything you can add to enlighten The Committee would be helpful."

"Yes, Ma'am. When I arrived at the residence, I noted that the patient was a larger man. I decided to give a barbiturate to calm him before administering the pre-shift medications." Thad was standing on point; he was, after all, a medical professional.

"So, you do admit to giving the additional medication?" Her tone didn't waver. It didn't judge. This was all just so much busy work to her.

"Yes."

"Dr. Bodaway, did you administer this extra step because the citizen was your brother Thomas?"

"No, Ma'am. I respond to all edicts from The Committee in accordance with the mandated protocols and the instructions on the pick-up sheet. I added the medication to subdue a larger patient." Thad tried to keep his voice steady. As the medication wore off, the pounding in his head got louder, and his mouth was dry. A sticky sweat collected on the back of his neck.

"Do you do this often? Administer additional drugs without notating them in your collection notes?" This was a male voice. A stern, sarcastic lilt pulling up the word *notes*. He recognized Dr. Regent immediately.

"Not often, but occasionally, I will administer this medication, especially if the citizen is particularly agitated or large. As far as I know, there is no protocol for listing additional medications; only a checklist to ensure the proper medications for each collection are administered as instructed. Since the barbiturate would not interfere with the ordered medications, I did not notate it because I didn't think it was required." His voice was steady, even if his heart was hammering against his chest. Though still stinging, his eyes had stopped watering, and the fog from the sedative was finally lifting. His mouth and throat were dry, and the bile he was trying to keep down was forcing its way up into the back of his throat.

There was a movement of papers and a few whispers from the front of the room. Then, a more defined movement of chairs, followed by louder voices.

"Dr. Bodaway. Please give us a few minutes. We need to review the protocol parameters you received." He recognized the voice as Dr. Metcalf, the new Committee Chair.

He wanted to ask for water but didn't want to seem weak or nervous or raise any other suspicions they could form when he heard the whir of the TALUS move toward him.

"Doctor Metcalf," The TALUS' metal voice erupted in the room. "This man has been sedated for several hours now, and there is a danger of dehydration. Please procure some water for Dr. Bodaway."

"Is that really necessary? We are almost through here." This was Dr. Regent.

"Yes, Doctor. That is the protocol. Dr. Bodaway should have been given water as soon as he regained consciousness. The Collectors did not administer water. This must be corrected immediately."

His job was completed; the TALUS moved back to the front of the room as a Collector brought a water bottle. Thad forced himself to drink slowly. He tried to appear calm. But his throat was dry as sandpaper, and he gulped at the water until it trickled out of the corners of his mouth. And just as he felt somewhat calm, he thought of Saige, and his throat closed again. He hoped he would be with her again when he opened his eyes the next morning. Of course, he would be with her again. *He had to be with her again. He had to.* He took a long breath, which opened his chest a bit, and then the thought of her soothed him. Calmed him. The pulse throbbing in his temples began to slow, and the vise that seemed to grip his throat eased.

And then The Committee took their seats again.

"Dr. Bodaway, we have reviewed your protocols, and you are correct; there is no provision for recording other medications administered or other medical attention given to the citizen about to be collected. You will have a revised set of protocols requiring you to report all and any additional medications or medical treatment, whether related to Shifting or not, in all reports from now on. Do you understand these new protocols, Doctor?" It was Dr. Metcalf delivering the edict.

"Yes."

"And Dr. Bodaway, we appreciate your honesty and cooperation in this matter, especially considering who this particular citizen happened to be."

"Yes, ma'am." Thad offered nothing. Explained nothing.

"You have proven over the years to be a reliable resource, and we do not wish to appear insensitive to those who have already proven their loyalty, but be clear here: any additional breaches or the slightest inkling of inappropriate responses, and this becomes a Shifting matter. Do you understand?" Her voice was now drilling into his brain with its politeness.

"Yes. Yes, I do."

"Just one other issue, if you would indulge the committee." This was Dr. Regent. Thad pushed back the anger in the pit of his stomach.

"Yes, Sir." The sweat on Thad's neck trickled down his back in a long, slow, greasy stream that collected at his waistband, soaking into the fold of his shirt.

"This is regarding your son, Ziph."

"My Son? I don't understand."

"Your son has notified this committee that he is dissatisfied with his placement. He feels that you are not giving him the proper encouragement for his aspirations. He has requested that he be reassigned to a member of The Committee to secure his future. Are you aware of his dissatisfaction?" This question was tricky.

"I know that Ziph is very dedicated to The Committee and its function. I am also aware of his aspirations to serve on this Committee. But I was not aware of his dissatisfaction with our instruction." Thad hoped he was coming off as a concerned and loving father and that the bile that now clogged the back of his tongue did not register in his voice.

"We believe so, too." Dr. Metcalf was pulling the reins again. "We have decided to grant Ziph his request. Your wife has been memory reorganized and will no longer remember that you had a son. His room has been dismantled and removed. We are telling you this as a courtesy. You will also not remember that Ziph was ever your son." Her voice poked at him with that tediously boring edge to it. Thad flinched at the mention of Saige being 'memory reorganized.' He hoped, for the millionth time tonight, that Saige's dosing had worked.

"I understand. I'm glad he had the foresight to contact The Committee to serve the Committee as he sees fit." But this was not the end.

He could feel something coming.

"Just one last question, Dr. Bodaway." Dr. Regent paused and cleared his throat. "Do you know why Ziph should be suspicious of you and your wife?" And there it was, the true reason for the meeting.

"No, Sir. I do not." Thad's voice was flat. He tried to keep his eyes from narrowing and his jaw from clenching.

"Ziph seemed to feel that there was something not quite right. He has searched your house and tested your medications and has found nothing. But still, his suspicions remain. Why do you think that is, Dr. Bodaway?" Now, the tone was sterner, more accusatory.

"I don't know, Sir. Perhaps his own frustration in wanting to serve The Committee better was transferred to annoyance with us for not pushing him harder in that direction. He could have confused frustration with suspicion." Thad set his jaw, not in an angry line, but in what he hoped would be interpreted as confident and honest.

"Perhaps you are right, Doctor. An impetuous, ambitious child who wants more can easily misconstrue feelings at that age. And I assume you have no objections to Ziph being placed in a more suitable environment?" This was Dr. Metcalf again. She was a good choice for Committee Chair for this session. She was loyal to all things Committee and a dedicated and respected doctor. She believed she was serving the people, doing her best to help heal a sick society, unlike Dr. Regent, who was about power and control. For him, it was The Committee above all else.

"No, Ma'am. Ziph should be placed in the best environment for his ambitions." Thad relaxed his shoulders. Well, at least that was partially true. There was more shuffling of papers, squeaking chairs, and whispers.

Then, the two Collectors returned and stood on either side of Thad.

"We thank you for your cooperation, Dr. Bodaway. You will be returned to your home, and of course, your memory of this meeting will be altered; you will only remember the new protocols regarding medication and medical treatment." The decree came from Metcalf.

"Thank you. It is a pleasure to serve The Committee." He gave the expected response and tried to say it as humbly as possible, even as his anger rose at the realization that Ziph had turned them in. He could have lost everything because of Ziph. He could have lost Saige.

The TALUS whirred its way around the room and stood in front of Thad. It was an eight-foot intimidation of metal and power. *Oh, what now?*

Thought Thad.

"Dr. Bodaway, do you believe The Committee has handled this matter fairly and impartially?" The metallic voice was disquieting with a blend of soft concern and artificial digital resonance.

"Yes."

"Dr. Bodaway, do you believe you have been heard fully?"

"Yes."

The TALUS clicked and spun, then circled his chair as a pinch warmed Thad's arm. His head was filled with the echoing whir as the TALUS moved to the front of the Chamber.

6
_____

Z*iph* was glad when the pinch in his arm roused him from sleep. The Committee had pulled him from class two days ago, and he freely spoke of his suspicions about his parents or, as he suspected, parental charges. He had no evidence. Had seen no breach. Had heard no anti-Committee whisperings in their conversations. But there was something about his parents that just didn't feel right. And he told The Committee just that. He had come up empty-handed after searching their medical kits and personal medications, but he still passed on his suspicions to The Committee.

He only did this because he wanted to be placed elsewhere and be the son of someone prominent on The Committee so that he could move into a position of power and respect. He told them he wasn't getting the push to serve that he thought he deserved. He knew he could serve this Committee well; even as a nineteen-year-old, he could serve even better than most adult citizens.

The Committee was pleased and said they would consider his suggestion. They had long considered placing a junior member on The Committee with full voting powers. They assured him he would be rewarded for his loyalty and honesty. He had thanked them. Told them his reward would be to serve, which he knew would please them.

"I do have one request."

"What sort of request?" Dr. Metcalf asked.

"I would like to be reassigned without a Shift." "That is a request we will deny," said Dr. Metcalf.

"Wait." Dr. Regent held his hand up to Dr. Metcalf. "Why do you want to be reassigned without a shift?"

"I know that I have been Shifted on several occasions. I knew every time I was placed with a host family. I always break through the Shift. I also remember previous placements. It's a waste of time to Shift me."

"You always knew? And do you remember past placements?"

"I do remember some, not all," Ziph answered. "I would also like to have access to my files. I want to see if my memories of these placements are accurate."

"Dr. Regent, is this something you were aware of?"

"Yes. I just became aware of this aspect of Ziph's previous shifts."

"This is a problem. This should have been added to your reports before the committee considered this request."

"As I said, this information was gathered in the last few hours. I suspected that something like this was going on. I would like the opportunity to follow up on this. I will update the portfolio." Dr. Regent slid through the pile of folders until he tugged at the tag of a section and flipped and opened the folder in front of Metcalf. "I believe this will give you some insight into why this is an interesting development." He tapped the page and sat back, drumming his fingers on the other folders.

"Okay, Hmmmm, I see. If you are sure this is pertinent, I may be inclined to grant these permissions. But," she added, twisting up her mouth a bit. "I want weekly updates, especially on this particular matter."

"Agreed."

"But I still am filing my concerns and slight objections to allowing this to go forward without a Shift. I think this is a dangerous thing, especially in this circumstance." Dr. Metcalf moved her focus back to Ziph. "But I must admit that I, too, am interested in finding out how you remember these placements without having a bleed-back. Have you ever experienced a bleed-back?"

"No. I just know that I am not a part of the family."

"And other families? Have you known that as well?"

"Yes. Well, yes and no." Ziph shifted his weight onto the heels of his feet. "Sometimes I realized it after the fact."

"After the fact?"

"Yes, when I was placed elsewhere a few times, I remembered where I was before and..."

"I would really like this discussion to be in a more clinical rather than casual atmosphere." Dr. Regent interrupted.

"I need to know more about this before you get my approval." Metcalf tried to say this authoritatively, but it cracked when Regent slammed his fist down.

"That's what the damned research is about. I'll not have it undocumented in a casual conversation."

"Again, I have to raise my objections."

"Noted. Can we move on now?" Regent hated what felt like permission-gathering sessions. He wished he could just be done with this stupid woman once and for all. He was going to do whatever he saw fit anyway. He needed everyone to get on board and just get on with it now. This new development with Ziph was very interesting indeed. Ziph's awareness that he had been shifted without the bleed-backs fascinated him. Could Ziph possibly be a second biological source? First, the Shift-resistant, and now the possibility of Shift without damage? Suddenly, everything he had seen for this project seemed possible. This increasing phenomenon of Shift-resistant people who pulled out of the shifts within a few days proved to be only one aspect. And now, this shift-resistant child could break through shifts without any residual damage. He could hardly contain his excitement. Everything about Ziph would be charted, from his reactions to his memories to the damage left by the failed Shifts. By this time next week, he would know the inside of this child's brain better than anything else he knew in this world. And then, the real research could begin.

"Okay, Ziph, much against my better judgment, you will get your wish. But let me assure you that I will intervene and immediately act if you get out of hand." Dr. Metcalf peered over her glasses at Ziph. "And again, I must admonish you to stay away from the Bodaways. They were not completely Shifted. They only received suggestive memory realignments, so they are a bit precarious. Seeing you could easily break through the suggestion and create a rather, shall we say, inconvenient situation." Dr. Metcalf was using her school matron voice, and Dr. Regent wondered if Ziph was as irritated by this as he was.

"Thank you. I appreciate the opportunity to serve." Ziph bowed and then added, "But what do you mean? Why weren't they Shifted and separated?" Ziph slowly clenched his hands into fists, which he hid behind his back. He knew how anger showed on his face; his face would already be flushed pink around his hairline, and his eyes hooded and sunk deeper into his already pronounced cheekbones. His face became a collection of shadows and hollows when he was angry, and he looked ghoulish enough with these long, skinny arms and thin shoulders without the added betrayal of his face.

How did he expect them to take him seriously? He had to get control of his emotions and level his voice, or he would be tossed aside, and then he would have lost all respect from The Committee.

"Mr. Bodaway, check your tone. You are not a member of this Committee yet," Dr. Metcalf snapped.

"Do not call me Bodaway," he said with a sneer. "I have told you there is something suspicious there, and you have ignored me."

"No. We have not. We have taken your request quite seriously. We have spoken with Dr. Bodaway and have set some measures to ensure his constant monitoring and..."

"Monitoring? If I lived there and could not find anything, how would monitoring help?" Ziph shook his head and began to pace.

"I think you do not know your place here, young man. Check yourself before we Shift you to garbage detail." The rebuke came from Dr. Regent, whose voice bellowed across the room. "And, if you interrupt another member of this Committee, you will spend a few days in a very uncomfortable medicated delirium."

"Yes, Sir. I apologize, Sir." Ziph gained some control over his voice as he attempted a partial bow in submission to Dr. Regent, but his face was still burning with anger. He spread out his fingers to release the fists he still held behind his back and forced his shoulders down, willing them to loosen. "You are not yet privileged enough to know the proceedings of this Committee. But rest assured, we have considered everything. Now, I'd like to get to the matter at hand, your reassignment." Dr. Metcalf cleared her throat and rearranged several papers in front of her. "We have carefully considered who should be your mentor, and since you have requested that you go through this readjustment without a Shift, we have decided that you have the intelligence to go forward. This is a very special privilege, Ziph. I hope you treat it as such."

"Thank you, Ma'am. I certainly will. May I ask who I am to be assigned to?" His fingers stopped rolling into fists, and a more natural color returned to his face.

"That would be me, young man," Dr. Regent said, pulling his glasses down and peering over the frames at Ziph as he stared the boy down. "We decided you needed a strong and effective mentor, and I have volunteered. But let me assure you, Mr. Bodaway, that outbursts like this one today will absolutely not be tolerated." He knew Dr. Regent intentionally used his current last name to antagonize him. He clenched his jaw so he wouldn't take the bait.

"I am honored that you have chosen me. I will try to meet your expectations." Ziph made another slight bow to Dr. Regent.

"We will begin processing your papers, name change, and other necessary credentials. Until that process is completed, you will remain in the dorms. Once your training is completed, you will reside at Dr. Regent's residence." Her voice dismissed Ziph.

"Training?"

"Yes, since you will now be considered a possible successor to The Committee, there is quite a bit of training and orientation. You will not be allowed to leave until you prove you can handle this responsibility."

"Especially," Dr. Regent interrupted, "In the light of some of the attitude we have seen here today. Leaders do not behave this way. You do want to be a leader, don't you, young man?"

"Yes, Sir. Very much so."

"Good. Then we will begin the training process immediately." Dr. Metcalf shuffled more papers and then began to sign the pile she had organized in front of her.

"Oh, and young man," Dr. Regent admonished, "Again, and I will not move on this point, do not speak with or come into contact with the Bodaways. This is not a matter up for discussion. I will hold you responsible if anything happens to them. Whatever you think of them, The Committee still considers the Bodaways valuable assets. Very valuable assets, understood?"

"Yes, Sir. Understood."

Not quite, Ziph thought as he exited the committee chamber. *They are up to something, and I want to know what it is. They all think that because these two idiots created the meds, they are with the program. I know they aren't, and I'm going to prove it. If only they knew how much I hated being their son and having to put up with all that sweetness and civility. It makes my skin crawl. I would have ended up stuck in some dank research facility, never seeing the light of day. That's never going to happen now.*

Ziph wandered the corridors and headed to his favorite place, the Memory Shift Lab. He loved to watch these idiots lose their silly little lives; how he enjoyed watching their eyes go blank and dull. It always gave him a chuckle when they awoke to a whole new crappy little life. That was never going to happen to him. He was much too smart ever to be that insignificant.

The prospect of having Dr. Regent in his corner was interesting, unlike that milky-white Mrs. Metcalf. What could he ever learn from her: proper fashion and professional etiquette? He already had the plan in his head. Had spent those quiet, dull family reading nights with the Bodaways researching the members of The Committee. He knew their weaknesses, fetishes, and every hidden secret pushed under the rug. He was going to have fun discrediting them. Yes, everything was falling into place nicely. How was he ever the son of those two meek and appropriate idiots? How could he ever reach his potential if he had stayed with them?

But he had to admit that Dr. Regent was a little intimidating. Cruel even. But that never really worried Ziph. Besides, he had the biggest file on Regent. The doctor had many secrets, and Ziph was planning to exploit every single one of them. Yes, this changes everything. He settled into an observation booth as a young girl was brought in for her seventh Shift. She was crying, kicking, and clawing the face of a Collector. *Oh yeah*, he thought, *what I could do to her that she wouldn't even remember in her shiny new life.*

What Ziph was searching for had nothing to do with serving The Committee. He had been searching for other answers if he was honest with himself. He wanted to know why these families could not embrace him as their own and why he always felt as if he observed his own life from the outside. Each family experience had been worse than the last. His obsession with understanding this grew into a gnarled ball in the pit of his stomach. He knew it was wrong to blame everything on the Bodaways, but they had been the one family he wanted to fit into. The one family that mattered to him. That was done now.

He had welcomed that pinch in his arm and the hiss of sedation that blended with the foggy murmur of the Collector's voices in the other room. He had stolen one last glance into their room as they propelled him down the hallway and let out the unchecked *Mom* before he could stop himself. He hated that he had sounded so vulnerable and scared and felt a split second of regret. He had loved Saige. Had wanted her to love him back. But he wasn't hers. And she wasn't his. *That*, he thought, *is my biggest regret.* But this wasn't the time for regret or sadness. This was the time to stop being a child from a powerless family and stick with the plan. There was no time for all of this sentimental emotion; all that was important now was his place on The Committee.

Yes, everything would be very different now.

7

The sun was rising over The Forty, and Chase was exhausted beyond the need for sleep. He had been ready to drop when they had to do the whole building-jumping thing to escape from the Collectors. This new place was safer, but it was a two-hour ride from the city, and the drive back always pushed his limits. He knew they were safer living this far out despite the rumors of chemical poisoning and Virus scares. Usually, Sam drove back, but Chase was too worked up after the near run-in with the Collectors in the hallway. And Ziph. Seeing Ziph just brought it all back. He was jumpy and edgy and told everyone to sleep so he could drive quietly and try to deal with it all.

Sam had been awake for about fifteen minutes, studying Chase behind his dark glasses. Something was making Chase skittish, but it was more than that; it was like he was somewhere else lately. He was even more shut off than usual, setting off all of Sam's warning flags.

"So, uh, what happened to you back there?" Sam said. "Not used to seeing you so spooked."

"Yeah, spooked. Let's call it that. Could you see the hallway from where you were?"

"No. I had just entered the hallway when I saw your hand go up. I got Kalare and Jo-Jo into the stairwell and was headed back for you when you got to the stairs. You usually get a rush from coming that close to The

Collectors. This was different."

"Yeah, this was different. They were taking my, uh, some kid out. Some kid I used to know."

"Oh, I get it. Somebody you knew well?"

"No, he was somebody that, um, well, it just brought up some issues for me." Chase tried to pass it off casually. He wasn't ready to go there. Not even with Sam. He realized he was thumping his foot. "Maybe justice is served sometimes."

"Yeah. Justice. I think we need to find new suppliers. This is the third close call this week."

They could smell the ocean long before reaching the small neighborhood of crumbling houses surrounding the forty-story hotel. The houses gave them a natural built-in level of security, and the beach and ocean kept them safe from danger on the other side. They could station someone to guard a few blocks from The Forty, which had a central high-rise with three wings extending from the main building. These sections were ten floors high and could easily be used as ground guard posts.

They set up one wing as a makeshift hospital, putting people there when they got sick. They had no medical equipment, and no one had any medical training, but at least they could keep the kids with runny noses and bad coughs separated from the others. Most of the lower floors of the main building were already boarded up, so any activity on the bottom floors was obscured. Using the upper floors gave them a vantage point, kept everyone centralized, and gave them some cover if anyone came to the hotel. There were enough beds, blankets, and other furniture left behind that they could use. Most of it was in pretty bad shape, but at least they had something to sleep on.

This was probably the best spot they'd lived in so far. There was no running water or electricity, but they got a small portable stove and propane bottles on one of the raids so they could at least cook.

They had skids of bottled water that worked out fine for washing and cooking, but Chase would give anything for a nice hot shower.

There were about twenty of them now. Their numbers shifted from day to day. Chase tried to do most things democratically, but ultimately, he depended on Sam and Kalare to help him make decisions. Chase, Kalare, Sam, and now Jo-Jo did the food and supply runs. Chase and Sam usually stayed closer to the ground floor while Jo-Jo and Tya cared for the kids on one of the upper floors. Kalare hated kid duty and would rather be out playing sentry with a gun slung over her chest. She saw herself more on Sam and Chase's level than on Tya and Jo-Jo's. Even though Jo-Jo was coming along, she was still a bit too girly for Kalare's taste. She respected Chase and did what he needed, but at times, she felt pushed out of the buddy thing Chase and Sam had going. She wasn't exactly one of the guys, but she wasn't one of the girls either.

Chase and Kalare stretched as they got out of the truck. Jo-Jo ran on ahead, pulled off her jacket, and sat just a little too close to Kit, who was standing guard in the first row of houses. They could hear her flirty giggle, then Kit's deeper laugh in response. Kit had wandered into one of the squatter houses right before they moved everyone out to The Forty. He kept mostly to himself and volunteered to stand guard all night, which was fine with Chase, since they never knew who might wander out and find them. He also stayed behind with Tya to help with the kids whenever Chase took the others out on food runs. Kit never shared why he was on the streets; he just shrugged and said, 'Everybody has a story, so what? We are all here either way.' Chase certainly understood not wanting to relive it whenever you met someone. So, he took Kit at face value and asked him along when they moved out to The Forty. He was a strong point guard. Taking in someone new, especially someone strong enough to use as a guard, was always dangerous.

"I think Jo-Jo has a crush."

"Yeah, not sure I like that."

"They are cute together, don't you think?" Kalare smiled. "It might be good for her."

"I guess. Something about him doesn't seem right." Chase draped his arm around her shoulders. She was a few inches shorter than him, making for a very comfortable nook to lean into.

"Really? I thought you were okay with Kit?"

"You know me, Sam." Chase shrugged and let out a small chuckle.

"Sometimes it takes a while for me to get there."

Tya appeared in the doorway, broke into a jog, threw her tattooed arms over her head, and ran toward Sam, the early morning light glinting off the piercings on her face. She let out a shriek that landed somewhere between a mouse's squeal and a hawk's cry. Her long, straight, ponytailed hair bounced out from the top of her head like a long horse's mane, accentuating the arched angle of her eyes and cheekbones. This week, her hair was jet-black and fell across her face, creating a ghostly pallor along a porcelain cheekbone. Her hair bounced back and forth with each exaggerated step she took. Sam towered over her short frame, and she looked even tinier, jumping onto him and wrapping her legs around his back. Sam wrapped his arms around her as she covered his face with kisses. "You were gone so long. I was lonely."

"We had a few close calls and couldn't get any meds. We have to make another run." Sam was trying to talk between a barrage of kisses to his cheeks, lips, and forehead. He started laughing so hard that he lost his balance, and they both fell.

"Ah, felled again by the dread, tiny four-foot kissing woman."

"Hey!" Tya said, feigning hurt feelings, and then she kissed him with more serious intent.

"Thought you were shy." Sam returned the kiss.

"I was. Now, I'm not. Are you hungry? There's food. You guys should eat." She stood, slid Sam's backpack onto her right shoulder and curled her other arm around his waist.

Chase smiled when he heard Sam laugh. He liked Tya. She was good for Sam. Her playfulness brought out the softness he tried so hard to hide. Tya had only been with them for about six months. She was picked up for Shifting after her parents turned her in for being rebellious. She had run away several times and returned with another tattoo or a different color streak in her hair each time. They finally turned her in when she came home one night drunk with three new piercings on her eyebrow, lip, and nose. But she didn't respond to the pre-shift drugs, and when the collectors got her to the transport, she elbowed the one holding her and broke his nose, then took his gun and shot both the Collectors. She wandered around the docks for a couple of weeks, trying to find food. The first time Sam saw her, she was beating up a shop owner who tried to grab her for shoplifting. She was sweet, funny, and shy, but could fight back like a beast when she needed to. She had totally captured his heart. She liked caring for the kids and had no interest in guarding or going on the raids. She kept the kids fed and clean, or at least as fed and clean as she could.

"Thanks, but I'm too tired to eat. I just want sleep." Chase yawned as he reached the entrance to The Forty. He was exhausted now that all the tension from running into Ziph was fading. *Ziph.*

"Sam, give me a few hours and then get everyone together. We need new ideas for getting supplies so we can cut down on these night raids.

I'll call Seth to see if he can set up anything for us."

"You got it, Brother." Sam picked Tya up and threw her over his shoulder. "Now, what's this rumor I hear about food?"

Chase collapsed onto the mattress, fully clothed; he was too tired to undress. He fell into a deep sleep quickly, but the dream woke him in a sweat. Why had he seen Ziph tonight? He was just getting to the point where the dreams had stopped, and now they were back again. Chase wished he could have gotten a better look at what was happening back at the apartment complex. Maybe he was getting Shifted, but that was probably just wishful thinking. He couldn't see the man they were dragging out. But he knew who it was. And if Ziph was with the man, he had a pretty good idea of what was happening. That's what kept tugging at him. The memories he had managed to push back on the ride home rushed at him all at once now. That place was where he became Chase and lost so much. He couldn't think about that, but his brain couldn't focus on anything else. Either way, sleep was not going to come. He pulled off his jacket, went into the bathroom, and splashed water on his face from a water bottle on the sink. He finished off the water in large gulps. He had to find a way to let this go. This wasn't doing him any good. He had to stop thinking. And suddenly, he was starving.

8

After they had taken Thad and Ziph, after they had whispered the new orders, after they had removed everything from Ziph's room, after the apartment was quiet for what seemed like hours, Saige turned her head and quietly sobbed into her pillow. Maybe she didn't want to take the drugs anymore. Maybe knowing how all this really worked was too much. So, what if she were reassigned? She would always be a doctor, that she knew for sure. Maybe all this knowledge was more than she could bear, especially if she lost Thad. She rolled over to his side of the bed. She could still smell him on his pillow and pulled it close to her. Then she realized that all of Thad's things were still there. The Collectors had not erased him from existence as they had with Ziph. This was a relief, just as overwhelming. She pressed her face into his pillow and breathed in that familiar, soapy scent that always filled her with a sense of security. She thought again of his dark hair falling into his eyes as they took him away. Tried to hold on to the memory of his face, hair, shoulders, and feet, his limp feet, as they dragged him from the room. Had she really seen the glint of blue from his eyes, or was it just her imagination? She remembered his arms around her, the warmth of his hand on the small of her back, and the softness of his fingertips along her cheek. This is why; she reminded herself. This was always why. Thad.

Saige stared at the clock, rolling numbers one through sixty. And then again and again until her vision blurred the numbers. Then she heard the snap of the lock on the front door, the sweep of wood against the rug, and the rustle of cloth on cloth. She closed her eyes as they pulled Thad down the hallway, set him on the bed, whispered something into his ear, and left the room. She waited for the closing click before opening her eyes. Even just the pressure of him lying beside her slowed her heartbeat. Just his scent calmed her. She watched the clock flip for a few more minutes until she finally heard his breath catch as he rolled over to her side of the bed, his arm wrapped around her and pulled her to him in one motion. His lips were at her ear, and she could feel the air tickle at the small hairs of her neck as he took a long, deep breath and released it.

"Saige," he whispered. "Are you still my girl?"

"Always." She turned and muffled her cries into her pillow. He held her until the sobs became hiccups; the shaking became slow breathing. He pulled at her shoulders to turn her to face him. Her dark eyes searched into his shaded blue to be sure he was still there. Still Thad.

"I thought. I was. I wasn't sure," she whispered. She softly touched his cheek as if he were a hologram that might disintegrate at her touch. When he remained solid, she tangled her fingers into the hair at the nape of his neck.

"I know. I know." He explored her eyes and ran one fingertip along her cheek, jawline, and lips. He pressed his lips to hers and kissed her with just a hint of pressure on her lips, then a tenuous but more intentional pressing. He had come so close to losing her again tonight. Then the desperation hit him, and he buried his face into her shoulder, her hair. He allowed himself one relieved sob before wrapping arms and legs around her, pulling her closer to him, into him, under him. He rose onto his knees, tugged back the covers, then threw them to the ground and yanked at her sweatpants to pull them off in one motion.

"I need you now." He said to her, pulling off his shirt.

"You have me."

He lifted her shirt and buried his face into her chest, listening to her heartbeat race as he stroked her back, leaned onto his left hand, and slipped his right hand down her side and over her hip. When she shifted, his hand reached low and slid his fingers down so he could linger for a few minutes at her favorite spot. She tried to reach down to touch him, but he whispered, "No," and waited for her familiar gasp as his fingers slid into her.

"Now," she said.

He pulled onto his knees, pressed down with his hips, and slid into her, fast and hard.

"I can't go slow."

"Then don't go slow." She arched her hips to him and wrapped her arms around his back.

"I thought I lost you tonight." She said, trying not to cry, but the tears spilled out anyway.

"Never," he said. "You'll never lose me." He lost himself to the rhythm then, forgetting everything except her, the feel of her, the smell of her; she was the only thing that existed for him now.

She pulled her legs up, locked her ankles around his thighs, and forced him closer. She wanted him to crush her until it pushed away all the terror she had felt tonight. And when he pressed even further into her, she let it all go until nothing existed but the rhythm of their breathing, the collision of desperate hands probing, and the agreement of their bodies folding into one another.

Light filtered into the room, and they woke to a tangle of blankets, sheets, arms, and legs. Neither spoke. Neither wanted to talk about what came next.

"You know what we need?" Thad said, handing Saige a cup of coffee. "A real day off; let's get out of the city for the day."

Thad realized that between his inquisition with The Committee and the reports from Thomas and Ziph, he was definitely on The Committee's radar now. They wouldn't just let it go. There was no way to know if they erased the memory of Thad's breach from

Thomas. For all he knew, Thomas had been instructed to report back on all of his movements. But that same stinging fear hit in the center of his chest: What if Saige was no longer the woman he thought she was? What if she turned him in or, even worse, informed on his every move? Then he guessed he wouldn't care if they Shifted him. He would have lost her anyway.

His heart ached for his brother and the things he assumed Thomas would never remember about them. But something else was nagging at him, something else he longed for; it was right there on the periphery of his memory. Something nudged at him more and more lately, hovering just beyond his understanding, just beyond his reach. He felt an ethereal loss he couldn't explain.

It wasn't about Ziph or Thomas. This was something else. He still wasn't sure how he felt about the loss of Ziph. The most attainable emotion he could identify was one of relief. The guilt about that would haunt him for a bit. But he always suspected that if he were Shifted, it would be at the hands of Ziph. The loss of Thomas hurt. Hurt badly. Not the betrayal but the loss of him. The next time they met, Thomas might not even know they were brothers. He didn't know what he would do if he ever lost Saige. Even the thought of it killed him a little each time it pushed into his mind. But he wouldn't care what they did with him if he ever lost her. None of it would matter. And maybe that would be when he could move into action. *Maybe.*

He knew he had to tell Saige about everything that had happened in the last thirty-six hours. But now that morning was here, he wasn't so sure. What does he tell her? Where does he begin? Does he tell her everything? And he meant *everything*. And what if, after he did, she didn't see him the same way? Would there even be a place for him anymore? Would she agree to leave with him? Even though she had fought him on that point so many times in the past. One thing was certain: if The Committee was watching them, as he suspected they were, they might not have any other choice but to leave everything and go. But go where?

There were stories of people who had fled the city and found

themselves in the unprotected sector. But the warnings about contamination remained widespread. Despite that, there was a rumor of a
gathering force of people opposed to The Committee. Maybe he
could find a way to contact them. But how does he go from working
for The Committee to fleeing The Committee, to joining others who
have escaped and are actively fighting The Committee? How does he
get from here to there? Where does he even start? And he realized he
had to start where everything begins. He had to talk to Saige.

"Yes," Saige said around a bite of scrambled egg. "I would love to
get out of this city." She almost called out for Ziph and caught herself.
That would be the first red flag. He guessed someone was listening,
and he realized it was safer to assume so. At some point during the
night, as she stared at those numbers on the clock ticking by, she had
decided it was time to tell Thad everything.

No matter the consequences. She had started remembering
things lately, and she had to find out whether they were, in fact,
memories or just bad dreams that lingered after she woke up. She
knew she had been having these bouts of false memories for years
now, so many flashes of places and people that she assumed didn't
exist. She blamed it on lack of sleep and working too hard. But she
couldn't shush the voices in her head so easily anymore. Maybe she
was crazy. Maybe all these years of being stuck in a lab day and night
were catching up to her. But Thad had a right to know whatever was
going on, especially if she was losing her mind. The hallucinations
and dreams were more defined and more frequent lately. What if
they weren't really dreams? What if everything in this life was manu-
factured, and she was remembering her real life? What if she had
been Memory Shifted and didn't remember? What if Ziph was not
her son? What about the boy in her dreams? The boy whose face she
could never see? She knew instinctively it was her son. The tilt of the
head seemed so familiar; what if he was real? What would she do
then?

They dressed quickly after a light breakfast. Thad pushed water,
and Saige pushed orange juice. As soon as they were in the car, a
darker mood took over. While Thad was sure this was the right next

step, the possibility of having misread each other could prove lethal. Saige was chewing on her cuticles when Thad reached over and pulled her hand into his and lightly kissed her fingertips. He shook her hand until she looked at him. Then he grinned at her.

"Still my girl?"

"Always," Saige gave him a sad smile. Everything was coming out more seriously than she had intended.

"Do you remember the cabin?" Thad said with a mischievous smile.

"The one by the lake?" The seclusion of the cabin was like their other universe. They had honeymooned there long ago, and the days were sun on bare skin and the ease of effortless afternoons when Saige and Thad tangled around each other exploring the depths of a new openness. It was a honeymoon freed from laboratories, security badges, military escorts and the demands of a new life and a new assignment. She had never wanted to leave.

The cabin was just a short drive south along the line of hills that ringed the city. This more secluded area was included when the city's parameters were set. It seemed like a good place for the more elite and military heads to live, especially when the crime rate and virus-sick wanderers overran the streets. But the seclusion created security risks, and in the end, the renovated high-rises proved a more secure option where they could be guarded and safe; and of course, monitored by The Committee. Since the cabin was within the parameters of the guarded sections that didn't require permission, certain citizens were allowed to use the few functioning homes that dotted the landscape. Thad thought it was the perfect place to say what needed to be said.

"I think that would be a lovely way to spend the day." Saige reached over and threaded her fingers into the cluster of curls resting on his neck. It would be the one place they could speak freely. It was then that she knew they understood each other fully. Thad accelerated the car, and the city skyline shrank behind them.

9

"I don't know what we should do with that one," Dr. Metcalf said as she rearranged papers on her desk.

"Why do we keep shifting him around? It's obvious he's going to be a problem." She was sunk into the oversized desk chair behind her enormous, ornate, wood-carved desk, making her look like a marionette caricature of herself. The office was decorated like a museum from some obscure, overstuffed period in France, and it gave Dr. Regent an itching in the back of his throat every time he stepped into her office. He tried to move slowly, afraid he would dislodge some fragment of dust that would choke his last breath out of him. He much preferred the clean lines and sterile cleanliness of his own office to the frilled lace and wall hangings. He could see the dust piled on them from where he sat. The dust was so thick it changed the deep red and gold to a pale yellow that ghosted along the top edges like phantoms about to leap from the darkened corner. He needed to get this meeting over with quickly.

"He's very promising. I want to give this one more try," Dr. Regent lowered his glasses and peered at Dr. Metcalf over the rims. There were so many things he was grooming Ziph for; so many plans that could use someone like him. This new development was going to prove to be very auspicious, very auspicious indeed.

"I thought the Bodaways would be a good placement, but he seems to have actually gotten worse in a less violent atmosphere. And this whole business of accusing them, I don't think he understands the value in these two. I never agreed with removing their son and replacing him with Ziph. It seemed a cruel thing to do to loyalists." She got out of her chair, crossed the room, pulled a small box from the over-stacked bookshelf and sprinkled food into a small fishbowl that held a gasping, half-dead orange fish. Dr. Regent shifted in his seat. The sight of the half-lilting fish nauseated him.

"This was the one memory shift I regret, placing Ziph with them." Dr. Regent cleared his throat with a guttural grunt. "Especially when their son eluded The Collectors and consequently was never Shifted."

"We have tried to keep tabs on the boy. He was along the docks a while, but he's either died or has left the city. Either way, it solves our problem, doesn't it?" Dr. Metcalf had seated herself back behind her desk and was sipping tea out of a ridiculously small teacup.

"Look, the Bodaways are the most important aspect of this research. We need to ensure that Ziph lets go of this vendetta against them. He could compromise everything with that temper of his. And now this incident with Thad's brother is also a bit troubling. We weren't going to shift Thomas completely, but after Thomas reported to the Collector that the protocol wasn't followed, we had to do a complete wipe. Thaddeus did administer the correct medication, as he should have. Do you think we need to put more surveillance in place?" Dr. Regent never let an extra layer of protection go. Although he couldn't think of any more precautions they could take against the Bodaways. They were already monitoring all research at the lab, car GPS, phones and security tags. The information from the TALUS, which they had programmed to serve as Thad's advocate, was downloaded weekly. He really couldn't see what else they could do other than inject devices. But he didn't think they were there yet. Not yet, anyway.

"I don't think so. They have instructed the wife to report anything unusual, and I think the surveillance already in place is fine for now. We gave them both the day off to clear their systems of the drugs administered last night. We don't want them to make an error in their research because we responded to a complaint. But we have to look like we are doing our due diligence. They are at a lake house, and tomorrow we will resume daily routines." Dr. Metcalf concluded and shifted papers in front of her into a separate pile. She took the pile and handed it across the desk to Dr. Regent, had to half-lay across the large desk to take it from her hand.

"That is all the necessary forms to transition Ziph. I hope you know what you are doing there." She let go of the folder as if it burned her hand, and she was glad to be rid of it.

"I have a few ideas on how to cope with him, but I also don't want to risk triggering isolated memory recalls at this juncture." *And I am really going to enjoy knocking that little brat down a peg or two. That's why I didn't want him shifted. I want him fully aware, with his total memory intact, when I crush him,* thought Dr. Regent.

"Be careful there. I think he is dangerous and should be Shifted into a low-level job here. I know he is loyal and seems like he would be a good soldier, but there is something about that boy that is fairly disturbing." Dr. Metcalf had worked with that type before. One minute, they shake your hand, and the next, they slit your throat. She was glad he hadn't become her responsibility. She would not have been able to sleep with him in her home. It was bad enough that he was roaming the halls here. Who knew what he was going to get into next?

"Oh, I think little Ziph might just have met his match." Dr. Regent chuckled. He was going to enjoy this. Yes, he was going to enjoy this very much.

"Shall we move on to new business?"

"Ah, yes. The dispersal project." Regent shuffled a few papers just for effect. He knew the results and the problems like the back of his hand. The damn synthetics just weren't sustainable, but there was no way he was going to give any of that away to Metcalf. "We have procured a new laboratory to re-synthesize the pre-shifting. I want a two-pronged approach involving water and airborne dispersal. Water is easy, aerosol is a bit more complicated. The aerosol is the preferable goal; easier delivery and less manpower." Dr. Regent coughed and cleared his throat several times before nodding to Dr. Metcalf to continue.

"Will this help alleviate the personnel strain?" Dr. Metcalf looked through a report on her desk. "Oh, never mind, I do have that. We would still use collectors, but the subjects would not have to be removed from the home for memory reassignment. Full Memory Shifts would still require collection. That should cut down the workforce by half."

"Yes, the dispersals will have everyone prepped, so incidents could also be handled on the spot. Someone could simply call the Collectors from the workplace and escort the offender to a designated quiet room. The whole affair is completed in less than five minutes. Also, we would no longer need the physicians to go along, so they could devote more time to research."

"Do we keep certain populations from being dosed?"

"At this point, our only alternative is to fit special water filtering and air filtering systems into specific offices and residences. Obviously, we don't want to dose committee members, program associates, or physicians. If a problem arises, it will be handled on a one-on-one basis. I think this is the best next step given the encouraging results we have seen in this program."

"And the Bodaways?"

"We are still waiting on their blocking mechanism research and possible conversion to a vaccine, but we need an organic source. The synthetic preliminaries are promising but weak." Dr. Regent sat back and frowned. He hadn't meant to play that card yet. He shuffled through another folder as if he were looking for something. Since he had stuck his foot in his mouth, he may as well lay the groundwork now. "I think the biologic portion of this research needs to become our central focus very quickly."

"Are we still using an isolated prisoner populace in our first rollout?" She slid the remaining papers into a larger file and placed it on the shelf behind her.

"Yes, these test subjects are our priority, and then we can compare them to the untreated. Of course, we are still a long way off from the most effective use, but we are getting closer every day, and this airborne dispersal is the most crucial piece. Once we have that in place, all systems are set to move on to the next stage. As I said, the Bodaways' initial results are still in the first stages, but it seems promising, very promising."

"So, it seems we are right on track. Thank you for spearheading this dispersal project. Keep me informed."

"Yes, right back on track." Dr. Regent mumbled as he slipped his papers into his briefcase, nodded and stepped into the cooler air of the hallway. These meetings that kept up the pretense of Metcalf running things were getting tedious. But it was necessary if he was going to accomplish what he needed to in the next six weeks. The more it looked like she was pushing the charge, the more he could focus on other, more sensitive areas. So, he was forced to play this little game for now. But he had to deal with Ziph quickly. He had to get Ziph under some sort of control. Although he knew a Shift would help subdue him, it would take at least three months to get him back up to the levels he was testing at now, and he needed Ziph's intelligence quotient to be at its highest for what was coming next.

He knew he had a soft spot for the Bodaways, especially Saige. He also knew it clouded his judgment sometimes and that he gave in to things that he wouldn't under other circumstances. But after all, it was Saige. He knew from the start that he had found a gem in her. He put everything into her from the very beginning, and except for her needing a little prodding along the way and a little gentle direction to get her moving, it had all worked out marvelously. Yes, his little gem was working out quite well despite the occasional interference of Thaddeus. And although Thaddeus was a bit harder to handle, in the scheme of things, he had also grown fond of him. After all, he was taking care of Regent's most precious commodity: Saige Bodaway.

10

eth pulled out the earpiece and dropped it onto the shoulder of a crisply ironed, buttoned-down pale blue Oxford shirt. He ran his hand through short-cropped blonde hair, removed his glasses and rubbed at his eyes with the heels of his hands. He was about to click off when he heard *aerosol dispersal*. He had to have heard wrong. *Was that right? Did I hear that right? Were they talking about dosing everyone?* He restarted the file, wiggled the earpiece back into his ear, and watched it a third time, staring angrily at the casual images of Drs. Metcalf and Regent. He had been updating settings for the Committee Chair's office. The previous Chair had all devices set to respond to voice and movement. The new Chair had requested that these settings be switched back to manual, and he was in the process of doing so when the recording clicked on automatically.

Seth's official title was Senior Specialist, Security. This meant he had the highest clearance level in the facility and access to everything: Committee files, research lab testing and reports, basic information storage, personnel files, and, most importantly, security. Along with his own research, he provided and monitored security and maintenance for all conference rooms, Shift Labs, and all records associated with the program, including extension labs and side projects. It was his job to keep everything interconnected and in running order. More importantly, it was also his job to keep unauthorized personnel from accessing anything outside of their specific sphere. He was the invisible fly on everyone's wall. He monitored, categorized and filed everything. A pin didn't drop without his recording and logging it. A lot of the conversations were typical office chatter, but a good deal of the information fell into the top-secret category, if terms like that even existed anymore.

His office was a littered cave of confusion. Rather than have the multiple screens spread across a wall that other employees might see, the monitors and recording devices were layered around him like a fortress. He was encased in an ever-expanding bank of equipment that kept all eyes from his screens. The walls behind his desk were littered with sheets of paper tacked so densely that they created several layers along the walls and in the corners above and around his desk. This wall of papers blocked any cameras that might have been installed behind him. He was pretty sure he had them all blocked but took as few chances as possible. The Committee, knowing he was monitoring their every move, decided it was in their best interest to allow him his space. They overlooked the messiness of his office, seeing it as quirky idiosyncrasies.

What the Committee didn't know was that this was also home base for all of Seth's special interests. For those he trusted, he supplied information, hard-to-obtain items, forged security papers, safe transport, and the occasional friendly syntH packet. He had a circuit of servers and connections across the city that was accessed through a central hub buried deep in the network's workings. Although Central Security could access his files and monitor his search histories, no one could decipher his encryption. After a few months of weekly meetings where he was asked to explain what was found, they just gave up on monitoring him, deciding it was a waste of manpower. His security clearance process had been exhaustive. There wasn't a blip that came up that caused even the slightest concern. He stood firm on this investigation, reminding them that he was the head technician who supervised the setup for the entire network. Since they didn't even understand him when he explained the files, they relied on their vetting and allowed him to do his job without interference.

Seth used this, like everything else, to his advantage.

He separated the audio file, pushed an earbud into the slot and transferred it onto an external drive. He hit playback and listened to be sure the audio copied correctly. He typed *anoot. 9. Chaser* into his phone, made three more copies, and then filed the audio clip under an obscure name in a utility file several layers in. He renamed the video file and saved it in a different directory. He pulled up the work order, typed in "COMPLETED," and closed out the file. Only the completed work order remained on Dr. Metcalf's server. No one would be looking for the file since the request for manual audio verification had been completed.

He stared at the blank screen for several minutes and decided to take the chance. He took the back stairs up three floors to Thad's desk and wrote: Hey Doc, I have preliminary results on new security updates for your lab.

I think you need an Exit lockdown.
Let's meet in the morning.
S

He taped the note to Thad's keyboard as his phone buzzed. He glanced down at the message, typed "SET," hit Send, and then deleted both texts. He exited the building through the usual checkpoint and headed to the garage. He flipped open the glove box, popped off the panel behind the lock and disabled his GPS. He slid all of his access cards into a thin lead-plated envelope, sealed it and popped open a back compartment. He switched off his phone, removed the battery, slipped it into another envelope, dropped both into the compartment, then clicked the cover back into place. He pulled a second phone from the center console, powered it up, typed in GO, and hit send to a multiple-user list. A few minutes later, the phone buzzed, and the message read: GO2-9. He pressed the ignition button, said, "Music on," and all eight speakers vibrated the floorboards as he pulled out of the garage and into heavy late-afternoon traffic.

Seth stood on the roof shivering, smoking a cigarette that only made him shake more. He hated this part of the city. The creepy, tall, windowless skyscrapers that stared back were filled with dark holes that dwarfed the few buildings with electricity. He would rather be sitting in his sterile lab safe inside his massive bank of equipment and monitors.

"What is it with you and this roof?" Seth said as Chase and Sam came over the side of the building. "I'm not the athletic type. And I still don't understand why you don't just use the back stairs?" "Hey," said Sam.

"You know, exercise, wide open spaces, keeping up my youthful figure. So, what's the emergency?" Chase was not in the mood. Three nights in a row at this building was more than he could take. But Seth was an old friend and his main source for meds and other hard-to-get supplies, so he dropped everything when Seth needed him; he was the only person besides Sam that Chase trusted in this way.

"I have the meds you asked for and a first-aid kit." Seth handed him a stuffed backpack.

"I also have something you need to hear. I don't even know what to say about this." Seth held out the earbud. He noticed his hand was shaking from more than the cold. This had really rattled him. He wasn't even sure why. It certainly wasn't the worst thing he overheard in that place.

Chase slipped the earbud in and pushed it to play. After a few seconds, he paused the recording and looked at Seth. "Is this for real?"

"Afraid so."

Chase clicked it again and listened to the rest of the recording.

When it finally ended, he pulled the earbud from his ear and handed it to

Sam. "Not good."

"Can we keep this?" Now, Chase's hand was the one that was shaking.

"Yeah. It's all yours. I might have a favor to ask of you, though. I mean, I know you hate the grown-up types and all, but I think I need an extraction. And I might need it very soon."

"Who?"

"The Bodaways. As you heard, they are being targeted. I know they think they are in the clear, but if Ziph has anything to do with it, he will destroy them. I have a meeting with Dr. Bodaway tomorrow. I don't even know how to broach this with him, but if they need extraction, will you do it?" Seth was shaking from the cold. He took a long drag on his cigarette, hoping the nicotine would warm him. It didn't help.

"Oh, Seth, man, I don't know. I mean. Shit, man. I don't know." Chase's voice cracked.

"You can give them the option without any names and locations, right?" Sam asked. "I mean, we need to be sure we are still safe if they don't want to go along with it."

"Sure. I mean, I wouldn't give names, locations, promises or anything. That's all up to you. You guys need to meet with them and sort all that out. Like I said, they might not even be open to it. I just have this bad feeling." Seth shrugged his shoulders. "They've been really good to me. I kinda feel like I owe them."

"I'll meet with them, but no promises. If he's all big-man-doctor, it's a no-go. I don't need that shit. We got things going pretty smoothly now, and the last thing we need is some outsider being all parental." Chase was growing angrier as he spoke.

"Yeah, parental. Wow. Shit. Oh man. I'm sorry. I didn't even think about that. I just thought of you guys because you are so far out there now, it would probably be safer than stashing them somewhere in the city." Seth took another drag from his cigarette. "You know what? Forget I even brought it up. I'll find another way."

"No. No. I get it. I'll meet with them. Leave a Chaser with a double twist message, and I'll know that's what it's about."

"This is scary shit." Sam handed Chase the earbud. "Thanks for the meds and the intel. You should come visit." Sam grinned. "It'll be like a day at the beach."

"Is it thirty stories up?"

"No," Chase smiled. "Forty."

11

T *had* and Saige pulled up to the cabin and left everything they brought from home in the car. They carried only the bag of new clothes they had bought on the way up to the cabin. The day was cool, but they stripped off their clothes and left everything in a pile on the porch before entering the cabin and showering to remove any small listening devices that might be on their skin or in their hair. They double-checked each other's ears and hairlines, then changed into clean clothes, shivering on the porch as the late-afternoon sun fell behind the trees encircling the cabin.

They walked around the lake, not speaking; speaking would make it real. It amazed Thad how they did all these things as if they were instinctively falling into a familiar pattern. They walked halfway around the lake before he could even decide where to begin.

"I've been dosing you for six months," Saige said. It broke the silence around and between them and should have been more ominous, but Thad broke into a throaty laugh.

"That means that I've been double-dosing you." Thad shook his head. "How?"

"Orange juice."

"Water. So, we are saying the same thing?" Saige searched his eyes.

There was so much at stake.

"Yes. I think so." Thad took her left hand and kissed her palm. "I'm sorry I did it behind your back. I didn't know where you stood, and I didn't want to lose you."

"I felt the same way. I have been taking the meds for three years, but I waited to dose you because it seemed so devious." Saige said.

"I started dosing around the same time."

"I don't know, I just felt that something wasn't right. I was scared that we had been shifted. But I couldn't pull any of it out of my head." Saige rubbed her temples. "It's like something got lost in there that is really important, but I can't figure out what it is."

"Me too. I felt like something was lost. I had this sadness for no reason." The muscle in his jaw started flexing, and his anger from last night flared again. "So, they shifted us."

"Yes. I think so. But when? Was it Ziph, do you think? Something is not right there." Saige flushed with a surge of guilt. "Does that make me a bad mother?"

"No. Ziph went to the committee about us."

"So, he was inserted." Saige felt this as confirmation, not a realization. Somewhere deep inside her, she already knew it was the truth.

"I think so. And worse, I think he replaced our real son. I think I lost my son. Our son." Thad's eyes filled with tears, but he pushed them back. There was so much more to talk about. He would never get through it all if he lost control of his emotions.

Saige touched the side of his face.

"I'm so sorry. I think I feel that loss too. But it's obviously rising to the surface much stronger for you. Our minds are amazing; that's why Shifting never holds. Repressed memories are intricately embedded and triggered by so many sensory responses that there is no way to erase them completely." How could she feel a loss she didn't even remember? They worked for these people, and they had taken their son away and replaced him like he was a piece of old furniture. She felt sadness, but she could see Thad's anger beginning to surge.

"I think I put us under the microscope," Thad said, and then he couldn't hold back his tears. "They got Thomas."

Saige wrapped her arms around him and let him give in to his loss. It's one thing to have a feeling, which could be a remnant of a dream or a focus on a fear. But it was something else altogether to realize that it was reality. Saige pulled Thad onto the ground, and they lay there wrapped around each other, staring at the sky in silence.

"What do you mean you put us under a microscope?"

"They had me do Thomas' collection."

"Oh, Thad. I'm so sorry."

"That's not the worst part. I shot him with a Barbiturate instead of pre-shift. And he told the collectors."

"No! How could he? I don't understand."

"He looked me straight in the eye and said I'd made a mistake. Told the Collector it had to be reported."

"What did you do?

"I gave him the prep drugs. What else could I do at that point? I told the collector I gave him a sedative because he was agitated. I can't believe he turned me in. And can't believe I almost lost you over it." Thad pulled her closer and placed a kiss on the top of her head as he breathed in the scent of her hair. He always pulled everything about her into his senses as if every embrace was the last time he would hold, smell, or have her.

"So, they took you in front of the Committee?"

"Yes, they are rewriting our protocols. I noted that I wasn't required to report additional meds or treatments. And that was fine until Ziph came up."

"So, Thomas and Ziph. This is bad. What did you say about Ziph?"

"You know, the usual bullshit; that he could best serve the Committee, exceptional boy, glad the Committee was willing to give him the appropriate instruction. The usual. I guess they believed me since they sent me home. Erased Thomas, though. I guess at least I tried. I want to go through that room when we get home. There has to be something somewhere about our son. I'm convinced there was one now. But was he Shifted? Is he a runaway? How do we even start a search for him?" Thad's head was beginning to pound again. "Saige, if our son is out there, I want him back." And then after a beat, "No, I *need* him back."

"So now, what do we do? Saige chewed on her lip.

"I don't know. It's tricky. Too tricky. If my brother was willing to turn me in, how can I trust anyone else?" The weight of his brother turning on him was still a punch in his chest.

"Do we stay? Can we just go back to work like nothing has changed, knowing we have been betrayed and shifted and lost our son? Can we really do that?" Saige was finally more angry than afraid. If there was any loyalty left in her at all, it had been stripped away. After all, they showed no loyalty to her, her husband, or her family. She would focus only on her family now. She was ready to do whatever was required to keep her family safe.

"I think we need to make plans. First, I have anti-shift meds stockpiled in case we have to leave. I guess I should tell you that I have been getting provisions together. I've been doing it for a while now. I have them stored all over the city where we can get to them in a hurry." Thad had thought this through so many times. He had already planned and organized their escape. And as much as he had thought about and planned all this, he couldn't believe they were actually here.

"You have thought about this, haven't you?"

"Yes, for a while now."

"And what do you have?" Saige asked.

"A little bit of everything. I'll show you." Thad stopped and kissed her. "I didn't mean to leave you out of it. I just wanted to keep you safe."

"We are decided then?" Saige's voice cracked as she tried to stop a sob.

"Yes. If you are with me, I can take whatever happens." Thad smiled. "Last night, I knew that if they Shifted me, I would remember you and vowed to come find you, that no matter what, I would find you. My last thought was that today would be different. I didn't think it would be this kind of different." Thad looked away. "And, well, there's some other stuff…"

"Such as?"

"Oh, well, yeah. I guess I need to come clean. Try not to overreact, okay?" They were sitting cross-legged, facing each other, and he reached out and pushed a stray piece of hair away that had fallen across her cheek.

"Why am I suddenly just a little bit afraid?" Thad's demeanor had been changing all afternoon. He was less reserved, less guarded, as if he were suddenly more comfortable in his own skin. These new pieces of him seemed somehow familiar. He leaned over, kissed her softly, pulled back, and grinned.

"Every time I think I've gone through it all, I realize there is another thing I've kept from you. I didn't realize how many things I didn't tell you over the past few years. I'm sorry. I wanted to, I mean, I wanted us to both do this, but I was afraid you would be in danger. I didn't care if they pulled me out, but I didn't want anything to happen to you."

"It's okay. No, I don't mean it's okay; I mean, okay, tell me exactly what you are talking about. How bad could it be?"

"Well. It's just that I've been buying guns.'

"Guns? You don't know anything about guns."

"Well, buying is a bit of an understatement. I've been stockpiling weapons for two years."

"Stockpiling weapons? You?"

"Yes."

"How many?"

"Warehouses. Two warehouses full, actually. And ammunition."

"Why?"

"Why?"

"Yes, why? You're a doctor, for God's sake. Why do you need two warehouses full of weapons?"

"Because a war is coming."

eth walked into the lab, shook Thad's hand, and slipped him the earbud. Thad stared into his palm and then back up at Seth, who put his finger momentarily into his ear as if scratching an itch, brushed his hand over his mouth, and glanced up into the corner at the mounted security camera without moving his head.

"If you are free right now for that security meeting, can you meet me out front in five minutes? I'm swamped for the rest of the day and was hoping we could do an off-site breakfast meeting."

Seth nodded toward the elevators and, without waiting for an answer, punched the down button. If he were going to do this, he would do it off the premises. At least if they turned him in or reacted badly, he would be out of the building and have some chance of escape. As good as the Bodaways had been to him, you could never tell who would turn you in, and Seth was taking every precaution.

Thad dropped the earbud into his jacket pocket and followed Saige to the elevator doors. This would almost be comical if he weren't scared half to death. But strangely, he seemed comfortable, like his reflexes were catching up. When he told Saige he was stockpiling, he had played it down. After recovering from the Shift three years ago, he had started making plans. At first, he collected the typical first-aid disaster stuff: bandages, various creams, and antibiotics like ciprofloxacin, which could be used for anything from skin and bone infections to urinary tract infections. He added a variety of pain medications with various strengths. He carefully sealed each container in an airtight pack to extend shelf life. He ensured that the warehouses for these medications were regulated to maintain even humidity levels to avoid corrosion or depletion.

Then he concentrated on the more complex equipment:

Microscopes, test equipment, and X-ray equipment, all the while thinking: *if it all goes to hell, what else would we need?* He quickly filled one storage unit, then two, three, and more. He had them categorized now: medications and first aid, medical and lab equipment, weapons, and food. The first Gun he fired kicked back at him, up his hand, and into his shoulder; it felt so comfortable, like that first taste of cool water after a long run when the more you drink, the thirstier you get. He consistently hit the center target within the first week of target practice. He started with handguns, small concealable .22 caliber dainty things that felt so small in his big-fingered hands he thought he would crush them if he squeezed too hard. He worked through various sizes and grips until he settled on his favorite: the Glock 19 9mm. He liked the stark military feel of the black metal in his hand; the grip was steady and didn't slip in his palm. It had a sweet center spot and kicked back up his arm with enough power that he felt secure in his target. It was now always snug against the ribs of his left side, resting in the leather custom-made shoulder piece. He moved from handhelds to larger weapons. He stockpiled everything he could get his hands on, including military-grade, sophisticated pieces that had cost him a bit more than he thought they were worth, but he couldn't be choosy about where he got them anymore.

The more he packed into the warehouses, the more he thought he needed. He now had enough to supply a small army. It was a satisfying but odd feeling. He struggled a bit with the hypocritical idea of it all, like he was betraying his oath as a doctor. He took that oath to save lives very seriously, and it wasn't like anyone was forcing him into this behavior. There wasn't even a real threat, just this feeling in the pit of his gut that told him to keep going. He also couldn't deny his casual comfort with these weapons or that this came so naturally to him. He wasn't so much being instructed about these weapons but almost felt as if he were simply remembering something so familiar he had forgotten. Something that suited him much more than his sterile white doctor's lab coat that always seemed to tug a bit too uncomfortably across his shoulders.

He also couldn't shake the feeling that he needed to be prepared to safeguard his family. He did many things that seemed that way recently, as if his body was responding to muscle memory or some internal instinct. And every time he tried to convince himself that he was going crazy, he remembered this feeling of loss that tugged at him; he had lost his son. It was a solid, dull, throbbing nudge at him that he couldn't shake. It woke him in the middle of the night, taunting him with every suspicion he held at bay during the day. He decided that whatever happened now, he would search for his son. He would get him back. He felt as desperate about this as catching that last glance of Saige as the Collectors dragged him off, the same pain in his heart, the same loss, the same determination never to be separated from those he loved ever again.

They left their bags and phones in the lab and took the elevator to the first floor. The TALUS was circling the lobby. They walked out across the expanse that was once a park and followed Seth to the noisiest intersection. He removed his badge, access key, and scanner pin, dropped them into his bag, and then held it open for Saige and Thad to do the same. He wrapped the flap around the bag three times and tossed it a few feet in front of him.

"Did you listen to that yet?"

"No, I wasn't sure what to do with it."

"Well, listen to that before I say what I have to say. It will explain a lot," Seth said.

Thad pulled the earbud from his pocket, slipped it into his ear, and clicked it to play. He tried to keep from jumping out of his skin so Saige wouldn't see his reactions as he listened to the recording. Saige watched his eyes shift from a hopeful blue to a grey, anger-tinged dullness; she knew this would be bad. The recording confirmed three things for Thad: the labs and offices were all wired for sound and video. Two: they were always under surveillance, even at home. Three: they had run out of alternatives and had to act now. And even though it was clear that they had no other choice, he was still worried about trusting Seth. Were they being set up? Was this the moment he lost his illusion of control despite the stockpiling and preparation? But the rest of the recording convinced him to trust Seth, as he realized this was no longer just about his family. Now, there was a deeper layer of danger for everyone that reached far beyond the small sphere of his family. And that thud of realization that he had been used to create it all just increased his growing anger. Regent would pay for that; if it were his last act on earth, that man would never hurt anyone he loved again.

Thad clicked the earbud off, removed it from his ear, and passed it to Saige. She placed it into her ear and clicked it to begin playback. When it finished, she removed it from her ear, and even though she was using all of her strength to keep all emotion from her face, her hand trembled as she shoved the earbud into Seth's hand as if tossing away something vile and wiped her hand down the front of her jacket, then shoved her hands angrily into her jacket pockets. How she hated looking weak.

"Look, as you heard, you are in a shitload of danger."

"Okay, wait. Where the hell did that audio come from?"

"I intercepted this while I was doing a standard audio check yesterday. I haven't searched for related files yet. Look, I'm taking a big risk here even bringing this up, but you guys have got to get out of here."

Seth stopped and looked from Saige to Thad. "Are you catching my

Shifting drift here?"

"Yes, I think we are. But how?" Saige asked.

"Look, people just see me as this invisible tech rat, and because of that, I know way too much of the shit that goes on around here.

Normally, I don't care who gets Shifted, reorganized, or whatever they call it this week. But I also know you guys. You don't deserve any of this. Plus, I really hate Ziph and how he is going for this big rise to power. Like I said, I hear everything. His manipulation to get in the back door onto The Committee is dangerous. If he's the future, we are doomed."

"Wait, what are you talking about? I thought he was Shifted the other night?" Thad tried to keep his voice down, but the anger was reaching up, constricting his throat.

"Yeah. Not so much. Without a Shift, Dr. Regent has taken him on as his son. He remembers everything that happened when he was with you. Regent will groom him to be a junior member of the Committee with a vote. Yeah. A vote. Not good. Well, Ziph's made you two his obsession, and he won't let it go." Seth leaned in and spoke even softer, "That audio file I gave you is seriously scary stuff. It's not just about you guys; it's about the new direction they are developing without your input. Look, like I said, I'm taking a big chance here, but I think you guys need to get out of here." Seth stopped speaking and looked back and forth from Thad to Saige. "Are you guys with me? Or am I somebody else tomorrow morning?"

"I think you are still you tomorrow morning," Thad said. "We already got here yesterday. The last three days have been, well, you know. And we didn't know where to go from here or who to contact. I thought I'd just get in my car and go. Is that ridiculous?" Thad swallowed the rising acid now burning at the back of his tongue. But something else seemed to be rising inside him; was it excitement?

"Um, yeah, that's not exactly a plan. Listen, I have a contact who can get you out of the city and into the unprotected sector. He's a little iffy about this. He's not a very trusting guy. He has kids he's caring for and doesn't want them to get hurt. I told him you could get him meds and some other stuff he needs. I can set up a meet for tonight at ten on your roof. You guys meet him, and then I'm out. He needs meds; you need to be alive. It's good for everybody, yes?" Seth shrugged his shoulders.

"Yes, we'll meet with him. What does he need? I already have some stuff. Tell him to bring a list. I'll bring a list of what I already have, and we can go from there." Thad felt an odd surge as if he negotiated like this every day.

"I'll set up the meet and relay the message. I'll be there for initial introductions. After that, I'm no longer the contact. It's all on you guys." Seth held out his hand, and Thad shook it.

"Thank you, Seth. I think you just saved our lives." Seth reached for his bag, but Saige stopped his hand.

"Seth, you said you know things?"

"Yeah. Unfortunately, sometimes."

"Seth, did they shift us and remove our son three years ago?" Saying it out loud was harder than she thought, and tears began to come to the surface. "Do you know?"

"Oh, Doc. Yeah. That was when they put Ziph in place. It wasn't right. That's one of the reasons why I'm doing this."

"Do you know where he is?" Thad's voice was on the verge of a tremble when he cleared his throat, and it came out deep and desperate on *where he is*. He cleared his throat again and looked away, feeling feeble and hating his emotions cracking to the surface like this.

"I can't say."

"Seth, we are remembering things. He's our son, and they took him from us. It's not right. Does he know who he is? Do you know? Please?" Saige was in tears now and didn't care.

"Okay, look, I know he wasn't shifted. He lived at the docks with other runaways for a while, but he's not in the city anymore. I can't give you any more information ."

"So, you do know where he is?" Thad was working the muscle in his jaw.

"Yes. But as I said, I won't say anything unless he agrees."

"But you will let him know we are looking for him?"

"Yes, but he gets to decide if he wants you to know."

"I understand. But you need to know I will not let this go until I find him." Thad said, leaning into Seth. "I will never give up until I find him."

"I get that. But I can't make these decisions. I wouldn't tell anyone about you either. That's how I keep my reputation and why people work with me. I'm sorry. I can't do more than tell him. Then it's out of my hands; it's just business. You understand." Seth reached over and picked up the bag. "I hope this won't come between us."

"I guess threatening to beat you up wouldn't help anything, huh?" Thad tried to drop a hint of humor into his voice but couldn't manage it. "Really? You'd beat me up for that?"

"Huh, sorry, not sure where that came from. Evidently, a part of me would like to. But no, no, I wouldn't. I understand your word is your currency. But I'll figure out a way to find him. You can bet on that." Thad grinned, but Seth swallowed hard. He hoped he was never on the other side of that dark, cold flash he saw in Thad's eyes. Maybe he had underestimated him after all.

The TALUS circled as the three went through the checkpoint and then the elevator. Thad thought *this was the strangest day of my life* as they headed toward their lab. But this was no longer their lab. Probably hadn't been for a long time. He didn't feel any particular sadness at the thought.

He realized the restless need to move on had been with him for a while.

As they rounded the corner to their office, Ziph paced the length of their lab. *What the hell is this now?* Thad thought as anger visibly rose to his face. But he remembered that Ziph should be a stranger to him, so he had to get his anger in check. *For now, but just for now,* he thought, squaring his shoulders.

"Are you lost, young man? This is a restricted area." Thad used as patronizing a tone as he could, walked past Ziph, and sat at his desk. It was hard to hold the anger in check, knowing Ziph had searched his home and belongings, seeking to erase them for political gain.

"Dr. Bodaway, I've been wanting to meet you," Ziph said as he held his hand for a handshake, looking for even the smallest hint of recognition. "Yes, you've gotten turned around. The classrooms are on the first floor, and you shouldn't be up here."

"My name is Ziph Regent, so that pretty much means I can be anywhere I please in this facility." He spat at Thad.

Regent? Oh yes, he's with Regent now. Can this get any worse? Thad began to absently move files around on his desk as if Ziph wasn't in the room.

"Seth," Thad said, dismissively moving his hand toward Ziph. "Can you handle this situation? Or do I need to call Main Security to have him escorted out?"

"Yes. Please take care of this. We don't have time for disruptions today," Saige said. She tried to sound as professional as possible, but she really wanted to slap Ziph across the face to put him in his place.

"Actually, you don't have access to anywhere in the building without clearance, and you must be twenty-one for that type of clearance. Oh, and that is your father's directive, so you should double-check that with him. I'll inform Dr. Regent that I will gladly issue you any type of clearance he authorizes. But you do not have access to this floor. I need a signed release, specifically naming which labs you require access to, the type of access, the reason for the access, and whether you need to be accompanied by a TALUS for your protection." This was more fun than Seth could ask for. He thoroughly enjoyed putting this little pompous creep in his place. It wasn't often that he could wield power, and, if he was being honest, he was sick of being ignored, so he cherished whenever he could use his little head-of-security badge to put arrogant idiots in their place, especially this runt who believed that his artificial privilege was reality.

"Oh, I'm sorry, and you are?" Ziph turned his belligerence on Seth.

"Security, Senior Specialist." Seth tapped his badge. "So have your dad call me, and I can take care of that if he would like. But as for right now, you are in a restricted, high-security area, and I have to escort you to the first floor."

"Who do you think you are talking to, you little tech geek? I'll have that badge and have you busted down to garbage detail." Ziph's face was flushing red. He forced his fingers flat against his thighs to stop them from balling into fists. No matter the extent of his ambition or the drive or cruelty in his mind, Ziph was trapped in the body of a nineteen-year-old boy. And he knew that boys, especially in this facility, didn't get any respect.

Saige went over to the bank of testing equipment and started pushing buttons, which made a series of clicks and buzzes that didn't do anything other than make what sounded like busy noises. It helped to calm the nervous ball unraveling in the small of her stomach. She needed to do something with her hands before she slapped him. She didn't trust herself to look him in the eye. Didn't trust herself not to fly at him in an uncontrollable rage. It had been years since she felt the kind of anger that was surging in her. Years since anything had spurned her into any sort of action. But that all seemed to melt away as she stood at the lab table and felt something that almost butted against her ribs. A reminder of who she had once been that she recognized and immediately shoved down with a deep, hard swallow.

"I'm assuming you can take care of this?" Thad said to Seth as the TALUS entered the lab. Thad was reaching his breaking point. He didn't think he could keep up this farce much longer without losing it. He just wanted to be out of here now. They had decided, and he didn't want to waste one more minute acting this role.

"Ziph Regent, you have not only wandered into a restricted area of the building but have violated the terms of your recent directive." The TALUS' voice echoed off the glass and steel struts of the lab's walls.

"Sorry for the interruption, Dr. Bodaway; I will have Mr. Regent removed from your office and have already put in a requisition for updated security procedures to be placed in your laboratory so this type of breach does not happen again."

"Thank you."

Three security guards, or more to the point, Collectors, rushed into the lab, physically picking Ziph up by the forearms and carrying him toward the door like a child being scolded for a tantrum.

"This isn't over. I'll be back, and you'll pay for this." Ziph tried to yell back over his shoulder, but the Collectors had too strong a grip on him, and he looked more like a long, skinny worm wriggling on a hook.

The TALUS, satisfied that the situation was now under control, turned to leave the laboratory but stopped inside the doorway. "Dr. Bodaway, you should be very careful."

"Careful?"

"Yes. You should also update your home's security. I will requisition this as well." The TALUS left the lab and followed in the direction the guards had taken Ziph.

"What was that all about? With the TALUS?" Thad had lowered his voice and bent to whisper this to Seth's left ear.

"I have no idea. The TALUS was assigned to you when the Committee brought you in the other night, but I'm not sure why he is still assigned to you. I'll check the requisitions and follow up with the new locks and security updates." Seth headed toward the elevator, and as the doors closed, thumbed:

> /anoot 9.Chaser.dbletwst

into his phone and pressed SEND. A few moments later, his phone buzzed and flashed:

> /gtg.c.

He slipped the phone into his back pocket before entering his office. He had to put a list of things in place before he met with Chase so that everything could be put into motion easily as soon as he was given the word. First, he pulled up the requisition for the TALUS, which, as he thought, had been signed off as completed this morning. He was pulling up the diagnostics when Dr. Regent's name flashed on the screen. *Oh, shit, this is bad.* Seth took a deep breath, so his voice would be level before hitting the connect button.

13

S*eth* pushed the roof door open and squatted against the wall. *I hate this damn roof.* He dragged harder on the cigarette than he intended and tried to control a spasm of coughs as Chase and Kalare jumped over the edge onto the roof.

"You know, you two are even starting to move alike. It's kinda creepy."

"Yeah, that's us, just a typical couple out for a nightly stroll up the side of a building. How are you, Seth?" Kalare said.

"But I am still the pretty one, right?" Chase flashed a big smile as he came up and planted a friendly slap on Seth's back.

"Umph, that's always been debatable. Okay, why the big 911?" Sam had come up over the side after them and stood up to his full height, stretching his back.

"I don't know, man. At first, I thought I might have overreacted, but now I don't think so. I'm really rattled. I think Ziph is a little out of control,

and I don't even think Regent can control him."

"Ziph." Chase spat the name. "What the hell does Ziph have to do with all this?"

"Found him nosing around in a lab this afternoon. In their lab, to be exact."

"Great. Okay, why should I care that they are in trouble?"

"These are good people. At least, I always thought so."

"Well, they do work for the Committee, so that makes me skeptical." Chase fumbled with his glove. "Why do I care?"

"Because you know what they do to people, The Committee, I mean. I met with them this morning, the Bodaways, I mean. I was there when the Ziph thing happened at the lab. I told them I might be able to get them out, but they had to come through with some stuff. I don't know, I

guess it was a kind of test. You know, I thought if they were a plant, there would have been a lot of questions: when, where, who; you know, questions like that. They had not a one. Didn't care how or where; just said they were all in. Agreed to everything: supplies, meetings, letting me handle all the details. They asked for a list of what you needed. He said he had a bunch of stuff ready to go and would give us a list tonight to see if there was

anything on it we thought we could use."

"Really? What kind of stuff?" Chase was hoping this would mean no runs for a while. This was the third night he had come into the city, and it was getting to him. He never thought of this place and the things he'd left behind most days. Every day, he tried to convince himself it didn't matter, that he didn't care. So, if he didn't care, why the hell was he having this indecisive battle? Why this indecision? He didn't want to bring these people into his world. A world where he could control who came into and moved out of his life. Everyone back at The Forty depended on him. He had to do right by them. He knew he shouldn't be distracted by the offer of supplies. And he tried not to let that sway his decision, but they desperately needed so much, and it was becoming obvious that he was falling short in supplying everything they needed. He wanted to make a good decision for the group. It had to be about the group, not his personal feelings. But these nights of scaling buildings and bumping into Collectors were getting dangerous and were yielding less and less. It would be better for everyone if they didn't have to come into the city.

"I'm not really sure what he has or what he can get. He said he would get a list together for us." Seth shrugged.

"Are you sure this isn't a set-up?"

"No. No, it's not. I went to them. I was the one who brought it up."

"Why would they be doing this? I mean, doesn't this make everyone a little nervous?" Kalare was swaying back and forth, looking around the roof as she spoke. "You know what I mean?" Her eyes stopped on Chase, but he wasn't sure what he saw there. Doubt? In him or just the situation?

"I know." Seth lit another cigarette, hoping the nicotine would warm him, but his hands kept shaking. Damn, he hated being up on this roof. "Look, I would never knowingly endanger any of you or the kids. It's been a rough couple of days for these guys. They looked a little shell-shocked this morning. Did I tell you his brother turned him in?"

"No shit." Sam shook his head. "That's cold."

"Yeah, right in the middle of a collection. They brought him before the Committee the other night. After he finds out his brother betrayed him, they tell him that Ziph did too."

"So, they just let him go after two accusations? Doesn't that seem strange to you?" Chase hated this whole thing more and more. But he wasn't sure if he saw any of this with a clear head; his brain had too much clutter, and he couldn't think straight. He looked over at Kalare again. Constant, tough Kalare, standing there like a natural-born soldier. She was rotating her gaze every few minutes like the ticking of a second hand on a clock. She took in the entire roof and then began again. Stopping and holding his gaze as her eyes flicked past him on their way to the other side of the roof. She was as comfortable in a flowered skirt as she was with her favorite bolt-action rifle slung over her back. She said she liked the push and pull of the bolt action because it felt solid and sure in her hand. Liked the heavy chunk of the bolt as she shoved it into place, and that she left her fingerprint on each bullet she chambered. It was like a tiny piece of herself penetrated each target along with the bullet. With her, it was always personal.

He broke eye contact with her by closing his eyes and swallowing down the tinge of guilt. There was still so much he needed to tell her. And even though he knew he would do anything for her, would do anything to keep her safe, he also knew that was just something he told himself to stop the guilt. So much he kept from her that he still couldn't tell her. She was still staring at him when he opened his eyes, eyebrows raised in unspoken questions.

"I know. Believe me. I know what I am asking you to do." Seth was saying as Chase returned to himself and tore his eyes from Kalare. "You guys just have to trust me." Seth put his hand on Chase's shoulder and shook it back and forth until Chase made eye contact. "Look, man, if you have ever trusted me, trust me now. How long have we been friends? This is a good thing for all concerned." Seth emphasized *good thing*.

"I do know that." Chase looked over at Kalare and then at Sam.

"Guys? Anything?"

"Well, no. At least not until we talk to them." Sam had come up behind Chase.

"We'll talk to them. I'll try to keep an open mind. It's just. You know." Chase shrugged and peered out over the city. He had already trusted Seth with so much and knew Seth would never knowingly put him in a compromised situation. But still, something was making the hair on the back of his neck prickle.

"Okay. I gave them the list of meds I couldn't get last time. I'm hoping they bring them tonight." Seth pulled out a small notebook and a well-worn pencil. "Now, he wants to know what we need. We have about forty-five minutes before they arrive, so let's get a list together for them."

14

aige and Thad had spent the afternoon gathering the meds Seth had asked them to bring as a show of good faith. It was a simple list: first-aid items like antibiotic and cortisone creams, bandages and wraps, peroxide and alcohol, broad-spectrum antibiotics, cough syrups, aspirin, and pain meds. She pulled everything from the supply shelves and went through the list one last time to be sure she had everything. Then she remembered Seth had said some of the kids were sick, so she included stronger antibiotics, cough syrup, and a variety of Albuterol inhalers and nebulizer units not on the list. She added several types of children's vitamins and holistic supplements before zipping up the backpack. This stockpile of medications that the Committee had just sitting here was ridiculous. She wished there was a way to empty these shelves and get them out to everyone who needed them. This was the emergency bunker reserve, which was kept in case The Committee lost control of the city. The department heads and their families would be well cared for during an attack.

Thad fumbled with his watch. He was completely withdrawn all evening. This was an odd quiet for him, as if he were on the verge of collapsing or exploding. He was making lists. Saige couldn't figure out if he were trying to keep himself occupied or just trying to be prepared. They both knew they could be walking into a trap and that these might be the last moments they spent together. But neither would voice that fear; instead, they busied themselves with packing and planning. Thad placed each list he had prepared into a different pocket, then obsessively took each list out, checked it item by item, and replaced it in its designated pocket. This was the evening ritual, except for the few times when he stopped pacing and looked at Saige. He even tried to crack a joke a few times but then took a deep breath and just walked away. They had already exhausted each other trying to talk through every possible scenario. There was not much left in them at this point. So, they settled for exchanging sad, nervous looks and limp smiles of encouragement.

They reached the top of the stairway five minutes early. Thad inhaled as he wrapped his fingers around the handle of the door to the roof and stared down at Saige. He closed his eyes and took a sharp breath, almost a sob, as he reached his arm out and pulled her to him.

"None of this means anything if I lose you." His voice vibrated through her hair and cracked slightly on *lose* before he cleared his throat, swallowed hard, and stepped back.

She wanted to reassure him, but all of her emotions were wedged into a tight ball in the center of her chest, and when she tried to speak, the words collided in her throat and cut off her air until her temples pounded. Instead, she slid his jacket over to the side, laid her ear against his chest, listened to the familiar steady rhythm of his heart, and concentrated on the rise and fall of his breath and the familiar heartbeat punctuating the end of each breath. This was what she had clung to for so many years. This familiar pace of falling, rising, falling again made her heartbeat slow to match his, and she inhaled, slowing her breath to move in and out with his. She reached her arms under the jacket and pushed her hands hard against his back, feeling his muscles tighten against the pressure. She slid her palms into the familiar arch of his lower back. Then she held him tight against her. Tighter, then tighter still, until everything was only their breathing together. She wished she could press so far into him that the rest of the world would disappear. After one last kiss, she looked into his eyes and nodded as if it could steady them for whatever awaited beyond that door. Thad inhaled one last time and held her gaze for one moment longer, like he always did when he thought it might be his last memory of her. Then he tugged at the bar on the heavy door and winced as the doorframe scraped against the door's metal.

They stepped onto the roof and stood for a minute, allowing their eyes to adjust to the darkness. Seth, two other boys, and a girl, all armed and standing in military formation, were a few feet from the doorway. Seth motioned for Thad and Saige to follow, then moved into a dark corner where the back wall met the abutment for the door to the roof. Thad and Saige hesitated a moment before following, fascinated by the city unfolding below them, but finally joined the huddle against the abutment on the other side of the doorway.

"Okay, look," Seth said as they approached the group. "I will introduce you guys and help with this initial contact, but after this, you have to devise your own system to communicate if any of you need me. I mean, if you *really* need me, leave a text message. You can put anything you want but have the following phrase in your message: *anoot.10.chaser.twist*. It means a night on the town. Add the time and chaser, so I know it involves Chase, and use twist as the code word for urgency, and you can let me know how urgent, you know: double twist, triple twist. Like that. Okay?" He reached into his pockets. "Here, throw away phones. Already programmed with access to me and to Chase. Do not take your phones. Do not take any of your security or access passes. They will track you. I'll leave them active, so you have more time to travel. The longer they think you are hanging out at home, the better lead time you will have." Seth looked at the four of them and did quick first-name introductions.

"Seth, *who* are you?" Thad said, pocketing the phone. He almost managed a smile.

"Just a tech rat. At least that's my superhero cover."

"Yeah, this is all nice and all, and I appreciate that you have a big problem, but I'm a little uncomfortable about this." Chase sounded more defensive than he wanted to; he wanted to sound more in control. He tried to sound like a man and not a little boy. "Look, we are just a bunch of kids left to ourselves. We have been on our own for, well, it doesn't matter how long; I don't want that dynamic to change. They trust me. I won't break that trust. That is all they have right now. And understand this: I won't risk putting them in danger."

"We understand that. We don't want to put anyone in danger either." Saige's voice cut through Chase, and he glanced over at her, felt the squeeze of anger release, and glared back at Thad, where he knew the anger would hold.

"So, I gotta ask, do you need us to just get you out of here? Do you need to stay with us for a day, a week or what? What are you looking for here?" Chase's voice was finally solid, strong. He fixed his eyes back on Thad. It was a challenging glare. Chase was standing his ground and setting boundaries, and Thad had to see that. No, Thad had to respect that.

"Listen, I get it; you don't trust me. I probably wouldn't trust somebody employed by The Committee if it were me," Thad paused; the thought of it churned the acid burning that hole deeper into his stomach.

"God, that does make us sound like a bad risk, doesn't it? I am willing to trust you and Seth with something that could cost me my wife's life and my own. It's already cost me, well, never mind about that now." Thad's voice cracked, and he stood on the roof feeling alien and out of control. Everything he said was bathed in helplessness, and he hated every second of it. He ground his teeth and cleared his throat. He had to do this for Saige. For his son. Goddamn that thought; *how was he going to find his son?*

"Look," he finally managed in a steady voice, "I got the supplies you asked for, and I understand your concerns. We all have concerns. You could have Collectors waiting for me downstairs right now. I don't know. But I have to trust someone. I certainly can't trust them anymore; I probably never could. I just hope you can see I'm not one of *them,* or at least not one of them *anymore.* I hope you'll be able to trust me. And I understand if every instinct tells you not to trust me but just know this: all I'm trying to do is save my family." Thad handed the backpack to Chase on the word *them*, more aggressively than he had intended.

"I added extra insulin and some asthma meds not listed just in case you needed them," Saige said.

"Thank you for this." Kalare took the bag from Chase. "I don't even know for sure what we need. There are some sick kids, but we have no idea about any of it. We are just trying to keep going. Thank you for the insulin.

It's the hardest to get and isn't always the right kind when we do."

"So, Seth said to give you a list. Here's our *if you're a superhero and can get everything on this list, I'll be your BFF* list." Chase handed Thad a piece of paper. Thad made a sound in his throat that was almost a chuckle and looked through both sides, nodding his head as he went through each item.

"Okay. I guess I'm your new BFF. This is all doable."

"You can get everything on that list?" Sam had been standing so quietly that he managed to slide into the background, and everyone jumped at his voice.

"Yeah. And then some." Thad was fumbling with the inside pocket of his jacket. "Now, here is what I can add to the list." Thad handed it to Chase. As Chase read the list, his hand began to shake. He looked at Thad, back at the list, and then at Thad, squinting his eyes into narrow slits. He was trying to hold onto his anger and determination not to do this, but the items on the list were things they could never get on their own. Chase let out a slow whistle.

"On the back is a list of some, um, shall we say, other stuff." Thad was staring at Chase, boring into his eyes. Chase looked up, and they squared off; anger and anxiety bounced between them. Chase turned over the list.

"Seriously, can I ask you a question?" Chase asked.

"Anything."

"What is someone like you doing with all this?"

"I guess that's a fair question. Three years ago, I suspected we were Shifted. I started having memory flashes or dreams and... Shit, never mind. It wasn't like a bleed-back or anything like that. It's more like I was; I don't know how to explain it. It was like something was missing. Not car keys missing; this was something big that was missing. Anyway, I just felt that something else was coming, and I wanted to be prepared," Thad said. Chase exhaled, looked over at Sam, and handed the list to him.

"Here, what do *you* think?" Sam let out a short whistle and handed the list to Kalare.

"Wait," Chase said to Sam as he moved toward the other side of the roof, and Sam planted his feet where he stood. Thad noticed the response and suddenly missed interacting with others who understood and responded to one word. It thudded against his chest as another empty spot he didn't know how to fill.

"If you got shifted, none of this would have mattered. You wouldn't remember doing any of this." Chase's voice was frustrated now. The anger was moving into something else, and Kalare snapped her head around to look at Chase and moved her position to where she could see his face.

There was definitely something else going on with him.

"That's true. That's why I started taking this." Thad handed Chase a vial of clear liquid. "I put it in water. It blocks the shift."

"And I started taking this." Saige handed Chase a vial with an orange-colored liquid. "I put it in orange juice. I knew something had been taken from us and never wanted to have that happen again."

"What do you mean? Something was taken from you?"

"Well, we are still putting that together. We think, no, we know they took our son. Anyway, you can start taking that. It will prevent the shift meds from working."

"Oh, right. Like I'm going just to take anything on your word." Chase handed the vile back to Thad, who popped off the cap and gulped it down in one swallow.

"See. Safe. Look, I'm not lying. I'm just trying to survive here." Thad pulled out another list and handed it to Chase. "This is the medical equipment I have. It's enough to set up a lab and a small but functional medical room. I'd like to take this with us now if you have room." "What's the catch?" Chase shook his head.

"The catch is, I don't want to lose any more of my family or mind. They just took my brother, who turned me in to the Collectors. And my other son, who was placed with us, turned me in to the committee." Thad's voice rose with a hoarse vibration in his throat that tinged the ending of each word with an acrid rasp. If he was putting on a show, it was a damn good one.

"And what about this son? This other son?" Chase looked at Saige because he knew if he looked at Thad, the anger would be more than he could control. But it was a mistake because her dark eyes were so framed in fear that he would have agreed to anything to take that fear from her.

"I don't know anything about my son. Our son. Just that there was one." Thad paused and cleared his throat. "I asked Seth to look into it, but he won't give me any information without his consent. I just know I have a son whose face I can't remember because they took the goddamn memory from me. My son is, God, it drives me crazy. Who knows where, and God knows how he is living. The thought of it kills me. He is out there on his own, and I can't even do anything for him. So, I can't, no, I *won't* lose anybody else." Thad ran his hand through his hair, turned his back on the group, cleared his throat again, and turned back. "Look, I'm sorry. That's another matter. That's not your concern and not why we are here."

"Is this really about your family? What about your research? I mean, you are setting up a lab, right?" Sam had stepped out of a shadow and stood beside Chase, arms folded across his chest, challenging.

"I'm onto something that will block the meds and the Shift completely, so I want to keep going, and Saige is getting some results using biological sources. I can't stop now; we can't stop now. Do you understand?

I can't stop. Not any of it, not the research or the search for my son."

"This is an awful lot to take in." Chase looked at Seth. "I didn't think they would be setting up a lab. I thought this was just a, I don't know, a rescue or an escape. What the hell, Seth?"

"I didn't know. We didn't talk specifics. Geez, Chase, this all happened within twenty-four hours."

"Look," Thad broke in, "I'm just trying to be honest."

Chase stared at his feet and started shaking his head. Kalare looked over at him and thought he was either going to cry or punch Thad. She couldn't understand why he was having such a visceral reaction.

"Are you okay with this?" Kalare said. "Because if you don't want to do it, we don't do it; we all already agreed to that."

"I know. I know. It's just...I don't know." Chase wouldn't make eye contact with Thad and instead stared at Kalare.

"Sam?" Kalare shifted her eyes to him without moving.

"Concerns?"

"Oh yeah, I have a million concerns, but we need everything on this list." Sam waved the list in her direction. "So, if you guys are cool with it,

I'm in."

"I know you have doubts. I would too if I were you," Saige said. "I know this is a lot to ask." She hated that she sounded so desperate. But desperate was exactly what they were.

"Okay. Okay. Everybody just shut up for a minute." Chase crossed the roof and looked toward the river, remembering the filthy house they had squatted in and how sick some of the kids were. Looking back at them, he felt a little snap as his resolve cracked. *Damn it. Damn them. Damn, this whole thing.*

"Okay." He paused and then firmer, "Okay. I think we can do this." Chase took Thad's list from Sam, folded it twice, and shoved it into his pocket. "Be ready tomorrow night."

"Tomorrow night. I'll get the things on your list. I just have one problem."

"Oh hell, another problem?" Chase bit his lower lip.

"Yes, the problem is I can't transport any of the things on that list I gave you. I'm being watched now. Can either of you arrange to transport it?

If you can, I can give you locations, passcodes, whatever you need to get them."

"You want us to transport this? Really?"

"Well, yeah, if you want any of it."

"So, you would trust us with all this?" Chase finally made eye contact with Thad, the challenge easing.

"I would. I do. I mean, I have to trust someone. I certainly can't trust anyone back there anymore. And if they get me, at least I'll know someone will use all that stuff well."

"I'll need a bigger truck, maybe two. Seth, can you get them?" Chase had pulled out the list and counted off items.

"Yeah. That's easy. Do you want a driver too?"

"Just to pick it up. I won't need it on the way back. I can take it from there." Chase looked over at Kalare. "Thoughts? Concerns?"

"Well, I think the truck is a good idea, but we need to do it tonight. Once they are gone, security will go crazy, and we'll have to stay away, so we might not be able to get the supplies out." She looked back and forth between Seth, Chase, and Sam.

"Yes? Okay, let me make a call." Seth moved away from them and spoke into his phone.

"Saige, we have a lot of sick kids. Are you strictly research, or can you help? I mean, I don't want to sound rude or anything, but we risk all this, and you need to do more than hang out in your laboratory and play with drugs." Kalare shifted the strap, so her gun hung at her left hip.

"No, not just research; I am a full MD. Is there anything else you need?"

"I don't know. Like I said, we don't know what's happening with some of the kids. I was hoping you could check them out when you get there." Kalare caught the narrowing of Chase's eyes and glared back at him.

"Okay, I have the truck and the driver. Doc, how many stops?"

Seth asked, covering the phone. Thad took the final list from his pocket.

"Here are the locations and the items at each location. Passcodes, entry codes, and anything else you need, including weights and the number of containers at each location. They are in fairly remote spots, so I don't think you will have any problems running into Collectors or anything." He handed Seth the list, and Seth walked away, talking back into the phone. "You are awfully prepared. I have to say this all makes me a little suspicious."

"Yeah, well, I had a few years to think about it." Thad shrugged. He had made his case; he was done begging for help. Either this worked out, or he would find another way.

"All set. The driver thinks he can pick up at all locations. He can meet for the handoff at three AM. Chase, does that work?" Seth was holding the phone against his chest.

"Three's good. Where?" Seth handed Chase an address.

"So, we are a go then?" Thad asked.

"We are a go. Be right here tomorrow at ten. Oh, and we usually scale the side of the building, so..."

"Really? I thought I could just disable my GPS, and we could load up the car. You know, it is a fully equipped medical transport, so it might be good to have on hand."

"I'll disable the GPS. I know I told you not to use your badges, but I have another idea that might buy you more time." Seth thumbed a note into his phone, switched it off, and put it back into his pocket.

"So, in the garage at ten?" Thad extended his hand.

"The garage at ten." Chase ignored Thad's outstretched hand and moved toward the other side of the roof.

"Coffee," Kalare said. "I would die for coffee."

"Coffee? I can do that," Saige said. "Coffee, I can do."

15

"You were instructed never, I repeat, never to come into contact with the Bodaways again, weren't you?" Dr. Regent was circling Ziph, slouched in the chair, resolutely glaring at Regent. "Do you know how easy it is to have a bleed-back the day after a memory realignment?"

"I told you I was going to continue my investigation." Ziph refolded his arms. "And then that giant metal guy extracted me. Me! Two Collectors escorted your son out. It was humiliating. Make them pay for this and that little twerp security guy who wouldn't let me in."

"First of all, the giant metal guy is a TALUS appointed to safeguard the interests of Dr. Bodaway. It's what he is programmed to do, you moron. Second, let's talk about this privilege you presume in this whole being my son business, and let me speak clearly here, you are nothing but my ward. You are not my son. You are a social-climbing amoeba that I should have Shifted back to menial labor, where you belong. You do not get to boss people around or demand that anyone be punished for doing their job." Dr. Regent slammed the book he was holding down onto his desk, pushed his glasses onto his head, and rubbed the reddish indentation on the bridge of his nose.

He had intended to hand the more tedious aspects of the

Committee work over to Ziph to be rid of them himself, but more to push busy work to keep Ziph out of his and everyone else's hair. But things with Ziph had gone from bad to worse. He hoped the post-shift memories Ziph was experiencing were worth all this. But the commotion Ziph created and the insane idea of demanding a full-scale investigation of the Bodaways were becoming a total waste of his time. His days were now about reining in this spoiled brat. Even a spoiled brat with tremendous potential was still a spoiled brat. Ziph had breached three labs today alone. This had to end.

Maybe he needed to try a different tactic.

"Ziph, listen, I understand your anger, and I can even see why you think we should take this course of action, but you have to realign your focus. You are missing a large piece of this puzzle. If you keep making this much of a commotion, and if I can't, correction, if *you* can't get yourself under control, I assure you, the Committee will step in. And by step in, I mean remove you from under my care. Then what will you have?"

"I thought you were The Committee?" Ziph's response was laced with sarcasm intended to upend him. Regent smiled. That was going to take a lot more than a sarcastic teenager.

"I am one part of it: just one small part. There are more moving parts than you could possibly understand. You need to back off and go to your lessons. That's what you have to do. And then, at the next stage, you will receive additional information. Information that will make all of this clearer." Dr. Regent readjusted his glasses onto the bridge of his nose and shifted his attention back to his book, dismissing Ziph. But Ziph was not ready to be dismissed. He stood, withdrew a folder from his jacket, and dropped it on the desk in front of Dr. Regent."

"What is this now?"

"Oh, I don't know. But I do know somebody has been a very bad boy with some appropriated money. I don't think all those moving parts will be happy about its big spearheading doctor pocketing the money meant for little kids. What did you do? Just leave them on the street alone. That doesn't seem like a very good daddy-figure image." Ziph smiled. No, Grinned.

"You are bluffing. And besides that, you were one of those street kids that I had some compassion for and look where that has gotten me."

"You are a liar!" Ziph had screamed at Regent; his voice had surprised even him. He wasn't quite sure where that had come from, but something was rising to the surface, and he did not want to see it. Regent snatched his glasses off and threw them onto his desk as he rose to his feet, rounded the desk, and loomed over Ziph.

"Am I? Hmmm. It seems your recollections have a few gaps at that. So, let me set the record straight. Your father beat your mother into a bloody mess one night, and you know what, Ziph? She didn't feel a thing because she was so strung out. Your father also took out three police officers and was working on a fourth when the Collectors got there and shot him. Yes, I said, shot him numerous times, if I recall, before he finally collapsed. We obliterated that piece of crap. And there, on the street, sat this little blond kid crying. He, correction, YOU had seen the whole thing. So, I had the Collectors pick you up and shift all that misery and horror out of your head.

This is why this system works. That is the scum we are taking off the street. The scum you came from, so think about that the next time you get that superior tone in your voice. You are the son of a junky and a murderer. You, my dear boy, are not my son." Regent's voice boomed, and Ziph's shoulders jumped slightly in the chair. Dr. Regent reached back onto the desk, picked up the folder, and dropped it into Ziph's lap without opening it. "Do your best. Better than you have tried."

"I will give you until the end of the day to list the Bodaways for Shifting, or the file gets sent." Ziph stood up and tossed the file back across the desk. "You can keep this. I have copies."

"What is it with you and these people? I don't get it. You do realize they started the whole thing, don't you? Without them, we don't have the meds, we don't have the Shifts, and we are chaos in the streets and prisons.

You understand, right?"

"What do you know about what goes on out on the streets? You never leave this complex. Even your apartment is here. You are so disconnected from anything but The Committee that you don't see anything."

"I see what is necessary to complete the work. I am warning you, once again, to stay away from the Bodaways. You have no idea the mess you are getting yourself into with this."

"I don't care. You have no idea what the other side of Shifting is like. Sure, for you, it's all about control and stopping the anarchy. But for those of us who have been Shifted, it's something else completely." Ziph took in a deep breath. Sadness shadowed the usual anger on his face. "Something happens when you are Shifted out for someone else. No matter how hard you try, they *never* feel the same about the kid replacing their own. They know. I swear they all *knew* I wasn't theirs. Oh, they were polite and nice. Well, some were, at least, those who didn't do things to you because they knew they could get away with anything, because no one was watching. I will say one thing: at least the Bodaways were nice to me. I wasn't their kid, and they knew it, and they were still so damn nice; maybe that's why I hate them so much. Because I knew they knew, I saw it in their eyes every time they looked at me. You took me and gave me to somebody who didn't know me. Or want me. Or love me. You can't program that in, can you?" Ziph was talking so low that Regent could hardly hear him. He was still as stone. The admission of his sadness had worn him out and drained everything from him.

"So why take it out on them? They lost their son, not you. You lost nothing. You were taken off the street and given a family; you should have been grateful."

"I'm not grateful. I want them to pay for it all. And I want you to do it, or I'll tell everyone that the great Dr. Regent is no better than a crook. And worse, a crook that throws kids like me away." Ziph turned but stopped at the doorway. His brief moment of humanness was gone, and his voice was cold, unmoving. "I have a follow-up with

Dr. Metcalf in a few hours. Send through the paperwork, or I will report."

Dr. Regent picked up the phone, punched a three-letter extension, waited for a tone, punched in six more numbers and on another tone, and hung up.

SETH HEARD the gunshot through his monitor. He opened the feeds to Dr. Regent's and Dr. Metcalf's offices and the Committee Chamber on his main monitor. Dr. Regent's window was a black screen. He opened the window, hit rewind, and stopped when he saw Ziph storm out of the room. Regent was seated at his desk. He picked up a file, plugged in a combination on the bottom left-hand drawer of his desk, and pulled out a pile of folders. He placed them into a metal tray and hit a red button on the control panel. There was an electronic flash, and the stack flared and disintegrated into ash. He spun the combination on the drawer and closed it. He reached down and pulled open his right bottom drawer, then pushed the phone, computer, books, and files off the edge of the desk with a loud crash.

He withdrew a bottle of single malt whiskey, a shot glass, and a revolver. He closed the drawer. Poured a double shot and downed it. He popped open the handgun's cylinder, slowly added bullets to each compartment, and poured another double shot. He lifted his glass to the camera in the corner and drained it. He picked up the handgun. A small grin escaped before he pulled the trigger and took out the camera.

No, no, no, no. Seth pulled out his cell phone and typed in: *anoot.7.chaser.quadrouple.twist.make.it.a.real.barhop.this.time.*

He put in the numbers for Chase and the Bodaways and hit send.

This was not good.

ZIPH STOOD at the back of Dr. Regent's office and watched the cleaning crew work. This was even more perfect than he could have hoped for. As the only legal son, he now had the authority to stand in for his father, regardless of his age. He made the appropriate commotion. Cried what he thought were very passable tears. The file was gone. Didn't matter. He had more copies. He headed for Dr. Metcalf's office as the cleaning crew finished up. This was going even better than he could have imagined. He would have the Bodaways collected in a matter of hours, and then he would be rid of them once and for all.

16

They had unloaded everything from the trucks about half an hour ago. Whatever else he was, Thad had come through with everything on the list, and it had filled three trucks. All of the passcodes worked, and except for a TALUS circling the last pick-up spot, everything had gone smoothly. Chase thought this might be a good omen, if he believed in omens, he reminded himself.

They were set to meet with the Bodaways at ten and had mapped out alternate routes back to The Forty. They would separate as they left the city, each taking a different route, with Sam and Jo-Jo in the truck and Chase and Kalare in the Bodaway's car. If they were followed, they would signal, and all would double back to the city, leading anyone following them away from The Forty. The last thing he wanted to do was lead the Collectors right back to everyone he had been protecting. That feeling still tugged at the hairs on the back of his neck, but he was in it now, whatever happened. His phone buzzed once, and he blinked, then tapped in:

/grt.bring.triple.

He stood over Kalare for a moment, watching her sleep. He drew in a long, stabilizing breath, held it deep within his chest, and released it in short, pushing breaths. Driving back to The Forty, he barely remembered anything but staring at the faded line in the highway until halfway home, when he finally decided it was time to tell her everything. She deserved to know everything: where he came from and who he was. He only hoped she wouldn't hold it against him or, worse, mistrust him. He took another quick breath and bent over to smooth her hair from her face. When she didn't stir, he ran his palm in tender circles along her shoulder until she let out a little groan.

"Kalare, wake up. Something's wrong. We have to head back to the city." He whispered into her ear.

"Mmmmm. No. Want sleep," Kalare mumbled.

"Kalare, sorry, we have to go now."

"What?" Kalare groaned again and squinted at him, coming awake.

"Oh, sorry, I was dreaming. Why do we have to leave now? Problems?" "I'm not really sure. Something is up, though." Chase leaned over and kissed her on the cheek. "I'm sorry. I know you're tired. You can sleep in the truck."

"Okay." She yawned and stretched like a sleepy cat. "Just give me like two minutes, okay?"

"I'll go get Sam and Jo-Jo.

"Should we take her? What if things get tricky? She's still a little skittish. I'm not sure we should take the chance." Kalare yawned again.

"Yeah, like she'd even let us leave her behind. Still, it might be good to have a fourth along."

"Whatever you want to do. She is getting to be a pretty good shot. So, um, can I ask you something?" Kalare pulled herself up and sat cross-legged on the bed.

"Oh-oh. I never like the sound of that." Chase wanted to run out of the room before he just blurted everything out.

"What is going on with you lately? You seem, I don't know, somewhere else." Kalare pushed his hair out of his eyes. "Look, I know some stuff happened to you. Stuff happened to all of us. It won't change how I feel. I hope you know that."

"I know that. Or at least I think I know." Chase leaned in and gave her a soft kiss. "You know how I feel about you, right?" His eyes softened into a warmer blue. "No matter what happens today, please remember that, okay?"

"Is that what this is all about? Trust?"

"It's not about that. Well, not just about that. It's just that I didn't understand why some things happened, and I thought that I was just, I thought that they, I don't know what the hell I thought. It's about me. I guess I just felt a little guilty about, you know, stuff."

"Stuff?"

"Yeah, stuff about moving forward. Not going back." Chase moved his eyes to the far wall.

"Back? Back to what?"

"I can't talk about this now." Chase stood up, walked to the doorway, stopped, and looked back at her.

"What?"

"Nothing." Chase grinned. "You just look pretty."

"Ewwww. Shut up." She said as she threw a pillow at him. "Clearly, you are suffering from sleep deprivation. Get out of here." But she broke out into a wide smile.

"Well, you do. I just thought I should tell you that more." Chase caught the second pillow she threw at him and smiled back at her as he stepped into the quiet hallway. *God, Kalare, I hope that's true. I hope nothing can change how you see me.*

Kalare pulled herself out of the cot. She didn't tell Chase she had a bad feeling, too. This time, the nervous twitch in her neck sent goosebumps along her arms and onto her neck. She bent and pulled all of her hair over so she could press her thumbs into the muscles where all the tension had settled into hard bands along her shoulder blades. It was making her head throb. *If I believed in omens,* she thought, quickly brushed the thought away, and stood up, stretching. That kind of thinking wouldn't help and would only make her jumpy. She missed her targets when she was jumpy.

She didn't like missing targets.

Jo-Jo and Kit sat next to each other at the table when Chase walked into the kitchen. Jo-Jo had her legs comfortably slung over Kit's thighs; they laughed at some private joke. Chase frowned; this was not good for JoJo. Kit rarely spoke, and he never really quite meshed with the group. It was more than his quiet detachment that tugged at Chase. He had hoped that as time went on, Kit would blend in, but he seemed as out of place now as the first day he wandered onto the docks. Jo-Jo was completely infatuated, and Chase hoped she saw something he didn't. Something just bugged him about Kit; he couldn't shake it. But he had other things to worry about today. He just hoped Jo-Jo didn't get hurt.

"Jo-Jo, change of plans, we need to leave in an hour. Kit, are you good staying with Tya and the kids?"

"Sure, man, whatever you need."

Whatever I need. Chase reached the front door as Kalare, followed by Sam, climbed out of the truck.

"You sure you're still good with this?" Sam slipped his blade into a pocket along the side seam of his jacket.

"Yup. Can't turn back now even if I wanted to."

"Well, you can. But you won't. Will you?"

"No. No, I guess not."

17

*C*hase, Kalare, Jo-Jo, and Sam arrived at the apartment garage two hours early. Somewhere between leaving Kalare and seeing Jo-Jo with Kit, he had decided to take her along. It made more sense to have two teams. The more backup they had, the less Chase had to worry about. *And,* he thought, *if she is with us, I won't worry about what trouble Kit is getting her into back there.* After sweeping the garage, Sam and Jo-Jo stayed behind, and Chase and Kalare made their way up the back steps.

"Where are we going?"

"You'll see," Chase said. But his eyes were set somewhere else. He stepped off the elevator on the floor where they had run into the Collectors two nights ago. Chase wasn't worried about running into anyone now. It was too early for the Collectors, and he knew the Bodaways hadn't left their lab yet, so he had the time. He reached the apartment door, pulled loose the knob plate, and popped the doorknob with the heel of his hand, and the door unlatched. He tightened it back into place, listened for a minute, took Kalare's hand, led her through the living room, through the hallway, stopped in front of a closed door, and took a deep breath.

"Chase?"

"No. Not yet." His voice sounded calm, but she saw his hand shake slightly as he opened the door. The room was changed. Of course, it would be. They would have changed it when they removed Ziph. He went over to the closet and pushed everything aside on the left wall. He hit the top right corner of a panel with the heel of his hand, and it dropped. Spray painted on a whitewashed surface was the word CHASE. There were three pictures tacked along the top: a woman, a man and a little boy, and one of all three smiling at an unseen camera.

"No Shit," Kalare said. "You're their kid?" It was then that she realized that Chase was crying, and she reached over to hold him, but he pushed her away.

"I had missed curfew again. That's why I rigged the doorknob like that, so I could get in when I missed curfew. He always got so mad about the stupid curfew and started locking the door, so I rigged the doorknob so I could sneak back in after they went to sleep."

"Ah, so you scaled down the side of the building to sneak out?"

"Yeah. That was how it started. I just thought he was being a dad, you know? Be in by curfew, do your homework, don't be a slob. You know, parental stuff. Now I understand it was because he knew about the Collectors and the Shifts." He paused, looked at her, shook his head, and let out a small chuckle. "But I was a stubborn kid. I wanted to be with my friends, so I found ways to get out and back in without them knowing. Anyway, that night I got here, and The Collectors were in their bedroom. They were already unconscious. I heard the Collectors say they searched my room, and I wasn't there, so I got by them and hid behind that panel in the closet. *I hid.* I was so scared. I hid like a little baby. They took them away, and I didn't do anything. *I just hid.*" He coughed, swallowed and took another breath. "I came back the next day, and all my stuff was gone, and they had replaced me with Ziph. I didn't even exist anymore. So, I snuck in and put this here, hoping they might find me, or this, or something. I don't know. I wanted to leave a memory, a mark, something to show that I was here. I didn't want just to be erased; you know?"

"Did you hear them the other night? They did miss you. They know, Chase, *they know,* and they are searching for you." She took his face into her hands, forcing him to make eye contact.

"This doesn't change how you see me?" His eyes were filled with guilt and shame and the moist redness of withheld tears, and he could only hold her gaze for a few seconds before turning away.

"No. How could it? You were a little kid. It wasn't your fault." Kalare pulled his face close to hers, so he had to look at her. "You wouldn't be here now with me if you had tried. They would have shifted you. And look. Look at what we are doing tonight. This is your chance to save them. Now you can save them. Now you are strong." She kissed him. "And brave." She kissed him again. "And I love you."

Chase grabbed her by the shoulders, pushed her back and smoothed her hair away so he could see her eyes.

"Do you, Kalare?"

"Yes."

"Even knowing this?"

"Especially knowing this."

He held her there, searching her eyes.

"Really?"

"Yes."

And then all of his resolve was gone. This place where he had lost so much and forced him to block out everyone he cared about compressed around him until there was only Kalare and her copper brown serious eyes staring back at him, unflinching, telling him she loved him.

"Yes," she said again. "Yes.

"I couldn't do this before." Chase paused and looked away. "I felt like I was hiding something from you and couldn't be honest enough to give you everything." He looked back at her. "I'm sorry."

"I understand." She reached over and took his hand. "But right now, all I want to do is kiss you." This time, when he kissed her, there were no walls between them. All the reasons he had always stopped himself from taking the next step didn't matter anymore. She had seen him at his worst, had accepted all of his secrets and still wanted him. No, loved him. They fell back onto the floor of the closet, and everything he had been holding in rose to the surface at once. They became a desperate tangle of jackets tossed off, shoes pulled off, shirts pushed off.

"Wait, wait," Chase said. "I want to see you. Can I see you? I don't want this to be groping in the dark. I want this to be you and me. Do you understand?"

"I don't want to grope in the dark either. I want to see you too. I want to see your eyes the whole time. That's how I'll know I'm safe. When I can see your eyes." Kalare smiled at him and got to her feet. She pulled off what was left of her clothing. She stood shyly, trying to stop the urge to cover herself.

"God, you're beautiful." Chase stood and went to her. He ran his hands along her shoulders, then followed the line down her arms and onto her thighs. "So beautiful." He dropped to his knees and began to kiss her stomach, her hips, the top of her thighs. He pushed his hand between her thighs and looked up at her.

"Is this okay?"

"Oh, god, yes." Kalare breathed out and tangled her fingers in his hair.

"How about this?" He said and bent his head to taste her.

"Yes." She said as she arched her hips toward him and let her fears drain out of her with the sensations that were running through her. Chase stood, and she ran her hands along that muscled torso she had seen so many times, moving under his shirt. The feel of him, as those muscles flexed now in a different way against her, filled her with more emotions than she could understand. She shook off the thoughts in her brain, trying to make sense of this and gave her body permission to enjoy every sensation gripping her now. She moved her hand across his thighs and slid one on either side of him. She smiled against the kiss he placed against her lips.

"What?" he breathed out.

"Nothing."

"No, what?" He said, trying not to explode at her touch.

"It just wasn't what I expected it to feel like." He giggled.

"You can tell me all about that later, but right now." He pulled her down onto the floor and got onto his knees and hovered over her.

"I love you, Kalare." He stared down at her with an intensity that could never hold a lie, and she believed him.

"I love you too, Chase." She said as a tear slid down her cheek. He leaned over and kissed her, then pulled himself back up on his hands.

"Are you still sure?" he asked.

"Yes."

"I'm not completely sure I know how to do this." Chase let out an embarrassed laugh, and Kalare kissed him softly.

"You are doing just fine." Then she whispered, "Here, let me help."

"You'll tell me if I hurt you?"

"I'll be fine. Just go slow." Kalare said as her hands tugged at his waist, pulling him toward her. All of his nervousness broke into wanting her more than he thought possible, and he kissed her with everything he had in him. And as they moved together, Chase let go of it all, here in the room that chained him to a past that no longer existed; he pushed everything into her without restraint. And he finally felt that he was home again.

Chase curled himself into Kalare's back, kissed her shoulder, wrapped his arm around her and pulled her closer. The red CHASE scrawled on the board stared back at him. But he wasn't that kid anymore. "I love you, Kalare." His voice was hoarse as he said it out loud for the first time. And after he had given her all he had, he realized that, finally, he wasn't scared to love her anymore.

"I know you do." She reached back and ran her hand through his hair and traced a single finger along the side of his jawline. "Now, let's go get your family out of here."

They tried to dress quickly between kisses and giggles. Chase reached over and pushed the board back up into the wall. Then thought better of it and popped the board back down, took the pictures and stuffed them into his jacket pocket, then pushed the board back into place. He closed the closet door behind him; he was finally ready to leave this life behind and move forward toward whatever was out there. As long as Kalare was by his side, he could handle anything.

18

had and Saige stared at the blinking message on the throw-away phones. Panic rose in Saige's chest as she realized that up until now, it all seemed like something they were talking about in theory. But suddenly everything seemed very real. They needed to leave now. Something went wrong with the plan. The departure time had been moved up, and whether she was ready or not, this was happening now.

The TALUS whirred into the lab.

"Dr. Bodaway. I understand you will be leaving the premises early. Are you having an emergency?" The TALUS' metallic voice reverberated against the glass walls of the lab. Thad thought he detected a hint of concern. He knew he was tired, and he also knew everything was just beginning. Had it really only been a few days since the collection call at Thomas' house? How could your entire world change in mere days? He took in a deep breath to center his voice before speaking.

"No. No emergency. They are updating the lab's security this afternoon, so it won't be quiet enough to get any work done here. We'll be working from home for the rest of the day. Thank you for your concern." "Yes, Dr. Bodaway." The TALUS spun and left the lab.

"What is with that guy?" Saige asked. "When did he become your buddy?"

"I have no idea. I wonder if it was because that kid wandered up here yesterday."

"I guess. I still can't get used to them, can you?" Saige said, letting out a shudder as she shook her shoulders. She added a few last-minute things to her bag before they headed to the elevators. It seemed odd to her that this would be the last time she would be here. This lab had been her home for so long, and she couldn't help glancing back and letting out a small hiccup of restrained emotion.

"I know. I'm sorry." Thad said, coming up behind her and wrapping his arm so that he was holding her elbow as if she might faint. "I'll make it all okay again. I promise." He whispered into her hair and gently backed her into the elevator, holding her close as the doors closed.

They pulled into their apartment garage and parked in their usual spot, except Thad backed the car in, leaving enough room against the wall for access into the back hatch. He pulled the metal GPS from the paper Seth had given him and dropped it between the wall and the cement bumper block. He crumpled the list with the instructions and shoved it into his front pocket. He wanted to do one last sweep of the apartment to be sure he hadn't left anything that would tip anyone off. He had made this sweep three times but still wanted to do it one more time. And then they would leave everything behind. Again.

Chase, Kalare, Sam and Jo-Jo were standing by their truck in the garage. Saige and Thad stepped out from behind their car and headed toward the elevator. Seth's car came speeding into the garage. He threw his car into reverse, blocked the row and ground the gears as he tried to get out and put the car into park at the same time. He ran toward them, spiraling his arms in a panic.

"They are right behind me. MOVE, MOVE, MOVE." Sam climbed into the truck as Kalare and Chase headed toward Thad and Saige. Jo-Jo jumped into the truck bed and slid the shortened barrel of her rifle into the precut hole. Sam pulled the truck into the center lane and blocked the aisle in front of Seth's abandoned car so that Chase had open space to pull out. Chase had pushed Saige and Thad into the back seat and climbed into the driver's seat, revving the engine when he fed it more gas than it needed. Kalare was standing next to the car, scanning the garage levels with her rifle.

"You two," Chase said to Thad and Saige, "Stay down. No matter what you hear. STAY DOWN!" Kalare opened the passenger door and was about to get into the car when the shots started. Two Collectors reached the railing on the second level of the garage and opened fire. Kalare brought up her gun and took out the first Collector. The second one ducked under the concrete barrier but managed to get a shot off, which ricocheted off the concrete wall behind the car.

"Get in," Chase shouted. "Get in the car, Kalare."

"Where's Seth?" She yelled back without turning.

"He's in the truck; get the hell in the car, Kalare." Chase realized he was screaming. He tried to pull back his emotions, but he couldn't. Everyone he cared about in life was in this garage, and he was afraid not all of them would make it out.

"I can get him; just hold one second. I can get him." She was aiming at the pole the Collector had ducked behind.

A black SUV smashed into Seth's car, slamming it out of the center aisle and into one of the pilings, and it burst into flames as the SUV headed toward the truck. Jo-Jo fired at the windshield, but the bullets wouldn't penetrate, so she aimed for the tires. She hit the right tire, the car swerved, and then she took out the passenger-side tire. The vehicle careened into two parked cars and smashed into the cement pillar at the end of the aisle. Smoke and blue antifreeze poured out of the front of the car as doors opened and three Collectors got out, aiming in her direction. Then Ziph got out of the black Sedan.

Sam pulled out his Springfield 9mm handgun, popped off the safety, and took out one of the Collectors.

"Here, Seth, you should be able to manage this," Sam yelled over the shots as he handed Seth the same make but a smaller model of the handgun he was using.

"No, man, I'm a tech rat."

"Take this, aim that way, pull the trigger, and try to hit something." Seth rolled down the window, started firing the gun with his eyes closed, and stuck his other finger into his ear. He jumped every time it fired and let out a hysterical sound that fell somewhere between a little girl scared by a spider and a rhesus monkey.

Jo-Jo took out another Collector and hit the third one in the knee, and he went down screaming.

"GO, GO, GO!" Sam screamed as Kalare finally got the Collector in her sights. Before she could pull the trigger, a shot came from behind and blasted into her shoulder. She went down, her rifle clattering into the floor of the garage. She collapsed halfway onto the seat, blood pouring from her shoulder.

"NOOO!" Screamed Chase as he tried to drag her into the car. Thad reached up and pulled the lever that dropped the back of the seat. Saige wrapped her arms around Kalare's waist and pulled her the rest of the way into the backseat. Thad reached up and slammed the passenger door closed.

"We got her." Thad yelled, "Go."

"Do something!" Chase pleaded with Thad. "Please, help her."

"Just go. Goddammit GO!"

Chase gunned the accelerator as another vehicle pulled into the garage from the entrance off Broad Street. If he didn't get moving, they would be blocked in. And now there were Collectors everywhere, and he realized they were trapped no matter what he did.

The TALUS whirled around the abutment on the far side of the garage and stepped through the center aisle and into the path of the oncoming car. When the driver saw the TALUS, he tried to swerve, but the TALUS caught the front bumper, flipping the car. Bullets pinged off the TALUS' metal as it turned toward the shots, and Sam heard a loud click as the TALUS' weapon slid out of a shoulder compartment. A high-pitched whine filled the garage until a small light flickered to green, and the TALUS fixed sites on the Collectors that filed onto the second level. Rapid-fire blasts started ricocheting everywhere as the TALUS stepped forward and shoved the flipped car out of the way, giving Chase and Sam a small but secure area to drive through. Chase slammed down on the accelerator as the TALUS took out the entire second level of the garage. Plaster and concrete showered down onto the car's roof and windshield and pelted JoJo, who was still uncovered in the back of the trunk.

Collectors were streaming in on the third landing as the TALUS swiveled and refocused its weapons and opened fire again. Sam followed Chase through the small opening and watched the TALUS advance on the swarming Collectors as it engaged a second weapon. The last thing Chase saw as he glanced back was Ziph walking out of the opposite side of the garage.

"I've been hit," Jo-Jo said.

"How bad?

"Not sure. My thigh."

"Front or Back?"

"Back."

"Tie something around it. I'll get you into the cab in a minute." Sam pushed in the clutch, downshifted and skidded into the exit ramp following Chase out of the garage.

"Hey, Seth, you okay, man? You're, ah, looking a little green there."

"Are you kidding me?" Seth dropped the gun as if it were electrified.

"Don't throw up in my truck, Seth."

"I'm not going to throw up, Geez. What am I, like a little girl?" Seth said as he heaved and threw up all over his own shoes.

"Seth, what the hell? I just told you not to throw up in my truck."

"Are you kidding me? Do you realize we almost died back there? You had me shooting a freakin' gun? A gun, Sam, and you're worried about a little throw-up?"

Jo-Jo had come up to sit at the back window and began to chuckle.

"It's not funny." Both Sam and Seth whined at the same time.

"Um, yeah, it is." Jo-Jo giggled. "Oh man, does it smell in there."

"I know that's why I didn't want him to throw up in my truck."

"Sam, was Kalare hit?" Jo-Jo was resting her head against the metal frame of the small back window of the truck, wincing.

"Yeah, she was hit. Don't know how badly, though. Are you okay back there?"

"Yeah, I think so, not bleeding too much; hurts like hell though."

"Ah, come on, Seth, again? Really?" Seth was retching for the third time but had subsided into dry heaves.

"Oh god. I'm gonna be sick again. Can't we pull over or something?" Seth asked.

"No, we can't pull over. Stop throwing up in my truck, Seth." Seth retched again.

"Oh, Geez, at least open the window, will you?" Sam switched into fifth gear and hit the accelerator harder to catch up with Chase.

Saige was holding pressure against Kalare's shoulder. She was losing too much blood. The bullet had hit her just under the shoulder blade and had not exited. Saige's hands were red, and the cloth she had been using to hold pressure was soaked through.

"Chase, we need to stop. I need to get her stabilized."

"No way. We can't stop."

"We have to. I can't do what I need to do for her with the three of us crammed into this back seat. And I need Thad to hold her while I work on her to keep her from bouncing around."

"Okay. Wait, I have an idea. Can you give me about five minutes?" "Five minutes? Try to make it three."

"Doc?" Saige looked up and met his eyes in the rearview mirror. "I can't lose her. She's everything. You have to save her." "I don't lose patients," Saige said.

A few minutes later, they pulled over into a loading dock between two tractor-trailers. Chase got out, fumbled with some keys and opened the back of another truck about ten feet away. He pulled down two ramps and got back into the car. Thad slid out of the backseat and opened the rear compartment. He unclipped the straps on the gurney and then lifted Kalare out of the backseat and moved her onto the gurney. Saige crawled in beside her when Thad moved to the trailer.

"Hold on back there, it's gonna be bumpy," Chase shouted back to Saige. Chase hit the accelerator, bounced up the ramps, skidded into the empty tractor-trailer and slammed on the brakes. Kalare yelped as the car jolted to a stop. Chase jumped down from the trailer as Sam lifted Jo-Jo to him into the trailer. A stain of wet blood coated her leg.

"Shit. Were you hit, too?"

"Yeah, it's not bad. We got the bleeding stopped now. How's Kalare?" Jo-Jo said.

"Don't know. Bad, I think."

Seth bent over and threw up. Again. Chase started to tug on the ramps as Sam hoisted Seth up and set him on the floor of the trailer.

Sam locked the ramps back into place and lifted Seth's legs into the
trailer.

"Do not throw up on me. Do you hear me?" Seth groaned and curled up into a ball.

"Chase, how's Kalare?"

"They're working on her. I'm trying to give them space. They said they needed about fifteen minutes."

"I got this, go take care of your girl."

"I don't think I could drive anyway." Chase's voice was shaking. His arms were folded across his chest, and he was pacing in tiny circles at the back of the trailer.

"Chase, I got this. Go sit with her. Give me the keys. I'll get us home."

They heard sirens all around them but couldn't tell whether they were approaching or heading back toward the apartment building. They could only stay here a short while. If the police set up checkpoints, they would be caught. Finally, he couldn't stay away anymore and went to the back door and watched them working on Kalare. Kalare was lying on her side, an IV bag hung on the handle in the ceiling, and they were wrapping bandages around her. Something plastic was sticking out of her chest, but the blood seemed to have slowed.

"How is she?"

"She's as stable as I can get her here. Her lung collapsed, but she's breathing better now. I need to get the bullet out, and I can't do that here. We should get moving. I'm not exactly battlefield experienced." Saige frowned, feeling inadequate. She hoped her skills weren't so rusty that she would make a mistake.

Chase pounded on the side of the trailer three times and felt the shudder of the engine kick over and the shift from the crunch of tires on gravel to the smooth hum of paved road.

"Thank you." Chase cleared his throat to stop his voice from cracking.

"Well, don't thank me yet. We have a long way to go." Saige smiled weakly.

"Thad, Jo-Jo was hit in the thigh, I don't know how bad. Can you take care of her?"

"Sure. Stay here in case Saige needs anything. I'll take a look at JoJo." Thad reached over and kneaded Chase's shoulder. "She's in good hands."

Sam didn't run into any roadblocks. There was no sign of any activity at all. As a matter of fact, it was almost too eerily quiet. They reached the bridge, and the city was left behind as it was getting dark. Jo-Jo was now riding in the cab with Sam. Thad had pulled the bullet from her thigh and stitched her up. She was in some pain but tried to hide it and refused to take anything for the pain.

Thad had given Seth several shots for nausea, but they didn't seem to help much, and he finally fell asleep curled up near the rattling door of the trailer. Chase was in the car with Saige and Kalare; Thad was sleeping on the trailer floor and jumped up when he felt the truck lurch to a stop.

Chase had drifted off to sleep holding Kalare's hand and opened his eyes when he felt the truck stop. Kalare was still out, but Saige was wide awake, listening through the stethoscope on Kalare's chest.

"How's she doing, Doc?" He was feeling every emotion at once. Kalare was hurt. Saige was here, with him, and taking care of Kalare.

Thad was out there watching over them. He was completely overwhelmed by it all.

"Her heart sounds steady. She's in great shape, so that always helps.

How's Jo-Jo?"

"Okay, Thad got the bullet out and stitched her up. She's in the cab with Sam. I couldn't drive. I couldn't leave Kalare."

"I know. I'm glad you were here. I'm sorry she got hurt helping us."

"I'm glad you had all this equipment. She would have..." Sam opened the door to the truck and pulled out the ramps.

"If I could get a couple of you to help with the gurney." Thad pulled the back door open and threaded two poles through the folds along each side of the gurney. Saige and Thad took the front, and Sam and Chase took the back, and they carried Kalare into The Forty.

Saige poured alcohol onto the kitchen table, opened a pack of linens, and spread them over the table. "Let's cut her out of those clothes before we put her down here." Saige was saying as the small generator Thad had hooked up kicked in.

"I'll get those machines plugged in so we can hook her up," Thad said as Saige connected the monitor wires.

"Listen, Chase, I don't know how long this is going to take. Go, get some rest or something to eat. We've got this."

"No. I'm not leaving her."

"Chase, she's going to need you when she wakes up. She needs you to look rested and strong. We've got this." Thad pulled Chase to his feet and walked him toward the hallway.

"Okay. I just, you know, don't want to leave her if..."

"We've gotten her this far, haven't we? We'll get her there.

Promise," Saige said.

After pacing the hall of The Forty for an hour, Chase went outside to get some fresh air and looked up to see the TALUS standing about fifty feet from the entrance. Seth had a panel open in the back and was typing on a keyboard.

"Oh, what the hell is this?" Chase asked.

"Well, as far as I can tell by the diagnostics, when they programmed Big-T. to keep an eye on Thad, there was some command that was put in so that it bonded with Thad. They do this when a TALUS represents a citizen because the programming allows for a certain amount of empathy and compassion toward the person they advocate for; think of a really kindhearted lawyer that isn't a complete skeeze. Now, this particular TALUS, which I think was originally planned as a military rather than a domestic servant, reinterpreted that command to a protection mode."

"Which means?"

"Which means that The Committee has, in effect, given Thad a giant metal guardian, who also seems to be integrating Thad's feelings for those around him as well. This is probably why they rotate them out so often." "So, what does this all mean?" Chase asked.

"What this means is that we have an eight-foot, fully armed, self-generating, non-traceable TALUS as our guardian angel. Here, watch."

"Big-T, this is Chase. He's Dr. Bodaway's right-hand man."

"Good morning, Chase."

"You have got to be kidding me. Is that why he showed up at the garage?"

"Yup. Main objective is to protect asset Thaddeus Bodaway and any extended family members."

"You said untraceable. You're sure it's not sending any information back?"

"No. It was never set up for mobile updates. They had to manually plug in and download data. I've checked all GPS and tracking connections to the home base computer. He is completely isolated from the mainframe. No one would even be thinking about tracking him. No one would expect him to follow Thad. It's pretty cool, don't you think?" Seth was grinning.

"No. It makes me nervous."

"What the hell?" Thad said as he came through the door. "Why is that thing here?"

"Good morning, Dr. Bodaway. What do you require?"

Thad looked at Seth, then Chase, and then at the TALUS.

"No. Nothing. I mean, I think we are good here," Thad said. He shrugged at Seth. "Is this safe?"

"Yeah, I'll explain it all. Just tell him to make sure the perimeter is clear. Oh, and I changed his name to Big-T."

"Great," Thad said. "Big-T?'

"Yes, Dr. Bodaway?"

"Can you keep watch to be sure the perimeter is clear?"

"Yes, Dr. Bodaway. As you wish."

"Oh, Big-T? Call me Thad."

"Yes, Thad." Big-T changed direction and began to circle The Forty.

Kalare came through the surgery fine. She lost a lot of blood, and she's weak, but it all looks good. You can go see her; she should be waking up soon." Thad was holding Chase's shoulder, and Chase leaned in and hugged him. Held it for a few seconds.

"Okay, Seth, fill me in on this whole Big-T thing. I guess nothing, and I do mean nothing, could surprise me at this point." Thad had thumped Chase with an encouraging hand on his back and turned to Seth.

Chase ran toward the entrance to The Forty, stopped and turned to Thad.

"Thank you for everything. It means more than you know." Chase stood for a minute as if he wanted to add something, but then turned and ran into The Forty.

Chase came into the room quietly. Saige was checking monitors.

"Hi, Chase. She's doing very well."

"Is she really going to be okay?"

"Yes. She needs lots of rest, and she'll have a nasty scar, but she's going to be fine.

"Thank you. Thank you so much." Chase leaned in and rested his head next to Kalare on the bed. She started coughing and tried a few times to open her eyes before she could focus on Chase's face. She gave him a weak smile.

"Hey."

"Hey," He leaned over and kissed her softly on the forehead, smoothing back her hair. "Are you still my girl?"

"Always," Kalare whispered.

Saige let out an audible breath, and Chase looked up at her and smiled.

"Hi, Mom."

19

"**G**et a car over here immediately to pick me up," Ziph screamed into his phone. He walked out of the first level of the garage as the TALUS opened fire on the second level. He had to admit, he was surprised. They must have reprogrammed the TALUS. That was simple enough to do. Seth probably did that. He was just another traitor to do away with. He didn't really care that they had found help; it was *who* helped them that infuriated him. He saw that street rat, saw the resemblance and knew immediately it was their son. He knew it. *Knew it.* They had probably known about each other the whole time. That's why he always felt like an intruder. He *was* an intruder. The Committee did this. He was glad he pushed Regent to shoot himself. Ziph was only sorry he hadn't been the one to pull the trigger. He didn't know how they found their son, but he was glad when he heard him screaming when that girl got shot. If it hadn't been for that street rat, they might have accepted him. There might have been room for him in their lives. They were all going to pay now. And everyone who helped them.

"Get an army over here to clean up that mess. I want a special detail to begin tracking the Bodaways. NOW!" Ziph shouted when the armed guards that had come to escort him back didn't move.

"We have other orders, Sir."

"Other orders? I'm giving the orders now. Get me back to Committee Headquarters."

"We have been ordered to take you to Directive Headquarters and not Committee immediately." The second guard opened the rear passenger door.

"Who gave you other orders?"

"As usual, from Command. Please get in, Sir." He stepped back respectfully, and Ziph got into the back seat of the sedan. He was confused. He was sure that he had gone through all of the information on Regent's computer. There was nothing on anything called Directive Headquarters.

Nothing in all of the files he had accessed. All orders appeared to come from The Committee. And *HE* was now the Committee. After they cleaned up the bloody mess that cowardly Regent left in his office, Ziph informed Dr. Metcalf that, as outlined in the regulations, he, as Regent's legal son, was taking over his position on the Committee. He forced her to release all passwords and access codes and to fully ordain him. She resisted until he persuaded her with that gun in her mouth; then she listened to him. Then she filled everything out, including a letter of resignation naming him as the new Chair of The Committee.

Once all paperwork was filed and he had his access codes and passes in hand, he promptly had her arrested for breaching regulations and helping the Bodaways escape. Who cared if it wasn't true? No one would question him now. He really wanted to get a sharp knife and run it across her throat so he could watch the life go out of her eyes, but he might need her. He was sure he wasn't going to get anything out of that tech geek. He had obviously been helping the Bodaways all along. The first thing Ziph was going to do was to get into Seth's office and find the trail. But it didn't matter. He would have them all hunted down, everyone who helped them in any way. He was going to enjoy torturing the Bodaways, *all of them*. He would do it himself; the ways he could inflict pain on them would be a lot of fun. They were going to pay for everything.

The car stopped in front of a one-story square building that looked like a warehouse. A single guard sat at the entrance. The guards pulled him from the car and into what looked like the lobby of an office building. A single desk sat in the middle of the glass-enclosed front and back walls. The sidewalls were covered in a brown stained engineered paneling that looked more like a series of doors than solid walls. They pulled Ziph up to the desk and up to a scanner. Each guard leaned forward and scanned their left eye.

The guard motioned to Ziph to do the same.

"I am not letting you do anything until I speak to someone in charge. Do you know *who* I am? Do you?" Ziph shouted, pushing the guard's hand from his arm. "Get me someone in charge. *Now*." He forced the word 'now' in between gritted teeth. The rage in him was uncontrollable now. He wanted to gun them all down. *Why? Why can't they all just do what I say?* A panel on the left side of the room slid open, revealing an elevator. A tall, blonde woman stepped out and motioned the guards away as the doors slid shut behind her. Her hair was slick and straight, falling just below her ears. She wore a bright blue, form-fitting dress and high heels. Her nails were impeccably polished, and she moved more like a supermodel rather than some underpaid office assistant.

"Yes, we are quite aware of who you are, Ziph. This little coup you pulled today, while impressive, is not, I repeat *not*, how things are accomplished around here." She gestured to the security guard behind the desk, and he stood and passed her a handheld scanner.

"You see, Ziph, control, of all concerned, is the key. No one. Let me repeat that: *no one* has done what you did today. Well, at least not without some sort of repercussion." She nodded to the guard who held Ziph's head, and she scanned his left eye.

"Hmmmm. Interesting. It appears you are Regent's son only on paper. Not biologically. Well, this is merely a technicality that we may decide to leave in place or, you know, not." She motioned to the wall she had emerged from. "Shall we? There are some people who want to meet you. But be careful how you handle this. While you have shown some promise, this little temper of yours is proving to be a bit of a problem." "I don't understand," Ziph said.

"I know. But you will," she said. As she took Ziph's arm, the doors slid open and led him into the elevator. "I think we are going to have a very interesting conversation, you and I; a very interesting conversation indeed."

The doors closed, but the elevator didn't move until the woman punched in a code and placed her thumb on the pad to verify her identity. A small panel opened at eye level, and a metallic female voice said: "*Please step forward for optical verification, Dr. Taylor.*"

Dr. Taylor stepped forward, allowed the eye scan, then waited for a response.

"*Good evening, Dr. Taylor. The others are waiting for you in the main conference room. Please identify your passenger and have him step forward for optical verification.*"

"I'm not doing anything until you tell me where I am and what is going on." Ziph folded his arms across his chest. He hoped the stance would cover the fear now coursing through him. He had made a mistake. Without the protection of Dr. Regent, he was really just a boy with no power, and right now, he wasn't sure what scared him more: a Shifting or his own death.

"*If the passenger does not step forward for optical verification, he will be considered an intruder, and evasive action will be initiated.*"

Dr. Taylor opened a compartment and took out a small, clear plastic facemask with a small cylinder attached. She placed it over her face and closed the panel. She looked at Ziph.

"I suggest you comply." She leveled her eyes and shrugged. "Of course, it's completely up to you."

Fear motivated Ziph to step forward and allow the optical scan.

"*Good evening, Ziph. The others are waiting for you in the conference room.*"

Then the elevator plummeted down. Ziph backed against the wall, holding onto the railing. His stomach was churning, and he was afraid he was going to throw up. Dr. Taylor calmly opened the compartment and replaced the facemask.

"Ziph, you will find that you will get along much better around here if you stop fighting everything so much. The Committee may have put up with this childish behavior from you, but I assure you, we will not."

The elevator began to slow, which caused Ziph's stomach to heave in the other direction. He turned toward the padded wall of the elevator. It reeked of dust and grease and something he couldn't identify. This forced saliva to well up, which he tried to swallow and held onto the railing with his eyes closed as the elevator abruptly stopped. He felt dizzy and was gripping the rail with whitened knuckles. Just when he thought he would pass out, the doors slid open, and air rushed into the elevator, cooling the layer of sweat that had formed on the back of his neck. He turned around to face the doors again, reluctantly letting go of the railing. He ran his hands along the bottom edge of his jacket, trying to dry them, but couldn't seem to move away from the back wall of the elevator. The hallway behind was bright and buzzing with activity, and the light and noise seemed to burst in around him, making him woozy again. He leaned his head back against the wall and shut his eyes, swallowing hard. How could his mouth be dry and full of saliva at the same time? Dr. Taylor stepped out of the elevator.

"Ziph?" He opened his eyes but didn't trust himself to speak.

Both sides of the hallway were lined with labs and offices, each outfitted with floor-to-ceiling glass walls. The workers wore lab coats, maintenance uniforms, and all-white jumpsuits, similar to HAZMAT suits but thinner, more like a combination of paper and plastic, leading up to tight-fitting headgear that allowed full head movement.

"What is this?

"Ziph, if you will please step in for decontamination," Dr. Taylor said. She gestured to the frame. "You must be decontaminated before you enter the facility. If you refuse, these two gentlemen will assist you." Two large armed guards stood on either side of a square metal frame just beyond the elevator. They didn't make a move toward him but were clearly waiting for the signal.

Ziph stepped out of the elevator and into the frame. Blue lights began to glow from the four sides of the frame and from the cross-beams along the top. There was a rising hiss as the lights continued to brighten until a loud pop and flash that made Ziph jump. As the lights dimmed, a sizzle swirled throughout the frames, making Ziph think of bubbling, burning skin.

"Subject has been decontaminated and is free to be escorted after the identification badge has been administered."

Dr. Taylor unclipped a square device from the frame. It looked like the handheld optical scanner she had used in the lobby, but it was much smaller. She motioned for Ziph to come out of the frame.

"Left wrist, please." She held out her hand, waiting for him to comply.

Ziph held out his left arm as Dr. Taylor slipped her hand under his forearm to brace it. She placed the device on the inside of his left wrist and depressed the button on top. Something cut into Ziph's skin, and then he felt the burning heat sear deeper into his wrist. The image of burning, bubbling skin came back to him as he tried to pull his arm away.

"If you damage the installation of your ID, we will only have to do it again." Ziph stopped moving his arm but worked his jaw muscles as he ground his molars together. When she took the device away, his wrist was red, but the skin wasn't broken. He felt the boil still; it went to the bone.

"The redness and burning will subside in a day or so. This way." Dr.

Taylor moved down the hallway, not stopping to see if he was following.

Ziph decided to follow her. The two guards followed behind them. His stomach was churning, his head was pounding, his wrist was burning, and two armed guards were escorting him into some hellhole buried several stories underground. *This was not the plan. This was going all wrong.* They came to a slight bend in the hallway, and Dr. Taylor stopped at the only office with enclosed walls instead of glass. She tapped at a corner square along the doorframe, and a panel opened. She punched in a code, and an optical scanner slid up from behind the keypad. Dr. Taylor leaned forward for a scan, then motioned for Ziph to do the same. This time, he complied without argument. A door slid open into a conference room, where people were seated around a large mahogany table. Ziph stared around the room until his eyes landed on the person at the head of the table.

"You've had quite a day, young man," said Dr. Regent. "Let's see how we can clean this mess up, shall we?"

Ziph stood at the opposite end of the table, glaring at Regent; first confused and then furious. His momentary wish to be back under Regent's control quickly vanished. Now he simply felt like a fool, and that was unforgivable. He thought he was finally free of this idiot and in control, but he was right back where he started. No. This was much worse than that; they were going to punish him as if he were a rebellious child. He had played his hand and had lost.

"Well, I can only guess that you are a little confused. You see, when you threatened to expose the misappropriation of the funding, you didn't understand that I wasn't embezzling money. I was following through with how The Directive earmarked the money for further research. It was to be off the grid. I knew you wouldn't stop, so the only way to protect the continued research was to eliminate the source: namely, me." Dr. Regent had raised his arms. It was an attempt at humor, but Ziph was reeling from hunger and nausea and this calm explanation of a staged death.

"What are you talking about? I thought the Shifting was the thing?"

"Oh, my boy, this is the problem with nineteen-year-olds, even brilliant nineteen-year-olds; they don't have any vision. Do you really think the only reason we exist is to dose and Shift a few stupid criminals that we can't keep in line?" Regent shook his head. "Think bigger, Ziph. Get beyond your anger and think about a long-range, expansive use."

"So, what? Are you going to militarize this or something equally idiotic?"

"Now you're getting it." Dr. Regent motioned for Ziph to take the empty chair. Ziph shook his head, and Regent shrugged. "Look, we have a lot to fill you in on; you may as well sit and get comfortable. But suit yourself."

"I don't understand. The shifts are the new weapon?"

"No, you idiot. The Meds. The meds are the thing. They create the blank slate we can control."

"I don't understand."

"That my boy is an understatement. Imagine having the capacity to dose and manipulate on a large scale. And then, walking in and taking everything over, restructuring everyone on the spot to do your bidding and all without firing a shot. Not one single shot. Can you imagine it?"

It was then that Ziph noticed Dr. Metcalf sitting at the table.

"Ziph." She couldn't help but let a slight smile tug up on the edges of her lips as she tilted her head toward him. "Now that you are beginning to realize that this is much bigger than your little tantrum and need for a title, maybe you can make yourself useful."

Ziph moved to respond when Regent slammed his hand on the table with a loud bang.

"We don't have time for this. We will discuss your many missteps later, but you have managed to secure yourself a place on the Committee, no matter the means. We sanctioned the papers filed by Dr. Metcalf and her dissention, which again, the Board has noted." Regent rolled his eyes and motioned toward Dr. Metcalf. "Now, can we please get to the matter at hand?"

"Please do." Dr. Metcalf said curtly.

"Yes, Ziph, you are correct, we are, have militarized this. These medications were revolutionary. I know you hate the Bodaways, who, by the way, are off limits for any kind of retribution. This little rebellion has forced them off-site. They are working on new protocols to reverse and not just block the drugs. We need this technology. Everything depends on this new protocol. Except now, because of your little attempted coup and belligerent attitude, you have forced us to find a way to, shall we say, safeguard certain important, um, assets." Dr. Regent smiled. "I would like to say this is all playing into unintended plans, but unfortunately, we now have to take a few steps back before we can go forward."

"I don't understand."

"You were placed with the Bodaways intentionally because we knew they were experimenting with anti-shift drugs. They were using themselves as test subjects, and we hoped they would begin treating you as well, but they never did. Curious, don't you think?"

"What is it with you and those people? If you knew they were going against The Committee, why weren't they arrested and Shifted?"

"We Shifted them when we placed you with them. They lost six months of research as a result. We decided to give them a long enough leash to get back on track and see where they were going with it all. We found that the more intelligent an individual is, the more initial damage is done to brain function. But we also found that more intelligent brains healed more quickly and began to reattach and restore memories without experiencing bleed-backs. Now, as fascinating as this is, we didn't care about this because, for our purposes, all we need is the initial effect of compliance and memory wipe." Dr. Regent paused, "As a matter of fact, this idea became an interesting way to continue to get intel right from the source. So, you see, this idea of blocking was good, but the chance of a timed tactical reversal was brilliant. We were so focused on deployment from afar that we hadn't considered these other possibilities. We could be in the center of deployment and remain unharmed using the reversal drugs. We could potentially get any information we needed without the need for torture. This is very good news to us."

"My god, you actually admire these people."

"Absolutely. They are held in the highest regard. They are, after all, the minds behind all of this. They have, whether unknowingly or not, orchestrated this entire scenario," Dr. Regent smiled. "Now, I'm not saying that they are not a problem, especially out there in their new little hideout, and even though we can still monitor them, your little stunt caused them to move their lab. As a result, we no longer have the capability of accessing their research."

"You know where they are?"

"Of course, we do, my boy. We are the government. We have eyes and ears everywhere." Regent shook his head.

"So, you have someone with them?"

"Of course, we do. We know everything they are doing, including the new research direction. But that is a discussion for another day. I think we should stop here for now." Dr. Regent motioned to Dr. Taylor. "Dr. Taylor is going to be your escort and assistant for the rest of your stay here. You need to go and get settled in your new quarters, and I will meet with you later to discuss some more personal matters, which the board has graciously allowed me to do in private." Dr. Taylor stood and walked around the table to stand behind Ziph.

"What are you talking about, *new quarters*?" Ziph was gritting his teeth now, anger beginning to rise again. His hands flexed and unflexed at his sides as he took in a deep breath, trying to maintain his control.

"Well, you don't think we are going to unleash you to go out and create another disaster like last night, do you?"

"So, I am a prisoner now? With an escort?"

"No, not a prisoner. But you will remain here and attend some informational sessions. Also, some, shall we say, adjustment sessions." It was Dr. Metcalf who responded with a great deal of satisfaction in her voice.

"Shifting? You are going to Shift me?" Ziph slammed both his hands flat onto the table.

"Ziph, we would like to see you become a viable, productive member of this project. But these little temper tantrums of yours get in the way. You either get these outbursts under control and decide to be the person we need on your own or, well, yes, Shifting has been discussed." Dr.

Regent motioned toward the door, dismissing him.

"I will not be shifted." He was tired of fighting. He was tired of arguing. This was the moment that needed to define him.

"Then put that brilliant brain of yours to better use and stop acting like a child. You have already established yourself as the Committee's head. Either you get yourself in line, or the news will be released about your tragic death in the drug-related shoot-out at the parking garage." Dr. Metcalf's voice was level and admonishing.

"Drug-related? What are you talking about?"

"Well, we couldn't very well let the real news leak out that the head of The Committee had launched a military-style attack on its two most prominent doctors, now could we?" Dr. Regent's tone was as dismissive as the hand gesturing for him to leave.

"I don't care how you covered that up. Or what your intentions with the Bodaways are, what I want to know is, what are you going to do with me?" Ziph folded his arms defiantly across his chest and leaned against the wall. "Because I'm telling you right now, I will not allow you to shift me." "Well then, shall we see how to get you out of this mess?" Regent slid his glasses down his nose and peered over them. "Because I'm telling you now, they are ready to incinerate you unless you do exactly as I tell you."

20

They were setting up one of the larger generators when Chase reached into his pocket and handed Thad one of the three pictures of them he had hidden in the panel in his closet. At the time, it seemed like a just defiant little victory, as if he had beaten the Collectors at something by snatching the pictures. Now he realized it was proof of the past. This one picture would explain it all without words. He always stumbled on his words at important times like this. How do you say, *oh, by the way, the son you lost? The one you are looking for. Oh yeah, that's me, and how do you feel about that now that you know who I really am?* There really wasn't any good way to do this, so Chase had taken a deep breath and clumsily thrust the picture into Thad's hand.

Chase stared at Thad, searching his body language for some sign of his reaction. He saw it register in Saige's eyes as soon as he said, "Hi, Mom," and, after the momentary shock of it, she simply reached out for his hand and smiled before settling into muted tears. It was wordless between them. He was hoping it would be the same with Thad, but he wanted this to be private between them. Even though he knew Thad wanted to find his son. Chase just wasn't sure how happy Thad would be when he found out that he was their son. His guilt hung over him like seething clouds of doubt, always on the verge of deluge. How could he explain hiding in that closet, scared out of his mind, while The Collectors did their work? How could he expect Thad to forgive him for letting them break apart their family?

Thad stared at the picture for a long time. He couldn't trust himself to speak for several minutes, but when he turned to look at Chase for the first time, he recognized the younger version of himself staring back. All the things he had been trying to pull out of his brain for the past three years suddenly broke free and collided. For one brief second, he was in total bliss, and then the burning pain started in the back of his neck, spread to his temple and exploded in his left eye. He reached up and grabbed the side of his head, grunted something unintelligible and collapsed.

Chase put his hand on Thad's throat, feeling for a pulse and screamed for Saige.

"I don't know what happened. I handed him the picture of us, and he was fine, but then he grabbed his head and fell." They carried Thad to the bed next to Kalare. "What did I do?"

"I think he might have had a bleed-back." Saige pulled open each eye and moved a light back and forth. The exploded veins in his left eye confirmed the bleed-back.

"What?" Thad blinked his eyes and tried to focus on Saige's face, then looked around the room until he found Chase. He reached out his hand, and Chase grabbed it.

"I'm sorry. So sorry." Chase breathed in hard; his voice and hands were shaking. Thad shook his head and tried to speak, but Saige had slid in the needle for an IV and pushed a sedative. Thad's eyes began to close.

"Don't try to talk. You're okay. It will all keep." She listened to his heart, hoping for that steady rhythm she rested against every night. His heart was still beating rapidly. She pushed a corticosteroid and a diuretic, hoping the combination would prevent swelling in the brain. Once his breathing deepened under the sedative, she pulled open his left eye and watched as the spreading fissures in his eye slowed. She had already done everything she was trained to do as a doctor, and the nausea hit her as her adrenaline began to ebb in her system. As much as she tried to stay strong for Chase, a sheen of sweat was building up behind her neck and along her hairline. She swallowed to push down the nausea but could feel her body reacting and knew she couldn't stop it.

"What do we do now?" Chase was still holding Thad's hand and placed it across his chest but didn't let go.

"We wait. This happens sometimes when memories come flooding back too quickly. I thought he would be safe because he was so close to remembering you that he wouldn't have a bleed-back." Saige tried to keep her voice steady for Chase's sake; she tried to be the doctor in control. But this was Thad, and the nausea built into a shudder that started in the pit of her stomach and shot up into her chest and sweat-soaked temples. Her knees buckled, and she stumbled back, grabbing onto the side of the bed to steady herself. She had to sit down, or she was going to faint.

"Are you okay?" Chase grabbed hold of her forearms to steady her. His hands were so like Thad's, thick and strong and sure. She was losing her balance, and his hands moved up to her shoulders, guided her around, and sat her in the bedside chair. He stooped down in front of her but wasn't sure what to say, so he just held onto her hands, which were shaking and ice-cold.

"I'm fine. I'm Fine." She tried to push his hands away. She had to pull herself together. If she gave in to this now, she would dissolve into a puddle on the floor and would never find her way back to herself. It was like her mind was disintegrating, and she couldn't think. Her first instincts as a doctor were wearing off, and her brain was filled with a single repeated scream: *I can't lose him. I can't lose him.* Then she just couldn't hold on any longer and put her face into her hands and held her breath trying to stop an escaping sob.

Chase leaned over and wrapped his arms around her. She pulled back at first and rolled her hands into fists, trying to push him away. They were still strangers, with titles like 'son' and 'mother,' but they had lost all emotional connection to each other. Whatever they once were had been erased, and her instinct was to pull away while his instinct was to protect and encase her. *He is so like Thad,* she thought. The feel of his arms around her was more familiar than she thought it would be. Her fear was tinged with anger; so much had been taken from them with the Shift.

"I'm here, Mom," Chase whispered. "I'm here. I'll stay with you until he wakes up."

His voice reached down into her with something so familiar that she couldn't hold it all in any longer and sobbed into his shoulder as she let him hold her and comfort her. *This is my son. My son!* She thought as she let in all the emotions of the past few days. *And he was strong and solid.* He held her as she cried for it all: the loss of her son, finding her son, losing the life she thought she knew, and now, possibly, losing Thad. But Chase was here. *Her son was here.* And at that moment, he was everything she could have asked for in a son. When she had cried herself into wheezy, exhausted sobs and her breathing had finally eased, Chase took a deep breath. He slowly let his arms muscles ease, keeping her hands in his until they stopped shaking.

"Better?" Chase asked.

"Yes. I'm sorry. I don't know what happened."

"Well, you always did try to hide behind the in-control doctor thing." He laughed then. Maybe everything wasn't gone, at least not for him. "Do you think you can talk?"

"Yes." Saige cleared her throat. "Let me just check everything first. Chase watched her as her hands moved quickly and assuredly over the equipment. Adjusting this, listening to that, flicking the light into Thad's eye, frowning and then doing it again. These were the things he remembered most about her, these strong and sure movements that were an extension of her. Maybe it all would be okay after all. She finished, sat back down and let out a breath.

"What did you want to know?"

"Why was this so different for you when I told you?"

"I don't know. I guess everybody reacts differently."

"Maybe I shouldn't have just shoved that stupid picture at him. Did I cause this? Is it my fault?"

"No, Chase. It isn't your fault. There is no way to know how any of us will respond. I don't know, maybe realizing you were my son and remembering everything are two very different things. I don't so much remember as much as understand that you are my son. I still don't have the memory of you actually being my son. I know that you are, and that is enough for me. But for Thad, well, I think he wanted to remember. He needed to have

all of you back, so I think that's what caused this."

"So, I did do this by giving him the picture?"

"No. His brain did this. The meds did this. The Shifting did this. The Committee did this. You can't blame yourself. There was no way to know this would happen."

"So, what do we do now?"

"We wait. I'll keep him sedated. I gave him everything that we had that could relieve the pressure. We should know if it's working in a few hours. And then I'll see if I have to repeat doses or if we need to do something else. Unfortunately, I can't test him without more sophisticated medical equipment."

"Something else?"

"We don't have to talk about that now." She wasn't trying to spare him; she just couldn't think about any of that now.

"I know this is hard, but I need you to be honest with me about what is happening right now. What is the worst case?"

"I'll have to relieve the pressure."

"How?"

"Drill." Her voice cracked.

"Drill? Like into his head?"

"Drill. Like into his head," Saige repeated.

"Have you ever done that before?"

"I do things every day as a doctor that I haven't done before," she said. *Dear God, but not on Thad. How am I going to do that to Thad?*

Chase looked over at Kalare, who was still unconscious, then back at Thad, lying in the bed next to her, and then at Saige. "I don't know what to do. What do I do?" Chase felt the tears spill over and hated that he was being weak. No matter how hard he tried, somewhere in him was that fourteen-year-old scared little boy sitting in his closet, crying. He pushed away tears and pressed his palms against his eye sockets and clenched his jaw, trying to force himself to be strong. To be tough, to be the man he thought everyone wanted him to be.

"We just have to wait. That's all we can do." Saige placed her hand on his head and unconsciously wound her fingers into his hair. "But for now, you need to get out of this room and keep yourself busy. Go finish whatever you guys were working on. We can't rush any of this. The body heals itself, but it does it in its own time." Saige shrugged. "I know. I know it's not enough and it sounds weak and not very reassuring, but that doesn't make it not true." She noticed her hands were still shaking and shoved them into her jacket pockets.

"I don't want to leave you alone."

"I'm not alone. Go. I will call you if anything happens."

"Or if you need me."

"Or if I need you." She smiled. *Yes, so much like Thad.*

Chase went outside to work on the generator, but only sat on the ground, staring off into space. *How did all of this get so out of control?* He looked back at The Forty. This was supposed to keep them safe, yet they are in more danger than ever. The TALUS came around the corner of the building.

"Chase, do you require assistance?"

"No."

"Thad's vitals are improving. His prognosis is positive."

"Wait, you are monitoring his vitals?"

"Yes. I monitor Thad's vitals at all times."

"Do you know if he has pressure in his brain?"

"There is no pressure in his brain. There are some ruptured blood vessels in his left eye, but they should resolve shortly. Is there any other

information you need on his condition?"

"Big-T, does Saige know that you are monitoring his vitals?"

"I have not relayed this information to Dr. Bodaway."

"I could kiss you right now, Big-T." Chase jumped to his feet and ran toward the entrance to the Forty. "Stay right here, don't move."

21

The pain in Kalare's shoulder pulled her from sleep. She was still a little disoriented from the pain meds, but this time she knew where she was. Thad was sleeping in the bed next to her, and Chase, curled into the chair between them, was still holding onto his rifle. He was the only constant in her life. She knew he would be mad because she didn't just get into the car as he had asked, but she couldn't take the chance of leaving that Collector to get them. She knew she was stubborn and sometimes reckless, but she never did anything in half measures. Well, not anymore. She didn't think there would be a whole battalion of them, and she still didn't understand where they all came from. They had scoured that garage, and there was nothing. And then that damn shot that took her. It was careless. She had thought that she had made her final reckless mistake. It was Chase's voice that kept her going, had kept her some-what calm through the ride back to The Forty. She couldn't remember much else, but she did remember his voice, his hand holding onto hers, hot and trembling. She held onto the touch of his hand, the only thread that connected her to this world.

She thought of his face in that closet, staring at the red spray-painted *Chase* that demanded someone remember he existed. The sadness he felt at being forgotten tore through her heart. She would never leave him alone again. Never. She was glad that he trusted her enough to tell her the truth and wished she had been able to do the same. Her escape wasn't a clean one. She didn't know how to get out back then. She was better at hiding her tracks now. But she knew it was just a matter of time before her father found her again. He had too many resources, and she hadn't had any until she met Chase.

He had been watching her from the end of the aisle. Kalare was trying to steal food, but she was awful at it. She had been rummaging around the docks for the last two weeks. If she couldn't find food, she would have to go home.

"You're gonna get caught if you do that." His voice whispered into her ear. She hadn't heard him come up behind her, probably because she was rattling the bags as she was stuffing them into her pockets. She turned and bumped into Chase's chest, and when she looked up, all she saw was a smiling face and those blue eyes looking down at her.

"I don't know what you're talking about." She didn't know why she had snapped at him, probably because the world tilted a bit when she looked up at him. She didn't like that. Or maybe she had liked it too much.

"Hey, what's going on over there?" The shopkeeper yelled.

"Kissing. Kissing is what's going on, old man. Do you want to watch?"

"Don't steal from me. I will shoot you." The shopkeeper gestured at them with the gun.

"Yeah, yeah, I know. Always with the shooting." Chase put his hand on Kalare's shoulder and moved her toward the door. She giggled as they reached the sidewalk, and Chase pulled her to the side of the building.

"Here, take whatever you want." He pulled everything out of his pockets and piled it into her hands. "Take it all. I'll get more later."

"I can't. I..."

"Come on. Take it. You look like you need it." He started stuffing everything he could fit into her jacket pockets when she wouldn't take anything. "Take it. Like I said, I'll go back later and get more."

"*But he said he would shoot you.*"

"*Nah, he's a lousy shot.*" *Chase smiled.* "*He threatens to shoot me every other day.*"

"*Thank you.*" *Kalare swallowed, trying to push down the unexpected emotion rising in her over a bag of stolen chips.* "*I don't, I just, I don't know what the hell I am doing out here.*"

"*Yeah, none of us do. You don't have to tell me anything; I don't need to know. Listen, there's a bunch of us squatting near here. You're welcome to come. It's not the greatest, but it's dry. Well, sort of dry, but there is some food and a place to sleep if you want it.*"

"*Oh yeah. I don't think so.*" *Kalare shook her head and started backing up away from him.* "*That doesn't sound very safe to me.*"

"*Okay. I get it. I know how it is out here. But where are you going to sleep tonight? I'll make sure nobody hurts you.*" *He was suddenly serious.* "*It's not like that. I promise.*"

"*So, is this how you pick up girls? Offer them stolen food and a sort of dry place to sleep?*" *Kalare wanted to be tough, but there was something in those eyes that made her want to smile.*

"*Yes. That's what I do, pick up girls with shoplifted food. I'm a dazzler. Come on. It's not safe out here.*" *He put his hand on the small of her back and guided her down the street.*

"*It's right down here. I know this seems creepy, but I promise it's not. And if you don't feel safe when we get there, you can just leave and not shoplift somewhere else.*" *He grinned. His hand on her back was comfort and safety, and it burned through her jacket with its gentleness. Staring at him now, curled uncomfortably in the chair, she realized he had kept that very first promise he had made to her. He had kept her safe. She wondered when she would trust him enough to tell him her story. He was so brave, showing her where he came from. Risked everything between them to be honest with her. She couldn't even face where she'd come from for herself; how could she trust him with it? It could change everything. She just couldn't risk losing him.*

∾

CHASE STIRRED in the chair and opened his eyes.

"Kalare, you're awake." He smiled and uncurled himself from the chair. "How are you feeling?"

"So great." She managed a thumbs-up and smiled. "You know, ready to kick ass."

"I think you've had enough ass-kicking for a while. Are you in pain?

Do you want me to get my mom, I mean, the Doc?"

"Your mom. Huh, that actually sounded weirdly normal. Why is Thad in that bed?"

"He had a bleed-back. But you don't need to worry about any of that right now." Chase smoothed her hair back and kissed her forehead. "You just need to worry about getting better."

"I'm sorry I didn't get into the car when you told me to, I was just afraid he would get us," Kalare said. She reached for his hand.

"I know you, and I knew what you were doing. But Kalare, we both have to stop taking these chances. I don't ever want to come that close to losing you again."

"Did I scare you?" She ran her fingers across his cheek.

"To death."

"Sorry."

"I mean, you know, it would be a big hassle if something happened to you. I'd have to go pick up some other girl with shoplifted food. Because, you know, I'm a dazzler," he said as he leaned over and kissed her on the cheek.

"Yes, you are a dazzler." Kalare laughed and looked over at Thad, who was trying to lift his head. "Look, I think Thad is waking up."

22

Saige stood in the doorway of The Forty watching Thad and Chase walk next to each other. It seemed so normal. It had been two weeks since the shoot-out at the apartment, the TALUS coming to their rescue and the close call for Kalare. Two weeks since they had found their son, and Thad's bleed-back.

Chase was their son. It was incredible. It was all there. Saige saw it the minute he said *Hi, Mom. Hi, Mom!* It still stopped her breath every time she thought of it. Then he took the picture from his pocket: Chase as a younger boy, her and Thad sitting with him, smiling. It was all there: Thad's smile, Thad's eyes looking back at her. How had she missed it that night when they squared off on the roof?

Thad still had the remnants of ruptured blood vessels in his eyes, and his vision was cloudy but improving. He described the visual and physical electric flashes like a high-speed, muted hodgepodge. He couldn't decipher any of it at that speed, and his brain overloaded like a processor. His head still hurt, and he had to resist rubbing at his eye, which still felt like it wanted to pop out of its socket. But the memories were all there, and even though he wanted to talk to Chase about everything, Saige was afraid that he was still in danger and limited their time together or at least limited the talk about the past.

It did Thad a world of good just to see Chase, so she forced Thad to stay in bed and monitored their conversations; at the least sign of agitation, she would cut them short.

Chase filled in the gaps for them about the night they were shifted and about Ziph's placement. His days on the streets and how he cared for the kids. The boy she never knew was a man she could be proud of; a man much like his father, wanting to do the right thing.

Thad was showing no signs of danger from another bleed-back and wanted to get back to work. But Saige made him promise to do light work. So, he had supervised Chase, Sam and Kit as they set up the remaining generators and lab equipment. Jo-Jo was already back into her normal routine. Her leg was still tapped, but luckily the shot hadn't hit any major arteries. Kalare was still recuperating from her gunshot wound but was finally out of bed and beginning to move her shoulder.

Tya was helping Saige check out all the kids at The Forty. Tya did well with all the medical terminology and asked Saige a million questions about a million things. Saige took extra care with the young kids needing insulin, trying to distract them from the sting of the needle with silly faces. Then she taught Tya how to administer asthma medications and check blood pressure and blood sugar levels.

The last thing they set up was the lab. Chase helped Thad and Saige, and they gave him a quick tutorial on how to operate the equipment. Now that they had the recording and understood where The Committee was going next, they could adjust their approach to the anti-shift meds. But now there was a time factor they hadn't anticipated. The infiltration into the water system was easily reversed, but the airborne component was a concern.

CHASE WANTED to continue working in the lab because it felt like he was finally doing something about everything he had seen over the last five years. Even though both Thad and Saige insisted that Thad's incident was a mild case, his perspective had changed. He used to ignore those vacant, bleed-back, damaged people wandering the streets. But seeing how it tore through Thad had angered him, and he couldn't just sit back and accept these as common, everyday occurrences any longer. He wanted to work on something that would prevent the source of the bleed-backs: the Shifts. He felt that everything that had happened in the past few weeks had finally brought him full circle. If they had never been shifted, he would probably have worked with his parents in the lab. It felt like the pieces were all falling back into place. He had his family back. And he had Kalare. For the first time in a long while, he finally felt settled. Not happy; he wouldn't allow that yet. But this was all beginning to feel really good and almost as if he had a home for the first time in years.

Chase quickly picked up how to use the equipment. He remembered a lot of it from when he used to tag along with Thad as a small kid who liked to tinker with machines. Seth agreed to teach him some of the more intricate details about maintaining the equipment so Chase could begin to serve as backup for Seth. Seth hadn't intended on fleeing with them, but his presence at The Forty had proven to be invaluable. He and Chase were working on the computer setups, and Seth set up a backdoor com-link back to The Committee office. He was able to download a large portion of the data they had been working on and also took the time to erase several incriminating files and surveillance videos. He knew Ziph had seen him at the garage and that there was no going back for him, which he somehow didn't mind. He used his connections to get backup drives and servers set up in new locations, and he downloaded the rest of the information he needed so he could access it whenever he wanted. He closed all backdoor access points except one. Seth then changed all his passcodes and redirected access paths so he could still log in to the mainframe. He updated his security clearance as well, just in case anyone tried to block him. The TALUS was able to access information from its memory banks, and Seth was trying to figure out a way to connect him to the mainframe without triggering any security alerts.

ALL IN ALL, Seth thought they had a pretty good set-up, more than adequate. He was glad to be here with them and out of that lab, especially with the death of Regent and the arrest of Metcalf. But he knew if Ziph ever found them, he was in trouble. They had committed serious breaches on their way out, serious, treasonous breaches. Security breaches. NDA breaches. Grand theft breaches. But he wouldn't think about any of that now.

THAD WAS surprised by how easily he and Chase connected and how many things they approached in the same way. He tried to let the anger go; to be glad he had his son back. But now that he knew what his son had to go through without them, he was even angrier. He knew that Regent was dead and that Metcalf was no longer in charge, but it was becoming obvious that they were just taking orders. They had to find out where the orders for this new approach to water and airborne infiltration came from. It reeked of military involvement, and that wasn't good for anybody. Thad wished that they could just settle in here and make up for lost time, but he knew that what was set in motion the night they left was only the beginning.

How could he look the other way any longer? He couldn't. He wanted time with Chase, but he knew they had so much work to do. At least they were all together, and that loss he had felt for so long was gone. Now he had Saige and Chase to protect. No. Now he had everyone here to protect. This might be his way to make up for so many wrong turns. Clear his conscience. So many things had happened because they developed this one drug. There was so much he needed to fix, and now he had help, and that was a good thing, a very good thing.

WHEN THEY ORGANIZED the Lab at The Forty, and the TALUS became their unlikely protector, Sam was uneasy with, as he saw it, a new regime. He went out scouting the area for a new place. He thought he should be prepared to move the kids in case of an emergency. Although he tried to stay loyal to Chase, he already saw the split happening and knew it wouldn't be long before everyone began taking sides. He didn't feel that he could count on Chase anymore. Saige and Thad had brought The Committee right into the center of their lives, and Chase just couldn't see it. Even though he understood what they were trying to do, Sam knew he couldn't be a part of it. *This isn't exactly a mutiny,* he thought, *just a change of location.* He had found a warehouse that was easily accessible and didn't look like it would attract much attention. As he checked out the surrounding area to make sure it was safe before moving everyone out, he stepped into a clearing surrounded by a cluster of short buildings. It was then that he noticed the sandbags and barbed wire strung across each doorway.

This looks military, he thought as he heard the clicks of guns behind him. "You can stop right there," a male voice said from behind the barrier. "What's your business here?"

"Just out walking, looking round."

"For what?"

"A new place to stay."

"And you're coming from?"

"The hotel is about twenty miles out that way."

"The one with the TALUS guard?"

"Um, yup. That would be the one."

"So why are you looking for a new place?"

"Did I not just say that one has a TALUS guard?" Sam paused, waiting for a reply. None came. "Okay. Okay, so you got me. What happens now?"

"That depends on what you are really looking for."

"I'm looking to get a bunch of kids to safety before half of the Collectors in the city pay us a visit in the middle of the night."

"Gun down and any other weapons on the ground."

Sam put his gun down and pulled a handgun from his belt and a twelve-inch blade from his right boot. He pulled a six-inch dagger from his left boot; a Chinese throwing star from a side pocket in his right boot, and placed them all on the ground in front of him. And then he remembered his father's K-Bar tucked into the pocket of his left arm sleeve.

"Anything else?"

He pulled back the Velcro holding a flap closed on the right side, pulled out two more blades of varying lengths and a long, narrow piece of flint that looked like an arrowhead. He bent over and placed them carefully on the ground. Smiled and then did the same with the left side of the jacket, which held three spearheads and another throwing star that was more of a triangle.

"That's all of it."

"You sure?"

"Well, except for the ammunition, replacement blades, two replacement barrels and a new ballistic handgrip, but I can't do much with those without the guns, can I?" Sam backed up two steps and interlocked his hands behind his back.

"Smart Ass," The voice mumbled under his breath.

"Most of the time. It's a gift." Sam smiled. "Am I just supposed to stand here and talk to a disembodied voice all afternoon?"

Sam heard the scratching of movement as a tall man stood up behind the barrier. He had the look of a military man: broad-shouldered with well-rounded forearms beneath the rolled-up cuffs of an olive-green shirt, legs in fatigues, standing at the ready. His cap and dark glasses obscured most of his features, but it didn't take much to realize this was the man in charge. He held his weapon lightly, as if it had been with him since birth. He made a slight movement of his capped head, and three men came up beside Sam. He hadn't even heard them move in behind him. They were definitely military, but what the hell were they doing out here? One man took hold of his arm after patting him down and pushed him in the direction of the side door. The other men picked up his weapons, clinking the blades together.

"Careful with those," Sam snapped, "It won't take much to chip those blades, and they are ground to a perfect edge."

"Watch the blades." The man snapped and stepped out, moving toward Sam. "We've been watching you guys for a while. Didn't think you were going to turn into a government type, though." He put out his hand.

"Connor."

"Sam."

"Yeah, I know who you are. Come inside, and let's have a little chat."

Sam followed Connor around to the side door that slid open, letting Connor, Sam, and the three men carrying all of his weapons into a dimly lit, short hallway that opened into a large room. This was a war room filled with tables piled with papers. The walls were overlaid with maps and aerial photographs intersected and connected with multicolored lines. This was definitely not a group of feeble-minded stragglers, helplessly damaged by chemicals.

"Are you ready to hear this?" Connor gestured toward the wall at an aerial photograph of The Forty.

"Hear what?"

"The truth."

"Or at least your version of it?" Sam shook his head. "Everyone has been spoon-feeding me bullshit lately. What makes you any different?"

"Oh well, I guess you'll just have to decide whether or not all this is bullshit, won't you?" Connor pulled out a chair for Sam and gestured for him to sit. "Give him back his weapons, boys."

"But, Sir, we were instructed to..."

"I know what you were instructed to do. I'm rescinding the order. Give him back his weapons." Connor took a beat and then a step toward them. "Now." He lowered his voice; it was no longer a command but a threat. The men dropped everything they were holding onto the table in front of Sam, who swiveled in his chair to see around the men, keeping eye contact with Connor. *Yes, there was a lot they were going to talk about.*

23

"*Look*, Chase, I get it, I really do. But this isn't what the rest of us signed up for. I think it's great that you found your parents and even better that they still want to keep researching to fight this. But we are turning into what we left." Sam tried to control the frustration in his voice.

"What else are we supposed to do? Just sit out here and do nothing? We are all here because of what The Committee did, and now we have a real chance to change things. We can do something other than steal food and scrounge around the docks." Chase was shouting now. How could they not understand? How could they betray him like this?

"Well, let's not forget your parents' meds started all this. And they work for The Committee. Chase, they administered the shift drugs. I mean, it's great and all that they are trying to change that now, and I like them and all, but I have some mixed feelings about all this," Tya said. "Geez, Chase, when did you start to even give a shit about all this?"

"I don't know. I think I always did. That's why I kept trying to get back. I was raised in that laboratory. They never intended these meds to be used to control people like they are using them now. Sam, you know that."

Chase looked from Sam to Tya to Kalare to Jo-Jo, all sitting at the table staring back at him. Kit was standing by the window, watching Big-T circle the building.

"I don't know, Chase, one minute we are scavenging food, and the next we are setting up a research lab. Come on, even you have to see that it's weird." Sam put his hands out, trying to soften the conversation. He was sorry they were all ganging up on Chase; most of them wouldn't even be alive if it weren't for Chase. But they needed to have this conversation. Sam had a bad feeling and was going with his gut this time.

"Kalare?" Chase looked to her for support, or confirmation, or something. He wasn't even sure what he wanted from any of them.

"I agree. At best, it puts us in danger. At worst, we could be attacked, and everyone Shifted. Damn, Chase, look at the firepower they came after us with in that garage. Do you really think they'll just leave us alone after that? Do you really think it's over?" Kalare shook her head. "I'm sorry, baby. I don't want to go against you, but you have to see the point here, right?"

"You guys have had my back, always. So, I have to believe you have it now, too." Chase put his head in his hands. Was he really putting them all in danger? Was he wrong to have saved his parents? Was it wrong for him to bring them here?

"I mean, Chase, a goddamn TALUS is guarding us," JoJo pointed out the window as Big-T passed. "How do we really know it's not reporting everything we are doing? I know. Seth said he took care of that, but Seth was security and tech for them. Can we really trust him either?"

"I agree with Jo-Jo," Kit said. "We just took everyone in on faith because of you, Chase. Maybe we moved too fast."

"We took everyone here on faith. Even you. That's not the point." Sam snapped at Kit.

"You guys are killing me here." Chase got to his feet and paced around the room. "So, you are all in agreement then?"

"Yes, I think we are. It's not against you, Chase or even them. I just think we should get the kids out of here. If The Committee knows where your parents are, they are just waiting to come and get them. And if they don't know yet, they will. Even if your parents leave, I think this place has been compromised." Sam was not going to waver on this. He had everything in motion and planned to have everyone out of there and safe by morning. The tractor-trailer was already loaded with supplies. Connor and his men stood by to help transport the kids if needed. But he wasn't ready to tell Chase about that yet. So, unless there was a problem, he was willing to make several trips. It seemed like a better alternative than telling Chase about the whole Connor thing. Sam decided to save that as a last resort, especially if, as Connor suspected, The Forty was under heavy surveillance.

"Okay. Okay. What do you want to do?" Chase sat tentatively on the edge of the chair as though he was ready to run out of the room. This was killing him.

"Well, are you staying or leaving?" Jo-Jo asked. Chase looked at her and then at Kalare.

"I, um, I can't leave them here alone." Chase looked from one face to another. "Are you all going?" He stopped with his eyes on Kalare. "All of you?" He thought his chest would collapse in on itself. How could he choose? He couldn't leave his parents, but he couldn't leave everyone else, either. Were they right? Had he gotten so far off track?

"I'm staying," Kalare said. "I'll help with the move. Then come back here."

"I'm staying too," Jo-Jo said, looking back at Kit.

"I'm with the kids," Kit said, looking out the window.

"I'm with the kids too." Tya reached over and grabbed Sam's hand.

"Sam?" Chase asked.

"I'll organize and move everyone, then split my time between the two. I understand what you guys are doing here and want the kids to be safe. But I want you to be safe, too. It's not a betrayal, Chase. I've still got your back, but I think this is what we need to do." Sam knew he was carrying out a mutiny; he knew he was hurting Chase, but he had to follow his instincts. He was angry with Chase but knew he could still bet his life on him. Chase had proved that time and time again, and this wasn't about that. It was about keeping the kids safe.

"I guess you guys have this all settled then." Chase got up out of his chair and stood for a moment looking at everyone, then started to leave the room, remembered his rifle, and crossed back over to the table.

"Look, I've always trusted you guys. I'm sorry if I'm out of line and I've put you in danger. That was never my intention, but you have to know, if I had it to do all over again, I would still save them. I won't abandon them now, just like I wouldn't abandon any of you." Chase swallowed hard and cleared his throat. "So, you guys don't trust me anymore? Is that it?

"It's not about that."

"Yes, it is. It's exactly about that. Oh, you know what? screw this." Chase slapped the strap of the rifle onto his shoulder and stormed out of the room, mumbling obscenities as he pulled the door shut with a loud bang.

"This is bullshit. Let's get out of here. Let's go out on the beach." Kit grabbed Jo-Jo's hand and led her out onto the beach. Kit knew she had a crush on him, and he was okay with that, except that most of the time, he just wanted her to shut up. But if he had to be stuck with them, he figured

he should at least have a little fun. He grabbed her hand, pulled her down behind the remnants of a rock pylon, and pressed her against the rock.

He started to kiss her softly, and she kissed him back. But then he got a little rougher, and she pushed at him.

"Hey, what's your problem?"

"Oh, come on, you've been waiting for this, don't get shy on me now." He pushed in to try to kiss her again. She pushed his face away.

"Yeah, I wanted to kiss you when I didn't think you were a jerk." She pushed past him, but he caught her arm and slid his foot forward, knocking her feet out from under her.

"Come on, Jo-Jo, you've been sending out flirty signals since I got here. Suddenly, this is a big deal, and you're all shy?"

"Yeah, big deal, so I flirted with you. I thought I liked you, but now I can see that you're an asshole." She tried to push him off, but he had her hands pinned above her head with one hand and slapped her hard with the other.

"Don't call me an asshole."

"Let me go. Stop."

"Well, as you can tell, I like it a little rough."

"Well, I don't. Kit, stop it. Stop it now." She was trying to roll over on her side, hoping it would make him roll off of her, and when that didn't work, she tried to slide her leg in between his legs to get a good crotch shot with her knee, but he caught on and pressed against her leg with his hip.

"Come on, this is what you wanted; admit it." He took his free hand and started to slide it up her shirt.

"No, Stop." She was screaming now. "Get off of me."

She tried to tangle her leg around the inside of his ankle to twist him off, but he outweighed her, and she just couldn't move.

Kit saw the gun barrel shadow before he saw Sam.

"You got two seconds," Sam said calmly.

"Mind your own business, we're just having some fun. Right, Jo-Jo?"

"Jo-Jo?"

"Get him off me, Sam. I told him to stop. Then he slapped me."

"Okay. One." Sam loaded a shot into the chamber.

"Geez, okay." Kit jumped up. "What are you going to do? Shoot me?"

"I've shot people for less. Jo-Jo, come on." Sam leaned over and pushed Kit to the ground with one hand. "Don't move. Stay away from her.

I'll settle this when I get back." Sam pulled Jo-Jo to her feet.

"Why did you have to be such an asshole?" She said as she leaned over and slapped Kit across the face.

24

C *hase* was sitting on the beach that looped around the back end of The Forty when Kalare finally found him. She sat beside him for a few minutes before reaching over and putting her arm across his shoulders.

"It's okay, baby. It really is."

"No. It's not. I screwed things up." Chase looked at her and then at the sling still supporting her shoulder. "That would never have happened if I hadn't asked you to help."

"That was my choice. Not yours. I should have moved quicker. I screwed up,"

"But what the hell are we doing? We're kids, Kalare, kids. We should be going on dates. Kissing in the back seat of cars, and sneaking alcohol from our parents' houses so we can get drunk at parties. Instead, we are having target practice, plotting military maneuvers, and planning to take out government operatives with stolen guns." Chase ran his hands through his hair.

"You couldn't have known helping them would lead to all this."

"It's not just about them. Kalare, I sleep with my gun now. I sleep with my goddamned gun. I don't want this. I don't want to be responsible for any of this. I can't handle all this, Kalare. I just can't."

"You can always walk away, you know?"

"From what? Who? Who do I leave behind? You? My parents? The kids? Everything?"

"Well, no, but..."

"But what? How do I choose? Can I even choose? And now everyone is leaving."

"I don't think you should take that personally ."

"No? What do you call what happened back there, that little mutiny orchestrated by my best friend?"

"I wouldn't exactly call it a mutiny."

"No?" He was talking to her through his teeth now.

"Well, maybe."

"Yeah, maybe. I don't know what to do. I'm losing everyone again." Chase buried his head in Kalare's lap and wrapped his arms around her waist, holding onto her. She tangled her fingers into his hair with her free hand.

"You're not losing anybody." She lifted his chin to make him look at her. "You do have a choice."

"It doesn't feel like I do. Everyone has already made all these choices, and I get to choose which one I want to be loyal to. No matter what I do, I will let someone down." He tried to move his head. He tried to break eye contact with her.

"You know that's not true."

"I don't know what to do. I can't just walk away. I have to stay. Can you see that?"

"I know you have to stay. I understand more than you know. That's why I'm coming back after we move the kids. We all agree we have to move the kids, right?"

"Yes, I do agree with that. And the more I think about it, the more I think you should go with them. He held her eyes for a few seconds and broke away when he saw the spark of anger in them. "I'd rather know that you are alive and safe without me than with me and dead." He stood up and started to walk away.

"Oh no, you don't." Kalare stood. "Chase, stop. CHASE," Kalare screamed. He stopped and turned to face her. "You gave everyone in that room a choice. You can't make this choice for me. My being with you doesn't give you that right."

"What if you get hurt again?"

"What if you do, and I wasn't here to help? How do you think I will live with that? I didn't get into this for those kids or your parents. Don't you know that? I chose you, wherever that leads. And you chose me too. Only, I thought you chose me for me. Was I wrong?"

"No, but I have to, you are..."

"If you say I am your responsibility, Chase, I swear, I will shoot you right here and be done with it all. You know who I am. You have to remember." She held him by the shoulders, forcing him to look into her eyes.

"I can't see you like that again."

"You have to stop being scared because I got hurt. You have to remember who I am."

Kalare stood and planted herself in the spot. She wasn't going to waver. She wasn't going to flinch. She wasn't going to cry. She wasn't going to beg. She was just going to stand there until he saw her. Until he saw Kalare again: until he didn't see her as a fragile piece of paper about to flutter away on the slightest bit of wind. She would stand there until he remembered who she was and stopped living in the shadow of the fear of losing her.

Chase had seen her stand still and determined before, but this was something else. It was as if she were creating a gravity field around them, pulling him out of a parallel world. He looked at the sling, remembered the blood and her pale face in the car ride back to The Forty. Remembered how helpless he felt because all he could do was hold her hand.

He remembered her hooked up to machines and calling for him in her sleep. His heart ached when she didn't answer when he whispered *I am here. I'll always be here.* And how his heart nearly stopped when she opened her eyes with that soft, breathy *Hi.* And then he remembered before all of this, before that night in the garage. Remembered how her strength had sewn up all of his jagged edges and given him something solid to hold onto. She had saved him. Remembered her staring into him with those warm, understanding eyes when he told her who he was and how his entire body had come alive when he made love to her in his old room as if she had always belonged there with him. Remembered how she had accepted it all. And then he remembered why he loved her. And he saw her again as if she had been gone a long time. Or maybe he had been. But he was back now. He dropped his gun, ran to her, and wrapped everything he had in him around her.

"I choose you, too," he whispered into her ear. "I will always choose you."

"You know I'm staying, right?"

"Yeah, I know. I shouldn't have expected anything else."

25

Ziph paced the eight square feet of his tiny new room. The door slid into the wall with a soft metallic whir as Dr. Taylor stepped into the room and placed a tray of food on the small metal table, and the door slid closed behind her.

"I thought I wasn't in prison," Ziph said.

"You are not in prison, Ziph. You are under protection."

"Protection, prison, it's all the same if I can't even walk down a hall alone. I want to get out of here. I want to leave." He ground his teeth together, trying not to flex his hand into a fist and fling the tray at her.

"I'm afraid that is just not possible. You are not yet cleared for that. Maybe in a few days, but I suggest you have breakfast before we start today."

Her dismissive, detached tone hit his final nerve, and he couldn't control himself any longer. Before realizing what he was doing, Ziph had picked up the metal chair and brought it down as hard as he could across the back of her head. Dr. Taylor turned without flinching, without being knocked off her feet, without even the slightest break in her stride, wrenched the chair from Ziph, grabbed him by his shirt, and lifted him six inches off the ground.

"I told you this type of behavior would not be tolerated here. There will be repercussions for this." She tossed Ziph onto the bed and retrieved his breakfast tray.

"What the hell are you?" He screamed.

"I'm TALUS 396746."

"A TALUS? Are you kidding me? A robot is babysitting me. I want to see my father *now*," Ziph demanded.

"I will let him know you have requested to see him." Dr. Taylor turned and stopped in the doorway as the door slid open. "He will not be pleased about this."

He had to get out of here. The Directive did not deliver on any of the promises they made to him. Dr. Regent hadn't even come to see him in days, and he was getting a little tired of being treated like a criminal. He couldn't even get any of the staff to give him information. This was infuriating. He would go crazy if they didn't let him out of here soon. Then he heard the door slide open.

"Look, I said I wanted to see my father," Ziph said as he sat in bed.

"Why are you always creating such a commotion? You try my patience, boy," Dr. Regent said as he moved the chair closer to the bed. He motioned to Dr. Taylor to stay in the hall, and the door shut in her face.

"Really? You made a TALUS escort me around and hold me prisoner?"

"No, I allowed you to help us research the new model. You see, the other TALUS models kept bonding to the person we assigned them to, which is why the model failed. So, we wanted to test whether this new model would bond and become protective, even with someone as obnoxious as you." Dr. Regent opened a map and placed it across the foot of the bed.

"This is where the Bodaways are. Now, while I normally don't care about going in with a military presence, I understand many children are at the site, and I don't want that kind of blood on my hands. So, we have devised an alternate plan to intercept them on this road when they are moving supplies." Regent thumped his index finger on a spot on the map.

"Okay. Why now?" Ziph asked.

"Now, and this is what I keep trying to teach you about timing, we have intel that Saige has developed something new from a blood sample from someone who appears to be immune to the pre-shift medications. So that means she is developing this from a live biological culture rather than a synthetic compound. The source is from someone on-site. This holds great promise. Great promise, indeed. Now, we want to have her continue this research with her biological source, but we want her to do it here, where we have control. Understand? We are discussing an extraction without harming her or the biological source."

"So, we will kidnap her and force her to continue the research here?' Ziph asked.

"Yes. I would like to get both doctors, but she is on this track, so she is the one we want. At least for right now."

"Great, so where do I come in? Do I get to look at her through the glass and watch her do her research? Sounds like a load of fun."

"Well, Ziph, I thought you would like to be the one to, shall we say, extract her from her present circumstances." Dr. Regent stared over his glasses at Ziph. "But you have to promise to follow protocol, and I can't stress this enough: you must follow protocol. No firepower, no commotion like last time. Do you understand?"

"Yes. I understand. What do you need me to do?"

"Well, I thought you might enjoy being the one to look her in the eye when we take her in, you know, so she knows it was you. That might give you a little bit of satisfaction, yes?"

"Oh, yes," Ziph said, smiling for the first time in days. "Yes, Sir, I would very much like to help you with this extraction."

"Oh, so it's Sir now, is it?"

26

S *aige* adjusted the microscope's focus, wrote down a few notes, and replaced the slide with another from the pile in front of her. Halfway through the slides, she stopped, checked the sample number, refocused the microscope, and went to the cabinet to retrieve the sample: *Tya: Enzyme Sample # 7384.*

The day Tya helped her inoculate some of the younger children, she mentioned that she wasn't knocked out when they administered the pre-shift medications.

"What do you mean they didn't work?" Saige asked.

"I don't know. I got a little drowsy, and then they made me feel awake or itchy or something. I pretended I was out and then got away from them. I didn't think much about it. Is that weird?" Tya asked.

"Yes," Saige had said matter-of-factly. "Very weird. Would you mind if I took a blood sample?"

"Sure. I mean, if you think it will help." Tya had shrugged, not very interested in the science of it all. *Who cares if it didn't knock me out? At least I got away from them,* Tya thought.

Saige had begun isolating and testing enzymes from Tya's blood. She wished she were back in her old lab. This equipment was slow and more hands-on than she preferred, and these manual tests were taking forever. All the samples had the same negative result, and Saige was beginning to think it might have been a fluke. Or that they hadn't administered the pre-shift to her at all. And then, she saw this enzyme react differently. Finally, something; she hoped this was enough to move forward. She had convinced Thad and Chase to leave her there alone with the TALUS for security when they relocated everyone this afternoon. She had pushed Chase into the car and told him to make sure his people were safe and that the TALUS would be enough. But if she were honest, it was nice to finally have time alone in the lab. All of these chattering voices and the conditions at The Forty were beginning to wear her down. She longed for the disinfected quiet bliss of her lab.

She crossed over the main floor of The Forty, heading to the kitchen wing. She had been working for hours and needed some food and coffee. She missed her lab, missed her apartment and her freedom to come and go as she pleased. She missed being able to flash a badge and have people respond to whatever she needed or wanted at any time of the day or night. She missed the control. She felt like a prisoner here, always having to discuss everything a million times before reaching a consensus. She was tired of everyone always being on guard and worrying if someone would find them. She was tired of the suspicious stares from Sam and the others. She knew they were not happy about the research and having to keep her and Thad safe. She knew they felt a certain misguided loyalty because she had saved Kalare. But she wasn't about to give up her work for anyone.

Even finding Chase, which meant the world to her, wasn't enough reason for her to stop. But for Thad, this was all different. After the bleed-back and his recovery, after finding Chase and what The Committee had done in the garage, she knew he was ready to gather his family and just walk away. But she never wanted to walk away; not ever in her life had she wanted to walk away from the work. And even though Thad knew that she avoided the topic at every turn, if they never spoke, it wasn't there. But she could see it in his eyes that something else was happening, and it wasn't anything to do with the research anymore. Something new had come to the surface in him, especially since the bleed-back. But she wasn't ready to hear any of it. She was really only sure of one thing: Thad would keep her and their son safe. Well, he would keep her safe as far as she would let him. That was the tricky part because he knew by now that nothing, not even he, could keep her from her work.

She was walking through the lobby when she saw the dust trail from an approaching vehicle. She distractedly thought they would be getting back much later than this as she headed back into the lab. As much as she had enjoyed the solitude, she was glad they were heading back early. It seemed like a good idea to her to leave her there alone at the time. She had been working in the lab all night and wasn't planning on stopping until they got back anyway, but now she was feeling a little more vulnerable than she thought she would. It felt odd to be here without all the voices and noises; without Thad; without Chase. The TALUS stopped when it saw her in the doorway.

She wanted to share her results with Thad to see if he had any suggestions, even though this was new research and far from what they had been working on together. He didn't know that Tya was her biological source, and she wasn't ready to hear what he thought, which was why she hadn't told him. She even felt that this was hitting a little too close to home.

She knew Thad would see this as taking advantage of Tya; even she could see that. But she kept telling herself that it was more important for him to recuperate from the bleed-back and bond with Chase than to share the research. But now that she had finally gotten a positive result, she knew she couldn't hide it from him any longer. And, she reasoned, he couldn't possibly be angry with her after she shared the result. She would hold back her biological source as long as she could. If she could get him excited about the work again, none of that would matter anyway.

"Dr. Bodaway. Do you require my assistance?"

"No, Big-T. I was just taking a break. Are we all secure here?" She asked.

"All clear," Big-T responded and continued on his way around the building.

She decided to try to finish the last sample so she would have verification for Thad. She pulled the new samples and began piping droplets of the enzyme sample from Tya's blood into each compartment. She snapped each section closed, inserted it into the slot and hit the START button. She was hoping to duplicate the results from the other sample to make sure it wasn't a fluke. It was then that she noticed the TALUS had stopped moving and that someone was standing in the hallway behind her.

"Hi Mom, I'm home." Ziph's voice prickled up her spine. But she wasn't going to let this little runt get the best of her. She turned to him. He was leaning against the doorway, a small smirk on his thin lips and twirling an electro-prod used primarily for violent patients.

"Ziph." She said his name without emotion, just simply to acknowledge him. "If I'd have known you were coming, you know, cake and all that." She added as she shifted around so that she hid the display screen.

"So, what's in the machine?"

"Nothing you would understand. Where is your sidekick? Or are you the sidekick? It gets so confusing with all of these memory shifts going back and forth."

"So, you do remember me then? I thought so."

"Little man, what I have forgotten wouldn't even fit in your brain." He flinched at the *little man*. It had once been an endearment, but now it was clearly meant to demoralize him even more. He shrugged it off and advanced toward her.

"I'm here to take you back with me. How I get you there does not matter to me. My instructions were that you be returned alive; they said nothing about not damaging you in the process."

"I'm not going anywhere with you."

"I think you might. You see, Dr. Regent and a platoon of armed Collectors are waiting outside. We are going to intercept Thad and Chase and your whole little group."

"What do you want?"

"You, I thought you understood that by now. You and the damned research."

"And if I say no?"

"Oh. Please say no. We are running an interception that goes like this: you come with us, and we don't kill them all. You don't come with us, and we'll kill them all. Well, all except for Tya. You need her for the research, right?" He couldn't help it; he let the giggle escape his throat. It felt so good, bubbling up and out of his mouth, watching her eyes go from anger to defiance to realization. "There it is," he said. He swung the electro-prod in circles and walked up to the table with the samples. "Shall we start packing you up?"

Saige was running scenarios in her head since she saw him out of the corner of her eye. She knew Regent was either right outside or on his way. She also knew that anything she did would risk everyone's lives. Every scenario she ran ended with all of them dead. There was no other way but to go with him. No, she would go with Regent. She would not capitulate to Ziph.

"Where is Regent?" She pushed him away from the table. "And don't touch those, you moron, they are infectious."

"You go with me. Now."

"No. I don't. If I go back at all, I need a medical team in here to pack this up properly. I am in the middle of running protocols, and I will lose everything. I need a medical team. Call Regent now, or I will. And you know he'll take my call over yours every time."

Ziph grimaced. This wasn't nearly as much fun as he thought it was going to be, but at least he would deliver her, and he had been the one to drop it. He pulled the radio out of his pocket and was about to hit the button when Saige pulled it from his hand and pushed him back.

"Let the grown-ups handle this, okay, little man?" Saige pushed Ziph away from the table, pressed the talk button, and waited for the voice to crackle on the other end. "Regent, get your ass and your team in here..." she managed to say before she was hit from behind and everything went black.

27

Sam was driving the tractor-trailer with Tya in the cab; Jo-Jo and Kit were riding in the extended cab. Thad followed in his car, with Chase in the passenger seat and Kalare asleep in the back seat. Seth had stayed behind with the kids in the new location. They were making one final run back to The Forty, where Kalare and Jo-Jo would stay with Chase, Thad and Saige. Sam, Tya and Kit would be leaving to go back with the kids once they loaded the last of the supplies. The lines had been drawn. The separation had begun.

"You hanging in there, Chase?" Thad reached over and gave Chase's shoulder a squeeze.

"I don't know." Chase continued to stare out the window. "I feel like no matter what I do, I'm letting somebody down." Chase turned and looked at Thad. It was weird that, after five years without Thad in his life, they could be this close. How could Chase trust this man? He was so confused.

"I'm sorry. I didn't mean for us to complicate things. It's my fault this split is happening. I don't know how all this happened. One day, I was getting up every morning and going to work, and the next I was in this action movie."

"Oh, Come on." Chase turned and stared at Thad and took a deep breath. "Please, don't try to redefine this. You knew exactly what was going on. God, Thad, you were working with the Collectors. How could you do that?" Chase didn't want to be angry. He wanted to be on Thad's side, but Sam and Jo-Jo were right; this was, intentional or not, Thad and Saige's fault.

"I don't know. I ask myself that every day. I was trying to do something good. I was trying to help. That was how it started. And then everything happened around me, and I didn't know how to get out. I was afraid of so much. Mostly losing Saige. Wow. That really sounds selfish, doesn't it?" Thad uncurled his grip on the steering wheel and wrapped his fingers around it again, increasing his pressure until his knuckles whitened. "I tried to convince myself that you didn't know; that they were doing all these collections behind your back. I mean, I watched them prep you and Mom. I hid in that closet, hoping you would come back for me. But you were gone. Both of you were gone. Now I find out that you knew. *Thad, you knew.*" Chase didn't want to do this. He just got them back. But he couldn't resolve it; he couldn't wrap his head around the fact that they had assisted in the Shiftings.

"I know. I have no excuse. I just convinced myself that I was a doctor and that I was helping the people who they shifted. I don't know."

"Oh, come on. Are you even buying that yourself? Do you really believe that, Thad? Do you?" Chase was shouting now. "You Shifted your own brother; *your brother, Thad.*"

"I, I had no other choice," Thad said flatly. "I tried to help him, and he turned me in. I had to."

"You could have walked away. You could have just packed up and left. You could have looked for me." Chase turned and stared out the window. "Why don't you just admit that you loved the work? The research, that's why you stayed? Because you were so caught up in the research that you could ignore everything else. I mean, look at you guys, you just set up another lab and kept right on going without missing a beat."

"You're right. That's exactly what we did. We went along with the whole program. I did know. I knew it all. I thought I could change it. I thought I could reverse it. But I took the coward's way out and just worried about Saige and myself. I guess if I'm really honest, it was all about Saige, about not losing her, no matter the risk. I'm sorry, son."

"Don't call me that," Chase said.

Kalare reached her hand through the back seat and placed it on Chase's shoulder. He reached up and interlaced his fingers with hers.

"You know, guys, we can keep pointing fingers, or we can just get done what we need to get done." She was making eye contact with Thad in the rear-view mirror. Thad was fighting back tears; if she knew Chase at all, she knew he was doing the same.

"What the hell is that?" Kalare pointed to the line of vehicles blocking the road.

"Oh, that can't be good."

They were already flagging down the tractor-trailer. Thad thought of speeding off in the opposite direction but couldn't leave everyone in the truck. He pulled along the driver's side of the truck as Sam and Chase rolled down their windows and looked at each other.

"How did they find us out here?"

"No clue. Fight or surrender?" Chase asked.

"Fight, Brother, always fight." Sam locked eyes with Chase, and for just one second, everything seemed okay between them.

Thad, Chase and Sam got out and stood in front of the car, weapons pointed down but ready. A car door opened, and a very alive Dr. Regent stood in front of them.

"So," Dr. Regent said, "are we going to talk, or do you just want to shoot it out again?"

"Probably shoot it out again." Sam moved his left foot slightly so that he was no longer leaning on the front of the car.

"Talk about what?" Thad asked.

"Well, let's see you stole classified files, equipment, personnel and one enormous and expensive TALUS."

"Well, we had nothing to do with the TALUS. He just liked our company better." Chase took a step forward and pulled on the strap to his gun, leveling the barrel so he could get a shot off more easily.

"Look, I don't know what you think is going on here, but you look pretty good for someone who is dead. What did you think I was going to do with all our research after you shot yourself and Metcalf was put in jail? Hang out to see when it was my turn?" Thad was surprised at his casual tone of voice. Chase was right. He had been a coward. That ended right now. "If you know me at all, you know I protect my family and our research above all else."

"The Committee sees this a bit differently."

"Well, I can't really control what The Committee thinks now, can I? I had to make a choice, and with all that firepower coming after us, I figured I'd read the situation clearly. So, we got out. For all I knew, you were dead, Metcalf was shifted, and I didn't know who, if anyone, was in charge.

What did you expect me to do?"

"Yes, well, that was an unfortunate situation that needed some cleaning up."

"This reunion is touching and all, but what do you want?" Chase was rocking back and forth, shifting his weight from one foot to the other. He didn't know what was coming, but it wasn't good.

"Ah, the son. I see the resemblance: same glaring eyes, same jaw. We lost track of you about two years ago. You are a very resourceful young man."

"Yeah, yeah, yeah. You can kiss me later. Again, what do you want?"

"Kalare, are you coming out of the car?" Regent said. Chase turned to stare at Kalare as she got out of the car and stood next to Chase, holding her gun without her sling on.

"I do hope you have recuperated. I guess my men didn't realize who you were. Or maybe they did, and that's why you are still alive." Regent smiled. "You really should be careful of the company you keep, my Dear."

Kalare took a deep breath, looked at Chase and shrugged her good shoulder.

"What do you want, Daddy?" Chase flinched but didn't break eye contact.

"Daddy? Are you kidding me?" Sam pushed against Chase's shoulder. "Did you know about this?"

"He didn't. This is all on me."

"I can't believe the two of you brought all of this out here to us." Sam shook his head.

"Oh, so maybe your friends don't know as much about you as they thought." Regent chuckled. He loved this. Loved watching Kalare squirm.

She was his biggest disappointment.

"I appreciate all this cloak and dagger stuff, but I'm still not coming home." Kalare broke eye contact with Chase and looked at her father.

"Please just leave us alone."

"Don't flatter yourself, kid, I'm not here for you, or you, Thaddeus. You are right about one thing: out here, you are not a threat to anything. You or these little kids playing war."

"Then what do you want?" Thad asked flatly.

"I want the girl." Regent looked into the truck's cab. "Tya, come down from there, young lady, and we can all go our separate ways."

"No way," said Sam. "There is no way that is ever happening."

"Why do you want her?" Thad was trying to buy time. They were clearly outnumbered and outmaneuvered, but he was still trying to find a way out that didn't get anyone killed.

"Who cares, Thad? It doesn't matter why. She doesn't go with them," Sam shouted.

"Why?" Thad ignored Sam and held his eyes on Regent. "Really?"

"Because, my dear Doctor, that girl is the key."

"What key?"

"The biologic key." Regent was a bit ecstatic when he said it, but when the realization that Saige had kept this from him registered in Thad's eyes, it was as satisfying as a fine wine. They both understood that Regent had won this battle.

"So, if you will just come down from the truck, all of your little friends here will live. Oh, and all of your little friends that you so nicely transported and left under Seth's care. They all get to live too.

Nice work with reworking the TALUS, though. I'm assuming that was Seth. Sorry to lose that boy. He was good at his job, and I would have overlooked this little misadventure, but he's taken things too far for that." Regent was bored now. He had gotten what he wanted on all levels and was ready for this to be over.

"Nobody is going anywhere with you." Sam started toward Regent as Thad grabbed his arm and pulled him back.

"Everybody just needs to stay calm. Let me go back with you." Thad said. "I'll come back and do the research with you. Just let them all go. They're just kids."

"I'm sorry, Thaddeus, too late for that. We need the girl."

"There is no way I'm letting you take her out of here." Sam leveled his rifle. The shot rang out before anyone had a chance to react and hit Sam in the leg. He went down, and everyone dropped to the ground.

Chase dragged Sam to the back of the car and then stood as Tya got out of the truck. She walked out into the open space and stood between the truck and the car. Chase walked over and stood in front of her, shielding her. "Tya, go back with Sam. I'm not letting you do this." "Sam. Are you okay?" Tya's voice shook.

"Tya, get back here. What are you doing?"

"You can't just come here and take people," Chase said and then took out the Collector on the roof of Regent's car with a single shot. Then blasts came from everywhere. Chase, Thad and Sam opened fire, pulling back behind the car for protection. Kalare pulled Tya to the back of the car near Sam.

"Everybody just stay put," Kalare shouted.

Kit opened the cab door and pulled Jo-Jo down, holding a gun to her head.

"Kit, what are you doing?" Jo-Jo was sobbing.

"Oh, you thought this all meant something. Yeah, it didn't." Kit laughed as he pulled her up in front of him and started to back up.

"Kit, let her go. You don't have to do this." Chase wanted to shoot him and probably would have if Tya weren't in the way. Kit was moving her back and forth, making a clean shot impossible.

"Sorry, Chase. They pay better."

"I don't care about that. Just don't hurt her. How she feels about you has to mean something, doesn't it?"

"No, it doesn't. Dr. Regent, I'm coming out with the girl." Kit shouted as he pulled Jo-Jo closer against him, using her whole body as a shield. He walked backward toward Regent.

"Well, this is just another misstep, isn't it?" Dr. Regent gave a signal with his left hand.

A shot rang out and hit Kit in the back of the head, spraying Jo-Jo with blood and brain matter. Jo-Jo screamed and hit the ground. Chase pulled her behind the car, checking her head and shoulders for a wound. Kit lay dead in the space between the tractor and the car. They were all huddled behind the car.

"I'm not letting them take you." Sam hugged Tya to him. "I can't let you go."

"No, I agree that's not a choice at all. How do we get out of this? Thad? Anyone?" Chase looked at each of them, but they all knew they were outnumbered.

Thad was holding pressure on Sam's leg with both hands. Jo-Jo was rubbing her wet sleeves across her face, trying to get Kit's crusting blood off the side of her face, but was only smearing it. Kalare was staring at Chase; it was the first time he noticed her hands shaking. He wanted to hold her. He wanted to comfort her. He wanted to yell at her. But mostly he wanted to take her away from everything and trust her again.

"He won't stop. Trust me, I know," Kalare said. Chase stood and leveled his stare at her. Kalare saw the anger. She knew he felt betrayed. This was her fault. She knew Regent always found her, and she should have told Chase who she was before coming to The Forty. She had endangered them all.

"Things we should have known yesterday," Chase said to Kalare with a bite. "Where's his weak spot?"

"It used to be me. I don't think that applies anymore."

"Great."

"Look, don't put this all on me. He wants Tya because of your mother's research. Don't act like I am the only one responsible here."

"We don't have time for this shit, argue about that later, what do we do now?" Sam shouted.

"I go with them," Tya said. "It's the only way to keep everyone safe."

"No. No way. I won't let you." Sam grabbed her arm. "Please don't do this."

"This isn't going to get us anywhere, people. It's simple. The girl comes with us, or everybody dies. You have three minutes, or we blow everything up." Regent snapped his fingers, and car doors opened, guns clicked, and a line of men squatted, guns trained on them.

"I have to," Tya said. "I couldn't live with this."

"No, you can't. You can't. Chase, *do* something."

"This isn't your choice, and it's not Chase's choice. It's my choice. I'm not going to be responsible for a bloodbath." Tya leaned over and kissed Sam. "I love you; you know? Come rescue me." She turned toward Regent and raised her arms. "Okay, I'm coming out. Put your little guns away."

"Well, at least there is someone here with some kind of common sense." Regent motioned for Tya to hurry up.

"Not so fast. Everybody moves out, and nobody comes back for these guys or any of the kids. That's the deal, right?"

"That's the deal."

"Because if that's not the deal, I either kill you, myself or both of us, which means either way your life is over. Got it?" She looked back toward Sam, but she couldn't see his face. "I still might stab you in the eye for shooting him."

"Okay, move out." Everyone filed back into the cars and pulled out onto the road. Then there was just Regent and Tya staring at each other over the hood of a single black sedan.

"I love you Sam." Tya's voice cracked. She was frozen to the spot and didn't know how she was going to get into that car without Sam.

"You don't have to do this." Kalare stepped out from behind the car and stood by Tya.

"I have to." Tya hugged Kalare. "Please take care of him. Them." Tya started moving toward Regent.

"You don't have to do this, Daddy." Kalare grabbed Tya's arm, stopping her from walking to Regent. She stood next to Tya, staring defiantly at her father.

"You coming, little girl? I can still find a place for you."

"You just killed any chance of that ever happening."

"It's a shame, such promise," Regent said, shaking his head. "I'll never understand; such a disappointment."

"I was a *little girl,* not a test subject. The things you did…" Kalare broke off and looked at Chase. "I would take you out right now if I didn't know you'd hurt them."

"Then I guess you've made your choice." Regent motioned to Tya to move toward the car.

Tya looked back once before getting into the back seat. Regent closed the door, opened the front door and stood still staring at Thad.

"You know, Thaddeus, this would all be easier if you would just come back and do the work we hired you to do. That's all we really want," Regent said. He waited a beat, and when Thad didn't answer, he got into the car and slammed the door. The car backed up and began to turn around.

"This is your fault." Sam punched Chase in the face. He fell onto his hands and knees. Sam was right; this was entirely his fault, and he would get her back for Sam. He would fix everything. Chase saw movement in the back window of Regent's car and realized that it wasn't Tya staring out of the rear window; it was Saige. *They had Saige.* Chase's eyes locked onto her. It was the only thing he could see, Saige's eyes full of tears. And he stared at them until everything disappeared.

"Come on, Son." Thad hooked his hands under Chase's arms to help him to his feet.

"Don't. Just don't." Chase pushed Thad away. "Did you see Saige in the car? Did you? And you just stood there?" Chase was on his feet now, charging toward Thad, pushing at him repeatedly. "How could you let him take her?"

"I didn't know. I saw her when you did. There was nothing we could do. What did you expect me to do?" Thad shouted back at him.

"I don't know, something." Chase picked up his gun and started toward the truck.

"Like you did for Tya?" Sam blocked Chase's path.

"I did what I could, Sam. We all did." Chase opened his arms and shrugged his shoulders. "Who the hell expected that to happen?"

"I should have," Thad said. "I know how Regent works. I should have never left Saige alone at The Forty."

"No, you shouldn't have. I wanted to stay, but you both shoved me into that car. Now they have her, and we need to get her back." Chase screamed at Thad, getting so close he almost tripped over Thad's feet.

"What about Tya?" Sam moved toward Chase so violently that Chase thought he was going to hit him again.

"Do you want to hit me again, Sam? Go ahead, I probably deserve whatever you want to throw at me. Have at it."

"I told you that we were compromised. I told you we weren't safe, but you didn't listen to me, did you?"

"How was I supposed to know that Kit was working for them? None of us knew that."

"But they didn't care about us until you brought *them* here." Sam gestured toward Thad. "We were just a bunch of kids hanging out until it became all this Committee shit. You brought this all on us. I blame you for all of it. I'm out of here. We are done." Sam moved toward the truck.

"Seriously? After everything we've been through, and we're done?" Chase wanted to yell and scream, but everything was draining out of him now. He knew it all went bad. He knew it was his fault; he knew he had messed up. He looked over at Kit's body lying between the truck and the car. A dark pool had formed around his head, and bloodied footprints ran in confused circles around the body. That was his fault too.

"I said we are done. I'm heading back with the kids. Kalare? Jo-Jo? You with me or what?"

"I'll drive back with you," Jo-Jo said as he walked past Chase,

careful to step around Kit and the splatter around him. Then climbed
into the passenger side of the truck.

"Kalare?"

"Get back to the kids. Make sure they are safe. I have things to
settle here."

"Have it your way. There's a place with us when you come to your
senses about him."

"Come on, man, don't," Chase said as he headed toward Sam's
truck. "I can't do any of this without you."

"I said we're done. I meant it. Find somebody else to do this with
you. Maybe Daddy can be there for you now." Sam rolled up the
window, pushed in the clutch, and ground the gears until it popped
into first.

"Kalare, you might as well go with them. Unless that is, you have
more secret connections to The Committee you want to come clean
about." Chase wouldn't look at her. He couldn't; once his eyes met
hers, he knew his anger would rush out of him. He wanted, no,
needed his anger now. It was all he had that he knew was true.

"I really don't think that's fair. You were holding on to a pretty
hefty secret yourself." Kalare snapped as she walked away from Kit's
body and toward Chase.

"But I told you, didn't I?"

"Only when we were taking them here. Did you ever think we
should have known about their work before we decided to get them?
That's what we should have talked about. Not the sentimental trip
down memory lane we took five minutes before extraction. I would
have seen the danger and told you about Regent." Her voice shifted
from anger to guilt and back to anger. "If I had the time to really think
about it, I would have known this would happen. When it was just
about me running away, it was one thing, but helping his top two
researchers develop something that was against everything he was
doing? He would never allow that to happen."

"And you should have told me that you were Regent's daughter
that night. You should have given me that information before we
extracted them. I would have stopped it, or at least, I could have put it

together. You should have given me that choice. You had to know by then that they worked for Regent, especially after the whole connection to Seth and the lab equipment. You had to see it." Chase was screaming again, standing so close to Kalare he could feel her breath against his cheek as she exhaled, trying to control all of the impulses that flashed across her face. "That's why I told you who they were before I brought them out here. I wanted you to know who they were, exactly who I was bringing here. How come you didn't do the same? I asked you over and over what you thought about this. I'm not the only person who didn't put it together. No one did." He could see the hurt in her eyes, the anger, but mostly the fear. But he had to shut down. He had to cut all this emotion off. He had to think.

"You told me only about your parents. You knew, *knew,* the kind of research they were doing. You *knew* they worked for Regent. You *knew* it all and didn't tell me anything about who they were. They were your parents, and you wanted to save them. That's all you told me; that was all that was about in that apartment. Not the developers of the damn drugs; not the top two researchers for the entire program. Don't you think that should have been included in your little confession?" Kalare stood her ground, challenging him.

"Come on, guys. This isn't helping anything right now." Thad walked toward Chase and Kalare. "Let's get back to The Forty and see what

kind of a mess is there. We'll figure out what to do from there."

"Oh, will we? You. You ruined everything. I knew I should have just walked away. I knew this was all a mistake the minute he mentioned your name. You have destroyed everything I have tried to build in the last five years. I should have just walked away instead of acting like I was still that little kid hiding in that closet crying for his mommy and daddy." Chase was pacing between Thad and Kalare. "Forget all this. I can't do this anymore." He slung his gun across his back and walked away.

"Where are you going?"

"Don't come after me. Just leave me alone, both of you. I did this alone before; I can do it again." No matter what either of them said,

Chase wouldn't stop now, even though he didn't know where to go. He couldn't go back to The Forty; he had let Saige down again. He had screwed everything up with Sam the minute he didn't shoot Regent in the head. And he knew that's what he should have done. Just like Sam had done for him that night when he shot that Collector in the head without a second thought, it would have all ended there if he had killed Regent.

And Kalare, Regent's *daughter*; it cut him in a way he didn't understand. He knew he had done the same thing by not telling her about Saige, Thad, and their research. But somehow, this felt like a deeper betrayal. She should have told him. She should have trusted him more than that. And maybe she was right. Maybe he was just mad because he knew she was right. Maybe they were all right. He just needed to walk. He needed to get everyone's voice out of his head. And yet all he really wanted was to turn around and bury himself in Kalare's arms. He wanted to hold her and have her put him back together as she did before: before they knew who they were; before they both understood where they came from. He wanted to go back to when the past was safely tucked into occasional nightmares, and he could pretend none of it really existed at all.

28

"You didn't need to do it this way." Saige looked out of the back window and locked eyes with Chase on his hands and knees, staring at her in confusion. "I already told you I would do the research. You didn't have to try to destroy everyone.

"I told you; we needed the girl."

"And I told you there was another way." Saige stared out the back window until Chase and Thad became specks left behind on the horizon.

"What are you doing here, Saige? I'm so confused." Tya was shaking on the seat beside Saige, sniffling and wiping her nose on the sleeve of her hoodie.

"They paid a little visit to The Forty; promised not to kill Thad and Chase if I went with them. But as usual, Dr. Regent here has a penchant for drama and half-truths."

"So, what happens to us now?" Tya couldn't hold back the tears any longer. She hated crying in front of Dr. Regent, but she had used up all her self-control in front of Sam. "And what happens to them?"

"I don't know." Saige put an arm around her, trying to calm her.

"Nothing happens to them, right? That's the bargain. More to the point, what happens to us?" Saige spat the words at Regent.

"Now we, sorry, *you,* continue the work. How could you ever think you could achieve the levels we need in that hovel of a laboratory? I blame Thaddeus for this. No true doctor would have done that; set you up with such archaic equipment. Might as well have thrust you into the Stone Age." He shivered as if this were the most vital thing he had seen today. "You, my dear, will be placed in one of our state-of-the-art facilities to continue your work." Dr. Regent said calmly. "I think you will find it to your liking, and you'll have all the assistance you need."

"And what about me?" Tya asked.

"You, my divine little girl, will be our most esteemed guest. You will have your every need catered to twenty-four hours a day. You see, little girl, you are the future." Dr. Regent's voice gushed in a sadistic way that made Tya want to throw up.

"And what do I have to do?"

"Do? You don't have to do anything. We need blood samples. Good, healthy blood samples. So, you'll be put on a healthy diet, and we will monitor all levels to be sure you are in the best of health. You will have a private chef and a physical trainer and anything else your little heart desires."

"So, I'm your prisoner? And I obviously don't have a choice."

"Obviously. But we will make your accommodations comfortable. You can decorate your room any way you want and furnish it however you like. That's not something we normally do, but in your case, we are willing to make many exceptions." Dr. Regent waved his hand at her. "These are all very simple details to be worked out by whoever is assigned to you."

"Assigned to me? What do you mean by 'assigned to me'? Like guards?"

"Well, don't think of them as guards; think of them as assistants."

"Uh-uh, she's with me," Saige said. "She is either in the same apartment with me, or I won't do the research. I can't protect her from all of this, but I can protect her from everything else that happens in that place."

"Done. Since you are going to be monitored twenty-four hours a day

I see no harm in it."

"And you leave them all alone: Thad, Chase and the others? You don't retaliate." It was a statement, not a request. Saige drew in a deep breath. It felt as if her body couldn't get enough air. "If there is any retaliation, I won't do the research."

"No. No retaliation. Well, let's see how you do with the research.

I'm still not convinced you can get there without Thaddeus."

"You know if you go back on your word, I can destroy all progress on this research, right?" Saige swallowed hard. Her voice seemed to be sinking into her throat as if her tongue were pushing them down as she tried to get them out.

"I am more aware than anyone of your talents and exactly what you are capable of, my dear. Why do you think you are still alive? And as far as Thaddeus is concerned, well, he proved to be the best asset for the job, now didn't he? I've seen the man do deep cover, but this was exceptional work, truly exceptional." Dr. Regent turned toward Saige, intending to continue his point, but when he looked at her, his face went ashen.

"Deep Cover? Asset? What are you talking about?" Saige felt a thick patina of sweat cover her face, and a buzzing sound flickered in her ears before she felt herself career into the front seat. She wasn't sure if it was a reflexive response to her anger surging or the result of an unnoticed bump in the road that caught her off balance. But no, something else was happening. She was falling into the console in the front seat and a distinct heat rose within her, no, it was a searing strip of acid racing to the surface of her skin at the base of her neck; an intense electrical heat running in a line up her neck, into her skull and exploding in her temples: throbbing, no, ripping at her.

The bleed-back hit her like a shot of white-hot luminescent liquid that blasted into her eyes so that everything around her flashed in a silvery, brilliant haze and then crashed into blackness. Her body slammed onto the floor of the car, and her hands shook as the seizure took over. She could hear Tya screaming and Dr. Regent shouting, but in a far-off sort of way, as if she were listening through a long tube that echoed and muffled every sound. She felt rough hands lift her and place her on the ground, and just before she lost consciousness, she saw herself in another lab, in another time, a time before Thad, before Chase, before the Committee. And then she understood why she was here now. All the flashes she had finally lined up: the sealed lab; the bacterial research; the militarization of the drugs; the military escort to keep her in line, the military insignia on Thad's jacket. Not her true calling then, just another of Regent's plans. *Betrayed*. She thought. *Finally. Finally, truth.* And then the muted voices faded. There was nothing but cold ground beneath her shoulders, her legs. Her head buzzed like a burning electrical current. The muddy, underwater muffled incoherence shifted into silence as if time had stopped for a few seconds. And then the shock of intense waves of light and images from somewhere deeper, farther back, flashed at her like a relentless, ever-increasing reel of sound. Until a hum vibrated from her skin and into tissue, muscle and bone; then an engulfing darkness with only her voice crying out from the center of it all. Alone.

29

Sam pulled the truck behind the abandoned warehouse, turned off the ignition and looked over at Jo-Jo. She was splattered in Kit's blood with chunks of skin and brain matter mashed into her hair. She had fallen asleep about ten minutes ago, and Sam didn't want to wake her. He really used it as an excuse to just sit in the truck. He was still trying to calm down but couldn't stop rerunning every detail. He was looking for the place where he could have stopped Regent from taking Tya. Kept looking for the one thing he could have done, but every scenario ended the same way: either Tya went with them, or they were all dead.

"Any problems with loading the rest of the supplies?" Seth had just come out of the building when he saw the blood all over Jo-Jo.

"What the hell happened?"

"Regent happened. They took Tya and Saige. Kit's dead. He was working with Regent the whole time. Oh, and evidently Kalare is Regent's daughter."

"Wait, what? Regent's alive? And where are Kalare and Chase and Thad?"

"Don't know. Don't care. I left them where we were ambushed. Told Chase we were done, and Kalare stayed with him, so I guess that's that. And as far as I'm concerned, Thad can just go back from wherever he crawled out of." Sam punched the dashboard, and Jo-Jo jumped. Seth went around to the passenger side of the truck and helped Jo-Jo out.

"Were you hit?" Seth checked her face, neck and shoulders.

"No. No, it's all Kit. Oh God. It's all over me." Jo-Jo started pulling off her jacket.

"Get it off me, Seth, get it off me." She grabbed at the sleeves, pulled on the collar.

"It's okay, I'll get it. I'll get it. Come on, let's get you inside and cleaned up." Seth led her into the warehouse and into the bathroom. He had rigged up a hand pump to one of the showerheads. As long as the water stayed at a high enough level, the pump worked so they could shower.

Seth threw her clothes into a trash can and helped Jo-Jo into the stall so she could wash the blood out of her hair. And gave her a pair of his sweats and a T-shirt.

"You need to eat something."

"I can't. I just want to throw up."

"Okay, just try to get some sleep then. I'll get one of the kids to sit with you. I have to go see if Sam is okay."

"He's not. He got into it with Chase. Punched him in the face. It was not good. Well, none of it was good. They got Tya, Kit's gone, he, they, um, he..." Her shoulders began to shake violently as she sobbed. He pulled her to him and wrapped a blanket around her. He couldn't tell if she was shivering from cold or crying from shock. But he knew getting her warm was the one thing he could do for her.

"I know. It's okay. Sam told me. Don't talk about that now. Just try to sleep. I'll check back in in an hour. Just come get me if you need anything, okay?" He placed her on the cot and pulled another blanket over her. It only took a few minutes until she cried herself to sleep.

Kit, a spy? This was not something he saw coming. He was angry that Kit had used her. She deserved so much more than that. He waited until she was sound asleep before getting one of the older kids to sit with her. He went to his computer and logged in through the one back door access he had buried in the Committee system. Nothing. He tried to go deeper into the directory and hit a firewall. Seth tried several typical go-arounds and password access points, but nothing opened, and he couldn't get past the block. He copied the location and parameters, opened another window, pasted it in, and sent it to an encrypted IP address; he waited several minutes until it pinged back with an access code. He went back to the first window, entered the code, and the wall fell, and documents began downloading.

"Gotcha," he said aloud and then went to find Sam.

"Okay, so I tried to find anything on what happened tonight and needed to broaden what I was looking for because there was absolutely nothing about any of it. Nothing about the shootout in the garage, nothing about what happened to you guys, total silence on everything. I hit this firewall I had never seen before, which is kind of weird because I built everything in this system. This existed long before I came along. I don't know how I missed it. Anyway, I finally broke through the wall, but it logs into another facility run by something called The Directive. Near as I can tell, this is a whole other branch operating on a strictly military level. I think this might be where The Committee is getting the money to do military-type research. Now. Here's the creepy part, according to this, Saige is one of the Board of Directors."

"Are you kidding me?"

"No, it gets better. She is also verified for all security levels."

"Meaning?"

"Meaning she has the highest security level of anyone at the facility. She is like the queen and completely untouchable. Completely." Seth looked up at Sam. "Sam, do you get what this means? It means no one knew, not Chase, not Thad. Thad is not even in this system. Saige has been in this system from the beginning. From before there was a Saige and Thad or a Chase."

"Did she know? I mean, did she remember or was she Shifted?"

"Shifted, I think. It looks like right before the aggression trials started, her records end here, but not her clearance. That was never changed. There are periodic updates on her research, along with some language about parallel applications. I downloaded all that; it's going to take a while to get through everything. But I think I hit the mother lode here."

"And Thad?"

"Nothing here. I'll have to check other databases, but he was never employed here. He was never any part of The Directive. He doesn't show up at all until the aggression trials." Seth clicked into another screen and pulled up security video.

"How are you getting into all this?"

"Well, once I got through the firewall, I logged in with my usual credentials. I'm not going through the hack anymore. Evidently, I have clearance. It's possible they were going to pull me into this before everything went down." Seth clicked through several live security camera feeds until he landed on Saige and Tya. Saige was being rushed in on a gurney, and Tya was walking alongside, crying.

"That doesn't look good. I got the impression that Saige was fine in the car. I wonder what happened?"

Sam stared at Tya's image; she looked scared out of her mind. His anger pulsed in his jaw. They rushed Saige through a set of folding doors, and two guards pulled Tya into a room and locked the door. Sam was able to see her through the glare on the glass walls. After a few minutes, a tall blonde woman entered the room, placed a tray of food on a small table, said a few words to her, and then left.

"This is killing me, Seth. Where is she? How do we get her out?"

"I'm downloading specs, GPS coordinates and blueprints now. I mean, it's good in a way that they have her at a facility. But I'm confused as

to why they wanted her. Did Regent say anything?"

"Yeah, he said something about her being the key."

"Key? What key?"

"I don't know. Something about biologic or something."

Seth closed the windows and typed something, and a series of documents opened. He started minimizing and closing documents, then stopped and enlarged one. "Oh, I see where this is headed. You're not going to like this."

"Just tell me."

"They are going to use Tya as a biological source because one of her enzymes has an unexpected reaction to the Shift meds. They are thinking it is a natural resistance to more than just the shift meds; it looks like she is resistant to the entire process. Evidently, they have been looking for an organic source because the synthetics implode before they work. Some kind of antibody early response problem; they think they can avoid it with an organic compound." Seth whistled. "This is pretty scary stuff. But I don't understand what the advantage is to have an antidote if it's used in a military operation? What would be the point in an attack?"

"This is bigger than just shifting some idiots because they don't follow the rules, isn't it?"

"Yes. This is military grade shit. Serious military grade shit." Seth closed out a few more documents and started flipping through analysis reports connected to the research Saige and Thad were doing just before they left. He found one memo linking aerosol dispersal to a blocking agent for use by ground personnel administering it. That referred to Saige's current research and the need to keep pushing her to find a biological source. But still nothing on Thad.

Seth downloaded all related documents, minimized all windows, and then reopened the security feeds. He flipped through until he found the camera in the room where they were holding Saige. She was hooked up to heart and blood pressure monitors and IVs; they had placed electrodes in various spots on her head. He connected the medical equipment to monitor her vitals and soon began receiving brain wave patterns on a panel in the lower left corner of his screen.

"What is going on with her?"

"I'm waiting for them to update the entry, but it looks like she suffered a severe bleed-back in the car. Seizures, heart stopped, shocked and brought back. Holy shit, Regent saved her life. She's stable but critical. In a coma, not medically induced. I'll download all the records, but Thad will have to interpret everything. I have no idea what any of this actually means. Sam, I know you are angry, but we have to bring this to

Chase and Thad. And we have to get their help to get Tya out."

"I know. I know. I need his help."

"No, Sam, you need his friendship. You need to fix this. This is beyond anything that any of us could have guessed. Hell, I had an all-access pass and never knew about any of this. I'm not saying you don't have a right to be mad, but I think we all were running from something. Chase's something just happened to catch up with him today."

"Yeah, but *his* something put us all in danger and got Tya kidnapped. Look at her. She's scared to death, and God knows what they will do to her. I can't worry about Chase and his feelings right now. We need to get her out of there. Bring up those blueprints. You work on finding a way to bypass their security. If you can get through security, I'll get us in there. I want to have a firm plan in place before we go to Chase. This is my plan. He's not in charge anymore."

"Let me look at all of this stuff. You need to get some sleep, and then we can go over everything when I have a clearer picture of their security layout and exactly where in the facility they are holding them."

"No. No sleep."

"Look, we can't do anything today or maybe even tomorrow. We can see her. It looks like she's safe for now. And if Saige is out of commission, that means whatever research they were going to do is on hold. At least for the moment, you need to get some sleep. I'll wake you if anything changes. Okay?"

Sam paced around the building. He knew it was wrong to lay all the blame on Chase; they had all decided they would help Thad and Saige. They also knew they would continue their research. They all agreed. He didn't know why he blamed Chase. He just didn't know where else to put all the anger. And Tya, just giving herself up like that? He should have been able to do something to stop that. He should have just shot Regent.

That would have ended it all. But even as he thought it, he knew better. They shot him before he even got that Collector in his sight. They would all be dead now if Tya hadn't been brave enough to get into that car and do what was needed for the rest of the group and the kids. He just needed to find a way to get her back. That was the only thing he needed to do now. He would worry about Chase later. He wandered back into the building and checked in on Jo-Jo, who was still sleeping and curled up on the floor at the foot of her cot. He thought of Tya, alone and scared, in that glass room. He vowed to get her out, no matter who he had to take out to do it.

30

hase had been walking for hours. He circled back to The Forty, walked away and then turned back again. He listened to the rush of the ocean hitting the beach and felt the vastness of everything around him. The sky, the ocean and the beach. All of these things usually helped him, centered him. But nothing was helping today. After walking most of the night, he had curled up and slept on the beach at the spot where Kalare had stood so still just days before.

The spot where she dared him to remember who she was, and he had seen her. He believed that standing there with her was the one truth he had known in this whole mess. Kalare, determined to stay rooted in the sand until he remembered. Until he broke out of his fears and saw them both for what they really were. He reached into that moment and knew he had seen her so clearly then. And she had seen *him*, separate from where they began or who they came from. They knew more about each other in that moment than anyone else would ever know. They knew the most important thing: what the other would do when it was necessary.

How had he let the secrets of their past break into the present? It wasn't even really their past; it was all the stuff their parents had done. Judging her based on who her father was had been his mistake. He knew who Kalare was, and she was nothing like Regent. But it didn't help. He couldn't take back everything he had said to any of them. He felt completely alone and betrayed, and he couldn't change any of it.

31

Kalare stood and watched Chase for twenty minutes. She knew that now she was someone else to him, and he would never see her in the same way again. That was her biggest fear, which was why she had never told him she was Regent's daughter. She knew he would only see Regent when he looked at her. She finally took a deep breath, gathered all her nerve and walked toward him. Whether he wanted to see her or not, they needed to face each other's demons, or there would be no returning from this. And she was still rooted to that spot with him. Despite it all, she still chose him. She would always choose him.

"Hey."

"Hey. How long were you standing there?"

"A while. You were gone a long time."

"I was walking. Thinking." He looked over at her. She didn't look back at him. She couldn't. She knew the minute she looked into his eyes, all her reserve would be gone. She was ready to hear anything he had to say. She was ready to face it all. But she couldn't look at the hurt in his eyes again.

"Where's Thad?"

"Pacing The Forty. The lab and all the equipment were stripped;

all samples and reports were taken. All the computers are gone, too. Big-T was immobilized, so he's just standing there."

"Does it look like there was a struggle? Does it look like they hurt her?" Chase bit down, trying to stave off the guilt.

"No. Just moved everything out. Saige left a note for Thad. I didn't ask what was in it." Kalare paused. "Chase, can we get past this?"

"Which part?"

"The us part. Let's start there."

"I don't know. Ummm, I might have said some things." Chase tried a small chuckle, but he just didn't have it in him. He deserved whatever she said to him.

"I think we both might have said some things." She tried the same chuckle, but it came out more like a sob. "Chase, can you imagine, I came from *him*. I couldn't look you in the eye and tell you that. You would never see *me* the same again."

"You should have left that up to me. You shouldn't have thought so little of me that I would turn my back on you for that. I mean, look at my family tree; the originators of the entire nightmare." Chase shook his head. "We shouldn't have to carry that around inside us, all that guilt. I wish I had reacted better. I don't know why it made me so angry. It's crazy when I really think about it. How have we never met before? There were so many functions and so many ways we should have seen each other before. Don't you think?"

"I don't know. They didn't let me out much. I mean, *he* didn't." An angry edge caught on the *he*.

"Can I ask you something about him?"

"I guess."

"What did you mean when you said you were a little girl and not a test subject?"

"Oh. I forgot I said that. Okay. This is the hard part. This is the part I really don't want anyone, especially you, to know."

"It's okay." Chase reached for her hand. "Whatever it is, we will deal with it. I promise."

"Okay. He, um, tested the early protocols on me."

"What do you mean he tested them on you?"

"He would run me through IQ tests, inject me, then rerun the tests to record any changes in simple memory function. We probably never met because I pretty much lived in the lab. I was his personal lab rat." Kalare lowered her eyes.

"It's bad enough they were using the stuff on the prisoners, but to do that on his own daughter? How does somebody do that?"

"Oh, it wasn't just me. There were other kids there, too. A lot of them got really sick. I guess I was lucky; the drugs didn't bother me either way. I think the worst part was that he was my father. Never understood how he could do that to me."

"I'm sorry, Kalare. That should have never happened to you."

"None of this should have happened to any of us. It was, well, he was, I don't even know how to explain how cruel he could be. I finally couldn't take it anymore and ran away. But he always found me and dragged me back home. That is, until I met you. You kept me safe from him without even knowing it." Kalare was crying now, and Chase cupped her hand carefully as if trying not to damage a butterfly wing.

"Chase, you can ask me anything. I will never keep anything from you again. That is, if you give me the chance. I'll understand if you don't." She still couldn't look at him; she couldn't bear for him to look at her. If all that hurt was still reflected in his eyes, it would snap the last thread of hope his hand touching hers had created.

"I guess we both thought we had a lot to hide. I thought what I told you in the apartment was what I was ashamed of, but it turns out there was so much more." Chase broke off and kissed the palm of her hand. "I could kill him for doing that to you." Kalare could feel him shaking; could feel his breath on her hand, ragged and uneven with anger. She understood this kind of helpless anger.

"Yeah, I've been there. I stood over his bed one night with a scalpel in my hand and thought that just one quick swipe would end it all. Then I would be safe. Be free."

"Why didn't you do it?"

"Because it would make me just like him. I'm not like him."

"No. No, you're not."

"Look, Chase, none of this was ever a part of who we were. This is who they are. Isn't this why we are out here? To get away from all of them?"

"I wanted them back; needed them back so badly. But now I don't know what the hell I'm doing. I don't know who I am anymore. Am I like them? Is that what you see now when you look at me? God, they were the ones who did it all. All of it; they created it. And your father, how do we come back from this?"

"I don't care where you came from, who your parents are or what they did or didn't do. I chose you in that crummy, burnt-out squatter house because you were kind and sweet. You saw me. I was someone else when you looked at me, someone better than him. That was all I needed then. It should be all I need now. You are not your father, and neither am I." Kalare finally looked at him.

"No," he said. He was already staring at her and dared her to hold his gaze. "You are not your father." He smoothed the hair off her cheek and brushed his thumb across her lips. "He is a coward who hides behind gunmen. And you are, well, you're Kalare." He smiled. It was a small, weak upturn on the corners of his mouth, but it was a smile just the same.

"So Kalare, can we take my damaged parents and your deranged father and our screwed-up pasts and throw them away?" Chase enclosed her face in his hands, forcing her to keep looking at him. "I was angry because I didn't want to admit that you were right. You were right about everything."

"No, I was wrong. I should have trusted you about Regent. But I couldn't; I just couldn't stand that look in your eyes. You looked at me like, like I was..." Her voice broke, and she couldn't hold any of it back anymore. She jerked her head out of his hands and tried to get up, but he grabbed onto her waist and pulled her into his chest.

"No. Don't." She pushed at him and tried to get to her feet, but he pulled her closer, gathered her into him and wrapped his arms around her.

"Shhhhh. None of that matters anymore. None of it," Chase broke off and pulled her in closer. "I was wrong about it all. I should have walked away that night on the roof. I should have looked out for us."

She stopped struggling against him and fell into him, sobbing. He held her with everything he had in him, until her breathing eased from gasps, to sobs, to slow, stuffed-up breathing. And he felt it all fall away between them.

"Kalare, can you still choose me? Even after all this? Can you ever trust me again?" He whispered into her hair because he couldn't bear to see her face if she said no.

"Always," she whispered.

32

"**C**hase, I'm still pissed, and I don't really want to do this right

now, but I need your help." Sam stood in the empty room that once held Saige's lab. Bits of discarded paper and trash were all that was left of everything she had there. Her wedding band lay on a small side table next to the crumpled note she had left for Thad. Seth was organizing maps and satellite shots of an area south-west of the city.

"My Help? Seriously?"

"We found them, Chase. Tya looks fine, but Saige, well, there's a problem."

"Did he hurt her?"

"No, I don't think so."

"Well, honestly, we don't know." Seth handed Chase a pile of medical reports. "We aren't really sure what happened."

"Just tell me." Chase tossed the crumpled papers that littered the floor onto the table.

"She had a bleed-back, a bad one. She's stable but in a coma."

"I don't understand."

"I don't have all the information; I'm downloading it now. Thad will have to decipher it. But it looks like it happened on their way here." Seth thumped the map on the table.

"So, what do you need my help with then?" Chase tried to keep the edge out of his voice, but his anger was rising again.

"We have a plan to get Tya out." Sam walked over to the table with the blueprints. "We need to get into this complex. They are being held here." Sam placed his index fingers on the two points on the blueprints. "Seth thinks he has the security bypasses figured out. So, it should be simple to get in and out."

"So, wait, you plan to go in for Tya?"

"Yeah."

"No. That's absolutely not acceptable."

"I don't care if you think it's acceptable. All I am worried about is Tya." Sam shoved at the blueprints on the table.

"I'm not coming out of there unless it's with both of them. I am not leaving Saige in there. What is wrong with you, Sam?"

"You guys get Tya. I'll get Saige," Thad said from across the room.

"No way. You can't do that on your own." Chase began pacing around the table.

"This is not your call." Sam paused. "Look, no offense, but I really don't care about Saige right now. As far as I'm concerned, she brought this

on herself. Tya is the innocent one in all of this."

"That's just ridiculous." Chase slammed his gun down on the table. "Is this how you are going to get even with me? Leave my mother in there for them to do God-knows-what with her?

"Look, we don't know if she's still even Saige. She had a bleed-back. She's hooked up to like a million machines. She's not even conscious.

Right now, for all we know, she's broccoli."

Chase jumped over the table, grabbed Sam by the jacket, and pushed him across the room until they both collided with the wall. "Okay, stop, both of you. This is not productive." Thad untangled Chase's hands from Sam's jacket and pushed Chase across the room. "You both just stay in opposite corners. Whatever is going on between you two, set it aside and step the hell up. Your mother is sick, and Tya is, well, God knows what will happen to her now without Saige to protect her."

"Protect her? Saige is the reason she is even in there."

"This is not the time for this. Sam, get your head on straight. Argue about this later." Thad grabbed Chase by his arm and pulled him toward the door.

"Get off." Chase jerked his arm away and stood against the wall.

"Look, I need your help. It's as simple as that; I'm not here to be all warm and fuzzy with you." Sam straightened his jacket and leaned against the wall. "If you don't want to help, I'll go in on my own."

"And you'll get yourself killed in the process," Thad said.

"We get them both, or we don't go in at all." Chase picked up his gun. "It's your decision, but I'm not leaving my mother in there."

"But we have a better chance of just getting Tya. At least look at the goddamn plan, Chase."

"Not until it involves both. Call me then." Chase walked out of the room, slamming the door behind him.

"Let me talk to him," Thad said. "But, Sam, you do know this wasn't his fault any more than it was yours."

"He lied to me, Thad. Lied to me about all of it."

"A lie of omission? That's what tears you guys apart after all this? I don't buy it."

"A lie is a lie; omission or otherwise."

"Yeah, well, this is exactly what Regent wants, this kind of division. I've seen him do this a thousand times. And it always works because people have feelings. But he doesn't. He's a monster. Don't let him win."

"You guys do what you want. I'm going in for Tya."

Sam pushed past Thad, went to the table, and began shifting blueprints around.

33

Thad caught up with Chase on the beach, his head bent into his arms, shoulders shaking. He sat down next to him, waited a few moments, then wrapped an arm around his son. In the middle of all of this chaos, he got his son back. This time, he wasn't going to waste it on arguments about curfews and bad grades. This time, he was going to embrace it for the miracle it was.

"Listen, I get all this, but it's not going to help anyone for you guys to keep fighting each other. You and Sam need to solve this, but not today. Today it's about getting them out. I am promising you, I will not leave her in there." Thad turned Chase to face him. "Do you hear me? We'll get her out together, okay?"

"Was everything a lie?" Chase ran his hands over his face. "You guys? How you feel about each other? And me? Am I really your son? Was any of it real?"

"I know what I feel for your mother is real, no matter how they tried to manipulate it. Yes, you are my son, that is real. That's always been real."

"I'm so confused. I don't know how to feel about anything anymore."

"Well, I think the first thing is for you and Sam to stop trying to punch each other out. He is right about one thing; you both need each other, or this isn't going to work."

"I guess. Okay, what do we do?"

"First, we need to hear their plan. And you need to play nice. If we go in without having each other's back, we might as well just walk up to the front door with a white flag."

"But we get Saige out, right?"

"We get Saige out. I promise I will not leave her in there. No matter what."

"No bail-out at the last minute or if things get hairy? You promise?"

"I umm, I don't bail. Or at least I never used to. Whatever happens, I promise we all get out. One way or another." Thad pulled Chase over to him and held onto his shoulder.

"We can do this, Son." This time, Chase didn't object to being called his son.

34

"**O**kay, tell me your plan." Chase and Sam stood at opposite ends of the room and glared at each other; *at least they were back in the same room without killing each other,* Thad thought as he looked down at the blueprints.

"Wait, I know this place. I know exactly how to get in." Thad pointed to an access tunnel running along the back of the building. "Right there."

"Hmmmm. Let me check something out." Seth flipped the blueprint over and ran his thumb across the page, then entered a code into his laptop. "Oh, good. I thought they might have one of these. There is a safe room along here. See how all these levels are underground?" Seth paused. "The room we need is on the same level so that it can be used for operations control in case of a failure. It's perfect. I can get you in through all the security doors from there."

"How?"

"All my access codes are active."

"And?"

"Okay, guys, keep up. I have security clearance. I can shut the whole damn place down if we need it."

"Really? Seems too easy, don't you think?" Chase stared at the blueprints for a few minutes, then shook his head. "Seems like a trap."

"Well, since I was the one who assigned and revoked privileges, and I am here, no one would do it." Seth laughed. "They don't see me as a threat. Like I said, people always underestimate the tech rat."

"Okay, then how do we do this?"

"Well, Tya is going to be easier since she is so close to this access door. Saige might be tricky, though; the medical equipment alone makes it a problem." Seth accessed the feed to Saige's room. "See."

"What happens if I disconnect her?" Thad chewed at the side of his mouth to keep his anger in check. He couldn't take Saige seeming so helpless, hooked up to all those machines.

"Don't ask me. You're the doctor."

"So they tell me."

"I think that might be the only way to get her out quickly, though. A bit hard to slip out wheeling a gurney with ten machines in tow."

"I can get us a medical transport," Sam said from across the room.

"More secrets?" Chase tried to keep the edge from his voice, but he just couldn't shut the anger out.

"Yeah, you might say that. Do you care if it saves your mother?"

"No. Do you fill me in, or do I just trust you?"

"Just trust me." Sam crossed his arms over his chest and squinted at Chase. "Or at least, trust me on this, if we get caught, you don't want to know anything."

"Oh, I thought we were done?"

"Yeah, we're done, not stupid. I have a resource. Can you just trust me without needing to know everything?"

"Damn, you are stubborn."

"Yeah, I'm stubborn." Sam tried to hold it back, but a smile broke out on his face, and he turned away, so Chase didn't see his resolve cracking to let him back in.

"Anything else?"

"I don't think so." Chase folded his arms. "As long as you are sure this isn't a trap."

"Well, we're not gonna know for sure until we get in there. So, no guarantees." Seth minimized the windows on the laptop.

"Then I guess we are a go." Thad rolled up the blueprints and stuffed them into his backpack. *I promised her I would always get her out, and I will.*

But this will be the last time he ever takes her from me.

35

T*had* led them through the access tunnel. His body moved with an odd tingle as if his cells were in tune with his surroundings on a primal, instinctive level. He realized he was registering and acknowledging each sound as if he were taking inventory: elevator; air conditioner; door opening, man walking. He shifted his weight to lean into each curve with a cautious but determined gait. He gave in to that instinctive physiological movement and settled into it quite comfortably. As the first juncture of the tunnel came into view, he squared his shoulders, and the energy in him was a heat rising to the surface of his skin. It felt like that first time he had knocked Thomas down; the energy thrumming through his forearms told him he was in control. And he still liked it; he still liked it very much.

Chase followed with Kalare and Seth behind him and Sam, as always, bringing up the rear. Their first stop was a small operations center just past the first juncture, which Chase could now see. It was, as Seth had told them, used as a backup safe room in case of a breach or power failure. It was independent of the complex's power source and could serve as a central base. Seth, with access to all of the codes, could control everything they needed from the small operations center. Tya and Saige were still on the same floor, so that was easy, except it was heavily guarded. Access was easy, but they would have to deal with the guards one by one once they got into the hall. Thad moved through the tunnel, and Chase fell into a mirrored pace behind him, as if they communicated physically without speaking. It was an odd sensation, this idea of familiarity, and as much as Chase still had so much anger, he found he instinctively wanted to trust Thad, and, to his amazement, realized he already had.

When they reached the juncture, Thad motioned to the left. Chase slid past him and stood on the opposite side of the doorway. Seth tapped the corner of a recessed box, and a panel opened; he entered the access code and the light beeped green. The ocular scan slid up from behind the keypad.

Seth leaned in, scanned his left eye, and a soothing female voice said:

"Good evening, Seth."

The door slid open, and Seth bumped into the doorway, jumping slightly at the small swish of the door as it closed behind him. All of the computer bays were dark, except for occasional blinking lights here and there that indicated sleep mode. And that meant the center was not totally shut down. Seth let out a slow, stressed breath and sat down at the main terminal.

He logged in, overrode the keypad and ocular scan, and the door slid open. Everyone crammed into the tiny room, and he closed and locked the door. He pulled up the site map, found the controls for the doors he needed to access, opened a separate window for each door and moved them all to the right side of the screen.

He opened the hallway camera for the floor, Saige and Tya were being kept and hit RECORD. Then pulled up both of their room cameras and hit RECORD. He recorded a thirty-second interval, duplicated the feeds, looped the video, fed it back to the main security room and hit PLAY. He waited a few seconds for the feed to jump and change to the recorded loop. He minimized the looped feeds, left the live feed open, and moved them all to a second monitor. They had timed it so they would arrive during the last half hour of the midnight shift, when the guards would be tired and less alert. Thad and Sam were dressed in black like the guards; Chase was in a white Hazmat jumpsuit and mask. They hoped they would blend in, and with Seth working the doors and access panels from the control room, it would look like they were using authorized access cards.

Kalare had given in about staying back with Seth in the control room. They had all argued against her coming and wanted to keep her as far away from Regent as possible, but she didn't care about that. Chase had finally convinced her it was not the time for a confrontation. But she still refused to be left behind and agreed to stay in the access tunnel to get Seth to safety if the plan went wrong. She shrugged the shoulder strap into a more comfortable position and pushed back her concerns about this plan. This wasn't so much a plan as a snatch-and-grab, and that's what concerned her. They were entering a highly secure underground facility, and they had no idea what they would really find. Sure, Seth had access and understood how it all worked, but they were really jumping into the middle of an unknown. It wasn't so much that she was scared; it was more like every cell in her body was screaming and vibrating with adrenaline. And she kind of liked it.

"Okay," Seth said, "I think we are a go. If you stick to the plan, you should be in and out in ten minutes. I will open the doors as you get to them, then lock them behind you. I'll also monitor that they don't send any kind of alert. Once you are on their floor, the access door will remain unlocked for ninety seconds. Sam, that's just enough time to get Tya out of the first room and then just follow the same route back through the access tunnel." Sam nodded, and Seth looked at Chase and Thad, then motioned to an image on the screen.

"You guys have to follow that hallway to the end corner for Saige's room. You can't double-back down the hallway. I'll have to block the access door, so you'll have to use the alternate route through the maintenance stairwell, here, right behind Saige's room. When I jam the door to the access tunnel, it will also jam the elevators. That means the guards will have to circle back to use these back stairs. You'll have to move fast. If you can get two floors up, you should miss them. Remember to go UP. The stairs lead to the loading dock at the surface level. And then move across to here." He motioned to a door on the screen, and Thad nodded.

"This is the access door to the secondary tunnel, just across from the stairs. There is always one guard, sometimes two, stationed here. You need to take him out. Once you are off the floor, I won't be able to see you, so you are on your own. You don't need me to open the doors since they are manual. I will reset everything except the looped feeds. That should buy you some time to get out. Sam and Tya should be back here by the time I've shut down, and then we all meet at the entrance to the alternate access tunnel."

"That's all we have to do?" Chase chewed his lower lip.

"Well, we could knock and ask permission, but I don't think that's going to get us anything but killed," Seth said.

"Let's move." Thad drew in a deep breath and looked at Chase, who nodded. When the door slid open, he moved into the corridor with Chase and Sam following.

Thad reached the first juncture and pushed down on the handle as the door lock clicked open. He leaned into the hallway and peered down the scope of his rifle, then switched to the other side of the hallway.

"Clear," he said back to Chase and Sam.

The second juncture was a bit trickier. This section had several elbowed corners and other access doors. Thad felt way too vulnerable and was relieved when he heard the lock click and felt the handle slide down. He stepped into the hallway face-to-face with a guard. He lunged and hit the guard with the butt of his rifle, and the guard went down. Sam stripped him of his handgun, two-way radio and access passes. They pulled the guard's double cuff restraints from his belt and looped them through his wrists and taped his mouth. They moved him down the hallway, trying doors until they found an unlocked supply closet. They dropped him to the floor, pulled the pin out of the inside door lock and pulled the door closed behind them. Thad was getting a familiar hot rush up the center of his shoulder blades that always tensed up right before something went wrong. He wasn't sure he wanted to know why he remembered that, and at first pushed his thoughts back, but as he moved toward the final door, he finally let go and allowed all of his surfacing instincts to take over.

They could see Tya through the glass panels in her room. She stopped at each pass and stared out into the hall as if she were expecting them to round the corner any second. The door lock buzzed, and Sam stepped into the hallway, holding the door open. Tya let out a short yelp when she saw him and froze. She heard the lock click but couldn't seem to move.

"*Let's go,* Tya," Sam mouthed as he motioned to the hallway. She pushed on the door, it slid open with a tiny whoosh, and she stepped out into the hallway. Sam reached out, grabbed her by the upper arm and pulled her through the doorway as Thad and Chase pushed past her. The door locked behind them, cutting the two groups off from each other. They headed back down the access tunnel as Thad and Chase made their way toward Saige.

They pushed through as the lock clicked at Saige's room. They missed the beam break across the threshold along the bottom of the door. By the time Seth saw the red blinking light in the corner, it was too late. Two guards were heading toward the door to the access tunnel, and three were headed toward Chase and Thad. Seth had no way to warn them. He punched in a code and jammed the lock to the access door, which unfortunately sent more guards toward Chase and Thad. The guards would have to double back and use the same stairs as Thad and Chase. By the time they gained access, everyone should be safely in the alternate tunnel. This bought Sam and Tya time, but it would be more bad luck for Chase and Thad if they all ran for the stairs together.

Once they were in Saige's room, Chase pulled all the curtains closed.

"Saige. Oh, God." Thad's voice caught, and he realized his hands were shaking. He inhaled and closed his eyes, counting to three to steady himself.

He had to get her out.

He had to stop thinking.

"Can you hear me? Saige?" He unplugged all the machines so the alarms wouldn't sound, then began to strip off all the wires as if they were snakes sucking the life out of her. Chase pulled out the IV lines and taped her arm when he heard the guards running toward the room. Thad rummaged through the supply drawers and stood with something in his hand behind the opening to the door.

"Get her up. No. Wait." Thad slid toward the opening of the curtain.

The first guard pulled back the curtain and pushed through the opening as Thad brought his hand up and back in one motion. The guard's face went blank; he let out a slight gurgled noise as his hands went to his neck. Blood poured onto the front of his uniform. He pulled up his hands, studying the blood in confusion. Then he went down. The second guard tripped over the first and landed with a grunt on top of him. Thad pushed his hand hard against the guard's forehead, pulled his head back with a quick jerk and sliced him with the scalpel. He collapsed, choking. Thad did the same with the third guard. Chase pulled Saige from the bed, wrapped the blanket around her and carried her over to the door.

"Give her to me."

"I got her. Move."

"Chase, let me carry her." Thad's voice was thick with emotion. Chase passed Saige into Thad's arms and slipped through the opening in the curtain.

Chase led the way into the hallway and through the door to the stairwell. As soon as he pushed on the door, all the alarms went off. This was the only way up to the loading dock. They would have to deal with whatever the alarms brought, but right now the stairs were quiet and empty as they made their way up to the ground floor.

They heard guards running as Sam and Tya got to the Control Room. Seth clicked off the screens and dimmed the light as the guards ran by. They waited a few minutes, and the guards ran back past them and continued out of the tunnel. When Seth clicked on the screen, he saw that Saige's room was empty, and the three guards were bleeding on the floor of the room. He remotely locked the room's door and began shutting everything down. He prayed the looped feeds and logged out just as two guards breached the control room.

"What are you doing in here?' The guard pointed to the sign over Seth's head. "This is authorized access only."

"And I have authorized access." Seth handed the guard his credentials.

"Who are these people?"

"My assistants. Didn't you hear the alarms? They are my protection detail."

"Why do you need a protection detail?"

"Um, control room, access to the entire complex, access to everything."

"I have to call this in. Use of this room was not authorized." The guard reached for his two-way radio, and Kalare stepped out from behind one of the machines and smashed him in the back of the head with her gun. "Why does everybody talk so damn much? Let's move out. Now." Kalare had stepped into the hall when two other guards caught up to her. "Stop where you are, or you are dead."

"Yeah, don't think so. Down!" Kalare threw herself onto the floor, and Sam opened fire on the guards.

"Well, that exit is screwed," Kalare grunted as she got to her feet and stared at Seth, waiting for him to do something.

"There's another door to the alternate tunnel." Seth was moving in a little circle, trying to orient himself. "It should be right around this corner.

Yup, right there."

36

Chase led Thad, who was still carrying an unconscious Saige, through the door to the loading dock. They pulled up into a small abutment to catch their breath. So far, everything was clear.

"Yeah, um, that scalpel thing back there, that was a little scary for a research Doctor, don't you think?"

"There are a lot of scary things going on in my mind right now. You really don't want to know any of them."

"Yeah, remind me not to get on your bad side."

"Huh, yeah, well, it's not pretty from over here either. Let's get the hell out of here. We can swap scary mind stories later." Thad hiked Saige up onto his shoulder, and as they stepped out onto the shallow strip between two trucks, the three guards walked into the service entrance and saw them.

"Halt!" One of the guards shouted before he fired a warning shot over their heads.

Chase knelt, aimed and fired, hitting one of the guards in the head as he pulled his handgun out of its holster. Thad pulled a small metal pellet from his pocket, pressed the button and shouted, "Catch!" to the other two guards, who tried to run and pull out their weapons at the same time. The pellet exploded, sending them into the air, with arms and legs floating out like paper-filled manikins. Chase collapsed at Thad's feet, blood pooling. Thad put Saige down and pulled Chase up into a sitting position. Someone had managed to get a shot off before the explosion, or the warning shot had hit Chase, and they hadn't noticed.

"Chase, where were you hit?" Thad shook him until his eyes opened.

"I don't know. It knocked the wind out of me."

Then Thad saw the blood pouring from his left arm. He ripped the bottom of his shirt, wrapped it around Chase's arm three times and tied it as tight as he could get it.

"Can you stand?"

"Yes. Let's get her out of here."

"You go."

"No. I'm not leaving you or her here." Chase stood, lifting Saige.

"Come on; the access tunnel is right there."

"We can't. I shouldn't have moved her. She's not well enough to travel, and I'm not leaving her here by herself. Get yourself and your people out. They should be at the second rally point. Go." Thad was pushing him toward the access door.

"I'm not leaving her here, and I'm not leaving without you, Dad." Chase was using Saige's legs to push Thad toward the door. "Stop arguing and move."

"You have to get out of here. Now." Thad shouted as five guards turned the corner, and Thad opened fire, blocking Chase and Saige. "Go. Get her out of here."

Chase shoved Saige over his left shoulder as blood gushed from his upper arm and grabbed Thad by the belt, pulling him toward the access tunnel. The guards opened fire, and the shots pinged off the truck in front of them. He finally reached the door as Sam pushed it open, leveled his gun over Chase's head and opened fire.

"Dad, come on! I can't hold onto her much longer."

Thad stopped at the access door as Chase pushed Saige into his arms.

"Go. Get her out of here." Chase dropped the clip from his handgun and slid in a new clip.

"I'm not leaving you."

"I've got my backup; get her out of here." Chase held his hand out and smiled. Thad dropped the last three pellets into his palm and turned into the access tunnel. Chase pressed the activator buttons on all three pellets. He rolled them out toward the guards as they rounded the trailers that hid the tunnel opening, then leveled his gun. Chase and Sam fired side-by-side as if the past few days hadn't happened. As if the breach in their friendship had already been mended. The three pellets screeched and exploded, taking out the three guards and the two behind them as Thad reached out and grabbed both of them by the back of their shirts and pulled them into the tunnel.

"Chase, go tend to your mother. Sam, help me with this." Thad had pushed the door closed and was trying to raise the brass bar to block the entrance. They lifted it together and slid the heavy bar into the metal slots as the general alarm blared from the building. The guards would need heavy firepower to get through that door, and by then they would be long gone.

They reached the first of the old sewer exchanges, took a left fork, pulled the hatch shut behind them and finally stopped so Thad could check Chase's arm, which was still bleeding. Thad applied pressure, tore off the other side of his shirt, and tied it as tight as Chase could stand.

"I'm sorry, son, we can't wait here. Can you walk?"

"Yeah, I think so, a little dizzy. How is Mom?"

"Bad. I made a mistake. I shouldn't have moved her."

"Well, we couldn't leave her there."

"Um. Guys." Sam was pacing up and down the tunnel. "We have to get moving."

"I know. I know." Thad was mumbling to himself as he rewrapped the blanket around Saige and picked her up as gently as he could. "Sorry, baby. But I had to keep my promise, didn't I?" Then he refocused. "Sam, help Chase. He's hurt worse than he's admitting."

Two hours later, when they reached the final exchange, Chase's arm was still bleeding even though Thad had stopped three times to redress it. Saige was unconscious, and Thad had pulled so deep into himself that he was responding in grunts and head bounces. They finally stepped out of the sewer access tunnel to a line of military Deuces, with armed guards lining the street.

A tall blonde military type smiled at Sam.

"Well, that looked like fun."

"This is Connor. I called him for backup. This is Thad and Chase. Connor heads up a group on this end of the zone. We're going to his compound. It's safe."

"Compound?" Chase was trying to get to his feet again after half-falling over when they stopped.

"Yes," Sam said. "I'll explain everything later."

"What do we have here?" Connor said, looking at Chase's arm.

"Somebody get the Doc to stop this bleeding before he passes out, okay?"

"Right behind you."

Thad spun around at the familiar voice and stood face-to-face with his brother.

"Thomas?"

"Thad." Thomas smiled and slapped Thad on the back. "I see you guys have been busy."

"But how?"

"Long story for another time." Thomas pushed open one of Saige's eyelids flashed a light across her eye. "How is she?"

"Not good, severe bleed-back. She's been out for several days. I don't think I should have moved her."

"We'll take care of her." Thomas tried to take Saige from Thad, but Thad just held her tighter. "It's okay. You can let her go."

Thad couldn't relax his grip. A man in fatigues came up alongside him, saluted Thad.

"Sir, we are all set up for her. We'll take good care of her, Colonel." Thad stood helplessly watching as they carried her to the medical vehicle. When she was safely inside the vehicle, he turned his attention to Thomas.

"I can't get his shoulder to stop bleeding. It's a through and through, but it's deep."

Thomas cut off the bandage and ripped away what was left of Chase's shirt sleeve. He pulled a packet from his pocket, ripped off the top with his teeth and poured a white powder over the wound before wrapping it with clean gauze.

"Okay, that'll burn like hell for a few minutes, but it'll hold till we get back to the compound. It's good to see you, Son." Thomas ruffled Chase's hair. "You," Thomas said to a young man in fatigues. "Take him back to the compound. He's my nephew, so if anything happens in transport, it's your head."

"Yes, Sir." The young man, dressed in fatigues, saluted Thad before he pulled Chase, who had sunk onto the curb, up to his feet.

"Move out." Came the shout from the back of the truck, and Thad followed Thomas into a Deuce.

"Colonel Bodaway." The first man saluted. "We are happy to rescue you and your family." Thad automatically saluted back.

"Well, this is all very military," Thad said to Thomas, who let out a short laugh.

"I thought you might like it." Thomas smiled. "It's a bit overkill for what we needed, but most of them either served under you or know your reputation and volunteered to get you out. I guess we have a lot to talk about. Sorry about the whole turning-you-in thing that night. They had been onto me for a while, and I needed to throw them off so I could get out."

"Yeah, about that. You know, a heads-up would have been great."

"I couldn't take the chance. But we'll get that all sorted out." Thomas gripped Thad's shoulder. "Glad I could be here now, though."

"And we are going where?"

"We have a compound; I think you will find it's more than adequate.

We've been gathering people for the last five years."

"For?"

"Oh, big plans, I think you will approve, that is, if military Thad has come back to us."

"Yeah, he paid me a visit a few days ago. Weird thing to meet up with yourself, isn't it?"

"You know, I always liked Military Thad so much more than Medical Thad; he has a much better sense of humor. Good to have you back, brother." Thomas slapped Thad on the back. "I missed you."

Thad smiled. He somehow thought he was going to like military Thad more than Dr. Thad. This felt like he was coming home.

37

Regent watched the security footage for the third time. It wasn't that they had taken them. It wasn't that he had lost them. It wasn't even that they had gotten away. He would get them back; that was inevitable. It was that a tech rat and street rat who outsmarted him. That's what really put him out. He had developed a false sense of security that depended on the Shifts affecting Thad's memory of the facility and access tunnels. That was one of the reasons for that final Shift before placing them in Philadelphia: to erase the knowledge he had that could potentially turn back around on them. That's what they get for recruiting the best. And Thad was the best. Strong, smart and ruthless. He was the perfect black ops man. The mission was everything to him. He rarely even needed backup. He was that good.

And now this just seemed like so much history repeating itself. They had forced Saige to do the military research. Had to Shift her to get her to do it. She kept coming out of the shifts and trying to escape, so they had to get someone to escort her. Thad was the most reliable resource they had. He was always on point and never distracted. He would get the job done, no questions asked. It was a simple security detail; that was Thad's mission. Just get Saige from here to there. That

was all he had to do. But something happened when they met. Whatever it was between them continually broke through the Shifts. Even
when he was reassigned, he would find his way back to her. And then
Thad was about to execute an escape plan. They knew that if Saige
left with him, Thad had the training to disappear completely, and
they needed the research above all else. That was when they just gave
in and put them together. Shifting both of them into the aggression
trials. It still accomplished what Regent needed, and it kept Saige
happy. That was the only way he could get her to do anything; push
back the military aspect and make her think it was some goddamn
humanitarian cause. The knock on the door brought him back to his
screen.

"Come," he shouted. His head of security came into the room.
"Tell me."

"Nothing, Sir. They are off the grid. Completely."

"What do you mean, nothing?"

"We searched every bit of security footage. We have them going
into the access tunnel. They had to have found an intersecting
offshoot because we were right there, and it was like they vanished
into thin air. They are not at the hotel or the warehouse. As a matter
of fact, no one is at the warehouse. We've searched their apartment,
all known storage units, and checked every place the kid had
squatted over the past two years. Nothing. They are ghosts."

"That is not acceptable," Regent shouted.

"No. It is absolutely not." Ziph was in the doorway. "We did this
your way, old man, now we do this my way."

"You are dismissed." Dr. Regent said to the head of security. "Get
this place back on track, or you are out of a job."

"Yes, Sir." The guard turned, stepping around Ziph as he left the
room.

Ziph plopped down in the chair across from Dr. Regent, folded
his arms and cleared his throat. "Well, this is a mess, isn't it?"

"Don't start."

"I've met with the other members. You are officially off this case.
You have failed miserably. We all agree that you are too close to

these two. Have been from the beginning. We need them to do this research, and you have not accomplished that. I am taking over as of right now."

"No, you are not. This is my project; it has been from the beginning. I was the one who recruited Saige. No one takes this over, not even you. Do you think this is the first time these two have gone AWOL? It's just a matter of time, and we'll have them back. Meanwhile, I already have a team pulling off the information she was working on and setting up duplicate samples. We drew enough blood to begin some other testing, and by the time we hit another wall, we will have them back. This is not a fast race." Dr. Regent waved his hand at Ziph to dismiss him. "Don't you have classes or meetings or something you should be attending to?"

"No. This is the new priority. Not only did you allow a breach, but you also allowed the kidnapping of our most important asset. Well, two important assets, but I doubt that Saige Bodaway is ever going to be able to research anything but the inside of her eyelids now."

"You never had any respect for that woman. She's brilliant, you know."

"Not anymore. Now she's a vegetable, and we still need the research to continue. Effective immediately, we are replacing all security personnel. All of those access tunnels are being blown this afternoon, and we will be completely revamping our network. Do you realize that Seth simply walked in here, accessed everything, and manipulated our entire facility? Do you know how much of a fool you look right now?" Ziph looked across the desk at him and chuckled. "You suddenly seem very small and powerless. You used to scare me. Now you are just an old fool. Oh, and when we get your little protégés back, there won't be any special treatment. And you will have no say as to how they are handled. They are now my priority, and

I can do as I see fit."

Ziph snapped his fingers, and two guards entered the room. "Please go with these guards without a struggle. You have been tried and found useless. Enjoy your new accommodations."

38

Thad was repairing the blown stitches in Chase's arm for the third time.

Chase drummed his fingers against his thigh, trying not to pull back at the sting.

"You have got to sit still, or this is going to tear again. You have to let this heal."

"I know."

"What the hell were you doing with it anyway?"

"Wanted to see how much weight I could lift."

"Did you have to use your stitched arm?"

"Well, it is the one I shoot with, so, yeah."

"If you keep ripping these out, it's not going to be for long. You were lucky with this. You have to let it rest."

"Okay, okay. I get it. You can stop being *Dad* now." Chase jerked as the needle went into his arm.

"Stop moving." Thad gripped the bottom of his arm to hold it steady. "You know, you can rest for five minutes, Chase. We got them back, and no one is going to find us here."

"Yeah. Right. Stop saying shit just to make me feel better. You know I know better." Chase leveled his eyes at Thad when he shrugged.

"I guess I do at that. This was easier when you were fourteen."

"Yeah, it was great. Can I get out of here now?"

"No. You need to let this mend." Thad snipped the end of the last stitch and dropped the scissors into the tray.

"What I need is to get out of this bed. I can't just sit here and watch her like that. I can't stand it anymore." Chase looked across the room at Saige, who was surrounded by machines. They had turned off the alarms because they all jumped at every beep, but he could still hear the click and pop and swish of machines in motion. They were doing all the work for her.

She was still unconscious. It was driving him crazy.

"And I don't even know where we are and who ARE all these people?" The edge in his voice caught Thad off guard. Sam had found this compound, but it wasn't until now that Thad realized it might have felt like a betrayal that it was done behind Chase's back.

"Look, I get it. I know you're upset. I'm still trying to put all these pieces together myself. But for right now, you need to relax. But I know a lot of these men. I think we are safe here."

"Think? Is that good enough now?"

"Damnit, Chase, cut me a break here." Thad wrapped a final piece of tape around the arm and tore it off a bit more aggressively than necessary.

"Oww. Okay. Okay, don't rip my arm off."

"Sorry. Look, I get it. I do. But look at her. It's all I can think about right now." Thad's eyes rested on Saige. He watched her chest rise and fall in a rhythmic pattern that followed the hush of air moving through the machines. "Thomas is going to try to get the breathing tube out again today. If she doesn't start breathing on her own soon..."

"I know. I just can't think about that. I just can't. So, I can get out of here?" Chase didn't wait for an answer and was already halfway out of the bed.

"Go. I taped that arm down. I would say you shouldn't be able to blow those stitches again, but knowing you, all bets are off. Just try to keep it still and let me know if it swells. Do not rip that off."

"Yeah, no promises."

"God, you do have your mother's stubbornness for sure."

"Yeah, 'cause you're not stubborn at all, right?"

"Well, maybe just a bit." Thad smiled and shook his head. It felt good to have his son with him. Felt good to look into his eyes and see himself reflected. Sometimes, there was a little too much of himself staring back; sometimes, he saw Saige, and it warmed his heart. But God, he was a strong kid. Well, not so much of a kid anymore, but he was proud of the man Chase had become. Damn, proud.

"You'll stay with her?"

"Like anything could tear me away."

"I'll send somebody back with coffee and food. Eat it." "Okay.

"Hey, Dad? You look like shit."

"Yeah, I love you too." Thad ran his hand through his tangled hair. He hadn't left the room since they got back. He was afraid she would wake up, and he didn't want her to wake up alone. Didn't want her to be scared. *If she even remembers who I am.* He pushed the thought back.

He couldn't think about that yet. Not yet.

Chase followed the smell of food through the hallways. People he passed nodded at him, said "hey," and a few asked how he was doing or called him by name. It was all so confusing; all these people knew who he was, and he hadn't a clue about any of them. More accurately, they knew Thad, who apparently was some sort of military hero. People were shuffling food trays and sitting at tables in the large mess hall. Some were dressed in military fatigues, some in jeans and tee shirts. He was glad when he finally saw Sam, Kalare, Jo-Jo and Tya at a table in the crowded room and seeing them all safe and sitting together, suddenly overwhelmed him. It was the first time in months that they didn't have guns strapped to them. He inhaled and let the breath out slowly as his chest relaxed and popped. It was the first time he felt he had relaxed for a second in days.

"Hey, how's that arm?" Sam pulled a chair out next to Kalare for him.

"Not good, just pulled some stitches again. Listen, Sam."

"No. No talking. Not yet."

"How's Saige?" Kalare leaned over and kissed Chase on the cheek. "Any change?"

"The same. Just closed eyes and breathing." Chase looked around the room. "Wow, things look pretty organized here. How did you find this place?"

"I ran into Connor, or should I say was waylaid by Connor, when I was looking to move the kids to the warehouse. They had things organized, and so I figured we were all on the same side, and it was easier to join them.

We weren't doing so well on our own."

"No. I guess we weren't."

"Hungry? They have an ex-military cook here. The food's not that bad, and the coffee is even worse."

"Sounds yummy. Coffee would be great. Thanks. Hey, Jo-Jo, you okay?"

"Better, I think. Seth's been helping me." She smiled. "He's kinda cute, don't you think?"

"Adorable." Chase rolled his eyes but smiled at her.

"Tya, I should have done something to stop them from taking you."

"No. No apologies. We all got hurt in that shit. You guys got me out, and that's all that matters. Just remind me never to give blood ever again."

"Deal. So, are we good?" Whatever happened with Thad and Saige, this was his chosen family. He needed to know they still chose him.

"Look, Chase," Sam paused, "I don't know how to tell you this. We all had a meeting, and this emotional, touchy-feely stuff? Yeah, man, that has to go. It's just gotta go. We really can't take any more of it." Sam smiled. "We're all good, brother. It's all good, except for, you know, the touchy, feely, talky shit."

39

T*had* reached over and lifted Saige's hand. He and Thomas had pulled out the breathing tube three hours ago. Her breathing was shallow, but she was breathing on her own, which they considered a very good sign. They had done everything they could think of to do; they had given her all the meds they thought would bring her back. Nothing was working. Thomas and the other doctors felt as dead-ended as he did. They all agreed it was up to Saige to come out of it. It was all in her hands now, and he couldn't do anything but sit here and stare at her. He wouldn't leave her side. Kalare and Sam kept bringing him food, coffee and water, which were piled in uneven stacks on the small table next to her bed. He had lost his appetite but was chugging coffee simply to stay awake. He was already wired, and the coffee was giving him the jitters, but he wouldn't let himself sleep; he didn't want to miss it if she woke up. And as much as he knew how strong Saige was, he blinked away the overwhelming realization that he was rapidly losing hope. He didn't know if he could go on without her. Didn't think he had the spirit to do it alone.

He worried that he shouldn't have moved her, but he couldn't leave her there. Not in Regent's hands. How silly was it that a simple security detail changed his entire life? She got to him; from the first look she shot him through the pouring rain as he helped her and her soggy raincoat into the transport. He could still smell her perfume; he remembered how it filled his senses and mesmerized him in a way he had never felt before. But it was more than that; they got each other. He was glad when they extended the assignment, and by the time his new orders came through, he had convinced her to leave with him. He realized they had Shifted her into the research, but she kept coming through. Her mind was so strong; her will was even stronger. That's why the Shifts never worked on her. She was stronger than the drugs and smarter than her handlers. Every time they had them shifted and separated, it only lasted two or three days. They kept finding their way back to each other. They would always find their way back to each other. It was their vow.

He kept his promise to her: find and get her out. That was always the promise between them. Whoever broke through the Shift first would find the other. And they always did. He traced the side of her jaw with the edge of his thumb and smoothed her hair. *This can't be how it ends, not after all this.* He couldn't accept it. He pushed down his anger toward Regent; that wouldn't help now, anyway. He just wanted her to open her eyes. *Just open your eyes and know me. Please just open your eyes.*

He eased himself into the space next to her on the bed, wrapped his arms around her, and softly placed her head onto his chest. He pulled his fingers through her hair, brought the strands closer, so he could bury his face into her scent and breathed her in until his shoulders vibrated with the sobs of losing her. He always thought that he had saved her, but she was the one who had saved him. She gave him something solid and immovable to hold onto. It was all so easy before he met her; a soldier takes orders and carries them out. And Thad did his job well. He was dedicated to his job. He was a good soldier. The best he could be. Black was black; white was white, and decisions are easy when the world has no grey areas. He had moved through his life like that: from assignment to assignment, throwing everything he had into his missions. He had nothing to lose and nothing to win. He thought it was his calling because he was so good at it. But maybe there had been something more, he just never thought he deserved.

And then he met Saige, and then he had the whole world in her eyes to lose. Those dark, unfathomable eyes demanded more of him than he ever thought he demanded of himself. She demanded that he be more than just a soldier; more than just a pawn who racked up statistics toward a military objective. She demanded he be a complete man, and he didn't ever want to let her down. So, he became a better man, mostly.

Please wake up. Please.

He ran his fingertips along the edges of her hairline, where tiny hairs curled around the tops of the creases in her forehead, then traced the edge down her jawline to her lips. Those beautiful, full lips that always seemed to be smiling at him, even when they weren't. He had tried to become the man she wanted him to be. Tried even though his stubbornness and his linear military brain always got in the way. But he had tried for her. Everything was for her. But in the end, he was only a man. And being merely a man has its limitations. This was the greatest limitation he had ever faced. He could do nothing to help her. The only thing he could do was hold her close to his heart, and he fell asleep with her in his arms.

40

Saige nestled into the rising and falling of the chest she leaned on; this was a familiar breathing to her, something soothing and internal. She lay there listening to the intake of breath and the steady heartbeat: the rise, the fall. Intake. Exhale. Heartbeat. And then listened to it all again. This was a rhythm that held onto her like a resilient filament as she drifted from this awareness into blackness and back again. She tried to open her eyes. The light burned into them, and her temples began to throb, so she closed her eyes and let the steady rhythm of the heartbeat and breathing keep her balanced.

She had wanted to go. That was what she remembered now. The soft, encompassing feeling of quiet relief as she sank into a dark, quiet space. Her head no longer hurt. The electric spikes stopped. Her neck was free from the burning and the shooting pressure that made her feel as if everything would pop like a small bubble releasing all of its liquid onto a steaming tarmac that would evaporate everything she was. She remembered feeling her body ease, the muscles released of their tension, her legs letting go, her hands unclenching and falling, finally relaxing onto the ground. She felt weightless, as if she had left her body and was suddenly free of everything. She liked the feeling. Liked the freedom of it and the untethering of all connections.

And she was ready to follow it. Ready to move on and leave them all. Without her, they would be free. She could give them their lives back by just letting go of that last tiny silken thread that seemed to move through her chest, out of her left arm and stretch out until it found its other end. She didn't want to look back. Knew if she did, if she saw him, she would change her mind and come back. Come back to him. And just as she had made up her mind to break that last lingering ethereal thread, she had heard it. It was a soft pleading that seemed to carry the weight of the world in one word: *Saige*. And then it was too late. She knew it. She was already turning her heart back, back to him.

She pulled her head to the side when she could finally focus her eyes and stared up into the face of the man holding her. She stared at the line of the jaw, the arch of the brow, the path of the lips: things familiar and not. She felt comfort and panic collide. She struggled to replace the face with a name, but her mind was blank; no, not blank, deluged with images and emotions in an endless animation in her head.

The last thing she remembered was a car, or was it a hospital? Then there were shots? Running? Were these dreams? She closed her eyes and tried to fall back into the calm of the rhythm of his breathing, but her mind fired images at her in a dizzying scuttle that she hoped would stop if she opened her eyes again. She snapped her head back and looked at his face once more. That was when he opened his eyes and stared down at her. Those eyes so familiar, so close to something she knew; something she loved.

"Saige. Oh, Saige," he said, caressing her face.

But she could only stare at him. His voice was familiar, his touch comforting. She was so close to his name, or was it hers? And then she burst into tears.

"Saige? Honey? Do you know me?" Thad said. "Are you with me?"

"I don't know," she whispered. "I'm...I'm not sure."

"Okay. We take this slow." Thad stroked his fingertips lightly down the side of her face. "Do you know your name?"

"No," she said and frowned. "Did you call me Saige?"

"Yes. Your name is Saige. Does that sound familiar?"

"Maybe."

"I'm Thad."

"Thad. Thad." She repeated the name, feeling it in her mouth. "I know you're breathing."

"My breathing?"

"Yes. And, and your heartbeat."

"But not me?"

"No. I mean yes. I mean. No." She looked around the room, confused. "Where am I?"

"There's time for all that." Thad pulled himself off the bed. "You need to rest now."

"Wait. You're not leaving, are you?"

"No. No, I'm not leaving. I'll be right here." Thad couldn't pull back the shakiness in his voice, and for once, he didn't try. "I just need to get someone to, to um, check things..." But she was staring at him, and he stopped moving.

"I heard your voice," she whispered. "Calling me back. I. I wanted. I wanted to go. But you called me back."

"You wanted to go?" Thad's voice cracked, and everything drained out of him.

"Yes." Her eyes were searching his for something. His eyes gave her only tears.

"You heard my voice?" He picked up her hand and brought it to his lips.

"Yes. I. I heard you say my name. You sounded so sad."

"Do you still want to? Go away?" He held his breath, clutching her small hand in his big, clumsy fingers. Her voice seemed so frail; so tiny now, as if she would blow away like dandelion seeds free on the wind. He felt the weight of what he asked her burst in his chest and wished he could take it back. He didn't want to know.

"No. I, uh, came back. Um, want to stay." Her voice trailed off into an inaudible whisper.

"Why?"

"Why?"

"Why did you come back?"

"Thad," she said. "Always Thad." She had closed her eyes and said this in a whisper so shadowy it sounded like the release of a breath.

Thad pulled her wedding band out of his pocket and slipped it back onto her finger. She had lost so much weight that he had to move it to the next finger, and he closed her hand around it. He lost the sob he was holding in his chest. It burst from him as he fell into the chair. He leaned his cheek against the rising and falling of her small chest, holding onto her tiny hand and sobbed into the lowermost pieces of himself until everything he felt for her was opened and raw. And then, finally, he stood before the last secret he held in his heart. The secret that could destroy them; the secret he vowed never to tell her. But he knew now that no matter the consequences, he must tell her if he was ever to have her back completely.

41

Z iph paced back and forth at the rear entrance of the forty-story hotel. "Which idiot decided to do this?" He hovered over the Technician, trying to reconnect the TALUS. "This is the one thing that was connected to him. Do you understand? This could have led us directly to them."

"We were acting on orders, Sir."

"Whose orders?"

"Dr. Regent's orders. Sir."

"Oh, that idiot. It makes sense now," Ziph said, flinching at the mention of his former mentor. "That man could barely use his computer, let alone know how to utilize a delicate piece of equipment like this. Any progress at all?"

"No, Sir. The surge incapacitated him as we expected, but it was only supposed to be a temporary short. It should have restarted within an hour. The reboot from surge was built into its programming. So, we are not sure why that didn't work. I'm trying to get through these firewalls."

"Firewalls?"

"Yes, Sir. Some were built in. Some were added later. The complicated thing about this is that I'm not sure where the actual button to deactivate, or in this case, reactivate, is; each TALUS was constructed so that this particular feature was camouflaged. It was never placed in the same place twice and was always left out of the original specs. We didn't want to make it easier for the enemy to break in and steal any recorded intel. So essentially, it would be a useless piece of equipment to anyone but the owner. Also, there was a sort of fake restart that would cause the TALUS to come out of a reboot in combat mode."

"Meaning?"

"Meaning it would attack anyone present until the correct access code was entered."

"And?"

"And we don't know the correct code. Potentially, it could reboot and see us as targets to eliminate. Especially if it's initial Protection Protocol was intact."

"Well, that worked well, didn't it? We are blocked out by our own design. Is there anyone we can call who would be more familiar with this?

Maybe could come up with a go-around?"

"Seth, Sir."

"Seth. That imbecile. We are done here; pack this up and transport it back to The Directive. Maybe one of the idiots there can do something." Ziph headed toward the car. Six months had passed since they breached The Directive and kidnapped Tya and Saige. Everything had literally come to a standstill. They had no leads at all. Every street rat they brought in had not seen Chase or any of them since that day. They hadn't used a piece of technology for anything. There was nothing. Ziph's frustration was beyond out of control. If Regent knew anything, and Ziph was certain that he did, he wasn't talking. Regent made it clear he would not help unless restored to his position, but that was not part of the plan.

Ziph stood firm on taking his father's place at the head of The Directive. Although some members strongly objected, Ziph had been vetted, and their own rules stated he was in line to take over, regardless of the circumstances. When he finally got his hands on the files on Saige and Thad, they told quite a story. If he didn't hate them so much, he might have admired them. He finally understood what he once took as Regent's stupidity about the Bodaways. But all that he learned only made it more imperative to get them back.

The search for other qualified researchers, even the so-called up-and-comers at the new labs, only went so far. They had used up all the biological samples taken from Tya, with no new results. Wherever Saige was heading with the research was in her head. *And hopefully, it was still in her head.* But this standstill was troublesome. If he couldn't deliver the Bodaways to The Directive, he wouldn't be able to hold onto his position for very long. He had pulled out every nasty trick to get them to back his mission. And now they were out of biologic, had no results, and the Bodaways were still in the wind. They were so far off track, he didn't even know if one existed anymore.

There has to be someone else who can do this. There has to be. Ziph thought as he sat in the car staring at The Forty. *We should have never let them know we knew they were here. We should never have played that card.* Then he saw a single flash from the TALUS. Then another. On the third, it spun and pulled the technician by his throat and held him six feet off the ground.

"Ah, finally," Ziph got out of the car as the TALUS flung the technician to the ground. "Now we have something we can follow."

42

"**B**ig-T has been activated. I have no way of knowing if he rebooted on his own or if someone else started him up." Seth was clicking through screens.

"This isn't good." Chase was leaning over Seth's shoulder, staring at the information blinking on the screen.

"I programmed Big-T to give me one ping and a disconnect so it wouldn't lead them to wherever we were. It will take me a while to get full reads from him like I used to. Depending on how he was activated, I might not even be able to patch in."

"But we have to assume he's still tracking Thad?"

"Yes, Thad, you, Saige, and probably everyone at the Forty." Seth frowned. "Possibly even The Forty itself."

"Meaning?"

"Meaning if somebody rebooted him without entering the proper sequence, it may have triggered a combat response, especially when he discovers that The Forty is now deserted. Wait, let me see if I can pick up on the old signal." Seth typed in the GPS coordinates for The Forty and zoomed in on a 3D map.

"So, he is definitely still connected to Thad?" Sam was pacing around in a little circle behind Seth. This was all they needed. They were ready to launch their offensive at The Directive, even though he still didn't think they were ready, but was outvoted. Sam tried to convince them that the only thing they would have on their side was the element of surprise, but everyone thought they needed to strike fast. At least Seth was able to convince them to hold off until he could get more information. They would have changed all security, passwords and access immediately after the breach and might also have destroyed the access tunnels. If they went in now, they were going in blind.

"It's hard to tell, but we have to assume that they would try to use him to track us. They haven't been able to find us any other way. I mean, Big-T should have rebooted from a simple surge way before this." Seth looked over at Sam.

He knew Sam had been campaigning to have Thad and Saige moved since they arrived. The only problem was that Thad had moved into full military mode and, together with Connor, Thomas, and a few of the other higher-ranking guys, had pretty much taken over planning the next stage. Chase and Sam were pulled into the inner circle, but Sam had come to resent his place in the new hierarchy. It was no longer a fifty-fifty thing between him and Chase like it had been before.

All the kids had been moved to another facility, and this had become the home base of operations, whose primary concern was stopping The Directive. Chase had fit right in, but Sam had a harder time. This was only going to increase the chasm in the rift between Sam and Chase.

"This is really bad, isn't it? Can we intercept him before he gets here?" Chase drummed his fingers on the desk next to Seth. His hands were calloused and seemed to have aged in the last six months. His face had also grown a bit more rugged. He looked more like Thad now. There was no mistaking that they were father and son anymore. They moved in sync, as if they had never been separated.

"It's bad only if someone without the access code activated him. In that case, his programming would put him in full combat mode. But if he reactivates on his own, he will simply look for Thad. I think we could intercept him, but since I don't know how he was activated, I don't know what we would be walking into. It's dangerous." "Full combat mode?

"Yup. Meaning he will take out anyone there and then search for Thad. He is programmed to assume that Thad is in danger if an incorrect reactivation code was used."

"Which means he will lead whoever turned him on right to us," Sam said.

"Great. So, we are here again." Chase stopped drumming his fingers and looked over at Sam. Although he had tried to repair their friendship, things were never the same between them. And the whole move with Connor and his people only aggravated an already strained relationship.

Even though it was Sam who thought that combining forces with Connor was the way to go, he wasn't ever about overturning big government, but now everything was about stopping Ziph and The Directive. Sam resented the mass military component and the fact that the decisions were no longer in his hands.

Chase also knew he was trying to get Saige, and Thad moved to another site, and he knew that Sam had a point. They never wanted any of this. If they had never helped Thad and Saige, they would still be safely living at The Forty with all of the kids. He hadn't seen the kids in three weeks. Everything had changed so much, and Chase missed his best friend. For the millionth time, he thought back to that split second when he changed his mind and decided to help them. It was the look in Saige's eyes that tugged at him. The desperation in her voice asking for help; how could he turn her down? His anger at Thad and her soft, scared eyes had clouded his judgment and brought all this down on all of them.

He knew everyone thought he was Thad's boy, bent on joining Thad's crusade of revenge, but suddenly he wasn't so sure. Maybe Sam had been right all along. Maybe it was time to leave. But how does he do that now? Especially with Saige as she was, how could he leave her again? He couldn't see the path that brought him back to his own life, and he didn't like that one bit.

"I think we are. And I think we can't ignore it." Seth spun his chair around and looked at Sam and Chase. "I mean, I think we all knew this was coming."

"Yeah, but this is lousy timing. Let's go talk to Connor and the others and see what they want to do." Sam had already started for the hallway. After they rescued Saige and Tya, everything went completely dark: no computers, no cell phones, no Internet. Seth needed time to install a new encryption that would bounce their signal around so that it would be impossible to locate them. Once encryption was set up, Seth began accessing all the specs they needed.

Along with what he had already pulled from The Directive, he added a series of back channels that downloaded new information daily to servers scattered around the city. He had to access everything through a series of back doors, which he programmed to shift every twenty-four hours. Within a month of their break-in at The Directive, they were up and in full operation with everything rerouted to the dark net. They assumed they were secure. But now, the TALUS could wipe that all out. They would be exposed again. Sam didn't really care how much of a military hero Thad was; he still thought protecting Thad and Saige was a bad idea.

Regent and Ziph would never let them go. But he was outnumbered here. Even Connor bowed down to the mighty Thad. Sam had been scouting out new places. He planned on convincing Tya to leave with him. It was time to move out on their own, maybe further into the Midwest, where they could just start over and get away from everything. This deep military shit was not what Sam wanted. He looked over at Chase and ground down on his molars. It frustrated him that Chase had so easily adapted to this whole thing. Their friendship had suffered, but as much as Sam missed his best friend, there was no way they could mend things here. He didn't think Chase would leave with him, even though he knew that's what his friend needed. After all, that was his role, to have Chase's back and to tell him when he was off track. This was as far off track as any of them could get.

Sam knew that no matter the rift, he would always be Chase's right hand; he would always be there to defend and support his friend. No matter what happened between them. That was the only reason he was still there. He was ready to tell Chase that he wanted to leave and that Chase and Kalare should come with him. They wouldn't even have the burden of the kids anymore. The four of them could just set out to see what was out there, forget all this crap, and find some sort of life for themselves.

But now this TALUS thing was happening, and he knew two things: Chase would never leave his family with everything going on, and he wouldn't leave Chase to battle this alone. No matter the Military strength here, Sam had a bad feeling that Chase would be one of the casualties lost in the big picture of taking down The Directive. He couldn't let that happen. No, he wouldn't let that happen.

"Sam, wait," Chase said.

"Why?"

"Wait a minute. Seth, what do you think we should do?"

"I don't know. But the first thing was to move Thad. And I mean like, right away." Seth hit print and waited for the papers to drop into the basket. "I was able to access Big-T's GPS. He's still at The Forty, but there is definite movement. I'm hoping he just goes into circle The Forty mode, but

I think that's just wishful thinking at this point."

"Seth, get Kalare. Sam, we need to do this old school."

"I don't know. Full combat mode and only the three of us? Really?"

"Since when is it bad to be only the three of us?"

"Since all this." Sam gestured a circle with his arms.

"So, you won't have my back if I go?"

"Go where?" Kalare said as she came into the room. "I swear to god if you two are squaring off again, I'm going to just shoot you both."

"Big-T is awake."

"Shit."

"I want the three of us to go to The Forty. Sam?"

"Oh, now it's the three of us again, huh?" Kalare snorted sarcastically. "Are we out of the time warp, then?"

"Oh God, not you too?" Chase looked back and forth between Kalare and Sam and realized just how far the rift between them had grown. He couldn't even remember the last time it was just the three of them going off on a raid or even just hanging out. Kalare shrugged as Sam turned and started for the doorway.

"I can't do this without you," Chase said.

"Really, since when? Seems you and Daddy have been doing just fine without us so far." This was from Kalare. It hit Chase in some indefinable spot in his chest. He had been so caught up with everything that he realized he had even neglected Kalare. He couldn't remember the last time they had been together, alone. He couldn't even remember the last time he had held her close to him in the middle of the night. He had been holding vigil with Saige to the point that he slept in her room. He wouldn't leave her alone. Ever.

"Okay. Okay. I get it. You guys are mad. Got it."

"No, Chase, not mad. Invisible." Kalare was mad. He could see it on her face. Her face, which had never shown any emotion, was showing everything now.

"Let's go tell the big guys and see what they want to do." Sam moved his arm toward the door and did a mock bow. "I mean, that's how it is now, right?"

"I guess so." Chase wanted to reach out to both of them. He wanted to go back in time. He wanted to hold Kalare and feel her soft skin against him to feel her breath moving through her lungs, her heart beating against his chest. But he stood there, helpless.

"Um, guys," Seth said. "Big-T is moving."

43

Thad was helping Saige into a wheelchair when Chase and Sam came into the room. The doctors had set up a workout for her, and she was making progress. It was slow, but at least it was progress. The brain-bleed, or the seizure, or moving her, no one was really sure which, had not only affected her memory but her motor function as well. Her recovery was slow, much slower than Thad had hoped, and even though she was remembering people and places and many things about their life, something was missing. That spark that had once lit up behind her eyes was gone, and her mind just wasn't functioning on the level it had before the brain-bleed. Thad felt that only half of her had come back this time. He hoped the rest would fill in. Thad was losing the little bit of hope that had sprung up in him when she first woke up.

Chase crossed the room and bent over and kissed Saige on the cheek.

"Hey, Mom."

"Hey, yourself." She smiled up at him but knew instantly that something was wrong.

"What's going on? And don't give me the oh, nothing answer either."

"We have a problem," Chase said to Thad, ignoring Saige. "Jo-Jo, can you take Saige back to her room so we can talk to Thad?"

"No, she can't take me back to my room. I want to know what's going on."

"Mom, come on. You have to get better. You don't need to hear about anything that's going on. You know this place. There is always something going on."

"I'm really tired of you guys treating me like a cripple." Saige stopped and looked down at the wheelchair. "Okay, bad choice of words. But you can't all keep shoving me in that room, not telling me what's going on."

Everyone looked at Thad.

"Hey, don't look at him. Look at me."

"We don't think you are ready yet, Mom," Chase said. "All you need to worry about right now is getting better. Okay? Jo-Jo, can you take her back?"

"Come on," Jo-Jo said to Saige as she leaned over to release the brake.

"I said no." Saige pushed Jo-Jo's hand away. "Look, I know you don't hear what's going on in my head, and I know you guys think I'm not all here, but I can't get back to me if you don't treat me like me. I know I still have this physical thing going on, but I am aware. Do you understand? Aware?"

"Thad?" Chase shrugged. "A little help here?"

"Right. Welcome to my world. She's been getting ornerier and ornerier every day."

"Stop talking about me like I'm still in the damn coma."

"You guys are driving me crazy. Look, we have bigger things to worry about than whether you are in on conversations. And I do mean bigger things. Big-T woke up this morning." Everyone in the room turned and looked at Sam.

"A little finesse would be nice." Chase dropped down into the chair next to Saige.

"We don't have time for finesse. He's awake and moving. That's all we know right now."

"He's going to track me down, isn't he? Thad drummed his fingers on the table.

"Yeah, we think so. No way to tell if he rebooted on his own or if he's been reprogrammed." Seth stood in the doorway. He kept trying to find a good spin for this, but there just wasn't one. "But he is on the move, and we figure he's heading to you and that someone is following him. Or may have even already retrieved information on where we are. Either way, we're screwed."

"So, he's either in protect Thad mode or seek and destroy everything mode."

"Basically, yeah," Chase said.

"And I am putting you all in danger again."

"This has to end now." Saige was pulling at the wheel locks of the chair. "Look, Regent wants me. If he has me, this all ends, doesn't it? That makes everybody safe, right? He knows I am the only one who can give him what he wants. Why the hell don't I just give him what he wants? And then we can be done with the whole damned thing."

"No. That's not going to happen." Thad squatted down in front of her. "Things have changed. So many things have changed that you don't know about."

"Doesn't matter. Whatever has changed, it's still the same thing as always, Regent and me and the research. He always gets his way, one way or another. If anybody knows that it's you, Thad." Thad stared at her helplessly.

So, she did remember.

"Okay, it's time to fill her in. I'm going to alert Connor and the others about Big-T. Seth and Sam, with me. Chase, bring her up to speed and then meet us in fifteen." He leaned over and kissed the top of Saige's head and squatted back down in front of her. "Saige, do you still trust me?"

"As if I ever had a choice."

"You always had that choice."

"Did I?" Saige searched his eyes. She watched the shift from watery grey to blue. She registered each emotion as it clicked through him. She knew what she said had hurt him. She meant to hurt him.

She knew he loved her; knew *that*, at least, was real. But as for everything else, she didn't see how they resolved some of it. All of it in the name of love? She wasn't so sure she was convinced of that anymore.

"I think this is a private conversation we should have at another time." He tried to break from her eyes; they were dark and fixed, boring into him with accusation, but he couldn't look away. He leaned in and kissed her softly on the cheek.

"I swear, if you call me your girl, I'm going to run you over with this wheelchair." He backed up and stared down at her, feeling accused, judged and condemned. They didn't have time for this. And maybe she was right. Maybe it wasn't all done with pure motivations. Maybe he shouldn't have kept so much from her. But how could she not know it was because he was protecting her? How could she not understand everything? Especially, if she remembered it all? It was always about her. Always for her, she had to know that. Or was he just kidding himself about that as well?

"Chase, bring her to the war room in fifteen."

"Wait, did he say war room?"

"Yeah, he did. Jo-Jo, can you get Thomas? I want him here just in case, you know, just in case."

"Did you say Thomas?"

"Yeah. "You've missed a lot." Chase leaned over, relocking the wheels on the chair as she followed behind him and unlocked them.

"Chase, I swear if you don't stop that."

"What? You gonna run me over? Damn, but you are stubborn."

"Ha, like you should talk?"

"Yeah, wonder where I get it."

"Your father."

"Oh yeah, that must be it. Between the two of you, I didn't stand a chance, did I?"

"Not really. I think I hurt him just now."

"Ya think?"

"I didn't mean to."

"Yes. Yes, you did. And you know you did."

"I'm just, I feel, I'm just so damn angry."

"At him? Or yourself?"

"Myself? Why would I be mad at myself?"

"You keep blaming him, but where were you in all this?"

"What do you mean?"

"You know exactly what I mean. And so does he. We've had many conversations about this lately."

"About what?"

"Him, you, me all of it. You know, you're not the only one who is angry here. But one thing I do know: he loves you, Mom. He almost got himself killed getting you out of there. He never left your side until you opened your eyes. Didn't eat. Didn't sleep. I think if you had died, he would have just crawled in with you."

"I know. He brought me back. I didn't want to come back. He never leaves me there, even when I want him to. But, Chase, there's just too much. I. I don't know how to get past it. Everything between us, I don't think it was, it wasn't always, you know, so pure."

"I get that. Like I said, I've had many conversations with him. A lot of very loud conversations about all of this." Chase shrugged. "But ultimately, I think he's about doing the right thing. He was just as manipulated as you were. You know that, right?"

"I do. Well, to a certain point, anyway. But he kept things from me. Important things. How do I reconcile that?"

"I don't know. I guess you just find a way to get beyond it. There's nothing you can say to him that is any more of a hell than the one he put himself through when you were in that coma. Blamed himself for everything: Regent, the protocols, the shifts, and pulling you out of there. He is convinced he shouldn't have moved you. Said he had to keep his promise never to leave you there. Had to stand on his promise no matter what. When he had nothing else to cling to, keeping his promise was the thing that kept him here; kept him going. There were days when I knew you would come through, but I wasn't so sure about him. He is lost without you.

"So, he told you everything?"

"No. He's actually told me very little. But he questions everything, you know? That is, he questions everything but how he feels about you."

"Great, and I accused him of, well, he knows what I accused him of. I guess he is right, this is a private conversation we need to have with each other."

"Do you still love him, Mom?"

Chase held her hand. It seemed so small in his calloused and strong hands. The scene seemed reversed now, not like when he was a kid, and she held his hand to reassure him. But he wasn't a kid anymore. He hadn't felt like a kid in a really long time now. She looked frail and scared. And confused, and he hated seeing her that way. This wasn't her, and he hated Regent for making her this way.

44

T *ya* removed the flash drive from the computer and left the war room, making sure she had everything she needed. She went to her bunk and pulled out the already-packed backpack. She added the flash drive to a tiny compartment along the side and did a final sweep of the room. She pulled the folded note from her pocket and slid it under the fold of the blanket on Sam's bunk. With any luck, she would be long gone before he found it. She wanted to curl up on the bunk and fall into the scent of him. She wanted to take him and leave. She wanted so many things. But mostly she wanted him to stay alive and safe. *Bargains with the devil don't just take your soul,* she thought, *they take everything you have.* But at least he would be safe.

She cut through the dining hall and turned right into the hallway to Saige's room. The commotion caused by the TALUS was perfect cover. She couldn't look Chase in the eye. This would hurt him too. And Thad. Thad would never forgive her. But she had no other choice. No one did.

"Hey, Chase, your dad wants you in the war room. He told me to sit with Saige. Some stuff about Big-T."

"Oh, okay. I thought I was supposed to bring Saige there. Maybe something happened. I'll be right back, Mom. Do not give Tya a hard time.

And no running anyone over with that wheelchair until I get back, deal?"

He leaned over and whispered in her ear, "I love you, Mom."

"Oh, she's not going to give anyone a hard time, are you, Saige?" Tya watched Chase head down the hallway as she pulled the tiny aerosol pod out of her jacket pocket. She held her breath and turned her face away as she dispensed one spray into Saige's face. Saige slumped over in the chair. Her arm dropped, limp at her side. Her wedding band slipped from her finger onto the floor.

Tya unlocked all the wheels and headed down the hallway toward the small door at the end of the hall of the medical wing. She pushed at the heavy door, trying to maneuver the oversized wheelchair over the ruts when two large Collectors pulled the door open and hauled her out of the way. They lifted the wheelchair and carried Saige to the waiting black van. A third Collector reached out a gloved hand and clasped Tya by the upper arm and tugged at the backpack on her shoulder.

"No, let go."

The Collector tugged on Tya's arm for a few minutes, then shrugged, roughly threw her over his shoulder, and headed for the van.

"Get off me." Tya shoved against the towering Collector, trying to wrench herself free and kick him at the same time. But his grip was too strong, and her legs were too short. She looked like a small child throwing a tantrum, and he simply hauled her around and dropped her against the van's side panel.

"So? Did you get it?

"Yeah, I got everything, asshole." Tya shoved the backpack into Ziph's stomach with such force that it almost knocked him off balance.

"Well done."

"Yeah, it's just great. Okay? Happy? You win. But we still have a deal, right? You leave everybody else alone? Right?"

"Right, we still have a deal if you continue to cooperate."

She rammed her left shoulder against the Collector, and when he didn't let go, slapped her hand against her thigh.

"Can you get this goon off me?"

"Let her go." The Collector stood firmly, holding onto her arm. Ziph snapped his fingers at the Collector, and he released Tya's arm and opened the passenger side door.

"Get me the hell out of here before I change my mind."

"Absolutely." Ziph stepped aside with a mocking, courteous bow and flourish of his hand. "Milady."

"Drop dead." Tya looked back at the Van as they closed the door. Saige was slumped in the wheelchair, and her guilt surged. Ziph slid into the car next to her, grinning. *Finally,* he thought, *finally something went right.* Reactivating the TALUS had been a mistake. It had taken out three of his best men in the time it took Ziph to run to his armored car. And then the idiot just started walking around the building. He was glad they had moved on to the newer model. He didn't even bother trying to surge it again. Anything that it knew obviously didn't register because he should have immediately looked for Thad if he had still been functioning properly. *Let it just circle that damned building until it rusts,* he thought. *I have what I need now.* And, as predicted, Thad proved to be nothing more than a mere manipulated cog without Saige. Ziph had Saige and the biological source as far as he was concerned; the rest of them could rot.

"You do know this is a good thing, right?" Ziph said.

"You think so? Because it tastes like betrayal to me."

45

"**W**hat is taking you guys so long? Chase said as he rushed into Saige's room, only to find it empty. "Mom? Tya? What the hell?" He pulled the receiver from his pocket and snapped a button to static. "Dad? Dad? Are Mom and Tya there with you?" A crackle, some static and another crackle, "Dad?"

"No. Not here. Chase, move them along."

"They aren't here."

"What do you mean they aren't there?"

"Not here; as in it's an empty room. Maybe I just missed them. Let me head back to you." Chase clicked off his receiver and stood in the doorway, looking down the hallway in both directions. Then, turned back into the room. He saw the glint of metal on the floor and stooped to pick up the wedding band. "Shit." He bounded into the hallway as he heard footsteps approaching. It was then that he noticed the sliver of light coming through the side door. He pushed the door open and saw the scrapes from the metal chair wheels, the collection of footprints and the gaping hole along the fence. He pushed the radio's button.

"Dad. We've had a breach."

"Where?"

"North side entrance. Get here now."

Seth was running through the shots from the cameras on that side of the building, rushing through the time code as quickly as possible, until he saw the van and the black Sedan approaching. He hit stop, rewound to just before the van's approach, then moved forward frame by frame. Regent or Ziph had found them. They knew The Directive would be launching something. The activation of the TALUS coinciding with the abduction was just a bit too coincidental. And then there it was.

"Thad."

"Do you have it?"

"Yup."

Thad crossed the room and leaned over Seth's shoulder, ran it backwards, forwards and then again. Saige was out, but it looked as though Tya was being abducted as well. Or had she turned on them?

"Seth, can you tell? Is Tya going with them on her own?"

"No. Maybe. I mean, he is kind of dragging her along."

"Tya wasn't abducted." Sam's voice was thick with anger, frustration, or maybe both. "She left this for me." He handed the note to Thad.

"Well, that's just great." Thad threw the note down on the table; it read simply: *S- Don't be mad- I did it for you... T.*

"Don't be mad? Seriously? Don't be freakin' mad?" Thad began pacing the floor. "How the hell did this happen, Sam? Do you know?"

"No. Thad, I'm so..."

"If you tell me you are sorry, I will throttle you." Thad crumpled the note and threw it at Sam. "What I want to know is, why was no one monitoring these cameras?"

"I left Tya in here to watch the monitors like I've done about a million times." Seth was shaking his head. "How was I supposed to know she would do something like this?"

"Somebody should have."

"Anything?" Chase caught his breath when he saw the image on the screen. "Ziph. Freakin' Ziph? Are you kidding me? And Tya? Seriously?

Tya?"

"Chase, I..." Sam was stammering.

"Sam, no. Nothing. I want to hear nothing. My mother almost died last time. She's still in a goddamn wheelchair. And Tya? This is how she repays us for rescuing her? This is bullshit."

"What I want to know is," Thad said slowly, deliberately, trying to keep his anger in check. "One: what the hell is in that bag, and two: was she working for Ziph all this time?"

"I can't believe she would, I mean, she..." Sam started to defend her, but stopped and looked at the screen, and shook his head. There was no defense.

"I'm running diagnostics now." Seth had streams of data running on three screens. "I'll run them first for the past couple of days and keep going backwards. I back up to several servers at completely different intervals.

Each backup should mirror the other. If they aren't, I can pretty much figure out what was breached. I can compare them. It will tell me what was moved, downloaded or deleted. But it's going to take time.

"Time we don't have. Where's Connor?" Thad clicked the receiver and waited for the static to clear. "Somebody get me Connor, now." Thad had sent Kalare and Connor to walk the fence, searching for other breaches while waiting for the crew to fix the gaping hole they had made when they took Saige. This now seemed like a ridiculous waste of time since she was already gone. Thad thought. He wanted to scream at someone; he wanted to punch someone, oh hell, he wanted to kill that little wretch and imagined his hands tight around Ziph's throat as he watched his life slide from his eyes. He ground his teeth together until his jaw ached. All of these precautions, all this military power, and once again, he had lost her. *I swear I will kill them both, and no one, not even Saige, is going to stop me. Not this time.*

"Right here," Connor said as he rounded the doorway. "That was the only breach."

"We need teams out now."

"Already dispatched." Connor leaned over Seth and rewound the footage. "So, they just rolled up and waited for her. How the hell did this happen? Sam?" Sam handed Connor the crumpled note. Connor whistled.

"Not Good. Any idea what's in the backpack?"

"I'm running diagnostics. I don't think she was smart enough to cover her tracks, unless she was given directions, in which case we may never know what they got. I'll try to get this as fast as I can for you guys." Seth pulled up another set of files on a fourth screen.

"Anything else on other approaches?" Connor clicked through a few other camera shots before pressing the call button on the receiver. "This facility is FUBAR. Break it down." Connor clicked off his receiver without waiting for a reply.

"Seth, we need to dismantle this now."

"But I need to find out what she took."

"Whatever she took, they have it all now, so I guess it's a bit like closing the barn door in the middle of a fire," Thad said.

"Don't you mean closing the barn door after the cows get out?"

"Nope. This is definitely a fire." Thad had pinched out the image and had his thumb on the screen over Saige's slumped head. *This time, I am going to squeeze the life out of that little prick with my bare hands.*

46

The throbbing pain in her head was what woke Saige. It started somewhere at her temple and then wrapped around to the back of her neck. No. This was moving up her spine and into her head. Something was holding her eyelids in place; she couldn't open her eyes. The sounds around her seemed to form a single, loud, concussive hum. But one by one, she started to identify them: hushed voices, the squeak of shoes on tile, the soft crashing of moving material. Then the heart monitor beeped, the blood pressure monitor released and inflated, with something that sounded swift and watery, like a placenta-encased pulse. She tried to move her head, and pain seared into her spine.

"Saige, you shouldn't try to move." A disembodied voice wafted above her. She tried to form a word, but there was something in her mouth and throat.

"You have a tube down your throat, so don't try to talk, but I need to check some things. If you can understand me, squeeze my hand."

She felt her hand lifted and concentrated everything on pulling her fingers together.

"Good. Now I need to ask you some questions, so just squeeze my hand if your answer is yes and do nothing if it is no. Okay?" She squeezed.

"Do you know your name?" *Saige*. Squeeze.

"Do you know your husband's name? *Thad*. Squeeze.

"Do you know where you are?"

"Do you know why you are here?"

"Do you know your birthday? *June third*. Squeeze.

"Do you remember the protocol you are now working on?" *Biologic host*. Squeeze.

"Do you recognize my voice?" *Regent*. Squeeze.

"Good. Good. This is coming along fine. Just fine."

She tried to shake her hand but realized she couldn't ask questions and didn't seem to have the energy to manage it anyway.

"Saige, can you wiggle your toes?" She concentrated on her toes. Squeeze.

"Can you feel this?" She tried to pull her foot back from the pinch but was restrained so that she couldn't move her leg. She squeezed again.

"And this?" Squeeze.

"Excellent. This is coming along just fine. I know you are probably a little confused right now. But let me assure you that everything is going splendidly, just splendidly. I'm going to put you back to sleep now for a little bit." That made her panic, and she squeezed the hand.

"I know. I know you have questions, but you can't move yet. It could harm you at this stage. Trust me. You're in good hands, Saige. I'm handling everything." *Handling What?*

The heat moved up her arm, and as the hum hit her head, she thought she heard Regent directing someone to clean that damn drain. *Drain? Why did she need a drain?*

The first thing she registered was how dry everything was, as if someone had poured sand into her and left her out in the sun to bake. Her skin felt like a thin, delicate glaze that would crack into a million pieces if she tried to move. She ran a dry tongue over cracked, peeling lips. Her throat was raw when she swallowed, which only pushed the dryness further down, and she suppressed a thin cough.

She rolled her eyes back and forth under closed lids, hoping it would help her open them, but instead, her eyelids scraped against her eyes like sticky sandpaper. She finally forced her eyelids open, but even that small sliver of light felt like lasers slicing into her eyes, and she squeezed them shut again. She realized the thumping in her head was her pulse and began counting each thud in an attempt to focus her mind on something. As the steady pace of her heartbeat receded, she began to pick up other noises: a soft beep, a whoosh, the soft sole of a shoe scraping on a floor near her, the rustle of cloth against something solid. And then movement over her, a hand around her wrist, a finger on the pulse in her neck, the dull thud of plastic tubing moving against itself.

Then silence.

Where the hell am I?

Someone was back in the room with her; she had been somewhat aware of things moving around her for a while now. But hadn't tried to open her eyes after that one piercing jolt of light. She was listening for voices, hoping it would help her to figure out where she was. She hadn't heard the familiar voices of Thad or Chase or Kalare. This was a growing tightness in her ribcage. Her last conscious memory was in her room at the compound, but she didn't think she was in any room in the compound now. She didn't know how she knew she was some-where else, but nonetheless, she did. Nothing smelled the same, and there was a hollow, metallic sound to everything, almost as if she were in a metal room. The piercing pain in her head and the base of her skull had eased, but she could feel the electrodes under the bandages and suddenly had the urge to pull everything off and scream. But instead, she pushed open her eyes, which began to tear, even in the dimmer light; her eyes felt as though they were blasted with an atomic bomb flash.

"Ah. Good. I thought you might be close to waking." Dr. Regent leaned over her. He pushed each eye open wider and flashed a light across them, blinding her momentarily and sending tears streaming down her cheeks. "Good, Good. This is moving along nicely. Do you think you can try to speak? The tube was taken out yesterday, so your throat might still be pretty raw."

"Water."

"Ah, of course. But just a bit."

A nurse leaned over the rails on the other side of the bed and put a straw to her mouth. She took a few sips that did little to ease the dryness of her mouth and throat. She licked her lips, but her tongue was still too dry to have any effect.

"Just a bit more." Regent nodded to the nurse, then took the cup and dismissed her.

"Do you want to try to speak?"

"Where?" was all she could get out before her throat closed up on her.

"You're here at The Directive."

"Why?" Her voice was ragged.

Back here again?

No. Not again.

He'll kill me this time for sure.

"No, no. Don't panic. We have reversed the damage caused by the bleed-back. You won't need that chair once we get you a bit of physical therapy, and that's just to help you recover from being in bed; external massage can only do so much for the muscles. Oh, and your memory has been restored. I guess I should say, fully restored." He grimaced. "I imagine there are going to be quite a lot of questions with that." He shrugged, leaned over and gave her a bit more water. "All secrets, as they say, have been revealed. But I imagine that's a conversation for another day. It's time for the truth to be between us anyway."

"Mmph. Truth." She mumbled and closed her eyes. "Need to sleep."

"Yes, I imagine you do want to sleep, but it's time to get you moving. It's time to get you up. You spent six months in that chair, and the physical therapy helped, but now that we've fixed the damage, this will all go much faster." He placed the cup on the table, wheeled it out of the way and dropped the bar along the right side of the bed. He pressed a button on the hand pad, and her head began to rise.

"No. Stop. Dizzy."

"Okay, we'll just start with this now. But I want you out of bed in a few hours, if not walking." Regent fidgeted with the tubes to move them out of the way, so they didn't catch as he slid the bed into a full sitting position.

The movement of the bed made her seasick and woozy. She grabbed onto the blankets to steady herself.

"Oh, good, natural reflexes are already kicking in."

"Yeah. Great." She managed to say, but the dizziness was more than she could handle. She closed her eyes. "Too much."

"Still dizzy?"

"Seasick, dizzy. Shaky. Oh, and vomit, definitely going to vomit." She took the container and heaved into it several times, breaking into a cold sweat.

"Yes, I imagine that's from the regeneration. It will take a while for everything to adjust itself. Probably twenty-four hours as you start moving.

Your brain will continue to readjust as you get stronger."

"Regeneration? What?"

"Yes. Too much for now, we can talk about all that later."

"What the hell did you do to me?"

"Everything I could, my dearest daughter; everything I could." He smoothed back her hair and wrung out a cloth from an iced container on the small table and placed it on her forehead. "Everything is going to be all right now."

47

*Z*iph stood on the other side of the glass, watching Regent with Saige. *Ridiculous. This softness he had for her.* He envied it as he had envied Regent's interactions with Kalare. His daughters! How could he have known? And, if he had known, would he have chosen the same path? He understood it all now: the soft spot, the Directive giving Regent such free rein when it came to them; her. Especially *her*. But he had to admit he had a renewed respect for Regent, doing all this to his own daughter: the memory shifts, the coercion into the research, the rearranging of her life with each shift and Thad. It took a certain kind of messed-up to do this to someone. But to do this to your own daughter was cold, even for Regent.

Using Thad was a stroke of particular genius; he had to admit that creating the false protocols, using the memory shifts to nudge her toward him, manipulating so many parts, even the creation of The Committee, had been solely to continue her research. And she hadn't been aware of any of it. He had to bow to Regent; it had been a brilliant plan. He had even pulled it off pretty successfully for years. But now Saige knew it all. He wondered if Thad knew everything this entire time as well. Was he still on his mission, or had it all evolved from there?

The tissue regeneration was a component of the new biologic TALUS. They were moving away from chips and hardwiring toward biological sources. They were more dependable and less prone to destruction. As long as the biologic source was healthy and strong, and in this case, Tya's sourcing was nearly perfect. Shift resistant, drug resistant, virus resistant: it was nearly perfection wrapped in that idiot girl.

Genetics was a cruel master. Not only would it reverse the damage to the nerves that the bleed-back had destroyed, but the tissue would actually continue to regenerate and grow. Her motor function would be restored, and all her memory. She would remember everything: every memory shift, every exchange and manipulation that had been perpetrated on her from the start. Every memory, both true and false, was now accessible. And she would know which was true, which was a suggestion and which was implanted by him. It amazed him. *But he would never feel that kind of power surge through his brain.*

Ziph shivered, remembering how angry he was the first time he remembered only one Shift. He had a brief feeling of empathy for Saige. But then Regent bent over and placed the softest of kisses on her forehead, and his anger and frustration grew into a rage he knew was reaching an uncontrollable level. He had been displaced once again, and this time she was reborn perfect, with her brilliant brain fully restored. But all he wanted was her, Regent and that little wretch of a son dead. *They'll all pay for this, every one of them.*

48

Thad wedged the barrel of his rifle across his shoulders, dropped his wrists over the edges and stretched the back of his neck across the cool metal as he watched the last of the caravan pull out of the compound. Chase had been pacing back and forth, buckling and unbuckling the leather straps on his weapon, which was casually slung across his shoulder with the rifle at his back. He would stop every few minutes, turn to Thad as if he wanted to say something, then think better of it, grind his back teeth, and move in the opposite direction.

"You know, you didn't have to stay back with me. I know you are worried about Kalare. Maybe you should have gone with them." Thad crouched down, pushing his back against the side of the building and placed his rifle across his knees.

"No. I wanted to stay back with you. I didn't want you here by yourself. Kalare, she can pretty much take care of herself." Chase turned and faced his father. "Plus, I think we need to talk, and I didn't want anyone else around when we did."

"Talk? About what?"

"Just some honest talk." Chase walked toward Thad, thought better of it and moved in the opposite direction.

"You have questions. What do you want to know?"

"The truth."

"The truth? About what?"

"You're kidding, right?" Chase stopped pacing and stood three feet from Thad, who now saw Chase's face and the anger that was taking over.

"I don't understand. What exactly are you asking me?"

"Look, it just doesn't all add up for me. I show you a picture of us, and you have this big brain-bleed. Then you find out you're this super-hero military dude and nothing? You sink into it like a second skin without a moment's hesitation? I'm not buying it. Not for a second. You knew, didn't you? You *remembered* that part of it all, didn't you?"

"Define remembered," Thad said thickly.

"Well, at least you're not denying it. Since I don't understand any of this, maybe you need to start at the beginning. I know all the crap that Seth found, but all of this with you and Mom, that all goes way before all this protocol research, doesn't it?"

"Well, yes and no. I mean, I do remember things that your mother doesn't."

"Things you kept from her? Right? She doesn't know the whole story, does she?"

"No. She doesn't remember the whole thing. They were doing memory Shifts on her long before I came along. They were using another technique then, some sort of aversion therapy in an isolation tank. Or I should say Regent was. He had a singular agenda and used any resources he had, especially on his daughters. No one dared interfere either." Thad pulled his rifle off his knees and leaned it against the wall. He picked up a few stones that he rolled over and over between his palms. Chase watched the expressions move across Thad's face. He wondered if he was choosing where to start or what to leave out.

"I tried to step in and make him stop. Sometimes it helped; sometimes it only made things worse."

"Wait. Did you say his daughters? Are you telling me that Mom is his daughter?

"Well, yes and no. I mean, oh God, how do I explain this?" Thad threw the rocks he was holding and brushed his hands across his thighs. "They, he, the research center, I don't know exactly who started it. This was all way before I got involved; anyway, they created hundreds of embryos using a combination of eggs and sperm samples. He, um, spliced them? Do you understand?" Thad's voice caught, and he drew a deep breath.

"I don't know, spliced what exactly?"

"He used eggs and sperm from various sources and spliced them together to create a group of children that were bred to be superior in intelligence and physical capabilities. He called them his kids. A lot of them died still in the embryonic stage. A lot didn't make it past the first year. I think there were maybe twenty that either survived or weren't impaired."

"Impaired?"

"Yeah, I guess the splicing wasn't an exact thing. Some were mental impairments; some were physical. Of the twenty or so who showed superior testing, he whittled it down to three boys and three girls. They lived in a sort of barracks under The Directive. The girls did especially well, much better than the boys. But Saige was his star. She rose quickly above all the rest, and he took her under his wing as his daughter."

"And the rest of the kids?"

"Don't know. I assumed they were adopted out. Once he got the test levels from Saige, he only concentrated on her, and the rest of them were removed."

"Do you know for sure that she isn't his daughter? Did you ever have her tested to find out if she really is his?"

"Oh God, yes. Several times. There was never a direct link to his DNA. But no one could tell him anything about that. In his mind, she was his daughter, and that was that."

"Are you sure? Because that kind of makes, um, Kalare and me, um, you know. It could be a little weird if she were Mom's sister."

"Oh God. I didn't even put that together. No. They are definitely not genetic sisters."

"Does mom know?"

"Which part?"

"The splicing test tube baby thing."

"No."

"No? You never told her?"

"No." Thad looked up at Chase and shook his head. "I couldn't. She had her memory wiped and replaced with what Regent thought would be a childhood that upheld her intelligence and psychological balance. He had already Shifted her so much that by the time I came along, it was too risky. I was afraid she would, it would, God, Chase, I couldn't lose her. No, that wasn't exactly it." Thad paused and picked up another stone. "How do I make you understand? I couldn't stand to see her lose herself."

"Didn't you think she had a right to know?"

"Yes. A part of me did, but if I told her, if she knew that she was nothing but an experiment and something that Regent used as a lab rat during her entire childhood, what would that do to her? I just couldn't take the chance. It wasn't just the thought of losing her. I had seen the bleed-backs, even those from one Memory Shift; I couldn't imagine what years and years of Shifting had done to her. I just, I don't know, I just couldn't be the one to do that to her. I couldn't take away the life she thought she had."

"So, you did nothing?"

"I did the complete opposite of nothing. I did everything. I tried to get her away from Regent. I tried to build a life for her. I loved her. I loved her with everything I had."

"Was being with you one of the shifts? Did she even have a choice?"

"No. It wasn't a shift, although I think she is questioning that now. I'm assuming she has remembered some stuff between us. But how we were, are, that was the thing that caused all the problems with Regent. I was ordered to transport her, but I took one look at her, and there was no one else for me. She felt the same way. Then I started putting all the rest of the pieces together, and I could have killed Regent for what he did to her."

"Ha, get in line."

"Right. In the beginning, Regent tried to squash it, used memory shifts and some other, shall we say, creative persuasions to come between us. But it never worked. We both tried everything. We tried reasoning with him, we ran away, and we threatened him. We even tried just going along with it all. But, you know him; he's stubborn as hell."

"He's stubborn as hell?" Chase chuckled. "I think this was an even triangle."

"He didn't see it that way. He kept Shifting her in an attempt to change her feelings for me. And it almost worked a few times. The last few Shifts took her months to remember who I was, but she always remembered. She always came back to me, even when we had to start over.

She always came back to me. That's where the *'Are you still my girl?* originated. We needed some kind of code, and to everyone around us it was a cute romantic thing, but to us it was code for: *Are you still in there? Are you still you?"*

"So, what made him change his mind?"

"The memory shifts were starting to hurt her. I could see the subtle differences in her, and he saw it too. Her research was off. Her brain wasn't functioning in the same way. I didn't care about that. It was the little things about her that were fading. She was here, but she was losing parts of herself. And *that* killed me. I had no other choice but to finally reach a deal with Regent. I would keep her researching according to his agenda, and he would stop the Shifting and let us be together." Thad sighed and ran his hand through his hair. "So, we came up with the pre-shift trials. It was research that was needed, so he handed the whole thing over to us, and we relocated to Philadelphia. I found a way for us to be together and have some sort of normal life. And as long as Regent saw progress in the trials, he left us alone. Then you came along, and it seemed like the life we had always wanted. No, scratch that, it seemed like the life your mother deserved. So, I never told her. I just wanted a life with her, and I would take what I could have. This was the way we could have a life. Eventually, Regent realized that if she had you and me, she was content, and he could get her to do the work."

"Creative persuasion? You to her?"

"Oh, God, no. Never. Regent had his own special brand of persuasion for me. It was in the beginning when he realized how I felt about her. He used some very creative methods to get me to leave. But I was Military. I was trained to resist. He couldn't get around my training. He couldn't break me. So, he finally gave up, and we found another way. I made it very clear that I was not leaving her."

"So, he got his research, and you got her?"

"Well, it sounds a lot more calculated when you put it that way. But, yes, I guess that's true enough. Chase, you have to believe me, I loved your mother from the first time I saw her. I was trying to protect her. I might not have always done it the right way, but it was always about her. Always." Thad cleared his throat. "You have to understand, I was military. He was my commanding officer. I did as I was told. I was a good soldier. And then there was Saige, and everything changed. I changed. But I couldn't get her out. So, I did the best I could to give her some kind of life. Before that, she was, it was, God, she was just something for him to test and probe and experiment with; I couldn't leave her there like that. I promised her I would never leave her there like that."

"You have to tell her everything, you know that don't you? You have to tell her everything. She is remembering stuff, and she's really angry with you." Chase shook his head. "You have to be honest with her even if she hates you for it."

"I know. And she is going to hate me. I know she is remembering more than she is admitting. And I know she has been really angry with me, especially the past few weeks. But I couldn't talk to her about it. Not yet.

She wasn't strong enough. Or I wasn't strong enough."

"Why do you think she's remembering?"

"Well, lately she has made more than a few accusatory remarks that were just a bit too close to home."

"Like what she said about choices?"

"Yup, like that. Look, Chase, I don't know if I did the right thing every time. But I did the best I could under the circumstances. And I'm sure your mother isn't going to see everything I did as clearly defined as I did at the time. But I did what I did, and I guess I'll have to answer for that. But God knows, I love her. The thought of her not coming back to me kills me. But you are right, I have to tell her. Even if she hates me for it all, she deserves to know the truth."

"She's gonna go bonkers."

"Oh, I know. You know what amazes me? I can run into an entire platoon of armed men and not be scared enough not to engage. I know I can survive because of instinct and training. But then I think of facing your mother with this, and I am like a scared little kid. She is a force, isn't she?" Thad smiled and let out a slight chuckle.

"She is that. It's not going to be pretty."

"No, but it is time we had the whole truth between us."

"And what about Kalare? Is she? Was she? Is she, you know, one of those test tube experiments?"

"No. She's Regent's biological daughter. I mean, he used her, too, and was thrilled that she naturally showed better test scores without the genetic alterations. He thought it had to do with his superior gene set, but her mother was an incredible woman. So, I think it was more of that than anything."

"Kalare said she spent her childhood in the lab. Did you know her then?"

"No. By then, we were knee-deep in the pre-shift protocols and had little to do with what Regent was doing. I never met Kalare until that night on the roof."

"So, we are going to kill this sucker, right?"

"No. *We* aren't doing anything. Regent is mine. This, between him and me, goes back a long way, long before your mother. But that's a story for another day. This is my score to settle." Thad got to his feet. "Do you have any other questions?"

"Not right now."

"Chase, look, I won't lie to you. Well, at least not anymore. What I will promise is that if you ask me, I won't lie."

"And if I don't ask?"

"I guess you'll just have to trust me, and we'll take it all as it comes.

Is that enough for you?"

"I guess for now. Just don't lie to me, okay? I can take the truth; I just can't take all the lies and bullshit anymore."

"Speaking of taking things as they come." Thad pulled the strap of his rifle up over his shoulder and set the gun across his forearm. He motioned his head toward the road. Chase looked up and saw the flash of sunlight glint off the arm of the TALUS.

49

*A*t first, it was the slight tease of an electric pulse at the base of her skull, like a moth fluttering against her skin that grew hot as it increased. But it wasn't on her neck or the outside of her head; she realized it was *inside* and opened her eyes, blinking with the rhythm as the sensation warmed and stretched throughout the inner bones of her skull. She closed her eyes and felt as if a million fireflies were trapped, buzzing and bumping against her brain. She imagined their tiny lights colliding and looping together, forming fissures and connections that reached back and back into forgotten corners. *Did the brain even have corners or just dark, misplaced self-possessions that the mind could no longer bear?*

A divisive heat slid along the center at the top of her cranium, and she pulled her knees up to her chest and cupped her palms around the bandaged head. *I have to get these damned electrodes off.* But then she was lost to the pulses, connections, and things that now came to her like flashes of light, each holding a specific recall. But now she could absorb the flashes at her own pace and choose which to view and which to discard for later.

She smiled at the childhood doll she always had clutched to her chest. The dorms that were so cold and eerily quiet at night, except for the bleeps of machines and moans of the other kids in the dorm struggling from sleeplessness, or worse. Then so many were gone. She never knew why, just that every day more and more beds were empty until they were all gone without explanation, until it was just Saige alone in a new room. Regent sat in that ridiculously small red chair as he pushed puzzles, tests, and ever-increasingly complicated graphs and formulas at her while pretending to sip through the miniature teacup.

Then, as she got older, she realized she had legs that could carry her away. But he always made her come back. Then he would punish her. Then her increasing defiance, until finally, acquiescence. *No! Not acquiescence, not resignation, but Shifts. So many Shifts. All from the very beginning.*

She realized the punishments had always been Shifts, and the reward was an increase in the complexity of the tests he gave her. He pushed. She shoved. But eventually, he had won. She kept one small bit of defiance for herself: her stark boldness in the knowledge that she could solve anything he gave her. *No, it was that I could, and he couldn't, and I knew it; he knew it too.* She smiled and felt that same satisfaction rise in her that she had as a teenager. He could do whatever he wanted to her, but he couldn't match her brain or even catch her. She knew it gutted him, and she flaunted it because it was the only way to get at him. It was the only way to get to him. It was her only weapon.

The pulses increased, and the images shot at her like rapid eye movement, but she wasn't asleep. And the faint remembrance of her bleed back made her take in a terrified breath that she held for a few seconds. But the images flashed at her easily now, as if the memories were in her control and she could move through them without pain. She could look, choose, explore, and discard each tiny spec of light moving along the channels and folds.

She rapidly flipped through the teen years stuck in that lab. That folded evenly into medical school, which spun easily into the research. Then there were the moves from lab to ever-larger lab after lab. She saw the arguments between Regent and the research team.

Her refusal to work the military angle after, after, what? What was that lurking under the innumerable labs? So far tucked under her that she almost missed it, but she had touched it, and it opened to her. The Military angle, the training, the missions, and then the pull-back when she was shut into the labs. *I had left. I did. But the bastard brought me back.* And then the resolve and calmness between them. *After what? More shifts? Goddamn, you to hell.*

And then there was Thad. *Thad. More lies. More broken promises.* But just there, it caught her, dangling there lost within that brief first moment: the rain, the transport, the smell of him, those eyes holding her dead still as he reached his hand to help her up and into the vehicle. He stared at her through the rear-view mirror.

Are we moving sometime soon? I do have a deadline, you know. She had said to him, annoyed that he smelled so good that his eyes looked into her. She was annoyed that her body skipped with an electric charge as if it had been shot with a million needles. She was annoyed that even the rain seemed to stop for a few beats when their eyes met in the mirror.

And then all the pieces rushed in like a blizzard of images forcing each tiny flake to drop into place until it was all suddenly waist-deep before her. It overloaded her like carbonated bubbles rising furiously in a too-small container, and the more they crammed in, the smaller the space got, and the angrier she became. Until it was all there: how they met, how they fell in love, the fights with Regent, the lies, the deceptions, and the omissions: hers and his.

All of it was suddenly spread out like a vast desert of tiny specs, down to even the slightest and simplest of interchanged white lies. Then she saw Thad for who he really was, and just as she decided what to do about it, she saw herself standing beside him and looked into her own soul, just as he had looked into hers that first day. And then, in those damn blue eyes that stopped space and time, the whole truth was finally there. It was so much more than she thought she could ever bear. But she had to shut it all off before her heart let him back in again. But she knew it would happen. There was nothing she could do about her feelings for

Thad. She reached up to pull at the bandages on her head. She knew he had already found his way back into her heart. *Damn it. Damn, that stupid man.*

She sat up, looked around the room, reached down and pulled all the intravenous needles out. She pulled off the cuffs and tabs that had her pinned to the bed. She swung her feet out and dropped to the floor using her palms to balance herself. She didn't fall. She didn't lose her balance. A slow grin pulled her lips up. Then she slowly rose to her full height and rummaged around the drawers, found surgical scissors. She cut all the bandages and pulled them off. Underneath the bandages, the electrodes covered her head. She reached up and pulled at them slowly, first one by one and then in twos and threes. Her hair had been cut bluntly here and there to accommodate the electrodes. It was growing back in large lumpy patches everywhere. She pulled a razor from the side drawer, lathered her head with soap from the dispenser, and shaved off the clumped, gel-sticky clusters. She opened the side closet panel and pulled on the scrubs, a surgical cap and scuffed, soft-soled shoes that one of the nurses had hung there.

She found her way to the unsupervised bay of computers at the end of the hall. She logged in, pulled up the map, studied it for several seconds, then pulled up her security badges and hit print. She accessed her files, opened another window, typed an IP address and a code, then entered the command:

/COPY/SEND/DELETE/SIGN OFF/END.

SHE PULLED her badges from the printer, walked out into the hall and casually pushed the UP button for the elevator. Before anyone even noticed she was gone, the doors had closed, and the elevator was starting its ascent.

"Good morning, Dr. Bodaway. How may I assist you this morning?" A female metallic voice said cheerfully through the elevator speaker. Saige smiled. She knew exactly how she could be assisted this morning.

Saige entered the access code and placed her palm on the pad to the security office. Four armed Collectors stood and turned their weapons on her.

"Mr. Nelson, please instruct your men to lower their weapons." Saige was pointing to the senior security officer, who stood stock-still without issuing the command.

"I would do it now, Gentlemen, or this is going to get really messy, really quick." She didn't wait for them to lower their weapons, but instead crossed the room and shoved one of the officers aside so she could access his terminal. "I need the room. Get out."

"Mrs., Um, Doctor, Um..."

"You do realize I am the ranking officer in this room, do you not, Mr. Nelson?"

"Yes, Ma'am."

"And, still, you are not following my orders." It wasn't a question.

"Ma'am, we've been instructed to, Um, to..."

"I know what your instructions were. Check your COM. Those orders have been updated." Saige was entering information into the terminal. "Oh, there is also a list of weapons and supplies I require attached as well. I need them here in two minutes. So, I suggest you close your mouth and get moving."

"Yes, Ma'am." Nelson motioned the men out of the room, started to salute, thought better of it, gave a slight, awkward bow and exited backward through the door. Saige was signing off when the door opened, and Nelson and two other guards brought in the supplies she had requested.

"Mr. Nelson, I have updated security protocols and have added a few special orders. Please be sure that everything, and I do mean everything, is followed to the letter. Take specific note of my instructions for Tya, you know, the young girl that was brought in with me. Take care of that personally, yes?"

"Yes, Ma'am."

"I will also require your assistance in parking bay three in approximately thirty minutes. Have my transport ready to move. I will also require two additional vehicles and drivers."

Saige was removing her scrubs and pulling on the pants, boots and jacket she always kept in her locker and began slipping ammunition and small disc canisters into the pockets of her jacket. She strapped on a side leg harness to each leg, tightened the straps, loaded the weapons and slid them into the holsters. She pulled the final weapon, slipped it into the slot along her right arm and pulled on the Velcro straps to secure the weapon. She pressed her thumb to release the handgrip, tested the scope, and retightened the straps. She removed the scrub cap, scratched at her scalp and pointed to the beanie covering his head. He handed it to her, and she pulled the black knitted cap low over her newly shaved scalp.

"Why are you two still standing here? You have your orders. Get to them." Saige dismissed the two men. "Nelson, you have been promoted to head of security. Please recheck your COMS and dispatch my orders now.

Or do I need to get someone else to do the job?"

"No, Ma'am, I mean, yes, Ma'am. I will take care of the girl, and your transport will be ready in thirty minutes."

"You only have twenty-two now. You do understand what is going on here, right?"

"Yes, Ma'am."

"Then, I suggest you get a move on."

"Yes, Ma'am." Nelson moved out of the room as Saige pulled the self-destruct window open, checked the countdown, and selected *Silent Alarm NOT BROADCAST and Audio Ten Minute Warning.* She rechecked all of her pockets, clicked the safeties off on all the weapons, pulled on snug ballistic gloves and fastened the Velcro at her wrists. She pinched open the window to the images of Ziph and Regent. *Gotcha.* She whispered and made her way into the hallway.

50

S eth hovered over the final monitor as the technician hit the power switch and backed away from the bank of terminals set up in the bunker. They had moved everything to a new bunker, and it had taken much longer than he wanted to set up. By the time he connected with the TALUS, it was already at the compound. And he had no idea whether it was in attack mode or Thad-friendly mode. He activated the GPS and was at least able to track where the thing was, but not what it was doing. It would take at least another fifteen minutes before he could reestablish a connection; by then, it might be too late for Thad and Chase. He hoped they weren't just standing out in the open or, worse yet, just going to walk up to the thing and say hi. Seth had given Thad the override codes and voice commands, but had no idea whether those had been tampered with or changed. Everything was a gamble about how the TALUS would be reactivated. He pulled up the satellite image of the compound and stared at the heat signatures of Thad and Chase walking toward the TALUS. *Of course, they are just going to walk up to it. Why would they not?* Seth shook his head as he entered the codes and tried to connect to the TALUS before anything else could happen.

A monitor across the room beeped, and Seth stood up and looked at it. Several lines of information filled the screen, then another window opened, then another. Seth moved over to the monitor and started sorting through the pages until he found the one he was looking for, then clicked the window to open it full screen. Saige. He'd found her, or at least her feed.

"Thomas, we are live." Seth released the button on the receiver.

"Good. Give me five." There was a loud crackle of static before Thomas clicked off.

Seth walked over to the other monitor and checked the heat signals again. Still two. Still standing. At least that looked hopeful. He entered several lines of code, hit ENTER and waited for the ping. Nothing. He entered several other lines and hit ENTER. This time, he got the ping, and two windows opened: one filled with diagnostics, the other with the video feed. He watched Thad and Chase approach. *Where the hell is the audio?* He was clicking buttons when the other monitors started beeping rapidly. He looked over as the graphs and readings connected to Saige sped up, and three other beeping windows were added to the noise. *Oh hell. What was this?*

"What the hell is that?" Thomas shouted over the noise as he came into the bunker.

"Um, Saige?"

"Seriously? You got the connection?"

"Yeah, of course, I got the connection. Have no idea what the hell I'm looking at. Can you make anything out of this? Got four windows with readings. There are readings on heart, blood pressure, temp, and other crap; I think this looks like a neurologic feed. I've never seen anything like it." Seth enlarged the window to fill the screen.

"Oh, I see what you mean. It's more like a mechanized download, isn't it?"

"Yeah. That's what I'm concerned about right now. All of her other functions are amazingly normal. Much better than they were when we had her here. But this read-out has me a bit confused. Did they chip her?"

"Chip her? What do you mean?"

"I mean, it looks like the new TALUS model readout. It's partially genetic, partially electronic. You don't think they would have tried some new experiment on her, do you?" Seth hit a couple of keys, and the information split into two graphs on the screen. "See, this is her last neurological feed from the monitors here and look at the difference between

that and this new one. It's like, no, it can't be, can it?"

"You mean it looks like the brain activity is regenerating? Damn. This is amazing. Look at these readouts; it's like watching an embryo grow in time-lapse. Is there any way we can get a video connection? I want to see what she is doing." And then, suddenly, it hit Thomas like a punch in the gut: this was his project. It was the one regret he had in leaving it all behind. Now that the ass Regent was going to get all the accolades, when it was all his research and technique that even made this possible. He had to get Saige back here. He needed to see her through this. If Regent does one thing out of sequence, it could all go badly, very badly. It was time to tell Thad everything now. "And where the hell is Thad?"

"Thad's still at the compound; they were intercepting the TALUS. I have the GPS and satellite up on that monitor for them. Still trying to connect to the TALUS, but it's at the compound now, so whatever is going to happen is going down now." Seth motioned to the other screen.

"Them? Did Chase stay back with him?"

"Yeah. You know them. Cut from the same cloth, no offense."

"None taken. That's why he's military, and I'm a doctor. He flies into bullets, and I just take them out of other people. But the two of them together make up one big react-now-pay-later power duo."

"Well, that's true enough. Have you ever watched them? It's creepy.

They even have the same expressions."

"Yeah. They were always like that. Oh, wait. Something's happening here." Thomas tapped the monitor.

"It's slowing. Moving at the same rate as the previous, but different. Like it's more..."

"Complete. Yeah, like the holes have filled in. Fascinating." Thomas went over to the printer and pulled the read-outs off. "Amazing. Just amazing. It worked exactly as I thought it would."

"What?"

"Later."

The connection to the TALUS clicked, and a screen opened. Seth typed in the code, hit Enter, waited for the "access accepted" message, and then added a login and access code. The answering ping opened a window, and the diagnostics started running.

"Okay. Looks like the TALUS is in friendly Thad mode. I just need to make sure that he isn't sending back any information; although something tells me they really don't care about us anymore. They got what they wanted; I'm assuming." Seth continued entering information and scanning the diagnostics for the TALUS.

"More than you know, Seth. I need Thad back here. And I need him back here now. This timetable just got accelerated. And it's not a good thing." But the read-outs were incredible, even more promising than Thomas had hoped for. He had to remind himself that this was Saige, his sister-in-law and not just any other test subject.

But along with his fascination, he was angry. Not just because it was Saige that Regent used as a test subject, but also because Regent had stolen this from him. He would make him pay. He would make him pay dearly for this.

Seth's phone buzzed. He pulled it out of his pocket and slid his thumb over the screen to the message.

/anoot.now.40.SKSS.-c

He typed in:

/techno? And hit send.

A few seconds later, his screen lit up with:

/no.Tgood.SKSS.-c.

He typed in:

/c.in.40

Seth hit send, went back to the original text, added the addresses and hit send again. Kalare and Sam came into the room as their phones vibrated. They checked the message, looked over at Seth, shouldered their guns and left the room.

Seth clicked on the window connecting to Big-T. Figures and files were downloading; he selected *Quit after Download* and minimized the window. He opened several other windows to fill the screen. Thomas was standing near the printer, going through the read-outs on Saige as Seth slipped out of the room, hoping he wouldn't run into Connor in the hall.

"So, you want to do this without Connor and the fourth infantry?"

Sam didn't even try to keep the sarcasm out of his voice. "What? The

Calvary not living up to its reputation?"

"Sam, is that really necessary?" Chase was holding out his hand toward Sam, shaking his head. "I got it. Okay? I got it. You're pissed. Can you just listen for a minute?"

"Look, I don't blame you for being suspicious." Thad paused, took a deep breath and looked at Sam. "I cut you guys out. I get it. I was out of line. I asked for your help and then just barged in and took over like I was in charge."

"Aren't you?" This time it was Kalare.

"No. Yes. I don't know. I sure acted like I was. And if any of you tell me to go rot in hell, I guess I deserve that too."

"We got you out. We risked everything and then, what? We were reduced to just a bunch of kids again? Oh, except for your golden boy there. No offense, Chase, but you did just fall in step." Kalare was challenging him, and as much as this wasn't the time to bite back, he knew he had to have this inevitable conversation, so now was as good a time as any. If they were going in to get Saige and Tya, they might as well get it all out in the open now.

"I didn't fall in line. I was trying to get my parents, my mother, back."

"It wasn't just about that, and you know it." Kalare was soft but insistent. "You put us all in danger: all the kids, each other, and even yourself. I've never known you to be reckless, but you lost your center. You made bad decisions for us. We couldn't trust your judgment anymore." Kalare shrugged. It wasn't condemnation; it was just how it was.

"You could always trust me, Kalare." His voice dropped to a whisper. "Always."

"Humph." Sam folded his arms across his chest, emphasizing the sound reverberating in his throat.

"Look." Thad broke in, "Don't blame Chase. I know I did it; I dragged you all into this whole thing, especially Chase. And I knew it was the last thing any of you wanted. I don't know how many times I can apologize. But right now, I just want to find a way to get them back. And, no, Sam, I don't want the whole freakin' Calvary storming in. I just want to get in, get them out and be done with it."

"Tya too?"

"Tya too? What the hell kind of question is that? Especially Tya. If anybody got caught in the crossfire, it was her. I don't blame her for anything. I'm sure that Ziph handed her an ultimatum that she probably thought she couldn't get out of, and I certainly didn't make it easy for her to come to me. Ziph probably threatened to kill you. It's what I would have done." Thad shrugged his shoulders. Truth was truth. You use whatever gives you the result you want.

"Okay. This can all be sorted out later. Where are we then?" Sam squatted down, shading his eyes from the sun.

"Well, Big-T was reactivated and began receiving files this morning.

We are assuming that it is Saige."

"So, let me get this straight. Saige is communicating with Big-T? Is that what's going on?" Kalare leaned against the wall, twirling circles in the dirt with the butt of her rifle. "How do we know this isn't a trap?"

"Because there was a specific code that only Saige, Seth and Big-T knew. She used her access codes, and that signal downloaded all of her files, including all the medical procedures. She has sent the coordinates for a rendezvous point. Big-T is mapping the route now. She doesn't want us busting in like the brutes we are, I guess. She said everything was already in motion." Chase cleared his throat and reached over to put his hand on Kalare's arm. She pulled her arm away, and he backed up, hands raised.

"Okay. So that's how it is? I knew you were mad, but I didn't think. Well, I thought..."

"You thought I would hang out in the background while you played soldier? Thought I would just what? Wait in the wings like a high school girl? Do you even remember who any of us are anymore?" She shoved her hands into her jacket pockets. "God, Chase, you just shut off. You gave me everything and then nothing. Damn it." She couldn't keep the tremor out of her voice; now, it was all breaking the surface. "I told you everything.

Everything. And you just went away."

"I was here. I was right here."

"No." Sam moved closer to Chase. "You weren't."

"Holy hell. You guys are killing me. What do I have to do? I still trust you guys more than anybody else in this world. If I have to choose my team, this is it. But I guess you have to decide if you still trust me."

"It's more than just trusting you. Do we trust that?" Sam gestured at Big-T. "I mean, six days ago, Saige was in a wheelchair and was having trouble talking. Now she is communicating with Big-T and organizing her own escape? Isn't that a little bit too convenient? How do we know this is even her?"

"Thomas recognized the outputs. He had been working on some kind of regeneration procedure before he defected. He validated everything, the outputs and the test results. Said it worked better than he even thought it would. Right now, he's pissed that Regent stole his research. But, you know, that's nothing new for Regent." Seth looked over at Big-T.

"Everything downloaded here aligns with what I saw at base camp. It's basically a duplicate copy of what I accessed this morning. I think it is Saige. I don't know what she is planning, but she has top security clearance, even above Regent. She could shut that place down with a simple command and then just walk out the door."

"What do you mean, shut it down with a simple command? You mean like a self-destruct?" Kalare laughed. "Are you telling me that we've been running around playing with these little guns when we had a self-destruct this whole time? Seriously?"

"I don't think we actually have a self-destruct. Well, except for Big-T here, but I'd hate to lose the guy."

"Wait. He has a self-destruct?" Thad walked to Big-T.

"Well, yeah. All TALUS models do. It's a safeguard against capture. First, they are programmed to blast everything in sight, but if overpowered, they go into self-destruct mode." Seth closed the back panel. "It can be programmed, but I think he is better used as an asset than a weapon, don't you?"

Thad scratched his head and squinted at Seth.

"Thad?"

"What? I'm thinking."

"No. You're not. We are not self-destructing, Big-T." Chase glared at Thad.

"I don't think we need it. I think Saige may be able to override security and just walk out of The Directive on her own." Seth ducked back behind Big-T and closed the second panel. Big-T shifted position and faced

North. "I think he's ready whenever you guys are."

"So, what exactly is the plan here?" Sam unbuckled the gun strap and massaged his right shoulder.

"So, you're going with us?"

"Of course, I'm going with you, you idiot. Who's going to cover that weak left arm of yours?" Sam looked at Kalare and tilted his head in question. Kalare responded with an affirmative nod.

"Well, there kind of isn't a plan. We just thought we would go." Chase said.

"Just go? As in, just walk up to the door and say hi. Is it time for tea?"

"Basically. Well, maybe not exactly go to the front door, but we need to at least get to the rendezvous point. Then we assess and go from there." Thad looked from face to face. "Look, I know we have that whole military thing back there, but with you guys, I don't know, I just think there's a personal stake here for each of us. We can always get Connor and the rest of them to come in as backup if needed. And as for Saige, trust me,

I've seen her come out of these things determined and in motion. It's actually a bit scary. You only know her as this meek little research scientist, but let me tell you, that woman has tusks; big, nasty tusks."

"So, we're going old school?" Sam stared at Chase.

"Yeah, old school. That is, if you still got my back."

"I always had your back, Brother. Even when I didn't think you were thinking straight. Especially when you weren't thinking straight, and I wanted to choke you. I still had your back because that's when I knew you needed me the most."

"So, we are really doing this thing?" Kalare had picked up her rifle and slung it over her shoulder.

"Yeah, we are. Seth, you are welcome to come with us, but we could really use you back at Basecamp running things from there."

"Oh, I'm definitely with you on that, Thad. I'm not exactly warrior material. You guys with the guns should go and do all that stuff. I have Big-T on remote, so I can keep tabs on you through him and then track everything else with Saige's credentials."

"Try to stall Connor if you can. I'll call when we are on site. But Conor should be ready for back-up if we need it."

"I'll take care of it. I'd better get back before somebody misses me." Seth circled the car and stopped next to them. "You guys bring them back, okay?"

"We'll see to it." Thad thumped on the roof of the car, and Seth drove off.

"Well, Big-T, I guess we are ready to roll."

"Dr. Bodaway has sent a message for you, Thad."

"Okay."

Make sure you don't get yourself killed.

I want to do that myself.

Shit. She remembered. "Chase, I might need you to run interference for me."

"Oh, no. Uh-uh. You are on your own. That is one scary woman when she's angry."

"Yeah, she's great, isn't she?" *And, angry or not, she's still mine,* Thad thought and didn't even bother suppressing the grin.

51

aige stepped from the elevator and drew in a deep breath. Not to steady her nerves but to clear her mind of all of them: Chase, Tya, Sam, and Thad. Especially Thad. She couldn't do this if she thought of Thad. This was personal. This was about pure revenge. She had forgotten this part of herself. Had forgotten everything but the medical training. The memory Shifts had washed away all of the rest of it. But now it was all there: accessible and ready for use. So, she had as much under those Shifted layers as Thad. *No. Not now. Later. I'll deal with Thad later.*

Ziph and Regent were still arguing when she reached the office. Their faces were red, and Ziph was leaning over the desk, jabbing a finger into Regent's chest. His jacket sleeves rode up his long, lanky arms so the slim forearm stuck out pale and brittle. *I could snap that in half.* She thought and checked her watch. *15 minutes. I have to move now.* She clicked the button on the side of the weapon on her arm. The handgrip slipped into her palm. The trigger chamber swung open with a soft click. She placed her thumb into the indentation, saw the green flash, and took her first step.

Thad stepped out from behind a support column, grabbed her by the left arm, and pulled her into him.

"What the hell are you doing here? I told you to wait by the transports." Saige pulled her arm free. "Why do you always have to do this? Why do you always have to be the goddamn hero? I don't need saving anymore. If I ever did."

"I can see that. What were you just going to walk in, shoot up the place, and walk out?"

"Yes, that's exactly what I am going to do. And now, thanks to you, I only have twelve-point-three minutes left to get it done."

"Oh God, Saige, you didn't, did you?"

"I did. In twelve-point-one minutes, this is all gone, and everything goes with it. And I'd really appreciate it if you didn't stop me." Saige rechecked the weapon and, with two strides, was standing in Regent's office.

"Oh, my Dear, we were just talking about you." Regent rose from his desk chair as Saige leveled her right arm, closed one eye, checked the scope, and adjusted her arm height. Then, the target set, she looked at Regent.

"I just want one thing. No, two things. One: I remember everything, you sick, twisted son-of-a-bitch; I want you to know I was the one who brought it all down. Me. Alone. I brought *you* down. And two: I want you to look me in the eye and know I did this when this bullet hits your brain. I want to see it in your eyes."

"Did what?"

"*T-Minus Ten Minutes.*" The electronic ten-minute fail-safe final alert sounded.

"You didn't." Regent stood frozen halfway between her and the desk as Ziph rose and started for her.

"I wouldn't do that, you little shit." Thad was across the room and jammed the barrel of his handheld into Ziph's neck. "Give me a reason. Just one little reason." Thad pulled Ziph toward the door. "Saige, we have to go."

"Uh, huh. Be right there," Saige said to Thad and then looked back to Regent. "Are you looking into my eyes? Do you want to see it?"

"Yes, but Saige, my Dear..." The shot hit him squarely and neatly in the center of his forehead. It was an insignificant little circle of darkness. It seemed so inconsequential until the bullet exploded the back of his head into a mash of brain tissue and blood, spraying everything in the room behind him. He crumpled to the floor. Saige stood over him. *That was almost too quick. Almost.*

"Saige, now. We have to go." Thad was holding the elevator door open with one foot, and Ziph was crumpled onto one knee with the other. Saige turned, rechecked the weapon as she entered the elevator, pulled her glove off, and pressed her palm onto the pad.

"Dr. Bodaway, your transport is ready. You are at the five-minute point of no return; do you wish to override the self-destruct sequence?"

"Where are Chase and the others?"

"In the lobby, I hope."

"Do not override sequence."

"What the hell are you doing, you stupid woman?" Ziph was on the verge of screaming or crying; it was hard to tell. Thad pushed down on his shoulders, leaning on a pressure point as Ziph struggled, then went limp with a small sob. Thad could feel him trembling and pushed back the small jolt of sympathy rising in his chest. He pushed his knee hard into Ziph's back, hoping he wouldn't piss his pants in the elevator.

"It all ends here. But you, oh, you are not getting out of it all that easily." Saige's voice was calm, direct, and level. Her eyes focused on the numbers clicking rapidly upward until they stopped on the L. "Scan lobby and report," she said.

"Three occupants: two males, one female."

"Identify."

"Bodaway, Chase; Regent, Kalare; one unidentified male."

"Open doors."

"Yes, Dr. Bodaway. This is also your two-minute warning to evacuate the premises."

Saige pushed through the doors as they opened and headed to the door.

"Saige, wait." Thad pulled up next to her. "Take him." He thrust Ziph toward Chase and Sam. "Saige, you have to stop it."

"No."

"Saige." He was shaking her now. "Saige, you can't kill everyone here. It's not you."

"It ends here."

"Yes. Saige, listen to me. You can't live with this. Stop it. Stop it now."

"No. It all goes away now. Except for him. I'm not done with him yet." Saige pointed her weapon at Ziph.

"Mom. Mom. Look at me." Chase was tugging at her left arm, trying to get her to look at him. He pulled a gloved hand up to her chin and forced her head in his direction. "If there is anything in you that is still you, you know you can't kill everyone here."

"Of course, I can't kill everyone here. What is wrong with you two today? I evacuated the building except for that idiot and the dead piece of filth downstairs two hours ago."

"Oh God, Saige. Oh, God." Thad was saying as he grabbed her shoulders and hugged her to him. "Come on, let's get the hell out of here."

"Wait," Sam said, "Where's Tya?"

"I left instructions that she be escorted from the building to the transports, but I don't know if she got out."

"We can't leave until we know for sure. I'm not leaving her here to die."

She heard the humph of air as the shot hit him. Thad's jacket flared up, and Saige felt the stream of sticky blood on the hand she held against his back. She looked over Thad's shoulder to Kalare, crumpled on the floor. Saige raised her weapon and shifted position as the elevator doors closed in front of Ziph's grinning face. Then she watched the numbers plunge downward as Thad collapsed at her feet.

"I'm going after him. Sam, get Kalare up and get all of them out of here." Chase was already halfway to the elevator.

"No, damn it, Chase, No. I need you." Kalare had reached Saige and was pulling Thad up off the floor.

"I have to, Kalare. I have to."

"No, you don't. Go. Take care of your family. I got it. I need to find Tya." Sam pushed Chase toward Thad and Saige. "They need you. I'll be fine." The elevator doors opened as Tya stepped into the lobby.

"Took your time about it, didn't you?"

"Tya. Oh god, I thought. I thought." Sam was holding her. "I thought I was too late. I thought I had, I..." All of his words melted into sobs.

You know what? Screw Ziph. Let's get out of here." Chase and Saige had Thad halfway on his feet.

"I can walk," Thad mumbled.

"Oh, sure you can."

"Saige? Did you shoot me? You did, didn't you?"

"It seemed like a good idea a bit earlier, but no, that would be Ziph."

"I knew you wouldn't do it." He tried to smile, but his legs went out from under him. "You look pretty." He said drunkenly.

"I guess you're not dead yet. Let's get you out of here."

"No? Are you sure I'm not dead? Sure feels like it." Then he gasped with a sharp intake of breath as the pain knocked the air out of him, and his head fell to the side.

"Tya, go. I'll be right there."

"No, Sam. No, I'm not leaving without you."

"I'll be fine. Trust me." Sam was pushing her toward Chase. "Chase, get her out of here."

Sam entered the stairway, and the automatic lock bar clicked when the door closed.

"Sam, damn it. Let me in there with you."

"No. I'll be right back. Two minutes, I promise." They were dragging Thad through the front door. "Kalare, can you get her, please? We only have seconds to go now."

"Come on. You know Sam. He'll be fine." Kalare pulled Tya toward the front door. Kalare wrapped her arm around Tya and propelled her through the door and onto the sidewalk.

They had cleared the front of the building when the first explosion hit deep underground like an echo of vague thunder as several other rhythmic blasts reverberated. *Research labs first.* Chase thought. *If they keep going off in sequence, he could still get out.* There was silence for a few seconds, and then the next boom hit just below their feet, echoing through the sidewalk and shaking the few trees that lined the parking lot.

The concrete walkways cracked and shook with the rumble of a retreating earthquake. The lobby belched out a cloud of smoke and ash. There was a brief silence, then the sensation of air rushing toward the building, and then the concussion blew out all of the glass. The next shock wave knocked them all to the ground as the blast took out the entire front of the building, and the back half of the roof collapsed. Torrents of glass, flaming plaster, and metal showered out onto the sidewalk and adjoining parking lot.

52

"*Seth*, I'm going to ask you one more time, nicely, and then I'm going to shoot you." Connor was looming over Seth. "Where are they, and what is going on?"

"Well, they didn't want me to tell you yet."

"So, they've gone? Alone?"

"Um, yeah." Seth started walking his chair back toward the door. "Look, I just do what I am told. They told me not to say anything." Seth continued to push his chair across the room; Connor's blond hair fell into angry, watery eyes as he walked along with the chair, bent over to within an inch or two of Seth's face.

"Where?" Connor seemed to shout even though he was now talking through his teeth. Seth jumped. Connor spoke in one-word sentences, trying to keep his rage under control. He had a feeling that Thad was going to pull something like this. *Damn fool that he is.* Connor looked down at Seth, shaking in his chair, and realized that Seth would either cry, puke, or piss himself, so he backed off and crossed the room. "Okay. You were following orders. I get that. Just tell me where and how long ago?"

Seth's phone beeped. He read the text and nodded.

"I just sent the coordinates. He wanted me to wait until I heard from him before I got you involved. But now they are in trouble."

"I know exactly what he thought." Connor's radio cut through with static.

"Connor, we're ready to roll."

"Sending coordinates now. Move out. I'll catch up." He clicked the radio off. "This isn't over, you little shit. If anything happens to them, I will personally pull you apart appendage by appendage. Gear up; you're coming with us."

"But," Seth said.

"You're not even going to try to give me shit, are you?"

"No Con...um, Maj...Um, Sir?"

"Shut up and get your stuff, you're riding with me, so you can explain what you guys have been doing all day and bring me completely, and I do mean completely, up to speed. Got it?

"Got it."

They felt the roadway rumble before they heard the explosions and saw the plumes of black smoke and ash rise in one large, billowing, cloudlike gasp before they could even see the building. The TALUS was moving in small concentric circles at the entrance to the parking lot.

"What the hell is that doing here?"

"Oh, did I forget to tell you that part?"

"Seth, I am going to beat the shit out of you just for fun." The crackle of the radio interrupted him.

"What? Anybody yet?" Connor yelled into the static on his radio.

"First Unit report."

"Yes, we are here. Five survivors. One badly wounded. The others have percussion and blast injuries. Oh, and one TALUS. What the hell is a

TALUS doing here?"

"Not sure yet about the freakin' TALUS." Connor glared at Seth.

"Who is badly wounded? Say again."

"It's Thad. Medics on site."

"How bad? Injuries?" Static. "Repeat, how bad?"

"Bullet wound."

"Repeat, how bad?"

"Well, Sir, it's hard to say. He just told us to put him the hell down, or he would stick his boot so far up our asses we would beg for him to shoot us."

"Ah, so not dead yet, I'm guessing." Connor let out a deep breath. The radio crackled again.

"Not yet, lost a lot of blood. We need birds here. Now." Thomas was trying to keep the tremor out of his voice.

"Birds already on the way." Connor clicked off his radio. "Idiot got himself shot. Again."

"Oh, he does that often, does he?"

"Ha, that's an understatement. That man definitely has a no-fear gene."

"You wouldn't say that if you had seen his face when he saw them load Saige into the van." Seth held the roll bar over his head, trying to keep from bouncing around on the seat.

"Saige. That's his flaw. She makes him reckless and stupid. Always has. Always will."

"Wait. Did he say five? Five people? There should be six. Someone's missing."

"Unit one? Unit one; come back." Connor waited through the static.

"Unit one here."

"I got a report of five, but it should be six. I repeat, recheck count for six on the ground."

53

is breath pushed out with a racking cough that brought up soot and sinewy mucus that clung to him like a parasite. His eyes burned, and he squeezed them shut as another explosion hurled tiny curls of smoke and flame out of the blasted windows. Hot ash fell around him in a slow, jittering motion that echoed the pulsating hum in his ears. Ash coated the sleeve of his jacket and began to collect in his hand. He tried to shake it off, and then realized he couldn't move his arm. He tossed that thought aside because it just didn't matter right now and instead watched the tiny burning smoke-tailed bits land on the walkway that led back to the building. They glowed red before popping into a blackish smoke plume that faded into grey, flaky ash, which fluttered along the sidewalk when he exhaled.

No, he thought, *it's really not like snow at all, is it?*

He couldn't hold onto any of it anymore: Thad, Saige, Kalare, Chase. He wanted it all done now; he needed a moment of quiet darkness free of their voices. He needed everything to go away, even for a moment. He curled his entire body into the next coughing spasm and looked over one last time at the demolished front of the building.

Damn you, Chase. Always so damn stubborn. He turned away from the approaching boots that crunched on the still-smoking debris on the sidewalk. He couldn't face any of them or take the look of either condemnation or sympathy from them. He would see everything he had already blamed himself for in their eyes. He had already let them all down and could do nothing about any of it. Not a damn thing. He squeezed his eyes shut against the stinging from the ash that clung to his face and eyelashes. But he didn't want to think about that either. Right now, he just wanted to sleep or die; he didn't care as long as it took him away from all of this obliteration. He dropped into the dizziness. Held onto the echoed spectral timbre of Chase's voice as if from a distant memory, saying: "I got you, Brother."

He allowed himself a small smile, took a deep breath, and then exhaled slowly as they carried him. A floating sensation like the shifting of a wave took over, and he let everything flow out of him. He felt oddly free, like when he balanced, one-handed, over the top of a roof cap when time stopped for a second of silent, suspended animation and control. He pulled in another breath and finally willed himself deeper into a sleep so dark he knew even he wouldn't dare to dream.

The End...

OTHER BOOKS BY JR

Codename Wolfe, The Omega Series, Book 1

Codename Raike, The Omega Series, Book 2

Codename Blade, The Omega Series, Book 3

Codename Havoc, The Omega Series, Book 4

Codename Cobra, The Omega Series, Book 5

Content Warnings:

The Codename Series is intended for mature audiences over the age of eighteen due to language, sexual situations, and depictions of trauma.

Please see my website for all content and trigger warnings: jrtootill.com

FOLLOW JR ON SOCIAL

Join our Omega Bionic Babes reader group here:
https://www.facebook.com/groups/omegabionicbabes

Social Media links:
<u>Facebook:</u>
https://www.facebook.com/JRTootill
<u>Instagram:</u>
https://www.instagram.com/jrtootill/
<u>TikTok:</u>
https://www.tiktok.com/@jrtootill_author
YouTube:
https://www.youtube.com/@JR_Tootill

JR's Website:
https://jrtootill.com/
Join JR's Patreon:
https://www.patreon.com/c/JRTootill
Get Omega Security Merch:
https://jrtootill.printify.me/

ACKNOWLEDGMENTS

First, to the lovely Alexa, who spent an entire summer helping me bring this book to life. Sharing the beginnings of this new path with you is a memory I will always hold close to my heart.

To all the fans of The Omega Series that have supported this little sci-fi story. Thank you so much for embracing this new world with me. This book existed when Omega was just a tiny concept, but if you look hard enough, I'm sure you'll see the seeds of Omega lurking within.

And finally, to Mr. Schmoopy, this is the book that started it all. Moved me from teaching to writing to independent publishing. And you've been there every step of the way. Through years of sending out manuscripts. Through the rejections and the hopeful responses that asked for a million changes, only to turn it down yet again. I was terrified to go independent. But you never doubted me. Not for one second. Thank you for it all: the videos, covers, ads and everything else you do behind the scenes as #videobycrog. You are my best cheerleader and Ben & Jerry's peddler! You get me...

ABOUT THE AUTHOR

 JR Tootill is an emerging author of techno thrillers. Her fascination with how people can rebuild their lives after hardship fuels her writing.

Her characters are sometimes broken, often battered, and always at a life-changing crossroads.

JR was a finalist in the Next Generation Indie Book Awards. She holds a Bachelor of Arts in Writing Arts and a Master of Fine Arts in Creative Writing. JR has been teaching creative writing at the university level for over fourteen years.